LISA KLEYPAS

DREAMING OF YOU

AVON BOOKS

An Imprint of HarperCollinsPublishers

This is a work of fiction. Names, characters, places, and incidents are products of the author's imagination or are used fictitiously and are not to be construed as real. Any resemblance to actual events, locales, organizations, or persons, living or dead, is entirely coincidental.

AVON BOOKS
An Imprint of HarperCollins*Publishers*
10 East 53rd Street
New York, New York 10022-5299

First Avon Books paperback printing: May 1994

Avon Trademark Reg. U.S. Pat. Off. and in Other Countries, Marca Registrada, Hecho en U.S.A.
HarperCollins ® is a trademark of HarperCollins Publishers Inc.

Printed in the U.S.A.

15   14   13

To Karen Churchill Bodager with love—
I'm glad I have such good taste in friends!

Chapter 1

*T*he lone figure of a woman stood in the shadows. She leaned against the wall of a crumbling lodging house, her shoulders hunched as if she were ill. Derek Craven's hard green eyes flickered over her as he came from the back-alley gaming hell. Such a sight wasn't unusual in the streets of London, especially in the rookery, where human suffering was visible in all its variety. Here, a short but significant distance from the splendor of St. James, the buildings were a crumbling mass of filth. The area was crawling with beggars, prostitutes, swindlers, thieves. His kind of people.

No decent female would be found here, especially after dusk. But if she was a whore, she was dressed strangely for it. Her gray cloak parted in the front to reveal a high-necked gown made of dark cloth. The lock of hair that strayed from beneath her hood was an indistinct brown. It was possible she was waiting for an errant husband, or perhaps she was a shopgirl who had lost her way.

People glanced furtively at the woman, but they passed her without breaking pace. If she remained here much longer, there was no doubt she would be raped or robbed, even beaten and left for dead. The gentlemanly thing to do would be to go to her, inquire about her well-being, express concern for her safety.

But he was no gentleman. Derek turned away, striding along the broken pavement. He had grown up in the streets—born in the gutter, nursed through infancy by a group of ragged prostitutes, and educated in his youth by criminals of every kind. He was familiar with the schemes used to prey upon the unwary, the few efficient moments it took to rob a man and crush his throat. Women were frequently used in such plots as bait or lookouts, or even assailants. A soft feminine hand could do a great deal of damage when it was wrapped around an iron cudgel, or when it clutched a stocking weighted with a pound or two of shot.

Gradually Derek became aware of footsteps close behind him. Something about them caused a warning prickle along his spine. Two sets of heavy footsteps, belonging to men. Deliberately he changed his pace, and they adjusted to match. They were following him. Perhaps they had been sent by his rival Ivo Jenner to cause mischief. Swearing silently, Derek began to round a corner.

As he expected, they made their move. Swiftly he turned and ducked beneath the drive of a clenched fist. Relying on instinct and years of experience, he shifted his weight to one leg and lashed out with his booted foot, striking a blow to the assailant's stomach. The man gave a muffled gasp of surprise and staggered back. Whipping around, Derek lunged for the second man, but it was too late . . . He felt the thud of a metal object on his back and a blinding impact on his head. Stunned, he fell heavily to the ground. The two men crawled over his twitching body.

"Do it quick," one of them said, his voice muffled. Struggling, Derek felt his head pushed back. He struck out with a clenched fist, but his arm was pinned to the ground. There was a slash across his face, a dull roar in his ears, hot wetness flowing in his eyes and mouth . . . his own blood. He sputtered a groaning protest, writhing to free himself from the searing pain. It was happening too quickly. He couldn't stop them. He had always been afraid of death, for somehow he had known it would come like this, not in peace, but in pain and violence and darkness.

Sara stopped to read through the information she had gathered so far. Peering through her spectacles, she puzzled over the new cant words she had heard that night. The language of the street changed quickly from year to year, an evolving process that fascinated her. Leaning against a wall for privacy, she pored over the notes she had made and scribbled a few corrections with her pencil. The gamblers had referred to playing cards as "flats" and had cautioned each other to watch out for the "crushers," which was perhaps intended to describe policemen. One thing she hadn't figured out yet was the difference between "rampsmen" and "dragsmen," both words used to refer to street thieves. Well, she would have to find out . . . it was imperative that she use the correct terms. Her first two novels, *Mathilda* and *The Beggar*, had both been praised for their attention to detail. She would not want her third, as yet untitled, to be faulted for inaccuracies.

She wondered if the men coming and going from

the gambling hell would be able to answer her questions. Most of them were quite disreputable, with unshaven faces and poor hygiene. Perhaps it would be unwise to ask them anything—they might not welcome an interruption in their evening revels. On the other hand, she needed to talk to them for the sake of her book. And Sara was always careful not to judge people by outward appearances.

Suddenly she was aware of a disturbance near the corner. She tried to see what was happening, but the street was shrouded in darkness. After folding the sheaf of paper she had stitched together to form a little book, she slipped it into her handbag and ventured forth curiously. A torrent of crude words brought color to her cheeks. No one used such language in Greenwood Corners except old Mr. Dawson, when he drank too much spiced punch at the annual town Christmas festival.

There were three figures engaged in a struggle. It appeared that two men were holding a third on the ground and beating him. She heard the sounds of fists pounding on flesh. Frowning uncertainly, Sara clutched her reticule as she watched. Her heart began to pound like a rabbit's. It would be unwise to involve herself. She was here as an observer, not a participant. But the poor victim made such piteous groans . . . and all at once her horrified gaze took in the flash of a knife.

They were going to murder him.

Hastily Sara fumbled in her handbag for the pistol she always carried on her research trips. She had never used it on anyone before, but she had practiced target shooting in a country field to the southeast of Greenwood Corners. Drawing out the small weapon, she cocked it and hesitated.

"Here, now!" she called out, trying to make her voice strong and authoritative. "I insist that you stop at once!"

One of the men looked over at her. The other ignored her cry, raising the knife once more. They did not consider her a threat at all. Biting her lip, Sara raised the trembling pistol and aimed to the left of them. She couldn't kill anyone—she doubted her conscience would tolerate it—but perhaps the loud noise would frighten them. Steadying her hand, she pulled the trigger.

As the echoes of the pistol's report died away, Sara opened her eyes to view the results of her efforts. To her amazement, she realized she had unintentionally hit one of the men . . . dear God, in the throat! He was on his knees, clasping the gushing wound with his hands. Abruptly he toppled over with a gurgling noise. The other man was frozen. She couldn't see his shadowed face.

"Go away now," Sara heard herself say, her voice shaking with fear and dismay. "Or . . . or I shall find it necessary to shoot you as well!"

He seemed to melt away into the darkness like a ghost. Sara crept to the two bodies on the ground. Her mouth gaped open in horror, and she covered it with her unsteady fingers. She had very definitely killed a man. Edging around his fallen body, she approached the victim of the attack.

His face was covered with blood. It dripped from his black hair and soaked the front of his evening clothes. A sickening feeling came over her as she wondered if rescue had come too late for him. Sara slipped the pistol back into her handbag. She was cold all over, and very unsteady. In all her sheltered twenty-five years, nothing like this had ever happened to her. She looked from one body to the other. If only there were a foot patrol nearby, or one of the renowned and highly trained city officers. She found herself waiting for something to happen. Someone would come across the scene very soon. A sense of guilt crept through her shock. Dear Lord, how could she live with herself, knowing what she had done?

Sara peered down at the victim of the robbery with a mixture of curiosity and pity. It was difficult to see his face through all the blood, but he appeared to be a young man. His clothes were well-made, the kind of garments that were to be found on Bond Street. Suddenly she saw his chest move. She blinked in surprise. "S-sir?" she asked, leaning over him.

He lunged upward, and she gave a terrified squeak. A large hand grasped the material of her bodice, clenching too tightly to allow her to pull away. The other hand came up to her face. His palm rested on her cheek, his trembling fingers smearing blood across the surface of her spectacles. After a frantic attempt to escape, Sara subsided into an unsteady heap beside him.

"I have foiled your attackers, sir." Gamely she tried to pry his fingers away from her bodice. His grip was like iron. "I believe I may have saved your life. Unhand me . . . please . . ."

He took a long time to reply. Gradually his hand fell away from her face and drifted down her arm until he found her wrist. " 'Elp me up," he said roughly, surprising her with his accent. She wouldn't have expected a man wearing such fine clothes to speak with a cockney twang.

"It would be better if I called for assistance—"

"Not 'ere," he managed to gasp. "Empty-'eaded fool. We'll be . . . robbed an' gutted in a frigging second."

Offended by his harshness, Sara was tempted to point out that a little gratitude wouldn't be amiss. But he must be in considerable pain. "Sir," she said tentatively, "your face . . . if you will allow me to get the handkerchief from my reticule—"

"*You* fired the pistol shot?"

"I'm afraid so." Easing her hand inside her reticule, she pushed past the gun and found the handkerchief. Before she could pull it out, he tightened his grip on her wrist. "Let me help you," she said quietly.

His fingers loosened, and she brought forth the handkerchief, a clean, serviceable square of linen. Gently she dabbed at his face and pressed the folded linen against the hideous gash that ran from his brow to the center of his opposite cheek. It would be disfiguring. For his sake, she hoped he wouldn't lose an eye. A hiss of pain escaped his lips, spattering her with blood. Wincing, Sara touched his hand and brought it to his face. "Perhaps you could hold this in place? Good. Now, if you'll wait here, I'll try to find someone to assist us—"

"No." He continued to hold the fabric of her dress, his knuckles digging into the soft curve of her breasts. "I'm awright. Get me to Craven's. St. James Street."

"But I'm not strong enough, or familiar with the city—"

"It's close enow to 'ere."

"Wh-what about the man I shot? We can't just leave the body."

He gave a sardonic snort. "Pox on 'im. Get me to St. James."

Sara wondered what he would do if she refused. He seemed to be a man of volatile temperament. In spite of his injuries, he was still quite capable of hurting her. The hand at her bosom was large and very strong.

Slowly Sara removed her spectacles and placed them in her reticule. She slid her arm beneath his coat and around his lean waist, blushing in dismay. She had never embraced a man except for her own father, and Perry Kingswood, her almost-fiancé. Neither of them had felt like this. Perry was quite fit, but he was not at all comparable to this big, rawboned stranger. Struggling to her feet, she staggered as the man used her to lever himself up. She hadn't expected him to be so tall. He braced his arm across her small shoulders while he kept the handkerchief clutched over his face. He gave a slight groan.

"Are you all right, sir? That is, are you able to walk?"

That produced a choking laugh. "Who the 'ell are you?"

Sara took a hesitant step in the direction of St. James, and he lurched along beside her. "Miss Sara Fielding," she said, then added cautiously, "of Green-wood Corners."

He coughed and spat a mouthful of blood-tinged saliva. "Why did you help me?"

Sara couldn't help noticing that his accent had improved. He sounded almost like a gentleman, but the trace of cockney was still there, softening his consonants and flattening his vowels. "I had no choice," she replied, bearing up underneath his weight. He clasped his ribs with his free arm and held on to her with the other. "When I saw what those men were doing—"

"You had a choice," he said harshly. "You could've walked away."

"Turn my back on someone in trouble? The idea is unthinkable."

"It's done all the time."

"Not where I'm from, I assure you." Noticing that they were straying toward the middle of the street, Sara guided him back to the side, where they were concealed in the darkness. This was the oddest night of her life. She hadn't anticipated that she would be walking through a London rookery with a battered stranger. He peeled the handkerchief back from his face, and Sara was relieved to see that the bleeding had slowed. "You'd better hold it against the wound," she said. "We must find a doctor." She was surprised that he hadn't asked about the extent of the damage. "From what I was able to see, they made a long slash across your face. But it doesn't seem to be deep. If it heals well, your appearance might not be affected greatly."

"It doesn't matter."

The remark sharpened Sara's curiosity. "Sir, do you have friends at Craven's? Is that why we are going there?"

"Yes."

"Are you by any chance acquainted with Mr. Craven?"

"I *am* Derek Craven."

"*The* Mr. Craven?" Her eyes widened in excitement. "The same one who founded the famous club and came from the underworld and . . . Were you really born in a drainpipe, as the legend says? Is it true that you—"

"Lower your voice, damn you."

Sara couldn't believe her good fortune. "This is quite a coincidence, Mr. Craven. As it happens, I'm in the process of researching a novel about gambling.

That's why I'm here at this time of night. Greenwood Corners isn't a very worldly sort of place, and therefore I found it necessary to come to London. My book will be a fictional work which will include many descriptions of people and places significant to the gaming culture—"

"Jaysus," he growled. "Anything you want—a frigging fortune—if you'll keep your mouth shut until we get there."

"Sir—" Sara tugged him away from a small pile of rubble, which he might have tripped over. Knowing that he was in pain, she didn't take offense at his rudeness. The hand clenched at her shoulder was trembling. "We're almost out of the rookery, Mr. Craven. You'll be all right."

Derek's head swam, and he fought to keep his balance. The blow to his head seemed to have knocked his brains out of place. Tightening his grip on the small form beside him, he matched his shuffling footsteps to hers. He leaned over her more heavily until the fabric of her hood brushed his ear. A kind of dull amazement took hold of him. Blindly he followed the talkative little stranger and hoped to God she was leading him in the right direction. It was the closest to praying he'd ever come.

She was asking him something. He fought to concentrate on her words. ". . . should we ascend the front steps, or is there another way—"

"Side door," he muttered, squinting from behind the handkerchief. "Ower there."

"My. What a large building." Sara regarded the club with awe. The massive building was fronted by eight Corinthian columns and seven pediments, and bordered by two wings. The whole of it was surrounded by a marble balustrade. She would have liked to have gone up the front steps and seen the famed entrance hall, filled with stained glass, blue velvet, and chandeliers. But of course Mr. Craven would not want to show himself like this in front of the club members. After she guided him to the side of the building, they descended a short flight of steps that led to a heavy wooden door.

Derek grasped the handle and pushed the door open. Immediately they were approached by Gill, one of his employees. "Mr. Craven?" the young man exclaimed, his gaze darting from the blood-soaked handkerchief clutched to Derek's face, to Sara's apprehensive eyes. "Good Lord—"

"Get Worthy," Derek muttered. He brushed by Gill and made his way through the small panelled antechamber. The winding staircase led to his private apartments. Contemplating the six-flight climb, he motioned abruptly for Sara to join him.

Surprised that he would want her to help him up the stairs, Sara hesitated. She glanced at the young employee, who was already walking away from them, disappearing down a wide, carpeted hallway.

"Come," Derek said gruffly, motioning for her again. "You think I 'as all night to stand 'ere?"

She went to him immediately, and he draped a heavy arm across her shoulders. Together they began the walk up the steps. "Who is Worthy?" she asked, sliding an arm around his hard waist to steady him.

"Factotum." Derek's ribs seemed to cut through his innards like dull knives. His face burned like fire. He heard himself talking, all the years of tutoring dropping away to reveal his thick cockney accent. "Worvy . . . does ewerything . . . 'elps me run the club.

Trusts 'im . . . wiv my life." He stumbled on the landing and gave a whimpering curse.

Sara tightened her arm on his waist. "Wait. If you
fall, I couldn't stop you. We must wait for someone
strong to assist you the rest of the way."

"You're strong enow." He began the next flight, his
arm gripped around her shoulders.

"Mr. Craven," Sara protested. Clumsily they ascended another two flights, Sara was terrified that he
might faint and fall down the stairs. She began to encourage him, saying anything she could think of to
keep him moving. "Almost there . . . Come, you're
stubborn enough to climb a few more . . . Stay on your
feet . . ."

She was breathing hard from exertion as they
mounted the last step and came to the door of his private apartments. They crossed the entrance hall and
came to a drawing room decorated with acres of plum
velvet and rich brocade. Her astonished gaze took
note of the gilt-embossed leather on the walls, the
regal parade of French windows, and the splendid view
of the city outside. Following Mr. Craven's mumbled
directions, she helped him to the bedchamber. The
room was lined with green damask and elaborate mirrors. It contained the largest bed she had ever seen in
her life. Blushing deeply, Sara reflected that she had
never been in a man's bedroom before. Her embarrassment was washed away in concern as Mr. Craven
crawled onto the bed, boots and all. He sprawled on
his back with a gasp and became very still. The arm
clamped over his ribs relaxed.

"Mr. Craven? Mr. Craven—" Sara hovered over
him, wondering what to do. He had fainted. His long
body was unmoving, his large hands half-clenched.

Reaching down to his throat, she unknotted his stained cravat. Carefully she unwound the cloth and pulled the handkerchief away from his face.

The slash went from his right temple, across the bridge of his nose, and down to the edge of his left cheekbone. Although his features were blunt, they were strong and even. His lips parted to reveal startlingly white teeth. Coppery smears of blood covered his swarthy skin, crusting in the thick lines of his brows and in his long eyelashes.

Spying a washstand across the room, Sara hurried to it and found cool water in the pitcher. After pouring a few inches of liquid into the basin, she brought it to the bedside table. She dampened a cloth and pressed it to his face, wiping away the blood and dirt. As she cleaned his eyes and cheeks, the water revived him, and he made a hoarse sound. His thick lashes lifted. Sara paused in her task as she found herself looking into intense green eyes, the color of grass on a cool spring morning. There was a strange sensation in her chest. Pinned in place by his gaze, she couldn't move or speak.

He raised his hand, touching one of the locks of hair that had fallen from her pins. His voice was hoarse. "Your name . . . again."

"Sara," she whispered.

Just then two men entered the room, one of them small and bespectacled, the other elderly and tall. "Mr. Craven," the smaller one said soberly. "I've brought Dr. Hindley."

"Whiskey," Derek croaked. "I've 'ad the piss knocked out ow me."

"You were in a fight?" Worthy bent over him, his mild face wreathed in surprise. "Oh, no. Your *face*." He stared disapprovingly at Sara, who stood by wringing her hands. "I hope this young woman was worth it, Mr. Craven."

"I wasn't fighting ower 'er," Derek said, before Sara could intervene. "It was Jenner's men, I think. Two ow 'em armed wiv a neddy jumped me in the street. This little mouse . . . pulls out a pistol an' shoots one ow the bastards."

"Well." Worthy regarded Sara with a much warmer expression. "Thank you, miss. It was very brave of you."

"I wasn't brave at all," Sara said earnestly. "I didn't stop to think. It happened very quickly."

"In any case, we owe you our gratitude." Worthy hesitated before adding, "I am employed by Mr. Craven to deal with disturbances on the floor, as well as"—he glanced at Craven's bloodstained body and finished lamely—"any other matters that require my attention."

Sara smiled at him. Worthy was a very nice-looking man, with small, neat features, thinning hair on top; and gleaming spectacles perched on his pointed nose. There was an air of patience about him that she guessed would not be easily shaken. Together he and the doctor bent over the bed, removing Craven's shoes and clothes. Sara turned away, modestly averting her gaze. She began to walk from the room, but Craven said something gruffly, and Worthy stopped her. "I think it would be best if you didn't leave yet, Miss—"

"Fielding," she murmured, keeping her eyes on the floor. "Sara Fielding."

The name seemed to awaken his interest. "Any relation to S. R. Fielding, the novelist?"

"Sara Rose," she said. "I use my initials for the sake of anonymity."

The doctor looked up from the bed with an expression of startled delight. "*You* are S. R. Fielding?"

"Yes, sir."

The news seemed to animate him. "What an honor this is! *Mathilda* is one of my favorite novels."

"It was my most successful work," Sara admitted modestly.

"My wife and I have spent many an evening discussing our theories on the ending of the novel. Did Mathilda cast herself from the bridge to end her misery, or did she choose to seek atonement for her sins—"

"Excuse me," said an icy voice from the bed. "I'm frigging bleeding to death. Mathilda can go tip a pike."

Sara frowned contritely. "Oh, I'm sorry. Dr. Hindley, please see to Mr. Craven at once." She turned her gaze to Worthy. "Where would you like me to wait?"

"In the next room, if you please. You're welcome to ring for tea and refreshments."

"Thank you." As Sara went to the drawing room, she wondered what it was about *Mathilda* that always inspired such interest. The book's popularity never failed to amaze her. There had even been a recent stage production of the story. People tended to discuss the character of Mathilda as if she were a real person, seeming to enjoy endless debates concerning the novel's conclusion. After writing the story of a girl who had run away from the country and fallen into the sinful ways of prostitution, Sara had deliberately left a question as to the ending. On the last page, Mathilda was poised at the edge of London Bridge, faced with the decision to end her ruined life or commit herself

to a selfless existence of doing good for others. Readers could form their own opinions about Mathilda's
fate. Personally, Sara didn't think it important to know
whether Mathilda lived or died . . . the point was that
she had learned the error of her ways.

Discovering that her reticule was hanging forgotten
from her arm, Sara delved inside and found her spectacles. She polished them on her sleeve until they
shone, placed them on her nose, and located her notebook. " 'Tip a pike,' " she mused, writing down the
unfamiliar expression. She must ask someone to explain it later.

Slowly she removed her cloak and draped it over the
back of a chair. She felt as if she were trapped in a temporarily vacated lion's den. After walking to the windows, she pushed aside the heavy plum-colored drapes
to reveal a view of the street. All of London was just
outside these thin panes of glass, a world of busy people absorbed in their own lives. She turned to gaze at
the gold mirrors adorning the walls, and the sumptuous furniture upholstered with painted white velvet.
The tables, inlaid with semi-precious stones, were
weighted with arrangements of fresh hothouse flowers. The room was beautiful, but too extravagant.

Sara preferred the small cottage she and her elderly
parents lived in. There was a kitchen garden in the
back, and fruit trees that her father tended meticulously. They had a small yard and paddock, and an old
gray horse named Eppie. The faded furniture in their
small parlor was constantly filled with callers. Her parents had many friends. Nearly everyone in Greenwood Corners had come to visit at one time or
another.

This, by contrast, was a splendid and lonely palace.

Sara stood in front of a vivid oil painting depicting Roman gods involved in some decadent celebration. She was distracted by a groan from the next room, and a curse from Mr. Craven. They must be stitching the wound on his face. Sara tried to ignore the sounds, but after a few moments, curiosity compelled her to investigate.

Coming to the doorway, she saw Worthy and Dr. Hindley leaning over Mr. Craven's head. His lower body, covered with a white sheet, was still. But his hands were twitching at his sides, as if he longed to shove the doctor away from him.

"We've given you all the laudanum we can, Mr. Craven," Dr. Hindley remarked, drawing another stitch through the cut.

"Damn stuff . . . never works on me. More whiskey."

"If you'll just be patient, Mr. Craven, it will be done in a few minutes."

Another pained groan erupted. "Damn you and everyone else in your stinking, bloodletting, bone-sawing, corpse-humping business—"

"Mr. Craven," Worthy interrupted hastily. "Dr. Hindley is doing his best to repair the damage done to your face. He is trying to *help* you. Please don't antagonize him."

"It's quite all right," the doctor said calmly. "By now I know what to expect from him." He continued to join the edges of skin with small, careful stitches.

All was quiet for a moment, and then Derek gave a muffled gasp. "Bloody 'ell. I don't care what it looks like. Leave me alone—" He made a move to get up from the bed.

Sara entered the room immediately. It was clear that Craven had a quick temper, but he must be coaxed into staying. It would be a shame not to let the doctor salvage what he could of his face.

"Sir," she said briskly, "I know it is uncomfortable, but you must let the doctor finish. You may not care about your appearance now, but you might later. Besides . . ." She paused and added pointedly, "a large, strong man such as yourself should be able to bear a little pain. I assure you, it's nothing compared to the suffering a woman endures in labor!"

Slowly Derek eased back to the mattress. "How do you know?" he sneered.

"I was present at a childbirth once in Greenwood Corners. It lasted for hours, and my friend bore the agony with hardly a sound."

Worthy looked at her pleadingly. "Miss Fielding, you would be more comfortable in the next room—"

"I'm distracting Mr. Craven with some conversation. It might take his mind off the pain. Wouldn't you prefer that, Mr. Craven? Or should I leave?"

"Do I have a choice? Stay. Flap your gums."

"Shall I tell you about Greenwood Corners?"

"No." Derek damped his teeth together and stifled a grunt. "About yourself."

"Very well." Sara approached the bed, taking care to preserve a discreet distance. "I am twenty-five years old. I live in the country with my parents—" She paused as she heard Mr. Craven's panting groan. The stitch-taking was hurting him.

"Go on," he said sharply.

Sara searched frantically for more to tell him. "I-I'm being courted by a young man who lives in the village. We share the same fondness for books, although his tastes are more refined than mine. He doesn't approve of the fiction I write." She crept closer and stared at

Craven curiously. Although she was unable to see his face, she had a good view of his chest, which was covered with a great amount of dark hair. The sight was startling. The only male chests she had been privileged to view before now were those of hairless Greek statues. Above his lean waist and midriff, his chest and shoulders were powerfully muscled, and splotched with bruises. "Mr. Kingswood—that's his name—has been courting me for almost four years. I believe that his proposal will come soon."

"*Four* years?"

Sara felt mildly defensive at his jeering tone. "There have been a few difficulties. His mother is a widow, and she relies on him a great deal. They live together, you see. Mrs. Kingswood doesn't approve of me."

"Why not?"

"Well . . . she doesn't consider any woman quite good enough for her son. And she dislikes the subject matter I have chosen for my novels. Prostitution, poverty . . ." Sara shrugged. "But they are issues that need to be addressed."

"Especially when you makes money off 'em?"

"Enough to keep my parents and myself in a comfortable style," she admitted with a smile. "You're a cynical man, Mr. Craven."

His breath hissed through his teeth as the needle pierced his skin. "You would be too, if you knowed anyfing about the world outside your stinking village." The ordeal was making his accent slip again.

"Greenwood Corners is a very nice place," Sara said, mildly provoked. "And I know a great many things about the world."

Derek held his breath for a moment, then let it burst forth. "Dammit, 'ow much longer—"

"A few more," the doctor murmured.

Derek struggled to keep his mind on the conversation with Sara. "Writing books about whores . . . I'll bet you newer . . . joined giblets wiv a man in your lily-white life."

Dr. Hindley and Worthy began to reprove him, but Sara smiled quizzically. " 'Joined giblets?' . . . I've never heard it put that way before."

"You 'asn't been long enow in the rookery."

"That's true," she said seriously. "I must make several more visits there before my research is complete."

"You're not going back," he informed her. "God knows 'ow you lasted this long. Bloody little fool, traipsing through the rookery at night—"

"This is the last stitch," Dr. Hindley announced, carefully tying off the thread. Derek sighed in relief and fell silent.

Worthy left the bedside and came to Sara, smiling apologetically. "Forgive Mr. Craven. He's only rude to the people he likes."

"Will he be all right?" she whispered.

"Certainly. He's a very strong man. He has survived worse than this." Worthy looked at her closely, his expression softening into concern. "You're trembling, Miss Fielding."

Sara nodded and took a deep breath. "I suppose I'm not used to so much excitement." She hadn't realized how rattled she was until now. "Everything happened so quickly."

"You must rest for a little while," Worthy urged, "and steady your nerves with some brandy."

"Yes . . . perhaps a splash, in a cup of tea." She twined her fingers together. "I'm staying with friends of my parents, the Goodmans. The hour is late . . . they might worry . . ."

"As soon as you're ready, we'll have a private carriage convey you anywhere you wish."

"Worthy!" Derek's disgruntled voice interrupted them. "Stop that bloody whispering. Give the country mouse some money and send 'er back where she came from."

Worthy began to reply, but Sara stopped him with a light touch on his arm. Squaring her small shoulders, she approached the bed. "Mr. Craven," she said calmly, "you're very kind to offer a reward, but I have enough money to suit my needs. However, I would be grateful if you would allow me to tour your club, and perhaps ask a few questions of your employees. As I mentioned earlier, I'm writing a novel, and you could help me—"

"No."

"Mr. Craven, it is a reasonable request, considering the fact that I saved your life tonight."

"Like 'ell you did."

Sara was taken aback. "But those two men were trying to kill you!"

"If they'd wanted that, I'd be dead now."

"Then . . . their purpose was to . . . to deliberately mark your face?" She recoiled in horror. "But why would anyone want to do such a thing?"

"Mr. Craven has many enemies," Worthy remarked, his round face troubled. "In particular a man named Ivo Jenner, who owns a rival club. But I wouldn't have expected Jenner to do something like this."

"Maybe not," Derek muttered, closing his eyes. "Maybe it was someone else. Worvy . . . take 'er out of 'ere."

"But Mr. Craven," Sara protested.

"Come," Worthy said, shushing her gently. He urged her away from the bedside. Reluctantly Sara followed him to the next room.

Left alone, Derek gave a soft laugh threaded with bitterness. "Damn you, Joyce," he whispered, and raised a hand to touch the stitches on his face.

After Dr. Hindley departed, Worthy rang for tea and stirred the fire in the grate. "Now," he said pleasantly, sitting in a chair near Sara's, "we may talk without interruption."

"Mr. Worthy, could you try to make Mr. Craven understand that I wouldn't be a nuisance, or inconvenience him in any way? All I want is to observe the activities at the club, and ask a few questions—"

"I will talk to Mr. Craven," Worthy assured her. "And I'll allow you to visit the club tomorrow while Mr. Craven is indisposed." Worthy smiled at her obvious excitement. "It is a privilege rarely granted to women, you know, except on assembly nights. There was only one other lady who has even been allowed to cross the threshold."

"Yes, I've heard of her—they called her Lawless Lily. She was Mr. Craven's paramour for a number of years, wasn't she?"

"Things are not always what they seem, Miss Fielding."

They were interrupted by a maid bearing a tray of tea and delicate sandwiches. Efficiently Worthy poured Sara's tea and added a liberal amount of brandy. Balancing the cup and saucer on her lap, Sara nibbled on a sandwich, feeling as if she were slowly awakening from a nightmare. She stretched her damp feet toward the warm fire, taking care not to expose her ankles.

"There is only one condition I must ask of you," Worthy said, settling back in his chair. "You must not approach Mr. Craven, or ask him any questions. In fact, I insist that you take care to avoid him. You will be free to talk to anyone else at the club. We will all try to be as accommodating as possible."

Sara frowned in disappointment. "But Mr. Craven could be of great help to me. There are things I would like to ask him—"

"He is an intensely private man who has spent his life trying to escape his past. I assure you, he will not want to talk about himself."

"Is there anything *you* could tell me about him?" She sipped her tea and watched the factotum hopefully.

"He's not easy to describe. Derek Craven is by far the most complicated individual I've ever met. He is capable of kindness, but . . ." Worthy drank some brandy and contemplated the rich amber depths in the glass. "I'm afraid that all too often Mr. Craven reveals himself as a man of ruined potential. He comes from a world more savage than you could begin to comprehend, Miss Fielding. All he knows about his mother was that she was a prostitute who worked at Tiger Bay, a dockland street where sailors and criminals go to be serviced. She gave birth to him in a drainpipe and abandoned him there. Some of the other harlots took pity on the infant and sheltered him for the first part of his life in local brothels and flash houses."

"Oh, Mr. Worthy," Sara said in a strangled voice. "How dreadful for a child to be exposed to such things."

"He began to work at five or six years of age as a climbing boy for a chimney sweep. When he became too old to climb, he resorted to begging, thievery, dock labor . . . There is a period of a few years which he will not speak of at all, as if it never existed. I don't know what he did at that time . . . nor do I wish to know. Somehow in the midst of it all he gained a rudimentary understanding of letters and numbers. By his teens he had educated himself enough to become a Newmarket bookmaker. According to him, it was at that time that he conceived the idea of operating his own gambling club someday."

"What remarkable ambition for a boy with such origins."

Worthy nodded. "It would have been an extraordinary achievement for him to build a small den in the city. Instead, he dreamed of creating a club so exclusive that the most powerful men in the world would clamor to be allowed membership."

"And that's precisely what he's done," she marveled.

"Yes. He was born without a shilling to his name . . ." Worthy paused. "He was born without a *name*, as a matter of fact. Now he is wealthier than most of the gentry that patronizes his club. No one is really aware of how much Mr. Craven owns. Landed estates, houses, streets lined with rent-paying shops and tenants, private art collections, yachts, racehorses . . . it's astounding. And he keeps track of every farthing."

"What is his goal? What does he ultimately want?"

Worthy smiled faintly. "I can tell you in a word. More. He's never satisfied." Seeing that she had finished her tea, he inquired if she wanted another cup.

Sara shook her head. The brandy, the firelight, and

Worthy's calm voice had all combined to make her drowsy. "I must leave now."

"I'll have a carriage brought around."

"No, no, the Goodmans live a short distance from here. I shall go on foot."

"Nonsense," the factotum interrupted firmly. "It is ill-advised for a lady to go anywhere on foot, especially at this time of night. What happened to Mr. Craven is an example of the dangers that could befall you." They both stood up. Worthy was about to say something else, but his words died away, and he stared at her oddly. Most of Sara's hair had fallen from its pins to her shoulders, the red glow of firelight dancing over the chestnut waves. There was something oddly moving about her quaint, old-fashioned prettiness, which would easily be passed over in this day when more exotic beauty was preferred.

"There's something almost otherworldly about you . . ." Worthy murmured, quite forgetting himself. "It has been too long since I've seen such innocence in a woman's face."

"Innocent?" Sara shook her head and laughed. "Oh, Mr. Worthy, I know all about vice and sin—"

"But you've been untouched by it."

Sara chewed her lip pensively. "Nothing ever seems to happen in Greenwood Corners," she admitted, "I'm always writing about the things other people do. Sometimes I'm desperate to *live*, to have adventures and *feel* things, and—" She broke off and made a face. "I hardly know what I'm saying. What must you think of me?"

"I think," Worthy said with a smile, "that if you long for adventure, Miss Fielding, you've made quite a start tonight."

Sara was pleased by the notion. "That's true." She sobered immediately. "About the man I shot—I didn't intend to harm him—"

"You saved Mr. Craven from horrible disfigurement, if not death," Worthy said gently. "Whenever you feel guilty about what you've done, you might remind yourself of that."

The advice made Sara feel better. "You'll allow me to return tomorrow?"

"I insist that you do so."

She gave him an enchanting smile. "Well, in that case . . ." Taking his proffered arm, she allowed him to escort her downstairs.

Derek lay stretched out on the bed. The laudanum coursed through his veins, making him sluggish, dizzy. It did little to numb the pain, or his self-disgust. His lips pulled into a bitter smile. He almost would have preferred it if his attackers had made a proper beast of him, instead of giving him a piddling slash that made him look less a monster and more a fool.

He thought of Joyce, and waited for a feeling of betrayal, anger, anything but this cold sense of admiration. At least she cared enough about *something* to take action, even if it was her own pride. Whereas he couldn't bring himself to care about anything. He had everything he'd ever wanted . . . wealth, women, even the pleasure of watching his betters scrape their boots at the entrance of his club. But over the past two years all his former voracious appetites had dried up, and he was left with nothing, a young man with a withered soul.

It was the absence of feeling that had driven him to Lady Ashby's bed, and ultimately had led to tonight's disaster. Joyce, with her sinuous body, blond hair, and catlike eyes, had stirred an interest that he hadn't felt in a long time. Mild though the feeling was, it had been enough to make him pursue her. He couldn't deny there had been many entertaining nights, filled with sophisticated games and sensual depravity . . . and it took a hell of a lot to make *him* feel depraved. Finally Derek had ended the liaison, disgusted with himself as well as her. The memory rolled over him, and he relived it in a drugged stupor.

"You can't be serious," Joyce had said, her silky voice amused at first. "You would never give me up." She stretched on the bed, her naked body unconcealed by the rumpled linen sheets. "Tell me, who would it be after me? Some bovine country maid? Some little actress with bleached hair and red stockings? You can't go back to that, Derek. You've developed a taste for finer things."

Derek had grinned at her confident tone. "You aristocratic ladies and your gold-plated twats. You always think it's such a honor for me to touch you." He surveyed her with mocking green eyes. "You think you're the first high-kick wench I've ever had? I used to have blue-blooded bitches like you pay me to do this. You've gotten it for free."

Joyce's beautiful face, with its narrow, aristocratic nose and sharply sculpted cheekbones, was suddenly pinched with rage. "You lying bastard."

"How do you think I got the money to start my club? They called themselves my 'patronesses.' " Derek gave her a hard smile, pulling on his trousers.

Joyce's red lips parted in a sneering laugh. "Then you were nothing but a whore? A male whore?" The idea clearly excited her.

"Among other things." He buttoned his shirt and faced the mirror to straighten his collar.

Joyce slid from the bed and strode to him, pausing for a moment to admire her naked body in the mirror. Married at a young age to an elderly widowed earl, she had satisfied her sexual urges by taking a long string of lovers. Any pregnancies had been terminated quickly, for she would never ruin her figure with children, and the earl had already begotten suitable heirs with his first wife. Joyce's cunning wit and beauty had made her a society favorite. A lovely predator, she devoted herself to ruining any woman whom she perceived as a threat to her own position. With a few carefully chosen words and some brilliantly engineered "coincidences" Joyce had been known to shred many a good reputation and cast innocent women into the depths of disgrace.

Derek also looked into the mirror, seeing what Joyce intended him to see, the erotic contrast between his clothed form and her gold-and-white nakedness. At times Joyce could seem as guileless as an angel, but he had seen her turn into a witch with wild hair and a contorted face, screaming at the height of ecstasy and clawing him with her long nails. She was the most wanton woman he'd ever known, willing to do anything for the sake of pleasure, no matter how debauched. They were quite a pair, he thought grimly, both of them existing only to satisfy their own needs.

Keeping her pale blue eyes on his expressionless face, Joyce ran her hand over his flat stomach, seeking his crotch with her palm. "You still want me," she purred. "I can feel how much. You're the most satisfying lover I've ever had, so big and hard—"

Derek pushed her away so roughly that she fell back

onto the bed. Expectantly she spread her legs and waited for him. Surprise dawned in her eyes as she realized he wasn't going to oblige her.

"It's over," Derek said flatly. "I'll pay all your debts on Bond Street. Pick out something from that little frog-eating jeweler you like so much, and charge it to my account." He left his black silk cravat hanging loose around his neck and shrugged into his coat.

"Why are you doing this? Do you want me to beg?" Joyce smiled provocatively. "I'll get on my knees before you. How would you like that?" As she sank to the floor and leaned her face toward the front of his trousers, Derek forced her up, clamping his hands on her shoulders.

"Listen to me, Joyce—"

"You're hurting me!"

"I haven't lied to you. I made no promises. How long did you think this would go on? We both got what we wanted. Now it's over."

She glared at him. "It will end when *I* say so, and not before!"

Derek's expression changed. "So that's it," he said, and laughed. "Your pride is hurt. Well, tell your friends whatever you want, Joyce. Tell them that you were the one to break it off. I'll agree with anything you say."

"How dare you speak to me in that superior tone, you ignorant cockney! I know how many thousands of boots you licked to get where you are, and so does everyone else! Gentlemen will come to your club, but they'll never invite you to their homes, or their parties, or let you eat at their tables or approach their daughters, and do you know why? Because they don't respect you—they regard you as something to be scraped from their shoes and left in the gutter where you came from! They think of you as the lowest form of—"

"All right," Derek said, a humorless smile crossing his face. "I know all that. Save your breath."

Joyce stared at him closely, apparently realizing her insults hadn't affected him at all. "You have no feelings, do you? That's why no one can hurt you—because you're dead inside."

"That's right," he said smoothly.

"And you don't care about anyone. Not even me."

His glinting green eyes met hers. Although he didn't reply, the answer was clear. Drawing back her arm, Joyce struck him with all her strength, the blow sounding like the sharp crack of a pistol. Automatically Derek moved to strike back. But his hand stopped before it reached her face. He lowered it slowly. His face was dark and cool.

"I can make you want me," Joyce said hoarsely. "There are things we still haven't done together—new games I could show you—"

"Good-bye, Joyce." He turned and left the room.

His refusal of her body was insultingly casual, as if he had turned down an unwanted offer of seconds at the supper table. Joyce flushed crimson. *"No,"* she snarled. "You won't leave me! If it's another woman, I'll claw her eyes out!"

"It's not another woman," came his sardonic reply. "It's just boredom." Suddenly his accent changed to coarse, flat cockney. "Or as you gentry likes to call it, ennui."

She ran out of the bedroom, still naked, calling after him as he went down the stairs. "Come back this instant . . . or you'll pay for this every day of your life! If I can't have you, no one will! Do you understand me? *"You'll pay for this,* Derek Craven!"

Derek hadn't taken her threat seriously—or maybe it was just that he hadn't cared. He had done what he'd planned with his life, never dreaming that at the end of the long, treacherous path success would be coupled with such disappointment. Now he had gained everything he wanted, and there was nothing to look forward to. Damn ennui, the mind-numbing clutches of boredom. A few years ago, he hadn't even known what the word meant. A rich man's disease, he thought, and smiled grimly in ironic appreciation.

Chapter 2

Sara dressed carefully for her visit to the gambling palace. She wore the best gown she owned, a gray-blue grenadine with three deep bias tucks at the hem, and a high-necked bodice ornamented with lace. She had very few clothes, but they were all made with good sturdy cloth. The gowns she preferred did not adhere to any particular style that would date them. She hoped the bloodstains could be removed from the garments she had worn last night. There had been quite a scene when Sara had returned at such a late hour, spattered with blood. In response to Mrs. Goodman's frantic questions, Sara had explained mildly that she had encountered a little trouble during her research. "Nothing to worry about—I merely stopped to give assistance to a stranger."

"But all that blood—"

"Not a bit of it's mine," Sara reassured her with a smile.

Eventually she had diverted Mrs. Goodman to the

problem of how to treat the stains. Together they had applied a paste of starch and cold water to her coat and gown. This morning the clothes were soaking in a mixture of gin, honey, soft soap, and water.

After pinning her hair up to stay away from her face, Sara covered the chestnut locks with a sprigged lace cap. Satisfied with her appearance, she searched through one of her trunks for a light cape. A glance through the small pane of her window had revealed that it was a typically cool autumn day.

"Sara!" Mrs. Goodman's puzzled voice drifted to her as she descended the stairs. "A magnificent private carriage has stopped right outside the house! Do you know anything about it?"

Intrigued, Sara went to the front door of the Goodmans' modest home and opened it a crack. Her gaze took in the sight of a black-lacquered carriage, gleaming ebony horses, outriders, and a coachman and footman dressed in buckskins, frock coats, and tricorns. Mrs. Goodman joined her at the door. All along the street, curtains were pulled aside and staring faces appeared at windows. "No carriage like that has ever been seen on this street before," Mrs. Goodman said. "Look at Adelaide Witherbane's face—I think her eyes are ready to pop out! Sara, what in heaven's name is going on?"

"I have no idea."

Disbelieving, they watched as the footman ascended the steps of the Goodman home. He was well over six feet tall. "Miss Fielding?" he asked deferentially.

Sara opened the door wider. "Yes?"

"Mr. Worthy has sent a carriage to convey you to Craven's whenever you are ready."

Mrs. Goodman's suspicious stare turned from the

footman to Sara. "Who is this Mr. Worthy? Sara, does this have anything to do with your mysterious behavior last night?"

Sara shrugged noncommittally. Mrs. Goodman had been distraught by Sara's late arrival, her disheveled appearance, and the bloodstains on her clothes. In response to the multitude of questions, Sara had replied mildly that there was nothing to worry about, she had been occupied with research for her novel. Finally Mrs. Goodman had given up. "I see," she had said darkly, "that what your mother wrote to me is true. Beneath that quiet surface is a stubborn and secretive nature!"

"My mother wrote that?" Sara asked in surprise.

"What she said amounts to the same thing! She wrote that you're in the habit of doing whatever you wish no matter how eccentric, and that you rarely answer any questions starting with the words 'where' and 'why.' "

Sara grinned at that. "A long time ago I learned not to explain things to people. It misleads them into thinking they're *entitled* to know everything I do."

Bringing her mind back to the present, Sara gathered her reticule and gloves, and began to leave with the footman. Mrs. Goodman stopped her with a touch on her arm. "Sara, I think it would be best if I accompany you, in the interests of your safety."

Sternly Sara held back a smile, knowing that the elderly woman's curiosity was running rampant. "That is very kind of you, but there is no need. I will be quite safe." She went to the carriage and paused as she glanced at the towering footman. "This was quite unnecessary," she murmured. "I had intended to walk to Craven's this morning."

"The driver and I are at your service, Miss Fielding.

Mr. Worthy is insistent that you should not go about London on foot any longer."

"Do we need to take the armed outriders as well?" Sara was embarrassed by all the pomp and show. The carriage would have been far more suitable for a duchess than a novelist from a small country village.

"*Especially* the outriders. Mr. Worthy said that you have a tendency to frequent dangerous places." Opening the carriage door with a flourish, he assisted her to the set of tiny carpeted steps. Smiling ruefully, Sara settled back among the velvet cushions and arranged her skirts.

When they arrived at the gambling club, the butler admitted her into the entrance hall with exquisite politeness. Immediately Worthy appeared with a courteous smile. He greeted her as if she were an old friend. "Welcome to Craven's, Miss Fielding!"

Sara took his proffered arm as he brought her into the club. "How is Mr. Craven this morning?"

"He's off his appetite, and the stitches are unsightly, but otherwise he is quite well." Worthy watched Sara as she turned a circle in the center of the sumptuous entrance hall. Her expression was transformed with wonder.

"My word," was all she could say. "Oh, my." She had never seen such luxury; the ceiling of stained-glass panels, the glittering chandelier, the walls lined with gilded columns, the heavy swaths of deep blue velvet. Without taking her eyes from the gorgeous surroundings, she fumbled in her reticule for her notebook.

Worthy spoke while Sara scribbled furiously. "I've told the staff about you, Miss Fielding. They are willing to provide any information that you might find useful."

"Thank you," she said absently, adjusting her spectacles and peering at the carving on the capitals of the columns. "This is an Ionic design, I believe?"

"Scagliola, the architect called them."

She nodded and continued to take notes. "Who was the architect? It looks like something by Nash."

"No, Mr. Craven felt that Nash's ideas were not sufficiently imaginative. Besides, Mr. Nash was quite elderly, and far too busy with projects for the king. Instead Mr. Craven chose a young architect by the name of Graham Gronow. He made it clear to Gronow that he wanted a building so magnificent that it would outshine Buckingham House."

Sara laughed. "Mr. Craven never does anything in half-measures, does he?"

"No," Worthy said ruefully. He indicated the entrance to the central hazard room. "I thought we might begin with a general tour of the club."

She hesitated. "That would be delightful, but I wouldn't like to be seen by any of the patrons—"

"You won't, Miss Fielding. It's too early in the day. Most fashionable Londoners do not rise until afternoon."

"I like getting up with the sun," Sara said cheerfully, following him to the central room. "I do my best thinking early in the day, and besides—" She broke off with an exclamation as she stepped through one of the doorways of the octagonal room. Her eyes widened as she stared at the famous domed ceiling. It was covered with lavish plasterwork and splendid paintings, and ornamented with the largest chandelier she had ever seen. The central hazard table was positioned directly beneath the dome. Quietly Sara absorbed the atmosphere of the room. She could sense the thousands of dramas that had unfolded here; the fortunes gained and lost, the excitement, anger, fear, wild joy. Several ideas for her novel occurred to her all at once, and she wrote as fast as possible, while Worthy waited patiently.

Suddenly an odd sensation crept over her, a ticklish feeling on the back of her neck. The movements of her pencil slowed. Disturbed, she finished a sentence and glanced at the empty doorway. An inner awareness prompted her to gaze upward to the balcony that overlooked the main floor. She caught a shadowy glimpse of someone leaving . . . someone who had been watching them. "Mr. Craven," she said beneath her breath, too softly for the factotum to hear.

Seeing that she had finished her note-taking, Worthy gestured to the exits at the other side of the room. "Shall we continue?"

They visited the dining and buffet rooms, a long row of elaborate card rooms, areas for smoking and billiards, and the concealed cellar where the club members could hide in the event of a police raid. Encouraged by Sara's questions and her rapt interest, Worthy told her all about the intricacies of gambling, the architecture of the building, even the lands of food and wine that were served.

Throughout the tour Sara couldn't dismiss the feeling that they were being followed. Frequently she glanced over her shoulder, suspecting she might catch someone watching them from a doorway or from behind a column. As the minutes passed, she began to see many servants bustling back and forth. Scores of housemaids crossed the halls carrying long-handled mops, buckets, and piles of cleaning rags. Door plates were polished, carpets were swept, fireplace mantels were wiped, and furniture was thoroughly dusted.

"How well-organized this place is," Sara remarked as they went up the grand central staircase with its heavy golden balustrade.

Worthy smiled with pride. "Mr. Craven has exacting standards. He employs nearly a hundred servants to keep the club running like clockwork."

Each of the six staircase landings branched off into long hallways. Sara noticed that Worthy's color heightened when she asked what those rooms were for. "Some of them are servants' quarters," he said uncomfortably. "Some are temporary residences for guests. Many are for the use of . . . er . . . house wenches."

Sara nodded matter-of-factly, knowing exactly what a house wench was. After the research she had done for *Mathilda*, she was very much against the practice of prostitution. She had sympathy for the women who were enslaved by such a system. Once they began on such a path, it was difficult, if not impossible, ever to turn back. One of her reasons for writing sympathetically about prostitutes was to show that they were not the amoral creatures people considered them to be. She didn't like the idea of Mr. Craven increasing his wealth by procurement—it was far more distasteful than gambling. "How much of Mr. Craven's profit is earned by the house wenches?" she asked.

"He takes no profit from them, Miss Fielding. Their presence adds to the ambiance of the club, and serves as an added enticement to the patrons. All the money the house wenches make is theirs to keep. Mr. Craven also offers them protection, rent-free rooms, and a far better clientele than they're likely to find on the streets."

Sara smiled ironically. "Better? I'm not so certain,

Mr. Worthy. From what I've been told, aristocratic men are just as adept at abusing women—and spreading disease—as poor ones."

"Perhaps you would like to talk to the house wenches. I am certain they will describe both the benefits and disadvantages of working at the club. They'll be straightforward with you. My impression is that they consider you something of a heroine."

Sara was startled by the remark. "Me?"

"When I explained that you are the author of *Mathilda*, they were all quite excited. Tabitha read the novel aloud to the others on their off days. Recently they all went to see the stage production."

"Would it be possible for me to meet some of them now?"

"At this hour they are usually sleeping. But perhaps later—"

A raspy feminine voice interrupted them. "Worthy! Worthy, you bloody idler, I been looking all ower the damn club for you!" The woman dressed in only a ruffled white wrapper that was slightly transparent, hurried down the hall to them. She was attractive, though her small face was coarsened by years of hard living. Rippling waves of chestnut hair, much like Sara's own, fell down her shoulders and back. She spared Sara only the briefest of glances.

Sara would have liked to exchange a few friendly words, but she knew from her previous experiences with prostitutes that they needed a fair amount of friendly reassurance before they would converse with someone like her. Out of deference, contempt, or shame, they usually avoided looking a "good woman" in the eyes.

"Tabitha," Worthy said calmly. "What is the matter?"

"Lord F again," came her indignant reply. "The cheap old rutter! 'E took to Molly last ewening an' said 'e'd pay for the 'ole night. Now 'e wants to leave without paying!"

"I'll take care of it," Worthy said calmly. He glanced at Sara, who was taking notes. "Miss Fielding, would you mind very much if I left you here for a few minutes? The gallery to your right is filled with many beautiful paintings in Mr. Craven's private collection."

"Please, go right ahead," Sara urged.

Suddenly Tabitha became very animated. "Is she the one?" she asked Worthy. "That's Mathilda?"

"Oh, no," Sara said. "I wrote the *novel* entitled *Mathilda.*"

"Then ye knows 'er? She's a friend of yers?"

Sara was nonplussed. "Not really. You see, Mathilda is a fictional character. She's not real."

The comment earned a chiding glance from Tabitha. "Not real? I read all about 'er. An' I knows a girl who met 'er. They worked the same street after Mathilda was ravished by Lord Aversley."

"Let me explain it this way—" Sara began, but Worthy shook his head as if it were no use, and ushered Tabitha down the hall.

Smiling thoughtfully, Sara wandered to the picture gallery. The walls were covered with paintings by Gainsborough, a horse and rider by Stubbs, two florid works by Rubens, and a magnificent Van Dyke. Drawing closer to a magnificent portrait, she stared at it curiously. The painting featured a woman seated in a large chair. Her young daughter stood nearby, a small hand poised on her mother's arm. The two were remarkably beautiful, with pale skin, dark curly hair, and expressive eyes. Touched by the tender scene, Sara spoke out loud. "How lovely . . . I wonder who you are?"

Sara could not help but be aware of the difference between the sparkling allure of the woman in the portrait and her own average attractiveness. She guessed that Mr. Craven was accustomed to very beautiful women—and she knew there was nothing exotic or remarkable about her. What would it be like to have the kind of looks that men found irresistible?

Although there was no sound behind her, a sixth sense caused her nerves to tingle. Sara whirled around. No one was there. Cautiously she straightened her spectacles and told herself that she was being foolish. Wandering further into the gallery, she looked closely at the sumptuous paintings. Like everything else in the club, they seemed to have been chosen for their ability to impress. A man like Mr. Craven would probably spend his life collecting valuable artwork, elaborate rooms, beautiful women . . . They were all earmarks of his achievement.

Slipping the notebook back into her reticule, Sara began to wander from the gallery. She thought of how she might describe the club and its fictional owner in her novel. Perhaps she would romanticize him just a bit. *Contrary to those who assumed he was completely without grace or virtue*, she might write, *he concealed a secret love of beauty and sought to possess it in its infinite forms, as if to atone for—*

All at once a powerful grip compressed her arm, and the wall seemed to open in a blur before her eyes. She was pulled off her feet, dragged sideways, so quickly that all she could do was gasp in protest as the unseen force yanked her from the gallery into a place of stifling darkness . . . a secret door . . . a concealed corridor. Hands steadied her, one wrapped around her wrist, one clamped her shoulder. Blinking in the darkness, Sara tried to talk and could only make a fearful squeak. "Who . . . who . . ."

She heard a man's voice, as soft as frayed velvet. Or rather, she *felt* his voice, the heat of his breath against her forehead. She began to tremble violently.

"Why are you here?" he asked.

"Mr. Craven," she whispered shakily. "I-its very dark in here."

"I like the dark."

She fought to catch her breath. "Did you really f-find it necessary to give me such a start?"

"I didn't plan to. You walked right by me. I couldn't help myself."

Sara's fear gave way to indignation. He was not at all sorry he had frightened her . . . He had intended to. "You've been following me," she accused. "You've been watching me all morning."

"I said last night I didn't want you here."

"Mr. Worthy said it was all right—"

"*I* own the club, not Worthy."

Sara was tempted to tell him how ungrateful he was, after what she had done for him last night. But she didn't think it wise to argue with him while she was trapped here. She began to inch backward, toward the crack of light where the secret door had been left ajar. "You're right," she said in a subdued voice. "You're absolutely right. I-I believe I'll go now."

But he didn't release his grip on her, and she was forced to stand still. "Tell me what made you decide to write about gambling."

Blinking in the darkness, Sara tried to gather her wits. "Well . . . there was a boy in my village. A very nice, intelligent boy, who came into a small inheritance. It would have been enough to keep him comfortable for many years. But he decided to try and increase his wealth, not by honest means, but by gambling. He lost it all in one night. At your club, Mr. Craven."

He shrugged indifferently. "Happens all the time."

"But it wasn't enough for him," Sara said. "He continued to gamble, certain that with each roll of the dice he would regain what he had lost. He gambled away his home, his horses and possessions, what was left of his money . . . He became the disgrace of Greenwood Corners. It made me wonder what had driven him to such behavior. I asked him about it, and he said he hadn't been able to stop himself. He was reduced to tears as he told me that after he had lost everything at Craven's, he sold his boots to someone on the street and played cards barefoot at a local gaming hell. Naturally this made me wonder about the other lives that have been ruined by cards and dice. The fortunes that are lost nightly at the hazard table could be used for much nobler purposes than lining your pockets."

She sensed his sardonic smile. "I agree, Miss Fielding. But one piddling book won't stop anyone from gambling. Anything you write will only make them do it more."

"That's not true," she said stiffly.

"Did *Mathilda* stop anyone from visiting whores?"

"I believe it made the public regard prostitutes in a more sympathetic light—"

"Whores will always spread their legs for a price," he said evenly, "and people will always put their money on a bet. Publish your book about gambling, and see how much good it does. See if it keeps anyone on the straight-and-narrow. I'd sooner expect a dead man to fart."

Sara flushed. "Doesn't it ever bother you to see the broken men walking from your club, with no money, no hope, no future? Don't you feel responsible in any way?"

"They're not brought in at gunpoint. They come to Craven's to gamble. I give them what they want. And I make a fortune from it. If I didn't, someone else would."

"That is the most selfish, callous statement I've ever heard—"

"I was born in the rookery, Miss Fielding. Abandoned in the street, raised by whores, nursed on milk and gin. Those scrawny little bastards you've seen, the pickpockets and beggars and palmers . . . I was one of them. I saw fine carriages rattling down the street. I stared through tavern windows at all the fat old gentlemen eating and drinking until their bellies were full. I realized there was a world outside the rookery. I swore I'd do anything—*anything*—to get my share of it. That's all I've ever cared about." He laughed softly. "And you think I should give a damn about some young fop in satin breeches throwing his money away at my club?"

Sara's heart hammered wildly. She had never been alone in the dark with a man. She wanted to escape— every instinct warned that she was in danger. But deeper still, there was a spark of unthinkable fascination . . . as if she were poised at the doorway of a forbidden world. "In my opinion," she said, "you use your poor beginnings as a convenient excuse to . . . to discard all the ethics the rest of us must live by."

"Ethics," he sneered. "I couldn't name one man, rich or poor, who wouldn't discard them for the right price."

"I wouldn't," she said steadily.

Derek fell silent. He was acutely aware of the small woman so close to him, buttoned and ruffled, cocooned in high-neck propriety. She smelled like starch and soap, like all the other spinsters he'd had the misfortune to meet . . . the governesses of his patrons' aristocratic sons, and the maiden aunts who chaperoned untouchable young ladies, and the bluestockings who preferred a book in their hands to a man in their beds. "On the shelf" was what such women were called—objects that had lost their freshness and were stored away until they might serve some convenient purpose.

But there was a difference between her and the rest. She had shot a man last night. For him. His brows pulled together until his wound ached.

"I would like to leave now," she said.

"Not yet."

"Mr. Worthy will be looking for me."

"I'm not finished talking with you."

"Must it be here?"

"It'll be anywhere I decide. I have something you want, Miss Fielding—permission to visit my club. What will you offer in return?"

"I can't think of anything."

"I never give something for nothing."

"What do you want me to offer?"

"You're a writer, Miss Fielding," he jeered. "Use your imagination."

Sara bit her lip and considered the situation carefully. "If you truly believe the statement you made earlier," she said slowly, "that the publication of my novel would serve to increase your profits . . . then it would be in your interest to allow me to do my research here. If your theory holds true, you stand to gain some money from my book."

His white teeth flashed in a grin. "I like the sound of that."

"Then . . . I have your permission to visit the club?"

He let a long moment pass before he answered. "All right."

Sara felt a rush of relief. "Thank you. As source material, you and your club are peerless. I promise I will try not to be an annoyance."

"You *won't* be an annoyance," he corrected. "Or you'll leave."

They were both startled as the secret door swung wide open. Worthy stood there, gazing inside the corridor. "Mr. Craven? I didn't expect you to be up and about so soon."

"Apparently not," Derek said darkly, his hands dropping from Sara. "Showing the place without asking my permission? You're bloody certain of yourself these days, Worthy."

"It was my fault," Sara said, trying to protect the factotum. "I-I *insisted* on having my way. The blame is all mine."

Derek's mouth twisted. "No one can make Worthy do anything he doesn't want to do, mouse. No one except me."

At the sound of Sara's voice, Worthy looked anxiously in her direction. "Miss Fielding? Are you all right?"

Derek dragged Sara out and pushed her, blinking, into the bright light. "Here's your little novelist. We were just having a discussion."

Sara stared through her spectacles at her captor, who seemed even larger and more imposing than he had last night. Craven was exquisitely dressed in charcoal-gray trousers and a snow-white shirt that emphasized his swarthiness. His tan waistcoat was made without pockets, fitted to his lean midriff with no hint of a wrinkle. She had never seen such elegant garments on anyone in the village, not even Perry Kingswood, the pride of Greenwood Corners.

But in spite of his expensive attire, no one would ever mistake Derek Craven for a gentleman. The jagged line of stitches on his face gave him a battered, rough appearance. His hard green eyes seemed to look right through her. He was a powerful man with street swagger and absolute confidence, a man who could no more conceal his appetite for the finer things of life than he could keep the sun from rising.

"I hadn't intended to show Miss Fielding the hidden passageways," Worthy commented, his eyebrows climbing up his forehead. He turned to Sara. "However, now that you know about them, I might tell you that the club is riddled with secret corridors and peepholes by which you may observe the action on the floor."

Sara slid a questioning glance to Craven, and he read her thoughts easily.

"Nothing happens here that I don't know about," Craven said. "It's safer that way—for the club members and for me."

"Is it really," she murmured. There was only the tiniest hint of skepticism in her voice, but it didn't escape his notice.

"You might find some of the passageways useful," he said smoothly, "since you won't be allowed to approach any of the guests."

"But Mr. Craven—"

"If you want to stay here, you'll abide by my rules. No talking to guests. No interference at the tables." He glanced at her reticule, which bulged with a suspiciously heavy lump. "Still carrying the pistol?" he asked, casually amused.

"I try to be prepared for any situation."

"Well," Derek mocked, "the next time things get tight around here, I'll know who to come to."

Sara was silent, her face averted. Unconsciously she had wrapped her fingers around the place on her arm he had gripped. Her hand moved gently, as if to rub the memory away.

So his touch repelled her, Derek thought, and smiled grimly. If she only knew the sins his hands had committed, she would never feel clean again.

Worthy cleared his throat and spoke in his official no-nonsense factotum's voice. "Very well, Miss Fielding. Shall we resume our tour?"

Sara nodded, looking back into the dark corridor. "I would like to see where this leads."

Derek watched with a reluctant smile as the two of them ventured into the passageway. He called after the factotum, "Keep an eye on her. Don't let her shoot anyone."

Worthy's reply was muffled. "Yes, Mr. Craven."

Derek closed the panelled door so that it blended seamlessly into the wall. He paused and steadied himself against a touch of dizziness. His bruised ribs had begun to ache. Slowly he made his way to his apartments and sought his opulent bedchamber. The headboard and posts of his bed were carved with cherubs bearing trumpets and dolphins rising on crests of waves. All of it was thickly covered with gold, which gleamed richly against the embroidered velvet bed hangings. Although Derek knew it was in bad taste, he didn't care. "A bed fit for a king" was what he had told the furniture maker, and the expensive design appealed to him. As a boy he had spent too many nights curled up in doorways and under rickety wooden stairs, dreaming of sleeping in his own bed someday. Now he had built a palace . . . only to discover that thousands of nights reclining amid gold and velvet would never take away the sense of deprivation. He still hungered for a nameless something that had nothing to do with fine linen and luxury.

Closing his eyes, he slept lightly, drifting into a troubling dream filled with images of Joyce Ashby and her glittering golden hair, her white feet splashing among rivers of blood . . .

Suddenly he knew he wasn't alone. He jerked awake with a slight gasp, his nerves clamoring in alarm. There was a woman by his bed. His green eyes focused on her, and his dark head dropped back to the pillow. "God, it's you."

Chapter 3

*L*ily, Lady Raiford, leaned over him, her dark eyes vibrant with concern. "Why didn't you tell me you'd been hurt?"

"It's not that bad." Although he wore an expression of annoyance, he accepted the little attentions she gave him; her soft ducking, the touch of her fingertips on his wound. Their relationship was that of amicable, bickering friends. They rarely saw each other alone, for Lily's husband, the earl of Raiford, possessed a jealous nature. "You'd better leave before Raiford finds us together," Derek muttered. "I'm in no mood for a duel today."

Lily grinned and settled back in her chair. "Alex trusts me," she said virtuously. "Besides, he knows I'm far too busy with the children to have an affair." The brief smile faded. "Worthy sent me a note this morning, saying you had been injured. Knowing his gift for understatement, I went mad with worry. It could have been a scratch or a fatal wound, or anything in be-

tween. I had to see for myself. Oh, your poor face,"
Her expression hardened, and for a moment her exquisite beauty was obscured by fury. "Who did this to
you?"

He shook off the hand she had placed on his arm.
"The odds are on Joyce."

"Lady Ashby?" Lily's velvet-brown eyes widened,
and she spoke impulsively. "Why in God's name? . . .
Derek, tell me you weren't having an affair with her!
Tell me you weren't like all the other poor rutting
fools who were so entranced by that false yellow hair
and lip-puckering and breast-jiggling that you fell
right into her greedy clutches. No, don't say anything,
I can see that you were yet another willing victim."
She scowled and said acidly, "It's written plainly across
your face."

The only reason she dared to speak to him so impu-
dently was the close, enduring friendship they shared.
Even so, she was treading dangerously close to the
limits. Derek shoved a pillow at her, much in the manner of a bickering sibling. "Get out of here, cold-
hearted bitch—"

She dodged the pillow. "How *could* you have an affair with Lady Ashby when you know I despise her
so?"

His mouth curved with a taunting smile. "You're
jealous."

Lily gave an exasperated sigh. "We're far beyond
that, and you know it. I adore my husband, I belong
to him completely—and he's the closest thing to a
friend you have. Both of my children refer to you as
'uncle'—"

"All very cozy," he jeered.

"There was never anything between you and me.

When I turned to you for help all those years ago, you pushed me into Alex's arms, for which I am profoundly grateful."

"You should be," he assured her.

Suddenly the tension between them dissolved, and they exchanged a grin. "Your taste in women is abominable," Lily said softly. She picked up the discarded pillows and placed them behind his head.

Derek leaned back and regarded her through slitted eyes. "Your style of nursing could kill a man." Gingerly he touched his stitches, which had begun to pull. Although he didn't admit it out loud, he knew she was right. She was the only decent woman he had ever associated with. He had loved Lily in his own way, but not enough to take the risk he knew he would never be ready for. He wasn't fit to be a husband or father. He had only the vaguest understanding of the word "family." Permanence, responsibility, commitment, the things Lily needed . . . those had never been part of his world. All he could be certain of were the material riches he had shored up in staggering amounts. If a place in heaven could be obtained with money, he would have cornered the market on eternity.

He watched Lily steadily, his expression closed. With her dark gypsy curls restrained in an intricate plait, and her slender form clad in an elegant gown, one would never guess that she had once been an outcast, just as Derek was. That had been the bond between them, the foundation for shared secrets and memories. Since her marriage Lily had graduated to the privileged society Derek was permitted to view only from the fringes. Aristocratic lords were seldom inclined to invite him to their estates, but their blue-blooded wives were more than eager to have him in their beds. For Derek it was a pleasurable form of re-venge, no less because it exasperated Lily.

"Tell me what happened with Lady Ashby," she urged.

"I broke it off with her a week ago." Derek smiled grimly as he remembered Joyce's snarling fury. "She didn't take it well. My guess is that she hired a pair of slashers to even the score."

"How do you know someone else wasn't behind it? Ivo Jenner, for example. He's always playing nasty tricks—"

"No. The bastards who jumped me last night went straight for the face." Ruefully he sat up and fingered the row of stitches. "A woman's brand of revenge, I'd say."

"You mean if Lady Ashby couldn't have you, she wanted to make certain no one else would want you?" Lily looked stricken. "Disgusting, vicious—and ex-actly what one would expect of a woman like her. Why were you involved with her? Has your life become so stale and dull that you simply couldn't resist her aris-tocratic charms?"

"Yes," Derek sneered.

"For years I've seen you hop from bed to bed. The more elite and snobbish they are, the more you want them . . . and why? Just to show the world that you can have the best, most sought-after females. Men like you regard women only as trophies, and it infuriates me!"

"From now on I'll hump all the homely, unwanted ones. Will that please you?"

Lily's small hands seized one of his, and she hung on in spite of his efforts to disengage her. "I'll tell you what will please me," she said earnestly. "It has broken my heart to watch you become so world-weary and cynical. I want you to find a woman, Derek. A nice, *unattached* one—not one of your usual debauched sophisticates. I'm not suggesting marriage, since you're so repelled by the idea. But at least take a mistress who'll bring a measure of peace to your life!"

He smiled derisively. "That's not why a man keeps a woman."

"Isn't it? I could name a half-dozen men whose mistresses are far more plain and matronly than their wives. A mistress is valued for the quality of companionship she provides, not the vulgar tricks she might know in bed."

"How do you know so much about it?"

Lily shrugged. "I've heard the fellows talking during hunts, and at the club, and over their after-dinner port. Most of the time they forget I'm there."

"Raiford should have put a stop to your hunting years ago."

"Alex is *proud* of my hunting," she replied pertly. "Stop trying to change the subject. What you need is a mistress, Derek."

He laughed, deliberately reverting to the thick accent he had worked so hard to overcome. "I gets all the tail I wants an' then some, lovey."

She frowned at him. "I said 'mistress,' Derek, not your usual parade of lightskirts. I'm suggesting you find someone who would be a companion. Haven't you ever considered spending all your nights with the same woman? Oh, don't make a face! I think you should find a nice young widow from the country, or a lonely spinster who would be grateful for your protection. If you like, I'll make a list—"

"I'll choose my own women," he said coldly. "God knows what kind of old crone you'd pick for me."

"Anyone I chose would easily surpass Lady Ashby!" She let go of his hand and sighed. "I'd better leave. It will harm my reputation if I stay any longer in your apartments—especially considering your fascination for married women."

"I didn't ask you to come," Derek retorted. But as she rose to leave, he snatched her hand and pressed a kiss to the back of it.

"Will you do what I ask?" Lily pleaded, squeezing his fingers.

"I'll consider it." His tone was so obliging that Lily knew he was lying.

Nevertheless she smiled and smoothed his black hair affectionately. "That's better. Someday you'll thank me for my sage advice." She began to leave, then paused at the doorway and looked back at him questioningly. "Derek . . . before I came up here this afternoon I caught a glimpse of the most unusual little person wandering about in the back rooms with the staff. She was asking all manner of questions and writing things down."

Derek settled back against the pillows, crossing his legs negligently. "She's a novelist."

"Really. Has she been published?"

"She wrote that *Mathilda* book."

"*That's* S. R. Fielding?" Lily laughed in surprised amazement, coming back into the room. "The famous recluse? How in heaven's name did you manage to bring her here?"

"She brought *me* here last night—after rescuing me from the slashers."

Lily's jaw dropped. "You're joking."

Suddenly he grinned at her astonishment. "Pulled out a pistol and shot one of them."

There was a moment of frozen silence, and then Lily began to howl with laughter. "You must introduce us," she begged. "If only she would consent to attend one of my soirées, or at least a salon discussion. You must help me persuade her to accept an invitation!"

"Just tell her you're Lawless Lily. She's here to research a book."

"How fascinating." Lily began to pace busily. "A woman who writes about whores, shoots criminals in the rookery, frequents gambling clubs, and is no doubt doing her best to dig up your dirty secrets. We'll be great friends, I think. What is she like? Old or young? Friendly or shy?"

Derek shrugged. "She's younger than you, about ten years. Quiet, spinsterish . . ." He paused as he remembered the discreet way Sara had glanced at him from beneath the lace frills of her cap, the little startled jump she had given as she realized she had been standing close to him. "Shy with men," he added.

Lily, who had always managed the opposite sex quite adroitly, shook her head. "I don't see why. Men are such straightforward, simpleminded creatures."

"Miss Fielding is from a village in the country. A place called Greenwood Corners. She knows nothing about men or the city. She wanders through the worst rookeries in London—to her, all problems are solved with 'please' and 'thank you.' Doesn't think anyone would rob or rape her . . . why, it wouldn't be polite. Do you know why I let her come to the club and poke her nose around here? Because if I didn't, she'd be visiting every gambling hell in the city and rubbing elbows with every thief an' murdering bastard what's ever shook an elbow at green felt!" He began to warm to the subject, the casual note disappearing from his voice.

"And she's almost engaged. Hell knows what kind of man would let her traipse through London alone, unless it's his plan to get rid of her! The bloody idiot!—I'd like to tell 'im what 'appens to women who walks in the city with frigging pistols in their readers—"

"Derek." There was an odd smile on her face. "Your cockney is showing."

He closed his mouth abruptly.

"That only happens," Lily murmured, "when you're considerably excited or angry about something."

"I'm never angry."

"Oh, of course not." She returned to him, skewering him with a level gaze.

Derek didn't like her expression, the superior look women wore when they felt they knew something a man was too stupid to understand. "I thought you were leaving," he said gruffly.

"I was, until you began making speeches about our Miss Fielding. What does she think of you? Appalled by your lurid past, as I would imagine?"

"She's in raptures over it."

"I suppose you've done everything possible to be offensive."

"She likes it. She calls me 'source material.' "

"Well, you've been called worse things. Especially by me." Lily regarded his slashed face with genuine dismay, "If only she could see you when you're handsome. How long before the stitches are removed?"

"She's not my preferred style," he said flatly.

"It's time I told you something, Derek . . . I've never been particularly impressed by your 'preferred style.' "

Derek's lips twitched with amusement "A fine romp I'd have with her in bed. She'd lie there and take notes the whole time. She . . ." He stopped as an image swept through his mind . . . Sara Fielding's pale, naked body beneath his, her arms twined gently around his neck, her soft breath rushing against his skin. The idea was disturbingly erotic. Frowning, he forced himself to concentrate on what Lily was saying.

". . . it would be far safer than the kind of liaison you had with Lady Ashby! You'll be fortunate if your looks aren't permanently ruined from this latest episode. Well, I'm going to make Lady Ashby regret this, mark my words—"

"Lily." Something in his voice hushed her at once. "Let the matter rest. You're to do nothing about Joyce."

Lily was made uncomfortable by Derek's sudden cool intensity. His was the kind of glance she had seen exchanged between men with dueling pistols in their hands, and between players who had staked their fortunes on the turn of a card. The men who won were always those who didn't seem to care. She both admired and feared such ruthless nerve. "But Derek," she protested, "you can't let her get away with this. She must be made to pay for it—"

"You heard what I said," Derek had never allowed anyone to settle his debts for him. He would confront Joyce in his own way and his own time. For now he chose to do nothing.

Lily bit her lip and nodded, wanting to say more but knowing the danger of provoking him. He would allow her friendly teasing and bullying up to a point, but there was a line she would never dare to cross. "All right," she murmured.

After holding her gaze for a moment, Derek relented. "Give us a kiss, then."

Obediently she pecked his cheek and gave him a

subdued smile. "Come to visit soon. The children will be fascinated by your stitches, especially Jamie."

He touched his forehead in a mock salute. "I'll tell 'em I was attacked by pirates."

"Derek," she said contritely, "forgive me for interfering. It's just that I'm concerned for you. You've had such a difficult life. You've lived through horrors that most people, including me, will never understand."

"That was in the past." He grinned and said in his old, boastful manner, "Now I'm one of the richest men in England."

"Yes, you have more money than anyone could spend in a lifetime. But it hasn't brought what you expected, has it?"

Derek's smile vanished. He had never confided in her the nameless hunger that gnawed at him, the emptiness that he would fill if only he could identify the craving. How had she guessed? Was it something she could see in his eyes, or hear in his voice?

Faced with his stony silence, Lily sighed and touched a lock of black hair that lay on his forehead. "Oh, Derek." Quietly she left the room while he stared after her.

Over the course of the next few days Sara was allowed to wander freely about Craven's, as long as she avoided the main rooms the patrons frequented. She was pleased by the gathering pile of notes she had amassed, which would allow her to write a detailed description of a gentleman's club. Soon she might extend her research to a few of the gaming hells in the outlying areas, but for now there was ample work to be done here.

She spent every morning sitting in the kitchen, the

largest and busiest room in the club. All of Craven's employees passed through the kitchen to take their meals and socialize, from the croupiers who ran the tables to the house wenches emerging after long nights of arduous activity.

The kitchen was well-stocked and meticulously organized. Three rows of assorted pots and pans hung over the heavy central worktable. The walls were lined with barrels of flour, sugar, and other supplies. A variety of sauces simmered on the long black stoves, sending a bewildering but delectable mixture of fragrances through the air. All of it was the domain of the chef, Monsieur Labarge. Years ago Mr. Craven had hired Labarge and his entire staff from an exclusive Parisian restaurant and had them all transferred to London. In return for their staggeringly high salaries, they provided the best cuisine in the city: a luscious cold buffet kept in constant supply for the club members and exquisitely prepared meals that were served in the dining rooms.

Monsieur Labarge was temperamental, but he was a genius. As far as Sara could tell, even Mr. Craven took care not to provoke him. Guessing at the chef's weakness for flattery, Sara made a special effort to praise his creations, until the ends of his mustache fairly quivered with pride. Now he insisted on serving her his specialties, many of them renamed in honor of *Mathilda*.

The kitchen was filled with constant activity; boys and scullery maids occupied with menial tasks of washing, chopping, scraping, and kneading, and servants laden with trays of food for the diners. The staff readily included Sara in their conversations as they related stories that ranged from ribald to touchingly sad.

They loved to talk and watch her write down what they said. Soon they began to compete to catch her interest. The prostitutes were especially helpful, giving Sara insights about the men who visited the club in droves . . . and about Derek Craven in particular. Sara particularly enjoyed Tabitha's lively chatter. Although they were quite different in temperament, outwardly they shared a striking resemblance, both of them the same size and height, with chestnut hair and blue eyes.

"I'll tell ye about the fine lords what come 'ere," Tabitha said, her blue eyes filled with a sly twinkle. "They likes the ruttin' awright, but they're the worst in the sack. Two shakes of a tail an' it's done." The other house wenches laughed in agreement. The four of them gathered around Sara at one of the wooden tables, while kitchen boys brought plates of delicate *omelettes à la Mathilda* and crusty rolls. "That an' the fine victuals . . . that's what draws 'em 'ere. But the cards is what makes 'em stay."

"How many men are you expected to consort with each night?" Sara asked in a businesslike tone, her pencil poised over her notebook.

"Whatewer we feels like. Sometimes we lets 'em 'ave a tiddle downstairs in the card rooms, an' then—"

"Tiddle?" Sara repeated, perplexed, and the prostitutes burst out laughing.

"Just a little touch an' feel," explained Violet, a short, robust blond. "An' if they like the goods, the usher takes 'em upstairs an' we does 'em over."

"Newer Mr. Craven, though," Tabitha said. " 'E newer asks any ow us to 'is bed."

" 'E gets it from 'igh-kick women," Violet commented sagely. "Countesses an' duchesses an' such."

At this mention of Mr. Craven's sexual preferences,

Sara felt her blush heighten to scarlet. The more she learned about him, the more of a puzzle he presented. His inner qualities were concealed by a smooth diamond-hard façade. He was a showman, first and foremost. Skillfully he provided a surfeit of elegant decadence that satisfied not only the aristocratic *belle monde* but also the shadowy world of libertines and courtesans called the *demimonde*. His courtesy to his social superiors was always slightly overdone, crossing the threshold of politeness into subtle mockery. Sara was certain he respected very few of them, for he was familiar with their darkest secrets. Through his own network of spies and informants, he knew about the lovers they took, the contents of their wills, even the marks their sons made at Eton and Harrow, and what they stood to inherit.

It seemed that few men felt comfortable enough to ask about the dreadful slash on his face. Members of the royal family; Wellington, the famed military commander; and the foreign diplomats who loved to lounge at the hazard-table all possessed an air of quiet unease when Craven was present. When he made a joke, they laughed a little too jovially. When he made a suggestion, it was usually followed with alacrity. Apparently no one cared to risk earning his displeasure.

As Craven had claimed the first night she had met him, he was never angry. Sara had observed that his mood could range from cold silence to biting sarcasm, but he never shouted or lost his self-control. He was a figure of mystery; arrogant, self-mocking, sociable and yet intensely private. Underneath his most congenial smiles lurked an ever-present shadow of bitterness.

Sara's attention was drawn back to the conversation as Tabitha mused aloud over Craven's preference for aristocratic ladies. "Won't touch anyone lower than a baroness." She laughed heartily at the sight of Sara's curiosity. "Ye should see 'em at the assembly balls, the 'ighborn bitches. Those fine ladies lust after our Mr. Craven, they do. An' why not? 'E's a good, solid man, not like their soft, lazy 'usbands what cares for cards an' drink more than women." She lowered her voice conspiratorially. "Built like a bull 'e is, an' just where it counts."

" 'Ow does ye know?" Violet asked suspiciously.

"I'm friends wiv Lady Fair'urst's maid Betty," came Tabitha's smug reply. "She told me once she walked in on the two of 'em by accident, ruttin' in broad daylight while Lord Fair'urst was gone to Shropshire."

The pencil dropped from Sara's lax fingers, and she ducked under the table to pick it up. She could feel her pulse racing. It was one thing to listen in detachment when a stranger was being discussed, but how could she ever face Mr. Craven again? Mortified, fascinated, she emerged from beneath the table.

"Newer say!" one of the women exclaimed. "What did they do?"

"Lady Fair'urst threw a royal fit. Mr. Craven just laughed an' said to close the door."

The whores giggled merrily. "What's more," Tabitha continued, "you can always tell what a man's got by the size ow 'is nose—an Mr. Craven's got a nice long one."

"It's not the nose," Violet said dismissively. " 'Tis the size ow the feet."

With the exception of Sara, they all cackled like a coven of amiable witches. Amid the hilarity, Tabitha leaned her head on her hand and stared at Sara as an idea occurred to her. " 'Ere's a plan, Miss Fielding—

why don't you bring Mathilda 'ere tomorrow to meet Mr. Craven? They'd make a grand pair."

The other women chimed their agreement. "Aye, she'd melt 'is heart!"

"Yes, yes, do!"

"She'd wrap Mr. Craven 'round 'er little finger!"

Even Monsieur Labarge, who had been eavesdropping on the conversation, broke in impulsively. "For *la belle* Mathilda, I will make the finest *gateau*, so light it would float in the air!"

Sara smiled apologetically and lifted her shoulders in a helpless shrug. "I can't, I'm afraid. There is no Mathilda. She . . . she's only a work of fiction."

The table was abruptly quiet. All of them stared at her with puzzled expressions. Even the kitchen boy had paused in the midst of stacking dishes.

Sara attempted to explain further. "You see, I created the character of Mathilda as the result of detailed research and discussions. She's really a composite of many women I encountered when I—"

"I 'eard as 'ow Mathilda's joined a convent now," Violet interrupted, and Tabitha shook her head.

"Nay, she 'as a rich protector. I've a friend what saw her walking along Bond Street, just the other day. Credit at all the finest shops, ewen Madam Lafleur's."

"What was she wearing?" one of the women asked eagerly.

Tabitha proceeded to describe Mathilda's lavish frock and the footman who had followed behind her. While the lively conversation continued, Sara reflected on what Tabitha had said about Mr. Craven and his affair with Lady Fairhurst. She wondered if love had been any part of his liaisons. He was a complex man, treading on the thinnest edge of respectability. No doubt it satisfied his sense of justice, carrying on affairs with the wives of aristocrats who secretly disdained him for his commonness. And it must be difficult for him to suppress a mocking smile as he counted his nightly earnings, the patrimonies he skillfully stripped from the young lords who considered themselves infinitely superior to him. It was a strange world he had created for himself. He was as apt to spend his time with the watchmen, pimps, and street urchins who were part-time employees of the club as he was with the highborn patrons. It was impossible to fit such a man into any category. Sara spent a good deal of time thinking about him, her mind filled with endless questions about who and what he was.

Sara paused in the midst of her writing in order to take a morsel from the plate of pastries Monsieur Labarge had sent up to her. The delicate layers of cake and coffee cream seemed to dissolve in her mouth. Flecks of sugar drifted to the polished mahogany in front of her, and she quickly wiped them away with her sleeve. She was sitting in one of the rooms of Craven's private apartments, working at his large mahogany desk. The stately piece of furniture, with its innumerable compartments and small drawers, was cluttered with intriguing odds and ends; pieces of string, loose coins, dice and cribbage pins, notes and receipts. It seemed as if he ritually emptied his pockets at his desk. She wouldn't have expected it of a man who conducted his life with such meticulous precision. As she consumed the last bite of cake, a few slips of paper piled in a corner of the desk caught her eye. Intrigued, she began to reach for the folded notes. Abruptly she stopped and scolded herself for even thinking of violating Mr. Craven's privacy.

She bent again to her writing, carefully dipping the ivory-handled pen in a pot of ink. But she was unable to resume her train of thought. Idly she speculated on what the mysterious notes might contain. Setting down the pen, Sara stared longingly at the slips of paper, while her conscience waged a war with her curiosity. Unfortunately the latter won out. Quickly she plucked the notes from their resting place.

The first note was a list of random tasks, with Worthy's name written across the top:

Worthy,

Riplace carpits in card rums 2 and 4
Credit to be rifused to Lords Faxton and Rapley until acownts seteld.
Have Gill sampel next brandy delivry . . .

Sara felt compassion as she glanced over the laboriously scrawled note. Craven's handling of the written word was nothing short of a massacre. On the other hand, there was nothing wrong with his mathematics. On a few occasions she had observed him multiplying and dividing figures in his head with bewildering speed, easily juggling betting odds and percentages. He could watch a card game in progress, silently calculate the cards that had been played, and predict the winning hand with unfailing accuracy. He glanced over the account books and rapidly totaled columns of figures without ever reaching for a pen.

His other talent was just as extraordinary—an apparent ability to see inside peoples' minds. He could unerringly sense a well-hidden vulnerability and skewer it with a casual remark. His alert gaze took note of every nuance in a person's expression, in a tone of voice . . . It made Sara realize with some surprise that he was every bit the observer she was, that he also felt a distance between himself and the rest of the world. At least, she thought, that was one thing they had in common.

Sara picked up the second note, which was inscribed in an elegant feminine style, all pretentious loops and curls. It was an odd, abrupt message which gave her a cold sensation.

> *Now you wear my mark for everyone to see.*
> *Come take your revenge if you dare.*
> *I still want you.*
>
>   *—J*

"Oh, my," Sara whispered, staring at the elaborately scrawled initial. She had no doubt the reference to a "mark" meant the slash on Craven's face. What kind of woman would pay to have a man's face ruined? How could Craven consort with such a female? Slowly Sara put the letters back in place, not wanting to see any more. Perhaps this "J" felt a kind of twisted love for Craven that was aligned with hatred. Perhaps Craven felt the same for her.

It was difficult for Sara, who had always known love as a gentle and comforting emotion, to understand that for others it was sometimes dark, primitive, sordid. "There are so many things I don't know," she muttered, taking off her spectacles and rubbing her eyes. Perry had always been helpless in the face of her "moods" . . . He saw little reason one should be interested in anything outside Greenwood Corners. She had learned to conceal her occasional frustrations from him, or he would give her one of his lectures about being sensible.

Her thoughts were interrupted by a quiet voice from the doorway. "What are you doing in my apartments?"

Sara turned in the chair and flushed. Derek Craven stood there, an unfathomable expression on his tanned face. "I'm sorry," she said with an appealing glance. "Usually I work at Mr. Worthy's secretaire, but he asked if I would use your desk today, since you were gone and he needed—"

"There are other rooms you could have used."

"Yes, but none that offered privacy, and I can't work with distractions, and . . . I'll leave now."

"That's not necessary." He walked toward her. Although he was a large, powerfully built man, he moved with catlike grace. Sara lowered her head, focusing on the desk blotter. Out of the corner of her eye she saw Craven touch her discarded spectacles. "How many of these do you have?" he asked, nudging them an inch across the surface of the desk.

"Only two."

"You leave them everywhere. I find them on bookcases, desks, edges of picture frames, wherever you happen to set them aside."

Sara picked up the spectacles and adjusted them on her face. "I can't seem to remember them," she admitted. "It's very disconcerting. I take an interest in something, and then just forget them."

Derek's gaze moved to the neatly formed sentences before her. "What's this?" Deliberately he leaned over her, bracing his hands on the gleaming expanse of mahogany. Stunned, Sara shrank in the chair, while his arms formed a cage on either side of her.

"I-I'm writing about the rookery."

Derek grinned at her overly casual tone. He knew exactly how much his nearness bothered her. Deciding to prolong her torment, he leaned over her more deeply, glancing at the tantalizing hint of fullness in her bodice and the flash of white skin above the lace at her neck. His chin nearly touched her lace cap as he read aloud from her notes. "The . . . city streets are . . . om . . ." He paused, concentrating on the difficult word.

Automatically Sara located the word with the tip of her finger. "Ominous," she said. "It means haunting . . . sinister." She straightened her spectacles as they slipped on her nose. "It seemed an appropriate way to describe the atmosphere of the rookery."

"I'll describe it better," he said flatly. "It's dark and it stinks."

"That's true enough." Sara risked a glance over her shoulder. He was close enough that she could see the grain of black whiskers beneath his shaven skin. His exquisite clothes and the pleasant trace of sandalwood scent couldn't conceal the brutality that simmered so close to the surface. He was a rough, masculine man. Perry Kingswood would be disdainful of him. *"Why, he is nothing but a ruffian!"* Perry would exclaim. *"A peasant in gentleman's attire!"*

Somehow Craven seemed to read her thoughts. "Your young man in the village . . . Kingsfield . . ."

"Kingswood."

"Why does he let you come to London alone?"

"I'm not alone. I'm staying with the Goodmans, a very respectable family—"

"You know what I'm asking," Derek said curtly. He turned to face her, half-sitting on the edge of the desk. "You spend your time with gamblers, whores, and criminals. You should be safe with your family in Greenwood Corners."

"Mr. Kingswood isn't pleased with the situation," Sara admitted. "We had words about it, in fact. But I was very stubborn."

"Do you ever tell him about the things you do in London?"

"Mr. Kingswood knows about my research—"

"I'm not talking about your research," he murmured, his eyes hard. "Are you going to tell him you killed a man?"

Sara blanched guiltily, feeling slightly sick as she always did when she thought of that night. She avoided his piercing gaze. "I don't think there would be much point in telling him."

"Oh, you don't. Now I see what kind of wife you'll be. Sneaking behind the poor bastard's back to do things he doesn't approve of—"

"It's not like that!"

"It's exactly like that."

"Perry trusts me," Sara said sharply.

"I wouldn't trust you if I were in his place." His mood turned caustic. "I'd keep you with me every bloody minute of the day—no, I'd have you fitted with a ball and chain—because I know that otherwise you'd be running off to do 'research' in the nearest dark alley with every cutthroat and pimp you can find!"

She folded her arms and regarded him with tight-lipped disapproval. "There's no need to shout at me, Mr. Craven."

"I'm not . . ." Derek's voice faded into silence. He

had been shouting, something he never did. Amazed, he rubbed his jaw and stared at her, while she returned his gaze like an inquiring little owl. Her fearless attitude provoked him beyond reason. Didn't anyone understand how much she needed someone to look after her? She shouldn't be allowed to wander through London by herself. She shouldn't be here alone with him, for God's sake. He could have ravished her ten times over by now.

As he continued to study her, he realized that beneath the cloud of frills and the spectacles, there was an attractive woman. She would be appealing if she didn't dress like a spinster. He raised his hand to her puffy cap, his fingertip brushing an edge of lace. "Why do you always wear this thing on your head?"

Sara's lips parted in surprise. "To keep my hair in place."

He continued to finger the edge of lace. A curious tension seemed to fill the room. "Take it off."

Sara could hardly find her breath for a moment. His intense green eyes remained on hers. No one had ever looked at her this way, making her hot and cold and unbearably nervous. She leapt up from the chair and backed away a few steps. "I'm afraid I don't have time to indulge your whims, Mr. Craven. My work is finished for now. I must go. Good evening."

She fled the room, leaving behind all her possessions, even her reticule. Derek looked at the little drawstring bag and waited for her to come back. After a minute had passed, he knew she would return for it later, when there was no chance of confronting him. He picked up the bag and sat more fully on the desk, swinging a leg nonchalantly. He loosened the silken cord and looked inside. A few pound notes . . . the tiny notebook and pencil . . . the pistol. Derek smiled wryly and delved deeper into the reticule until he found a few coins and a handkerchief. Extracting the neatly pressed square of linen, he held it to his face. He hunted for the scent of perfume or flower water, but there was none.

Lodged at the bottom of the reticule was the extra pair of spectacles. Derek examined them minutely, the round lenses, the dainty steel frame, the small curved earpieces. He squinted through them at the words she had written. After he folded the spectacles, he placed them in his coat pocket and closed the reticule. When Sara discovered the spectacles were missing, she would assume she had left them somewhere, as she often did. It was the first act of outright thievery he had committed in ten years. But he had to have them. He wanted to own a little piece of her.

Leaving the reticule as Sara had placed it on the desk, Derek jammed his hands into his pockets and began to walk with no particular destination in mind. He thought of the way Worthy had sung Sara Fielding's praises yesterday. Not even the former Lily Lawson, with all her sparkling allure, had been able to elicit such devotion from the factotum.

"She is a lady of quality," Worthy had said in response to one of Derek's sarcastic barbs. "Miss Fielding treats everyone she encounters with kindness and courtesy, even the house wenches. Before she leaves the club in the evenings, she voluntarily writes letters dictated to her by some of the illiterate members of the staff, so that they might send word to their families. When she saw that the hem of Violet's gown needed mending, she asked for a needle and knelt down on the floor to fix it. One of the maids told me yesterday that when she tripped with a pile of linen in her arms, Miss Fielding stopped to help her gather it up—"

"Maybe I should hire her," Derek had interrupted sarcastically.

"Miss Fielding is the most gentle, tolerant woman who has ever set foot in this club. And perhaps I should take this opportunity to tell you sir, that the staff has been complaining."

"Complaining," Derek repeated without inflection.

Worthy nodded stiffly. "That you have not been according her the proper degree of respect."

Derek had been dumfounded. "Who the hell is paying their salaries?"

"You, sir."

"Then tell them I don't hand out a bloody fortune in order to hear their opinions! And I'll talk to their saintly Miss Fielding any damn way I want to!"

"Yes, sir." With a barely audible sniff of disapproval, Worthy had turned on his heel and gone down the stairs.

Oh, Worthy was indeed taken with her. Everyone was. Derek had never dreamed that his territory would be so gently and thoroughly invaded—or that his employees would be such willing traitors. Sara Fielding's mysterious charm had captivated everyone in his club. They all strove to please and accommodate her. During the hours she sat at Worthy's desk, they tiptoed quietly through the halls as if in mortal fear of distracting her from her work. "She's writing now," Derek had heard one of the housemaids tell another reverently, as if some holy sacrament were being performed.

Derek hardened his jaw. "A lady of quality," he snorted aloud. He'd had his pleasure between the thighs of women with far superior pedigrees, ladies born with blue blood and illustrious names, generations of privilege and wealth behind them.

But Worthy had been right. Privately Derek admitted that Sara Fielding was the only genuine lady he had ever met. She had none of the vices that Derek could detect so easily in others. Jealousy, greed, lust . . . she seemed to be above such flaws. On the other hand, he sensed the reckless edge that might someday prove her undoing. She needed someone to keep her from plunging headlong into trouble, or at least to drag her out of it. It didn't seem likely that her hapless suitor Kingswood was up to the task.

Derek was certain that Kingswood would be slender and classically handsome in the mode of Byron. He would have a cultured voice, of course, and locks as fair as Derek's own were dark. No doubt Kingswood was a stuffy young country squire who couldn't understand recklessness. Eventually he would mature into a portly old gentleman who drank too much at dinner and would never let others finish their sentences. And Sara, as his loving wife, would tolerate his boorishness with a gentle smile, and save her frustrations for her private moments. When she had a problem, she would try to solve it herself to keep from bothering him. And she would be faithful to her husband. Only he would know the sight of her with unbound hair and a thin white nightgown . . . Only he would know the feeling of her sleeping trustingly against him. They would make love in the concealment of darkness and layers of bedclothes, their eyes closed, their movements governed by modesty and restraint. No one would ever awaken Sara Fielding's passion, strip away her inhibitions, taunt and tease her . . .

Impatiently Derek raked his hands through his hair and stopped in the middle of the empty hallway. He wasn't behaving like himself—he wasn't *thinking* like himself. He felt as if he should brace himself for some cataclysmic event. The air was charged with white-hot currents. His nerve ends seemed abraded. Something was going to happen . . . something . . . and all he could do, it seemed, was wait.

"Please let me out here," Sara called to the driver, tapping on the roof of the carriage. It was eight o'clock in the morning, her usual time to arrive at the club. Before they had pulled around to the front entrance, her interest had been caught by the sight of several loaded carts lined at the side of the building. They were different than the usual market wagons that brought deliveries of fresh produce to the kitchen.

The footman assisted her from the vehicle and inquired if it would please her to have them wait there.

"No, thank you, Shelton. I'll enter the club through the kitchen." Although Sara knew it was improper, she gave the driver a cheerful little wave as she walked away. He gave an imperceptible nod, although he had painstakingly explained to her yesterday that it would not do for a lady to appear familiar with the hired help.

"Ye should look down your nose all grand and haughty-like," he had instructed sternly. "No more smiles at me an' the footmen, miss. Ye needs be more offhandish with the servants—or what will people think of ye?" In Sara's opinion, it hardly mattered if she behaved without the expected hauteur, since she would soon be gone from London.

The sound of voices raised in debate rang from the alley. Sara drew her cloak more closely around her throat, shivering as the cold morning air struck her face. The carts were filled with crates of wine bottles. A short, rotund man waddled back and forth, shaking his finger and talking rapidly to two of Craven's employees. The man appeared to be a merchant defending the quality of his wares.

"I'd slit my throat before I'd water my precious vintages, and ye know it!" he barked.

Gill, an intelligent young man who had become one of Worthy's protegés, selected three bottles at random. He opened them and examined the contents carefully. "Mr. Craven was displeased by the last delivery of brandy. It wasn't fit to serve to our patrons."

"That was first-rate wine I sold ye!" the merchant exclaimed.

"For some dockside tavern, perhaps. Not for Craven's." Gill took a small sip, swished it around his mouth, and spit it out carefully. He nodded his approval. "This is acceptable."

"It's the finest French brandy," the merchant said indignantly. "How dare ye swill it like it was some stinkin' cheap ale—"

"Mind your language," Gill said, suddenly noticing Sara. He cast a quick grin in her direction. "There's a lady present."

The merchant ignored the new arrival. "I don't care if the Queen o' Sheba's here, there's no need to open them bottles—"

"There is, until I'm satisfied you haven't watered down your liquor."

As the two argued, Sara skirted around the side of the alley toward the kitchen entrance. Engrossed in the animated conversation, she didn't watch where she was going. Suddenly a huge, dark shape moved near the corner of her vision, and she gasped as she bumped into a tall man hefting a crate of wine on his shoulder. "Oh—"

Automatically he steadied her with his free arm. The hard band of muscle threatened to crush her. Sara's head fell back as she regarded the swarthy face above hers. "Forgive me, I wasn't looking—" She stopped and frowned in bewilderment. "Mr. . . . Craven?"

Derek bent to set down the crate, and then he loomed over her once more. "Are you all right?"

Sara nodded jerkily. At first she hadn't recognized him. He was always so immaculately dressed, smoothly shaven, every hair in place. Today, heavy black stubble shadowed his jaw. His broad shoulders were covered with a knit sweater and a rough coat. His wool trousers and scuffed boots had seen far better days. "Should you be exerting yourself like this?" she asked with a frown. "What about your injuries?"

"I'm fine." Derek had found it impossible to attend to his usual business this morning; poring over account books, combing through piles of promissory notes and bank drafts. Filled with frustration, he had decided to work outside where he could be of some use. He glanced at Gill, who was engaged in the argument with the wine merchant, and then back at Sara. The collision had dislodged her white cap. A band of lace drooped lazily over her cheek. One corner of his mouth twitched with unwilling amusement. "Your hat is crooked," he told her.

"Oh, dear." Sara reached up to her head, pulling the frilly headgear forward.

Suddenly he laughed. "Not that way. Here, I'll do it."

Sara noticed that his white teeth were slightly snaggled, giving his smile the appearance of a friendly snarl. It was then that she understood why so many women had been seduced by him. His grin held a wickedly irresistible appeal. She stared at his chest as he untied the laces and positioned her cap correctly.

"Thank you," she murmured, and tried to take the strings of the cap from his fingers.

But he didn't let go. He held the laces at her chin, his fingers tightening. Glancing up at him in confusion, Sara saw that his smile had vanished. In a decisive motion he pulled the concealing lace from her hair and let it fall. The cap fluttered to a patch of mud and rested there limply.

Sara lifted her hand to the loose braided coil of her hair, which threatened to tumble from its pins. The chestnut locks gleamed with fiery highlights, escaping in delicate wisps around her face and throat. "Mr. Craven," she scolded breathlessly. "I find your behavior untoward a-and offensive, not to mention—oh!" She stammered in astonishment as he reached for her spectacles and plucked them from her face. "Mr. Craven, h-how dare you . . ." She fumbled to retrieve them. "I . . . I need those . . ."

Derek held them out of reach as he stared at her uncovered face. This was what she had kept hidden beneath the old-maid disguise . . . pale, luminous skin, a mouth shaped with surprising lushness, a pert little nose, marked at the delicate bridge where the edge of her spectacles had pressed. Angel-blue eyes, pure and beguiling, surmounted by dark winged brows. She was beautiful. He could have devoured her in a few bites, like a fragrant red apple. He wanted to touch her, take her somewhere and pull her beneath him, as if he could somehow erase a lifetime of sin and shame within the sweetness of her body.

Forcing his muscles to loosen, Derek bent to scoop up the soiled puff of lace. Sara watched him in offended silence. He tried to brush off the lace cap, succeeding only in grinding the mud deeper into the pure white cloth. Finally Sara ventured to retrieve it from him. "I'm certain this will wash," she said crisply.

She was most definitely annoyed. Derek felt a rueful grin stealing over his face. As he handed the spectacles back, his bare fingers brushed her gloved ones. Impersonal though the touch was, it caused his heart to pump with unexpected vigor. He decided to charm her back into her usual pleasant mood.

"It's a pity to cover such beautiful hair, Miss Fielding."

Sara received the compliment with a forbidding frown. "Mr. Craven, I am hardly eager to hear your opinions about my appearance." She held the crumpled puff as if it were an injured pet. "Throwing my favorite cap into the mud—"

"It dropped," he said hastily. "I didn't throw it. I'll buy you another."

The frown lingered between her silky brows. "I'm not in the habit of allowing gentlemen to purchase articles of clothing for me."

"Sorry," he said, doing his best to look chastened.

The cold breeze gusted again, bringing with it the scent of a coming storm. Sara looked at the gray sky and wiped at an errant raindrop that had whisked against her cheek. "You'll catch a chill," Derek said, all solicitous concern. He found her elbow in the folds of her cloak. Before she could jerk her arm away, he ushered her down the steps of the nearest entrance, and opened the door for her. The warmth and light of the kitchen enveloped her in a comforting glow.

"What are your plans for this morning?" Derek asked.

"I am going to breakfast with Mr. Worthy. He is going to explain to me about the committee of lady patronesses that has planned the assembly ball for this evening."

His eyes glinted dangerously. "I don't recall giving him leave to tell you anything about my patronesses. Why do you have to know how everything works around here? Who does what, and why, and everything about the people I hire, how much frigging money I have, which side of my face do I start my shave every morning—" Breaking off with a beleaguered sigh, he drew the cloak from her shoulders. He took the bedraggled cap and handed it to a nearby kitchen maid. "Do something with this," he said brusquely. He turned back to Sara and took her arm once more. "Come with me."

"Where are we going?"

"I'll show you how they've decorated the hazard room."

"Thank you. That would be delightful." She followed without hesitation. "I'm looking forward to the ball tonight. We certainly have nothing to compare in Greenwood Corners."

"If you want to watch, you'll get a fair view from the second-floor balcony behind the musicians."

Sara didn't think that would provide a very good view at all. "I don't think I'll be noticed if I stand in a corner of the hall—"

"No. That won't work."

"Then I'll borrow a mask from someone, and come downstairs for a closer look."

"You don't have a suitable gown, mouse."

Mouse . . . Oh, how she disliked the nickname he had bestowed on her! But he was right. Sara glanced down at her heavy plum-colored gown and flushed. "I might have something," she said bravely.

Derek gave her a derisive glance but let her comment pass unchallenged. "Only the *demimonde* will attend tonight. The more debauched variety of aristocrats and foreigners, whores, actresses—"

"But those are precisely the kind of people I wish to write about!"

"You're no match for a crowd of randy bucks. They'll be drunk and ready for action, and they'll assume you're here for one reason. Unless you're prepared to oblige them, you'll stay upstairs where it's safe."

"I can take care of myself."

"You're not coming to the ball tonight, Miss Fielding."

Her eyes widened. "You're *forbidding* me to attend?"

"I'm advising you not to," he murmured in a tone that would have caused Napoleon to quail.

They entered the central hazard room, and Sara temporarily abandoned their argument. She'd never seen a place decorated so extravagantly. It was like a glittering underwater kingdom, reminding her of the tales of Atlantis that had enchanted her as a child. The walls were hung with gauzy blue and green silk draperies. A painted canvas studded with seashells gave the impression of a castle beneath the sea. Slowly she wandered around the room, inspecting the plaster sculptures of fish, scallop shells, and bare-breasted

mermaids. A gaudy treasure chest filled with paste
jewels was wedged beneath the central hazard table.
The doorway to the next room had been converted
into the hull of a sunken ship. Lengths of blue gauze
and silver netting were hung overhead, making it seem
as if they were under water.

"How extraordinary," she said. "It's beautiful, imaginative . . ." She turned a slow circle. "And when all the
guests are here, the women in glittering gowns, everyone wearing masks . . ." A feeling of wistfulness swept
over her. She smiled tremulously, lifting one of the
silken banners and letting it stream through her fingers. "I've never attended a ball before. Country
dances, of course, and the local festivals . . ." The silk
caught in the sudden vise of her fingers. She was lost
in her thoughts, forgetting the presence of the man
who watched her.

All of her life she had been quiet and responsible,
living vicariously through the experiences of others.
It had been enough to content herself with family
and friends, and to write. But now she regretted the
things she had missed. She had never made a mistake
more serious than forgetting to return a borrowed
book. Her sexual experience had been limited to
Perry's kisses. She had never worn a gown cut low
enough to show her bosom, or danced until dawn.
She'd never really been intoxicated. Except for Perry,
the men she had grown up with in the village had always regarded her as a sister and confidante. Other
women inspired passion and heartbreak. She inspired
friendship.

Once when she had been overtaken by a mood sim-
iliar to this, she had thrown herself at Perry. Filled
with a desperate need to be close to someone, she had

begged him to make love to her. Perry had refused, pointing out that she was not the kind of woman to be taken out of wedlock. *"We'll be married someday,"* he had explained with a loving smile. *"As soon as I can make my mother accept the idea. It won't take long—and in the meantime, you and I will pray for patience. You mean more to me than a hour or two of illicit pleasure."* Perry had been right, of course. She had even admired his concern for doing the right thing ... but that had done little to ease the sting of rejection. Wincing at the memory, Sara let go of the silken banner and turned to face Craven. He was watching her with the intense stare that always made her uneasy.

"What is it?" He reached out and took her arm, his fingers resting lightly on her sleeve. "What are you thinking about?"

Sara was very still, feeling the warmth of his hand sinking through the heavy material of her gown. He mustn't stand so close ... he mustn't look at her this way. She had never been so aware of anyone in her life. A mad notion crossed her mind, that he was about to take her into his arms. Briefly the image of Perry Kingswood's reproachful face floated before her. But if Craven did try to take a liberty ... no one would ever know. Soon she would walk away from him forever, back to her ordinary life in the country.

Just once let something happen to her. Something she would remember all her life.

"Mr. Craven." Her heart rose in her throat, threatening to obstruct her voice. "Perhaps you wouldn't mind helping me with my research. There is something you could do for me." She took a deep breath and continued in a rush. "Living in Greenwood Corners, one tends to have rather limited experience. Certainly I've never encountered a man like you, and never expect to again."

"Thank you," he said dryly.

"Therefore, purely in the interests of research . . . to broaden my scope of experience and so on and so forth . . . I thought that perhaps you might be willing to . . . that is, you would consider . . ." Sara balled her hands into fists and forced herself to finish bluntly. "That you would kiss me."

Chapter 4

*T*he temptation of it beckoned sweetly. Derek couldn't control the lurid thoughts that flooded his mind. Of all the women he had known, none had ever affected him like this. In his ruthless climb out of the gutter, he had used women, for pleasure and for gain. And he had been used in turn. But the game at which he was so expert had always been understood by his partners. Sara Fielding didn't realize what he was, and how much she had to fear from him. If it was the only decent thing he ever did, he would protect her from himself.

Carefully he reached out to her. His long fingers curved gently around her jaw, as if he were handling a precious object. Her skin was soft and fragile, like the finest silk. "Miss Fielding." His voice was hoarse. "I'd like to do more than kiss you." He watched as her lashes drifted downward, partially concealing her deep blue eyes. "I'd like to take you upstairs to my bed. And keep you with me until morning. But you . . . and me . . ." He shook his head, and his friendly, mocking snarl of a smile appeared. "Do your 'research' with Kingswood, mouse."

He was refusing her. Sara's cheeks turned rosy with humiliation. "I-I wasn't asking to come to your bed," she said tensely. "I asked for a kiss. One kiss isn't such an earth-shattering request."

Derek released her, the warmth of his fingers fading immediately from her skin. "For you and me, one kiss is a mistake," he assured her, and produced a half-hearted grin. Sara didn't return the smile. Faced with her puzzled countenance, he turned abruptly and strode away, leaving her alone in the sparkling room. His body was beginning to respond to her nearness, his loins awakening with throbbing awareness. If he stayed with her one moment longer, she would get far more than she had asked for.

Incredulously Sara watched his departure. It seemed as though he couldn't get away from her quickly enough. Her offer had been considered and summarily dismissed. Suddenly her embarrassment changed to baffled anger. Why had he refused her? Was she so unattractive? So undesirable? At least Perry had declined her invitation for reasons of honor. Derek Craven had no such excuse!

She glanced around the opulent room. There would be dazzling, sophisticated women here tonight. Craven would dance, flirt, and ply them with seductive charm. After midnight the assembly would begin to unravel. There would be drunkenness, gallantry, merriment, scandals brewing. Sara wrapped her arms around herself. She didn't want to watch from a safe distance. She wanted to be down here tonight. She wanted to become someone else, someone brazen enough to capture the attention of Derek Craven himself.

In her novels, her characters always acted with boldness. Mathilda, especially, had been fearless. If Mathilda had wanted to go to the assembly, she would have, and damn the consequences. A sudden blast of excitement made Sara's breath shorten. "I'll get my kiss from you, Mr. Craven. And you'll never even know it was I." Terrified she might lose her nerve, Sara flew from the room. Abruptly she checked herself. It wouldn't do to appear frantic. Busily she combed the club in search of Worthy. She finally found him at his desk, sorting through stacks of letters and receipts.

"Miss Fielding," he said with a smile, setting his papers aside. "I was told you had decided to delay our breakfast while Mr. Craven showed you . . ." He paused as he saw her expression. "Miss Fielding, has something happened? You seem agitated."

"I'm afraid I am. Mr. Worthy, I need your help!"

All at once the factotum's face changed, taking on a grim austerity that made him seem unfamiliar. "Is it Mr. Craven? If he's done anything to distress you—"

"Oh, no, if s not that at all. Mr. Worthy, it is imperative that I attend the assembly tonight!"

"The assembly?" the factotum asked blankly, and gave a sigh of relief. "Thank God. I thought . . . well, that doesn't matter. I promise you will obtain an excellent view from the balcony—"

"I want to do more than watch. I must be there. I must get a mask from somewhere, and a gown—nothing too elaborate, but appropriate to the occasion. Could you recommend a shop, a dressmaker, someone who would be able to help me at such short notice? Perhaps I could pay to borrow a gown and then return it later, or remake one I already have—"

"Miss Fielding, you are quite overwrought," he exclaimed. He took her hand and bestowed several fatherly pats in an attempt to settle her nerves. "You're not yourself—"

"I have the rest of my life to be myself!" she said passionately. "For just one night I want to be someone else."

Worthy continued to pat her hand while he regarded her with concern. His gaze was filled with unspoken questions. He considered several approaches. "Miss Fielding," he finally said, "you don't understand the atmosphere at these assemblies—"

"Yes I do."

"You wouldn't be safe. There are men who will undoubtedly make unwelcome advances—"

"I'm aware of that. I can certainly handle a harmless tiddle here and there."

" 'Tiddle'?" he repeated dazedly. "Where did you learn that word?"

"That's not important. The point is, I want to attend the ball tonight. No one will know. Not even Mr. Craven. I'll be wearing a mask."

"Miss Fielding, the mask is more of a danger than a protection. It's only a scrap of leather and ribbon and paper, but it leads people to discard their inhibitions, and then . . ." He paused to clean his spectacles. Vigorously he rubbed the lenses with his sleeve. Sara suspected he was stalling for time in order to think of a way to dissuade her. "May I ask what has caused this sudden determination? Does it have something to do with Mr. Craven?"

"Absolutely not," she said, a shade too quickly.

"This is strictly for the purposes of research. I . . . I'm considering writing a scene in my novel which includes an assembly ball, and since I've never been to one, this is my only opportunity to gain an accurate perception of the people, the atmosphere—"

"Miss Fielding," he interrupted. "I doubt that your family—or your fiancé—would approve of this."

"Mr. Kingswood isn't my fiancé yet. And you're right, he wouldn't approve. No one I know would approve." Sara smiled in delight at the thought. "But they're not going to know."

Worthy contemplated her for a long time, reading the determination on her face. He gave a reluctant sigh. "I suppose I could have Gill and one of the croupiers to keep an eye on you. But if Mr. Craven had any suspicion of this—"

"He won't. He'll never, ever find out. I'll be utterly discreet. I'll avoid Mr. Craven like the plague. Now about the dressmaker . . . could you possibly recommend a reputable shop?"

"Yes, indeed," Worthy murmured. "In fact, I believe I can do better that that. I think I know someone who will help."

Derek strode edgily about his apartments, trying to ignore the fever that coursed through his body. He hungered for a woman . . . for *her*. He had been fascinated by her since the first morning she had come here, with her fancy words and her ladylike manners, and her gentle wilfulness. What would it be like to wrap her in his arms and hold himself deep within her? Savagely he wished he had never met her. She should be married to her country suitor, and located well out of his own reach. She belonged with a decent man. A stab of

violent jealousy for Perry Kingswood caused Derek to
scowl.

"Mr. Craven?" came a steward's voice from the
doorway.

The servant approached with a card poised on a silver tray. Derek recognized the Raiford crest at once.
"Is it Lily?"

"No, sir. The caller is Lord Raiford."

"Good. God help me if I have to see any more
women today. Bring him up."

There was no man in England more different from
Derek than Alex, Lord Raiford. Alex possessed a self-
assurance that could only come from having been born
to a family of nobility. He was an honorable man with
an inherent sense of fairness. There had been struggles
in his life, grief and loss, which he had overcome hand-
somely. Men liked him for his sportsmanship and his
sense of humor. Women adored his easy masculine
charm, not to mention his looks. With his rich blond
hair and rangy build, he possessed a distinctively lion-
esque appearance. Raiford could have an affair with
any woman he wanted, but he was passionately in love
with his own wife, Lily. His devotion to her was a
source of amusement for the sophisticated members of
the *ton*. In spite of their mockery, many secretly wished
for the kind of loving and faithful union the Raifords
had, but in these days of arranged matches that wasn't
possible.

Alex tolerated Derek's friendship with his wife because he knew that if the need ever arose, Derek would
protect Lily with his own life. Throughout the years,
a friendship had evolved between the two men.

"I came to see if Lily had exaggerated about the
scar," were Alex's first words as he entered the library.

He studied Derek's dark face impassively. "It's not what I'd call an improvement."

Derek grinned briefly. "Piss off, Wolverton."

They sat down before the fire with snifters of brandy, and Alex accepted one of the cigars that Derek offered. After snipping and lighting it carefully, Alex inhaled with great enjoyment. His gray eyes appeared silver in the haze of smoke. He gestured to the scar. "How did it happen? A dozen rumors are circulating—none of them particularly flattering to you, I might add."

Derek gave him a level stare. "It doesn't matter."

Alex sat back and regarded him thoughtfully. "You're right. The scar is of no import, and neither are the rumors. What matters is that Lady Ashby did this to you—and having gone this far, she'll likely do worse." He held up his hand as Derek tried to interrupt. "Let me finish. There's good reason for concern. Joyce is a dangerously unpredictable woman. I've been acquainted with her for a long time. Fortunately I managed to avoid the mistake of becoming involved with her. But you—"

"It's over now," Derek said flatly. "I can handle Joyce."

"I'm not so certain. I hope you don't believe that by ignoring the problem, she'll go away. As far as I can tell, Joyce has made life hell for every man she's ever taken as a lover—though this seems to be the first time she's ever resorted to physical maiming." Alex's mouth tightened with distaste. "For all Joyce's beauty, I would never have the desire to lie with her. There's something emotionless about her. She's like a beautiful, deadly serpent. Why in God's name did you become involved with her? Surely you knew better."

Derek hesitated. It was a rare occasion when he confided in anyone—but if there was one man he trusted, it was Alex. "I knew better," he admitted, "but I didn't care. I met Joyce at Lord Aveland's wedding reception. We talked for a while. I thought she would be entertaining, and so . . ." He shrugged. "The affair began that night."

Alex began to ask something, hesitated, and looked disgusted with himself. "What was she like?" he finally asked, unable to hold back the question of purely masculine interest.

Derek smiled wryly. "Exotic. She likes tricks, games, perversions . . . There's nothing she won't do. I enjoyed it for a while. The trouble began when I'd finally had enough of her. She didn't want it to end." His mouth twisted. "Still doesn't."

Alex sipped some brandy and then swirled the liquid in the snifter, regarding it with untoward interest. "Derek," he murmured, "before my father died, he had a close friendship with Lord Ashby. Although Lord Ashby is an old man now, he's lost none of his mental agility. I'd like to approach him discreetly and ask him to put a stop to Joyce's antics before she does something worse than she already has."

"No," Derek said with a short laugh. "I'd be lucky if the old codger doesn't hire someone to finish me off. He wouldn't take kindly to the idea of flash gentry humping his wife. Don't interfere, Raiford."

Alex, who had always been fond of solving others' problems, was annoyed by the refusal. "What makes you think I'm asking for your bloody permission? You've damn well manipulated and interfered with my life for years!"

"I don't need your help."

"Then at least take my advice. Stop having affairs with other men's wives. Find your own woman. How old are you? Thirty?"

"I don't know."

Alex registered the statement with a blink of surprise, and then regarded him speculatively. "You have the look of a thirty-year-old. That's high time for a man to marry and produce legitimate offspring."

Derek raised his brows in mock horror. "A wife? Little Cravens underfoot? God, no."

"Then at least find yourself a mistress. Someone who knows how to take care of a man. Someone like Viola Miller. Were you aware that she and Lord Fontmere have recently broken off their arrangement? You've seen Viola before . . . a graceful, intelligent woman. She doesn't bestow her favors lightly. If I were you, I'd do whatever was in my power to become her next protector. I think you'll agree she's worth whatever price you have to pay."

Derek gave an irritable shrug, wanting to change the subject. "A woman never solves anything. She only causes more problems."

Alex grinned. "Well, you'd be safer with your own wife than someone else's. And you have little to lose by throwing in your lot with the rest of us."

"Misery loves company," Derek quoted sourly.

"Exactly."

Their conversation drifted to other matters, and Derek asked if Alex and Lily were planning to attend the assembly ball at the club.

Alex laughed at the idea. "No, I'm not fond of that crowd of scoundrels and whores called the *demimonde*—though my wife does seem to enjoy such gatherings."

"Where is she?"

"At the dressmaker's, having some new gowns fitted. Lately she's worn her damn breeches about the estate so often that our son asked why she didn't wear gowns like all the other mothers." Alex frowned. "Lily left in a hurry this morning. She wouldn't explain why. Received some note she wouldn't let me read. She's up to something. Damn that woman—she drives me to distraction!"

Derek suppressed a grin, knowing that Alex wouldn't change a hair on his wife's head.

"S. R. Fielding!" Lily exclaimed with a soft laugh, seizing Sara's hand and holding it tightly. Her dark eyes glowed with delight. "You have no idea how much I admire your work, Miss Fielding. I felt such kinship with Mathilda. She could have been modeled after me!"

"You're the woman in the portrait," Sara said in astonishment. "In Mr. Craven's gallery." The painting had captured the countess faithfully—except that on canvas she had looked far more serene. No artist's skill could ever completely capture her radiant self-confidence and convey the lively sparkle of her eyes.

"The little girl in the painting is my daughter, Nicole," Lily said proudly. "A beauty, isn't she? The portrait was completed a few years ago. The artist refused to sell it, but Derek offered him a ridiculous sum that he couldn't refuse. Derek claims anything can be had for a price." Her lips quirked. "Sometimes I think he's right."

Sara smiled cautiously. "Mr. Craven is far too cynical."

"You don't know the half of it," Lily said wryly, and dismissed the subject with a motion of her hands. Suddenly she was all business. "As Worthy described the situation, we are in dire need of a ball gown."

"I had no intention of putting you to such trouble, Lady Raiford. Thank you for agreeing to help me."

Worthy had arranged for Sara to be conveyed to Madam Lafleur's, the most exclusive dressmaker in London. Lady Raiford would meet her there, Worthy had said, and further made it clear that Sara was to allow her complete authority. "Lady Raiford knows all about this sort of thing. You must trust her judgment, Miss Fielding." Privately Sara suspected that Worthy was far from impressed by her own fashion sense. However, it was lack of funds, not taste, which had always determined her wardrobe.

Now Sara found herself in the famed set of rooms on Bond Street, lined with gilded mirrors and elegant pinkish-gray brocade. There was an intimidatingly regal ambiance at Lafleur's. Even the pleasant smiles of the assistants did little to calm her trepidation. The thought of how much her whimsy might cost was unnerving, but Sara doggedly ignored the nagging worry. Later she would moan and wince as she accounted for her wild expenditure. Later she would be prudent and responsible.

"Please call me Lily," Lady Raiford said. "And this is no trouble at all, my dear, especially in light of all you've done for *me*."

"Ma'am? Have I done something for you?"

"Saving Derek the way you did, never thinking of the danger to yourself . . . I'll be forever in your debt. Derek is a close friend of the family." Lily grinned cheerfully. "Quite an interesting man, don't you agree?" Before Sara could answer, Lily turned and caught the eye of a figure standing by. "Well, Monique?"

How long will it take to make Miss Fielding breath-takingly beautiful?"

The dressmaker approached them from the door, where she had been waiting tactfully. She welcomed Lily with a fondness that betrayed a long-standing friendship, and then turned to Sara. By all rights a woman of Monique Lafleur's stature and success would be aloof, proudly wearing an air of hauteur. Instead Monique was friendly and kind, with a smile as generous as her girth.

"*Chérie.*" She took Sara by the shoulders and glanced over her assessingly. "Ah, yes," she muttered. "I see there is much work to be done. But I do enjoy a challenge! Lady Raiford was right to bring you to me. When we finish, I promise you will be an *enchanteresse!*"

"Perhaps we could find something simple for me to wear . . ." Sara's words were lost in the sudden bustle as Monique gestured to her assistants. Lily merely stood back with a smile.

"Cora, Marie!" the dressmaker called. "Come, bring the gowns, *maintenant!* Quickly, there is not a moment to lose!"

Sara stared in bemusement at the armloads of richly hued silks and velvets that were brought forth. "Where did all these come from?"

Monique dragged her to an adjoining room outfitted with delicate rococo furniture, tasseled curtains, and mirrors even more massive than the ones in the front rooms. "The gowns belong to Lady Raiford." Deftly she turned Sara around and unfastened her bodice. "I design everything she wears. When the countess adopts a new fashion, all of London copies it the next day."

"Oh, but I couldn't take one of Lady Raiford's gowns—"

"None of them has ever been worn," Lily interrupted, following them into the room. "We'll have one of them altered for you, Sara." She turned her attention to the dressmaker. "The blacks and purples won't suit her at all, Monique. And nothing so virginal as the white. We want something bold and striking. Something that will make her stand apart from the crowd."

Sara stepped out of her gown and averted her eyes from the sight of herself in the mirror, clad in her chemise, thick white stockings, and heavy drawers. Monique cast a speculative glance at the serviceable undergarments, shook her head, and seemed to make a mental note of something. She reached for one of the gowns, turning it this way and that. "The pink?" she suggested, holding the shimmering rose-colored satin in front of Sara's half-clad figure. Sara held her breath in awe. She had never worn such a sumptuous creation. Silk roses adorned the sleeves and hem of the gown. The short-waisted bodice was finished with a stomacher of silver filigree and a row of satin bows.

Lily shook her head thoughtfully. "Charming, but too innocent."

Sara suppressed a disappointed sigh. She couldn't imagine anything more beautiful than the pink satin. Busily Monique discarded the gown and sorted through the others. "The peach. No man will be able to keep his eyes from her in that. Here, let us try it, *chérie.*"

Raising her arms, Sara let the dressmaker and her assistant Cora pull the gauzy peach-hued gown over her head. "I think it will have to be altered a great deal," Sara commented, her voice muffled beneath the

delicate layers of fabric. The gowns had been fitted for
Lily's lithe, compact lines. Sara was more amply en-
dowed, with a generous bosom and curving hips, and
a tiny, scooped-in waist . . . a figure style that had been
fashionable thirty years ago. The current high-waisted
Grecian mode was not particularly flattering to her.

Monique settled the gown around Sara's feet and
then began to yank the back of it together. "*Oui*, Lady
Raiford has the form that fashion loves." Energetically
she hooked the tight bodice together. "But you, *chérie*,
have the kind that *men* love. Draw in your breath, *s'il
vous plaît*."

Sara winced as her breasts were pushed upward until
they nearly overflowed from the low-cut bodice. The
hem of the unusually full skirt was bordered with three
rows of graduated tulip-leaves. Sara could hardly believe the woman in the mirror was herself. The peach
gown, with its transparent layers of silk and shockingly
low neckline, had been designed to attract a man's attention. It was too loose at the waist, but her breasts
rose from the shallow bodice in creamy splendor,
pushed together to form an enticing cleavage.

A broad smile appeared on Lily's face. "How splendid you look, Sara."

Monique regarded her smugly. "With a few alter-
ations, it will be perfect. This is the gown, *n'est-ce pas?*"

"I'm not certain," Lily said, pacing around the room
as she considered Sara from all angles. "Perhaps it's
just my preference for more assertive shades . . ." She
paused and shook her head with a decisiveness that
caused Sara's heart to sink. "No, it isn't spectacular
enough to achieve our purpose."

"Purpose?" Sara asked, perplexed, "There is no purpose other than to see me suitably attired. Surely this one is more than adequate?"

Lily slid an unfathomable glance to the dressmaker, who suddenly found a multitude of reasons to leave the room. Quietly the assistants followed. Baffled by their sudden departure, Sara fluffed the skirt of the peach gown and feigned unconcern.

"Perhaps we should have a little talk, Sara." Sorting through the other garments, Lily held up a mauve and violet creation and made a face. "My God. I can't think why I ever had this made." Carelessly she tossed the gown aside. "Exactly why is it *imperative*, as Worthy wrote, for you to attend the ball tonight?"

"Research," Sara said, not quite meeting her eyes. "A scene for my novel."

"Really." An odd smile played about Lily's mouth. "Well, I know nothing about writing novels. But I have a fair understanding of human nature. Perhaps I'm mistaken, but I assumed the point of all this was to make someone notice you." There was a subtly inquiring lilt to the last word.

Sara shook her head immediately. "No, my lady—"

"Lily."

"Lily," she repeated obediently. "I don't intend anything of the sort. I don't wish to attract anyone's attention. I'm nearly engaged to Mr. Perry Kingswood, of Greenwood Corners."

"Ah." The countess shrugged, regarding her with friendly sympathy. "Then I was wrong. Actually . . . I'd thought you might be entertaining an interest in Derek Craven."

"*No.* He's not at all the sort of man I . . ." Sara stopped and stared at her blankly. "Not at all."

"Of course. Forgive me. I was being presumptuous."

Sara tried to smooth over the awkward moment. "It's not that I don't think well of Mr. Craven. He's a unique sort of person—"

"There's no need to tiptoe around the truth. He's impossible. I know Derek better than anyone. Selfish, secretive, lonely . . . very much the way I was five years ago, before I married Lord Raiford." Lily stood behind Sara and began to unfasten the snug gown. "We'll try the blue velvet. You have the perfect complexion for it." Seeming disinclined to discuss the subject of Derek Craven any further, she freed the row buttons from the tiny silk loops that held them.

Sara frowned as she slipped the sleeves down her arms and stepped out of the gauzy peach circle. The silence became untenable. "But why should Mr. Craven be lonely?" she finally burst out. "He's surrounded by people all the time. He could have the companionship of any woman he desires!"

Lily made a comical grimace. "Derek doesn't trust anyone. After being abandoned by his mother and living for so long in the rookery . . . well, I'm afraid he doesn't have the highest opinion of women, or of people in general."

"He has a very high opinion of you," Sara said, thinking of the magnificent portrait in Craven's private gallery.

"We've been friends for a long time," Lily conceded, and added pointedly, "but nothing more. Oh, I know what the gossips claim—but the relationship was strictly platonic. Perhaps it doesn't matter to you. In any event, I wanted you to know the truth."

Sara felt an unaccountable leap of pleasure at the information. Aware of Lily's perceptive gaze, Sara struggled with an urge to confide in this sympathetic stranger—she, who had always guarded her own privacy so carefully. *I'm not going to the ball for research*, she wanted to burst out, *I'm going because Mr. Craven thinks I'm a country mouse. And I barely recognize myself . . . because suddenly I would do anything to show him that he's wrong . . . when it shouldn't matter. It shouldn't matter at all.*

"Mr. Craven forbade me to come to the club tonight," Sara heard herself say.

"Did he?" Lily responded immediately. "I'm not surprised."

"He claims I wouldn't be safe among the *demimonde*. Why, I've visited brothels and rookery gaming hells, and I've never come to any harm! It's not at all fair, especially in light of the fact that I'm the one who rescued him!"

"I should say so," Lily agreed.

"From the moment I arrived, he's wanted to send me back to Greenwood Corners."

"Yes, I know." Lily moved to fasten the blue dress. "Derek wants to be rid of you, Sara, because he perceives you as a threat."

Sara laughed incredulously. "Me, a threat? I assure you, no one has ever thought of me that way!"

"There is only one thing that Derek Craven fears," Lily assured her. "He's a complete coward when it comes to his own feelings. He's had affairs with dozens of women—and as soon as there's any danger of becoming attached to one, he'll discard her and find another. When I first knew him, I thought of him as an extremely *limited* man, incapable of love, trust, or tenderness. But now I believe those feelings are there. He's bottled them deep inside ever since he was a child. And I think the time is fast approaching when he won't be able to hold them back any longer. He's not quite himself these days. Lately I've seen signs that the wall he's built around him is cracking."

Troubled, Sara smoothed the velvet at her hips and stared down at the floor. "Lady Raiford, I'm not certain what you expect of me," she said honestly. "I love Mr. Kingswood, and I intend to marry him—"

"Sara," Lily interrupted gently, "you would help Derek greatly if you show him tonight that he's not as bloody invincible as he thinks. I'd like for you—or someone else—to find a chink in the armor. That's all." She smiled warmly. "And then you'll go back to Mr. Kingswood, who is a wonderful man, I'm certain . . . and I'll do my part to find the right woman for Derek." Lily laughed. "She'll have to be strong, wise, and patient enough to qualify for sainthood." She stood back to look at Sara, and a grin appeared on her face. "*This*," she said emphatically, "is the gown."

They sat together in the Raifords' carriage, drinking companionably from a silver flask that Lily had produced. Sara stared out the window from behind a tiny tasseled curtain, watching the torrent of people ascend the steps to the club. Women wore sumptuous gowns and masks adorned with plumes, jewels, and ribbons. Their escorts were attired in dark, formal attire and simple black masks that made it look like a highwayman's ball. The windows blazed with light, while the strains of orchestra music floated into the cold darkness of night.

Lily watched the procession and smacked her lips, savoring the taste of fine brandy. "We'll wait a few minutes more. It wouldn't do to appear too early."

Sara drew the borrowed cloak around herself and reached for the flask. The brandy was strong but mellow, a pleasant fire that eased the tautness of her nerves and the chattering of her teeth.

"My husband is probably wondering where I am," Lily remarked.

"What will you tell him?"

"I'm not certain yet. It will have to be something close to the truth." Lily grinned cheerfully. "Alex can always tell when I'm lying outright."

Sara smiled. Not only did Lily take pleasure in recounting outrageous tales of her past misbehavior, but she freely gave her opinions about anyone and anything. She had an amazingly cavalier attitude toward men. "They're easy to manage, and entirely predictable," Lily had said earlier. "If something is easily given, they're indifferent to it. If something is withheld, they want it desperately."

As she mulled over Lily's advice, Sara thought that perhaps she had been right about withholding. Perry Kingswood had always known that as soon as he cared to propose, Sara would accept. Perhaps if he hadn't been so certain of her, it wouldn't have taken four years to come to the brink of an engagement. *When I return to Greenwood Corners*, Sara thought, *I'll be a new woman*. She would be as self-confident and independent as Lily herself. And then Perry would fall madly in love with her.

Pleased by the notion, Sara bolstered herself with more brandy.

"You'd better go easy on that," Lily advised.

"It's quite bracing."

"It's quite potent. Here—it's time to put your mask on. Don't be nervous."

"It's a lovely mask," Sara said, toying with the narrow black silk ribbons before tying it in place. Monique had artfully fashioned it out of black silk and lace, and glinting blue sapphires that matched her gown. "I'm not nervous at all." It was true. She felt as if some reckless stranger had replaced her usual cautious self. The midnight-blue gown molded to her figure, cut so low that her breasts seemed ready to spill from the meager bodice. A broad satin sash fastened with a gold buckle emphasized her small waist. The mask covered the upper half of her face but revealed her lips, which Monique and Lily had insisted on darkening with the faintest hint of rouge. Laboriously they had arranged her hair in a cluster of curls on top of her head, allowing a few ringlets to dangle teasingly against her cheeks and neck. A perfume that reminded Sara of roses blended with some deeper foresty scent had been applied sparingly to her bosom and throat.

"A triumph," Monique had declared, gloating over the transformation. "Beautiful, worldly, but still fresh and young . . . ah, *chérie*, you will make many conquests tonight!"

"Stunning," Lily had said, beaming with delight. "What a stir she'll cause. You'll undoutedly hear all the gossip tomorrow morning, Monique."

"*Bien sûr*, everyone will come in to ask who she is, clucking like a flock of jealous hens!"

As the two had congratulated themselves, Sara had stared at the unfamiliar reflection in the mirror, her stomach jumping excitedly The image was that of an experienced woman, well-versed in the art of šeduction. "Not a mouse tonight," she had whispered with a wondering smile. "You won't even know me, Mr. Craven."

At the sound of Lily's vaguely anxious voice, Sara recalled herself to the present. "If you have any trouble tonight," Lily was saying, "just shout for Worthy."

"There won't be any need for that," Sara said airily, and tipped the flask for another deep swallow.

"You'd better say something to Worthy when you go in. He won't recognize you otherwise."

Sara smiled smugly at the thought. "Neither will Mr. Craven."

"I'm not certain I like the look in your eyes," Lily said uneasily "Be careful, Sara. Strange things have been known to happen at these assemblies. I ended up *married* after a particularly memorable one. Here, give me back that flask. I think you've had enough."

Reluctantly Sara gave back the brandy, while Lily delivered a final lecture. "Don't accept any wagers, or you'll be tricked into playing prick-the-garter with some randy buck before you know what's happened. And mind that you don't go to the back rooms with anyone—that's where people disappear for a convenient tail tickle."

"Worthy didn't tell me that."

"He was probably too embarrassed," Lily said darkly. "Those rooms are designed to muffle all sound, and they're filled with questionable pieces of furniture upon which all manner of sordid things have taken place."

"How do you know so much about them?"

"Hearsay, of course." Lily grinned in a way that belied her innocent tone. "Out of the carriage, minx."

"Thank you," Sara said earnestly. "Thank you for everything. I do wish you would let me pay for the gown, and the silk undergarments, and—"

"I won't hear of it," Lily interrupted. "You can tell

me all about the ball someday. That will be payment enough." She waved Sara away with a laugh.

The footman assisted Sara from the carriage, and she walked up the steps alone. Perhaps it was just a touch of giddiness from the brandy, but she was feeling most strange. The night was magical, menacing, kaleidoscopic. The marble steps beneath her feet seemed to shift like sands moved by the tide. Something was going to happen to her tonight. Whether the morrow brought happiness or regret, she knew that for at least a few hours she would have lived as boldly as she had always dreamed of doing.

"Madam?" the butler asked imperturbably as she swept into the entrance. It was his responsibility to filter out uninvited guests, otherwise the assembly balls would swell to unmanageable proportions.

Sara smiled faintly as she slipped off the black cloak, revealing the sumptuous curves of her figure outlined snugly in blue velvet. "Good evening," she said, lowering her voice at least an octave. "You must be Ellison. Miss Fielding has told me about you."

Ellison, who had confided everything to her, from his mother's recent illness to his fondness for kidney pie, clearly didn't recognize her. "You're a guest of Miss Fielding's?"

"I'm very close to her," Sara assured him. "She said I would be welcome tonight." She shrugged her silky shoulders. "However, if that's not the case—"

"Wait, madam . . ." A trace of wonder entered his usually impassive voice. "May I ask your name?"

She leaned close to him. "I don't think that would be wise," she confided. "I'm afraid my reputation would tend to make things quite inconvenient."

Ellison's face turned pink. It was easy to read the

thoughts that whirled through his mind. A beautiful, mysterious woman, with a vague connection to Miss Fielding . . . "M-madam," he stuttered in barely restrained excitement. "Could it be? May I ask if you are . . . M-Mathilda? The *real* Mathilda?"

Her red lips pursed thoughtfully. "It's possible." She handed her cloak to him and glided into the building. She felt no shame at her ruse. After all, if anyone had a right to assume Mathilda's identity, it was her creator!

A cluster of three young rakes who had stood behind Sara at the entrance stared after her eagerly. "Did you hear that?" one of them gasped. "Hang me if that ain't Mathilda."

"It could be a masquerade," one of his companions pointed out reasonably.

"No, no, that's her," the first insisted. "I've a friend who spent an evening with Mathilda in Bath last June. She's just as he described her."

"Let's follow her."

"Mathilda couldn't have been in Bath last June," the third argued. "I heard she was touring the continent with one of the Berkleys."

"Was that before or after she joined the convent?"

Sara did not notice the three men debating and following her. Having caught sight of Worthy, she made her way through the central hazard room. Her progress was impeded by a multitude of men suddenly offering to bring her punch, asking her to dance, pleading for her attention. Someone pressed a glass into her hand, and she accepted it with a smile. Pausing to sip the spicy mixture, she savored the flow of warmth through her veins. Gracefully she lifted a black-gloved hand to push a dangling curl away from her forehead, and smiled at the crowd around her. "Gentlemen," she said in a throaty voice, "you're quite a dashing assortment, and I'm flattered by your attentions, but you're all speaking at once. I can only manage three or four of you at a time."

They renewed their efforts enthusiastically. "Miss, may I escort you to one of the card rooms—"

"—a glass of wine?"

"—a sweetmeat or two?"

"—if would dance the waltz with me—"

Sara declined all the invitations with a regretful pout. "Perhaps later. I must leave to greet an old friend, or he'll be heartbroken at my neglect."

"I'll soon expire of a broken heart myself," one of them exclaimed, and the gathering attempted to follow Sara as she slipped to the side of the room where Worthy stood.

Smiling in triumph, Sara stood before him and made a small curtsey. "Well?" she demanded.

The factotum bowed deferentially. "Welcome to Craven's, madam."

As the factotum resumed his preoccupied perusal of the room, Sara frowned slightly and inched closer. "Are you looking for someone?" she asked in her normal voice, following the direction of his gaze. "Is something happening?"

Suddenly Worthy's eyes were riveted on her. He removed his spectacles, polished them roughly, and replaced them to stare at her in amazement. *"Miss Fielding?"* he asked in a shocked whisper. "Is that you?"

"Of course it's me. Didn't you recognize me?" She beamed at him. "Do you like the transformation? Lady Raiford is responsible for all of it."

Worthy choked and stammered, and could not seem

to reply. As he glanced at her lusciously exposed figure, his face turned pale with fatherly dismay. Sara accepted another glass of punch from a passing servant
and drained it thirstily. "How delicious this is," she exclaimed. "It's very warm in here, isn't it? That music is
enthralling—I can scarcely keep my feet still. I'm
going to dance tonight, the quadrille and the waltz
and—"

"Miss Fielding," Worthy gasped, "that punch is
much too strong for you. I'm going to have Gill bring
you a drink without spirits—"

"No, I want to drink what everyone else is drinking." She inclined her head toward him until her fruit-
scented breath fogged his spectacles. "And don't call
me Miss Fielding. There's no Miss Fielding here
tonight."

Worthy stuttered helplessly, polishing his spectacles
once more. In the space of a few seconds he prepared
a speech that would herald her immediate departure
from the ball. He had never suspected Sara Fielding
could be transformed into a blood-stirring temptress.
Everything about her was different; her voice, her
movements, her entire demeanor. Even the shape of
her face seemed to have changed. By the time Worthy
fitted the spectacles back onto his nose, she was gone,
whisked away by a pair of dandies who managed to
look bored and lecherous at the same time. The factotum began to signal frantically for Gill, hoping that
between the two of them, they could avert the coming
disaster. If Mr. Craven happened to see her . . .

Sensitive to Worthy's harried expression and wild
gestures, Gill approached from the opposite side of
the octagonal-shaped room. "Trouble?" the young
man asked.

"Miss Fielding is here! We must find her at once."

Gill shrugged, seeing no reason for concern. "She's probably in a corner somewhere, watching and listening to everyone as usual."

"Miss Fielding is not herself this evening," Worthy said tersely. "It's a dangerous situation, Gill."

"You sound as if you expect her to cause some sort of trouble," Gill said, and laughed at the notion. "That sweet, quiet little spinster . . ."

"That sweet, quiet spinster is capable of setting this entire club on its ear," Worthy hissed. "Find her, Gill, before Mr. Craven does. She's wearing a blue dress and a black mask."

"That describes at least two dozen women here," Gill pointed out. "And I don't think I could recognize her without her spectacles." He poked Worthy's arm, his interest occupied by a more urgent matter. "By the by, do you know what I heard just before I came over here? Mathilda may be attending the ball. Mathilda herself! Well, I'd like to hear Miss Fielding try to claim there's no Mathilda after *this*."

"Find her," Worthy said in a strangled voice.

"Mathilda?"

"*Miss Fielding.*"

"I'll try," Gill said dubiously, and sauntered away.

Worthy scanned the crowd for a sight of Sara's blue gown, his foot tapping the floor. As he considered alerting more of the club's employees to search for the elusive Miss Fielding, he heard a soft drawl that sent a chill down his spine.

"Looking for someone?"

After gulping painfully, Worthy turned to face Derek Craven's grim countenance. "Sir?" he croaked.

"I know she's here," Derek said, his green eyes hard

behind the stark black mask he wore. "I saw her not a minute ago. Slinking around to look for me, asking questions—she's as subtle as an elephant stampede. I hope I can keep from killing the bitch with my bare hands—or giving her a scar to match the one she gave me."

With equal parts of relief and horror, Worthy realized Craven was referring to Lady Ashby. "*Lady Ashby* had the effrontery to attend the ball?" Temporarily he forgot about the problem of Sara Fielding. "Would you like me to remove her from the club, sir?"

"Not quite yet," Derek said grimly. "First I'm going to talk to her."

Lady Ashby waited by a massive column, watching the milling crowd like a cat studying its prey. Her slender body was draped in a gold silk gown that matched her hair. A mask of gold and silver feathers covered her narrow, perfectly sculpted face.

Suddenly a clenching pain attacked the back of her head, as a large hand twisted in the mass of her curls. The unseen man behind her twined his fingers more tightly, preventing her from turning her head. Her breath escaped in a hiss of pain. Slowly she relaxed. "Derek," she murmured, staying perfectly still.

His voice was low and filled with hatred. "You stupid bitch." His hand twisted until she inhaled sharply and arched to ease the pull on her scalp.

"I wanted to see your face," she gasped. "That's why I came. I wanted to explain—"

"I know why you're here."

"It was wrong of me, Derek. I didn't want to hurt you. But you left me no recourse."

"You didn't hurt me."

"I can't let you leave me," Joyce said steadily. "I won't. I've been manipulated and abandoned by every man I've ever depended on. The first time was my father—"

"I don't care," Derek interrupted, but she continued insistently, ignoring the pain of his grip in her hair.

"I want you to understand. I was forced to marry at the age of fifteen. The bridegroom was as old as my grandfather. I despised Lord Ashby at first sight, the lecherous old goat. Can you imagine what it was like, climbing into bed with *that*?" Her voice turned acid. "His wrinkled skin, his bad teeth, his body shriveled with age . . . oh, quite the impassioned lover he was. I begged my father not to sell me to an old man, but he was mesmerized by the thought of the Ashby lands and wealth. My family profited greatly by the marriage."

"So did you," Derek pointed out.

"I promised myself that from then on I would take whatever pleasure I could find. Never again would I let anyone control me. I'm different from all the spineless bitches who allow men to mold their lives however it pleases them. If I allowed you to toss me aside so easily when you tired of me, I would be nothing, Derek. I would have been reduced to the state of the fifteen-year-old child I once was, forced to submit to the will of an indifferent man. I won't be abandoned, you smug cockney bastard."

She caught her breath as she was spun around and brought face to face with Derek's harshly shadowed countenance. He had removed his mask. "There's your revenge," he snarled. "Does it please you?"

Transfixed, Joyce stared at the stitched wound on his face. "I did hurt you," she murmured, sounding awed and contrite, and eerily satisfied.

Derek fitted the mask back over his face. When he spoke again, there was a weary note in his voice. "Get out of here."

She seemed to be empowered by the sight of his scar. "I still want you."

"I don't heel to anyone," he said roughly. "Especially not to a well-worn little purse like you."

"Come back to me," Joyce entreated. "I'll make life very sweet for you." Her smile was tainted with menace. "You're still handsome, Derek. I would hate to see your face cut to ribbons."

"Until you, I'd never met a woman who had to threaten a man into her bed." The barb found its mark—he saw a flush collect at the outline of her mask. "Don't cross me again, Joyce," he said through his teeth, taking her wrist in a grip that made her wince. "Or I'll make you wish you were dead."

"I'd rather have your retaliation than your indifference."

With a sound of disgust, Derek motioned for a club steward, who was standing several feet away and talking sotto voce with an exotically dressed woman. Quickly he approached them. "Take her out of here," Derek muttered, shoving Joyce toward him. "And if I see her back again tonight, I'll have your head."

"Yes, sir." The steward ushered Joyce away with quiet haste.

Feeling unclean, Derek took a drink from the tray of a passing servant and downed it quickly. He grimaced, disliking the cloying sweetness of the punch. It was strong stuff, the liquor passing smoothly down his gullet and settling with fiery warmth in his belly. He waited for it to numb the boiling resentment, the distaste, and worst of all the twinge of pity. He understood what it was like to rail against one's own help-lessness, the desperate struggle for dominance. Many times he had sought revenge for wrongs done to him. It would be the height of hypocrisy for him to pretend he was any better than Lady Ashby.

The noise in the room became almost deafening with the antics of the crowd at the hazard table. Derek hadn't noticed the unruly group before, having been completely immersed in the scene with Joyce. Setting the empty cup aside, he drew closer to the hazard table. He checked the work of his employees; the croupiers raking in the dice, the "flasher" hired to complain pub-licly about the bank's "losses" and thereby draw heavier play, the waiters who ensured that everyone had glasses filled with punch or wine. The only two who weren't attending to their jobs were the ushers, who were sup-posed to bring the club patrons upstairs when they de-sired to visit a house wench.

But no one wanted to go upstairs. The group of boisterous men, spanning all ages and levels of social consequence, was gathered around one woman. She stood at the side of the table, tossing dice from a cup onto the green felt. She was flirting simultaneously with at least a half-dozen players.

Derek smiled unwillingly, his bitterness fading a lit-tle. It had been years since he'd seen a woman handle a crowd of admirers so deftly—not since Lily in her gambling days. Fascinated, he wondered where the hell she had come from. He knew about all the new ar-rivals in London, and he'd never seen her before. She must be some diplomat's wife, or some exclusive cour-tesan. Her lips were red and pouting, her pale white shoulders enticingly bare above the blue velvet of her gown. She laughed frequently, tossing her head back in a way that caused her chestnut curls to dance. Like the other men present, Derek was captivated by her figure, the luscious round breasts, the tiny waist, all revealed by a well-fitted gown that was unlike the shapeless Grecian styles of the other women.

"A toast to the loveliest bosom in London!" Lord Bromley, a rakish young ne'er-do-well, exclaimed. Titillated and excited, the crowd raised their glasses with a cheer. Waiters rushed to bring more liquor.

"Miss," one of them begged, "I entreat you to cast my dice for me."

"Whatever good luck I have is yours," she assured him, and shook the dice in the box so vigorously that her breasts quivered beneath their shallow covering. The temperature in the room escalated rapidly as a host of admiring sighs greeted the display. Derek decided to intervene before the crowd's mood became too highly charged. Either the vixen didn't realize the lust she was inciting, or she was doing it deliberately. Either way, he wanted to meet her.

Sara cast the dice and laughed in delight as a triple came up. "House pays thirty to one!" the croupier called, and the group's roar of appreciation was equaled only by a clamor for the woman to roll the dice again. Before she could say a word, she was neatly plucked out of the crowd by a pair of strong hands.

The protests were quelled immediately as the men recognized that the abductor was Derek Craven himself. Their tempers were mollified as Derek motioned for a bevy of seductive house wenches, who filtered through the group with inviting smiles.

Slowly Sara looked up at her captor's masked face. "You took me away from the game."

"You were about to cause a riot in my club."

"*Your* club? Then you must be Mr. Craven." Her red lips curved provocatively. "I didn't mean to cause trouble. How can I make amends?"

He studied her intently. "Come have a walk with me."

"Is that all? I thought you might make a more daring request."

"You seem disappointed."

She shrugged. "With your reputation, Mr. Craven, it's only reasonable to expect an indecent proposal."

His mouth quirked with a subtly flirtatious smile . . . a smile unlike any he had ever given Sara Fielding. "There's every chance I'll oblige you."

She laughed throatily. "There's a chance I might accept."

All at once Sara thought she had given herself away. Something in her voice had awakened a spark of recognition. He was staring at her far too intensely. "Who are you?"

Sara tilted her head back to look at him, daring him to guess. "Don't you know me?"

The hint of a smile disappeared. "I intend to."

A sense of reality began to pierce the pleasant fog surrounding her. Sara became uneasy, taking a half-step away from him. "It's possible I arrived with someone," she said, wishing for the return of her earlier recklessness. She needed another drink.

"You're not leaving with him."

"What if I'm married?"

"You still won't leave with him."

Sara laughed and feigned alarm. "I've been warned about men like you."

He leaned close to whisper in her ear. "I hope you

didn't listen." His lips brushed the sensitive curve of her jaw. Sara closed her eyes while a nerveless quivering took over her body. She tried to summon the strength to pull away from him, but instead she stood against him docilely, as if she had no will of her own. There was the delicate catch of his teeth against her earlobe, and the low murmur of his voice. "Come with me."

She couldn't. Her knees were too weak. But somehow she allowed him to lead her to the next room, into the midst of the whirling couples. His supportive arm slid around her, and his vital grip enclosed her hand. So this was what it felt like to be held far too closely, to have a man stare at her with desire in his eyes. "You've never been here before," he said.

"You're wrong."

He shook his head. "I'd have remembered you."

"Actually," she said in a hushed voice, "I'm not here now. This isn't happening at all. You're just visiting a dream of mine."

"Am I?" He bent his head, his smiling mouth very close to hers. His breath was warm against her lips. "Then don't wake up, angel. I'd like to stay awhile."

Chapter 5

Derek Craven's arm was firm around Sara's waist as they whirled in an effortless waltz. He seemed to savor her tipsy playfulness. He flirted shamelessly with her, and pointed out the envious gazes of other men, and made Sara laugh by accusing her of collecting men's hearts as her playthings. When the waltz ended and a quadrille began, they drew to the edge of the room and accepted drinks brought by a passing waiter. As Sara watched the pattern of the dance, she stood close to Craven, swaying until their shoulders brushed. He grinned and slid an arm around her waist to steady her. Cheerfully Sara drifted back toward the skipping couples, attracted by the music.

Derek pulled her back deftly. "Not a quadrille. You're not quite steady on your feet, angel."

"Angel?" Sara repeated, resting back against him. Unladylike behavior, yes, but in the cheerful revelry of the ball, no one noticed or cared. "Do you give names to all your women?"

"I don't have any women."

"I don't believe you," she said with a giggle, leaning harder against his solid chest. Lightly his hands cupped her elbows, preserving her balance.

"Tell me your name," he said.

She shook her head. "It doesn't matter who I am."

His thumbs moved slowly over the gloved surface of her inner elbows. "I'll find out before the night is through." A waltz began, and she turned in his arms to look at him imploringly. "All right," he said with a laugh, guiding her back to the dance floor. "Another waltz. And afterward you'll take off your mask."

The words gave her an unpleasant start. It was the one threat that would break the magic spell wrought over the evening. Sara opened her mouth to tell him no, and then thought better of it. A denial would only make him determined. "Why?" she asked instead, making her voice provocative.

"I want to see your face."

"I'll *tell* you about my face instead. Two eyes, a nose, a mouth . . ."

"A beautiful mouth." His fingertip drifted over her lower lip with a light touch that she could have mistaken for a kiss, had her eyes been closed.

The vague smugness Sara had felt at being clever enough to fool him was gone, dissolving in a rush of warmth. She was drunk. "In one's cups" was the way her father had always put it. Yes, very much in her cups. That was the explanation for the aching emotions that surged within her. Tonight was supposed to be a game, and Derek Craven was nothing but a scoundrel. Why did his touch fill her with such longing? He was the embodiment of all the forbidden delight she would never experience. If only tonight would never end . . . If only Perry would hold her like this sometimes . . . If only . . .

"I want to dance for a long, long time," she heard herself say.

He took her into his arms and stared down at her intently. "Anything you want."

Derek didn't think he would be able to take his hands from her when the waltz ended. He couldn't risk letting go of her, the one gift Providence had ever seen fit to bestow on him. Everything else he'd had to work, suffer, steal, and cheat for. It had all required effort. But she had simply appeared, like a perfect fruit dropping from a tree into his outstretched hands. He was almost light-headed with desire. She must have felt it too. Her responses dwindled to wordless murmurs as she stared at him through the mask. She was beautiful, experienced, and worldly enough to understand and accept the terms he offered. Not like the other one. Not like the fine, innocent lady who was as different from him as ice from fire.

The hour grew late, and the club was strained at the seams. More guests had arrived, contributing to the happy mayhem. Couples were formed as lords, ladies, rakes, and prostitutes each sought a partner for the night. Usually Sara would have been shocked by the ribald jokes tossed back and forth, but a liberal quantity of alcohol had painted a rosy glow over the scene. She laughed at the lusty sallies she heard, even the ones she didn't understand. Frequently she was jostled against Derek in the crowded room, until he drew her to a more sheltered spot beside one of the marble columns. Sara was beseiged by invitations to dance, but Derek warded them all off with sardonic amusement. He had claimed her for the evening, and he had no trouble making it clear to those who tried to encroach on his territory.

"I don't recall giving you exclusive rights to my company," Sara said, nestled in the crook of his shoulder. She could feel the steady beat of his heart right against her breast, and the incredible strength of his body. The scent of brandy, the starch in his cravat, and the fragrance of his tanned skin formed a heady mixture.

Derek looked down at her with a grin. "Do you want to be with someone else?"

Sara considered that. "No," she said with a catch in her voice. "No one else in the world." It was the truth. There was only tonight . . . that was all she would ever have with him. She met his searching eyes and touched the lapel of his coat, smoothing it needlessly. In some distant corner of her mind a scolding voice intruded on the moment . . . Here she was, cavorting in a palace of sin with a scoundrel . . .

A scoundrel who was about to kiss her.

His fingers threaded through her curls, disarranging her hair, cupping the back of her head in a secure grip. There was the rasp of silk and velvet as the edges of their masks brushed, and then his mouth found hers. At first the kiss was cool and gentle. He took his time, tasting, slowly turning his lips over hers. Sara couldn't help thinking for a surprised moment that his kisses were rather like Perry's.

But it all changed in a quicksilver moment. His mouth became searingly hot, rubbing over hers until her lips were forced open. Sara quivered with astonishment at the intrusion of his tongue. Was this how other people kissed? Confounded by the intimacy, she pushed at his chest until he lifted his head and looked at her. There were flares in the depths of his eyes, like small, intense rushlights.

"N-not in front of everyone," she said, waving an unsteady hand at the crowd. The excuse was a feeble one. Not one pair of eyes was focused on them. All the revelers were absorbed in their own flirtations. Obligingly Derek linked his fingers around her gloved wrist and pulled her away with him, out of the central room, past the dining and card rooms, farther away until the music and chatter blended to a quiet drone. Sara stumbled after him, her grogginess clearing away. "Where . . ." was all she could manage to say as they strode along the hallway.

"To the back rooms."

"I . . . don't think that's a good idea."

His pace didn't ease. "We need privacy."

"F-for what?"

He urged her through a private door and into a softly lit room. Sara's wide eyes took in the sight of silk damask walls and the play of violet shadow on intricate plasterwork. A few pieces of furniture were placed around the room; a tiny round table and two gilt chairs, a pretty bronze screen with painted panels, and a chaise longue. Sara reared back in panic, but the door was already closed, and Craven's arms were around her. His hand clasped the back of her neck, and his voice puffed warmly into her hair.

"Easy. All I want to do is hold you."

"But I can't—"

"Let me hold you." He kissed her neck and crowded her more closely against him.

Slowly Sara relaxed. A pleasant languor spread from her head to her toes, and somehow she forgot there was a world outside the circle of his arms. There was only the warmth of his skin, banked within the layers of his clothes. And the movement of his hands as he worked the soft muscles of her neck and back. Even in her innocence, she was aware of the sinful knowledge in his touch. He knew how to hold a woman, how to seduce her away from inhibition. Blindly she lifted her face, and he kissed her. His lips seemed to wring her very soul from her body.

Sara clung to him, wrapping herself closer until her aching breasts were wedged against his chest. He took hold of her waist, pressing her to his groin. As she felt the hard, insistent protrusion of his body, she broke away awkwardly. "I-I've had too much to drink. I must go, I must . . ."

Derek gave a muffled laugh and stripped off his mask. Greedily he kissed her vulnerable throat, biting into the tender flesh. She gasped, trying to move back, but he caught the slippery waves of her hair in his fist. Murmuring reassurances, he nudged her off-balance and eased her down to the cushioned chaise. Objections wavered on her lips, all too quickly hushed by his mouth. He pulled the velvet bodice down until her naked breasts gleamed in the golden light . . . magnificent breasts with silken points. Fastening his mouth on a rosy nipple, he sucked and licked gently until she whimpered, her fingers tangling in his dark hair. He cupped her breasts high in his hands and used his lips, his teeth, and his tongue on them, as if he would devour the sweetness of her flesh.

Sara groaned and arched upward, pushing her nipple further into the depths of his mouth. She felt him pulling up her skirts, his powerful thighs clamping on either side of her hips. He crouched over her, kissing, cupping, stroking, until she was left with barely a shred of sanity. It was only that tiny scrap of consciousness that made her realize he had reached for her mask.

She twisted her head away with a gasping cry. "No!"

His hand curved underneath her breast, his thumb stroking the moist patches left by his mouth. "All right, then," he said softly. "Keep your disguise. I don't care who you are."

"I can't do this. You don't understand—"

"There's nothing to be afraid of." He dragged his lips through the deep vale between her breasts, each word he spoke a hot brand against her skin. "No one will know. No one but you and me." His hand searched the layers of her silk undergarments. One of his knees delved between hers. The weight of his body over hers was delicious. She wanted more, wanted him to press harder, deeper, until she was crushed beneath him. She had to stop him before the pleasure became disaster. But her trembling arms encircled him tighter, and the only sounds that escaped her lips were broken gasps.

Recognizing the signs of surrender, Derek kissed her with a mixture of triumph and relief. Tonight, at least, there would be no empty hours, no tormenting frustration. He would ease his needs within her, and use her to forget . . . he would give her all the pleasure he could never give Sara Fielding . . . *Sara* . . . Damn her for intruding on his thoughts even now. But perhaps that was only to be expected. In some ways this woman resembled Sara. She had the same flawless skin, and beneath her heady perfume there was the same delicate scent . . . She was the same size . . . shape . . .

He went still. The shock of it was like a hard blow to the chest. Roughly he pulled his mouth from hers and lifted himself up on his elbows. He hung over her, panting hard. The wracking breaths weren't enough to sustain him. Nothing was.

"It's not you," he said, the words torn from his throat. "Oh, damn you, it's *not* . . ."

Sara tried to turn away as his shaking hand descended to her face and removed her mask. Her dazed blue eyes stared up into his appalled ones. He was pale underneath his tan, the scar showing in harsh relief.

Derek would have thought his body could be no more aroused than it already was, but as he stared down at her, he became painfully hard. The frantic, exquisite throbbing of his blood made him flinch.

Sara moistened her lips. "Mr. Craven—"

"Look at you. Oh, God . . ." Derek's gaze burned over the gleaming rise of her breasts, her kiss-swollen lips. "I told you not to come here." His fingers sifted through the russet tumble of her hair. "I told you . . . Why?"

"R-research?" She offered the one stammering word as if it would explain everything.

"Christ." A frightening expression came over his face, dark and cruel and passionate. He looked ready to kill her.

Although it seemed to be a lost cause, Sara tried to defend herself. "I didn't mean for it to go this far," she babbled. "I'm sorry. It happened so quickly. I was drinking. It didn't seem real. And you were so . . . I . . . I really don't know how this all happened. I'm so sorry, so very—" She stopped, aware of how woefully inadequate the explanation was.

He was silent, his weight pinning her against the

chaise longue. The hard pressure of his arousal seemed to burn through the layers of their clothes. Uncomfortably Sara moved beneath him.

"Stay still!" Derek swallowed hard, his gaze traveling to the lush display of her breasts. "You and your . . . *research.*" He said the word as if it were obscene. His hand covered her breast, his palm rubbing over the nipple until it formed a tight bud. He tried to let her go, but his body wouldn't obey. Every nerve screamed rebelliously. He wanted her. He would have given everything he owned just to grind himself inside her. Breathing harshly through his teeth, he fought to contain his desire.

"I wanted to be someone other than myself," Sara said in defiant misery. "The kind of woman that you would . . . dance with . . . and desire. And even now . . . I don't regret what I've done. You may not feel any attraction for Sara Fielding, but at least you felt something for the woman I pretended to be, and that—"

"You don't think I want you?" he asked hoarsely.

"I knew when you refused to kiss me this morning—"

"*That's* what this is about? You wanted revenge because I didn't . . ." Craven seemed to choke on the words. When he managed to speak again, his voice was tainted with a cockney twang. "It wasn't enow for you that I've ached like a drawn dog ever since you came 'ere—"

"Drawn dog?" she repeated in confusion.

"Pulled away before the rutting's finished." He clenched his hands on either side of her face, glaring at her. "I wanted you this morning, you little tease. I've wanted to do you over since the first time I . . . *Be still!*" He snarled the last two words with a roughness that made her cringe. She stopped squirming at once.

Swallowing hard, he forced himself to continue. "Don't move, or I won't be able to stop myself. Listen to me. I'm going to let go of you . . . and you're going to leave. For good. Don't come back to the club."

"Never?"

"That's right. Go back to your village."

"But *why?*" Sara asked. Humiliating tears threatened to spill from her eyes.

"Because I can't—" He stopped, his breath rattling in his throat. "Jesus, don't cry!"

Don't move. Don't cry. Don't come back. Sara stared at him with glittering blue eyes. She felt wild, drugged, drunk with emotion. "I don't want to leave," she said thickly.

Derek's muscles trembled with the effort of holding still. He did not want to ruin or hurt her, and he was close, so close, to throwing away the few meager scraps of honor he possessed. "What do you want, Sara? *This?*" He taunted her with his body, urging himself against her in a crude thrust. "This is what you'll get from me. I'll do you over right now, and send you back to Kingswood a soiled dove. Is that what you want, to be covered by the likes of me?" He pushed again, expecting her to beg for her freedom. Instead she gasped and lifted her knees, instinctively making a cradle for him. He wiped at a fallen tear with his fingers. A guttural sound came from his throat, and he lowered his mouth to her face, licking at the silken trail of salt. It was going to happen. He couldn't stop it.

Pushing his hand beneath her skirt, he found the waist of her drawers and delved beneath them. He spread covetous kisses over her pale breasts and throat. She was everything he'd ever wanted, beauty and fire arching against his despoiling hands. His fingers wandered across the smooth skin of her belly, the white tops of her thighs. She started in fear, but he held her down and sifted through the patch of delicate curling hair until the soft core of her body became swollen and wet. Fondling her gently, he covered her mouth with kisses, while his breath rushed in rhythmic bursts. She writhed uncontrollably, making small, wanton groans that heated his senses to full boil.

Sara dug her fingers into the thick layer of his coat as she realized he was opening his pantaloons. Time stopped, like a whirling top snatched up in an unyielding fist. Pleasure unfurled and billowed in ever-widening waves as she yielded to the man intent on claiming her, the hard weight of his body poised to drive inside her. "Sara," he said over and over, his breath scalding her ear. "Sara—"

"Mr. Craven?" A quiet male voice broke the spell.

Sara gave a start of fright as she realized someone was in the doorway. She struggled to sit up, but Derek held her down, concealing her with his own body. He groped for his sanity. Finally he gave a savage groan. "What is it?"

Worthy's voice was strained. Keeping his face turned away, he spoke with great care. "I wouldn't have disturbed you, Mr. Craven, but there is a rumor that Ivo Jenner has been seen in the club. Knowing his wont to make trouble, I thought you should be informed."

Derek was silent for nearly half a minute. "Leave. I'll see to Jenner . . . if he's here." The last words were invested with heavy sarcasm, making it clear that he suspected the factotum had invented a ruse merely to rescue Sara.

"Sir, shall I have a carriage brought for . . . ?" Worthy paused, unwilling to voice Sara's name.

"Yes," Derek said tersely. "Get out, Worthy."

The factotum closed the door.

Sara couldn't seem to stop trembling. She clenched her arms around Craven's shoulders and buried her face against the humid skin of his throat. She had never experienced the pain of unsatisfied desire before. It *hurt*. It hurt like nothing she'd ever felt, and there seemed to be no remedy. Although she expected Craven to be cruel, he was kind at first, holding her tightly against his body and rubbing her back. "Dog-drawn," he said with a humorless laugh. "A few minutes and you'll be all right."

Wildly she twisted against him. "I c-can't catch my breath."

He clamped his arm across her hips and pressed his mouth to her temple. "Be still," he whispered. "Still." When her trembling eased, his mood changed, and he pushed her away abruptly. "Cover yourself." He sat up and clutched his head in his hands. "When you're ready to leave, Worthy will take you to the carriage."

Sara fumbled with her clothes, tugging at the bodice of her gown. Derek watched from the corners of his eyes until her breasts were concealed. He stood up to arrange his coat and pantaloons. Striding to the mirror that hung over the small marble fireplace, he neatened his cravat and raked his hands through his rumpled hair. Though the final result was not as immaculate as before, he looked presentable. Sara, on the other hand, knew herself to be a complete mess. Her gown was disheveled, while her hair cascaded in wild ripples down her back. She was on the verge of tears. Somehow she kept her face dry and her voice steady. "Perhaps we could both manage to forget tonight."

"I intend to," he said grimly. "But what I said before still holds. Don't come back, Miss Fielding." He strode to the door, pausing to deliver a savage aside to Worthy, who waited outside the threshold. "If it were anyone else but you, I'd fire you. After beating you to a bloody pulp." He left the room without a backward glance.

Sara reached for her mask and put it on. The door was closed, but she knew that Worthy was waiting for her. Slowly she stood up and rearranged her gown. Only by holding her hand over her mouth could she stem the sobs that threatened to erupt. She was swamped with self-pity, surpassed only by hatred of the man who had rejected her. *"Don't come back,"* she repeated his earlier words, turning crimson. She had felt anger before, but never this burning fury. A few weeks ago she wouldn't have thought herself capable of it.

Suddenly Lady Raiford's words crossed her mind . . . *"He's had affairs with dozens of women—and as soon as there's any danger of becoming attached to one, he'll discard her and find another . . ."*

Perhaps at this moment Craven was looking for another woman, one who would suit his standards, whatever they happened to be. The thought caused Sara's insides to boil. "Well, Mr. Craven," she said aloud, her voice shaking, "if you don't want me, I'll find a man who will. D-damn you, and Perry Kingswood too! I'm not a saint or an angel, and . . . and I don't want to be a 'good woman' anymore! I'll do what I please, and there's nothing anyone can say about it!" Her rebellious gaze flew to the door. As soon as she walked through it, Worthy would take her outside to a carriage. No argument would persuade him to let her stay.

Frowning, Sara glanced around the room. The shape of it, four panelled walls with blunted corners, was familiar. It reminded her of another room upstairs, which featured a bookcase that opened into one of the secret passageways. There was no bookcase here, but the panels were about the right shape . . . Quickly she stripped off her gloves and strode to the walls, running her hands over the edges of the panels. Pressing, tapping, she hunted for any sign of a concealed door. Just as she began to give up hope, she found a tiny catch. Triumphantly she eased the panel outward, revealing a dark passageway. With a mutter of satisfaction, she stepped inside and closed the panel.

Feeling her way along the narrow hall, she progressed several yards and paused at the sound of clinking dishes and silver. She could hear the muffled, imperious voice of Monsieur Labarge, the chef. The noises were on the other side of the wall. He was shouting angrily at some hapless assistant who had apparently doused a fish with the wrong sauce.

Having no desire to make a grand appearance in the kitchen, Sara passed the hidden doorway and forged ahead. After a long journey through the darkness, she stopped at a small enclave that she guessed opened to one of the less frequently used card rooms. Sara pressed her ear to the crack of the door and squinted through a peephole. It seemed the room was vacant. Digging her nails into the side of the panel, she tugged until it opened with a protesting squeak. Her skirts rustled over the sill. Closing the panel, she sealed it once more and gave a triumphant sigh.

An unexpected voice made her start. "Wery interesting."

Sara whirled around and saw an unfamiliar man in the room. He was stocky and tall, with a clean-shaven jaw and blondish-red hair. He removed his mask to reveal an attractive but battered face, with a crooked nose and a lopsided smile. There was a healthy dose of cockney in his accent. He pronounced the "v" in "very" as if it were a "w"—just as Derek Craven did in his occasional lapses. Although there was something secretive and guileful in his light blue eyes, his grin was so winning that Sara decided she had nothing to fear from him. Another cockney in well-tailored clothes, she mused.

She smoothed her wild hair and gave him a hesitant smile. "Are you hiding from someone?" she asked, with a nod toward the closed door.

"Could be," he replied easily. "An' you?"

"Very definitely." She pushed some of her wild curls back and tucked them behind an ear.

"From a man," he guessed.

"What else?" She shrugged in a worldly-wise way. "Why are *you* hiding?"

"Let's say I'm not a faworite of Derek Crawen."

Sara gave a sudden wry laugh. "Neither am I."

He grinned and gestured to a wine bottle poised on one of the card tables. "Let's drink to that." He filled a glass and handed it to her. He lifted the bottle to his lips and swigged the rare vintage with a carelessness that would have caused a Frenchman to cry. "Fine stuff, I s'pose," he commented. "All the same to me, though."

Sara tilted her head back and closed her eyes, rolling the exquisite flavor in her mouth. "Nothing but the best for Mr. Craven," she said.

"Pompous bastard, our Crawen. Though I newer likes to insult a man while drinking 'is stock."

"That's quite all right," Sara assured him. "Insult him all you like."

The stranger surveyed her with frank appreciation. "A pretty piece, you are. Did Crawen break it off with you, then?"

Sara's bruised vanity was soothed by his admiring gaze. "There's nothing to break off," she admitted, lifting the wine to her lips. "Mr. Craven doesn't want me."

"The bloody fool," the stranger exclaimed, and smiled invitingly. "Come with me, my little tibby, an' I'll make you forget all about 'im."

Sara laughed and shook her head. "I don't think so."

"It's my beat-up mug, aye?" He rubbed his battered face regretfully. "I been sent to dorse too many times."

Realizing he thought she was rejecting him because he wasn't handsome, Sara interrupted hastily. "Oh, no, it's not that. I'm certain many women would find you appealing, and . . . did you say 'sent to dorse'? Isn't that a pugilist's term? Were you once a boxer?"

Looking self-important, he stuck his chest out an extra inch. "Ewen now, I could beat any bruiser to the punch. They filled the stands to watch me in a set-to . . . Sussex, Newmarket, Lancashire . . ." Proudly he pointed to his nose. "Broke three times. Near ewery bone in my bloody face 'as been broke. Once I almost 'ad my brains knocked out."

"How fascinating," Sara exclaimed. "I've never met a fighter. I've never even been to a prizefight."

"I'll take you to one." He jabbed the air with his fists in a couple of combinations. "Nothing like a good match, 'specially when they spill the claret." Seeing that she didn't understand the term, he explained with a grin. "Blood."

Sara shivered with distaste. "I don't like the sight of blood."

"That's what makes it exciting. Me, I used to fill buckets durin' a set-to. One back'ander, and *ffshhh* . . ." He mimicked a spray of blood coming from his nose. "They pays more when you bleed, too. Aye, fighting made me a rich man."

"What is your occupation now?"

He winked slyly. "I 'appens to operate an 'azard bank myself, on Bolton Row."

Sara coughed a little and set the glass down. "You own a gambling club?"

He took her hand and kissed the back of it. "Ivo Jenner, at your service, m'lady."

Chapter 6

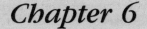

Sara lifted her mask and stared at him incredulously. The mischievous twinkle in Jenner's eyes was replaced by surprise as he saw her face. "What a beauty you are," he muttered.

Suddenly she gave a burst of laughter. "Ivo Jenner? You're not at all as I imagined you. You're actually rather charming."

"Aye, I'll charm the drawers off you tonight, given 'alf a chance." He came forward to refill her glass, plying her with a liberal dose of wine.

"You're a rogue, Mr. Jenner."

"That I am," he agreed readily.

Sara ignored the wine and leaned back against the wall, folding her arms across her chest. "I think you would be wise to leave as quickly as possible. Mr. Craven is looking for you. Why did you come here tonight? To make mischief, I assume?"

"Wouldn't think of it!" He looked wounded at the very idea.

"I've heard from the employees that you're constantly scheming to plant spies here, summoning the police to conduct raids during the busiest times . . . Why, rumor has it that you even caused a kitchen fire to be started last year!"

"Bloody lies." His gaze flickered over the half-exposed mounds of her breasts. "There was no proof I 'ad anyfing to do with it."

Sara regarded him suspiciously. "Some even suspect you of hiring men to attack Mr. Craven in the rookery and slash his face."

"No," he said indignantly. "That wasn't me. Eweryone knows Crawen's fancy for 'igh-kick women. It was a woman what did it to 'im." He snorted. "Pull a cat's tail, and she'll scratch. That's what 'appened to Crawen's face." He smiled insolently. "Maybe it was you, aye?"

"It was *not* me," Sara said in annoyance. "For one thing, I don't have a single drop of blue blood—which makes me completely uninteresting to Mr. Craven."

"I likes you better for it, love."

"For another thing," she continued pertly, "I would never dream of slashing a man's face just because he didn't want me. And I wouldn't chase someone who had spurned me. I have more pride than that."

"An' so you should." Ivo Jenner laughed low in his throat. "A prize wench, you are. Forget about Crawen. Let me take you to a better place than this. *My* club. The pigeons aren't as fine—but there's deep play an' all you wants to drink—an' no Derek Crawen."

"Go somewhere with *you?*" Sara asked, picking up her glass of wine.

"You'd rather stay 'ere?" he countered.

As Sara sipped the fruity beverage, she contemplated him over the rim of the glass. She began to feel better than before, a little less hollow. He had a point, she thought. There were no possibilities for her at Craven's, not with Worthy and probably the entire staff ready to "escort" her out. Furthermore, this would be a chance for her to continue her research on gaming clubs. Of course, Ivo Jenner was not the most trustworthy of men. But neither was Derek Craven. And—childishly spiteful though it was—the idea of fraternizing with Craven's business rival was not without appeal.

After replacing her mask, Sara gave him a decisive nod. "Yes, Mr. Jenner. I would like to see your club."

"Ivo. Call me Ivo." Grinning widely, Jenner donned his own mask. "I 'ope we can leave without being caught."

"We'll have to stop at the front entrance. I'll have need of my cloak."

"We'll be stopped," he warned.

"I don't think so." She threw a reckless grin in his direction. "I'm feeling very lucky tonight."

He chuckled and crooked his arm invitingly. "So'm I, love."

Brazenly they walked into the main rooms and along the outskirts of the crowd. Jenner proved skillful at maneuvering his feminine prize out of the reach of the exuberant guests, alternately exchanging laughter and threats as he shouldered his way through. Arm in arm, he and Sara made their way to the front entrance of the club. They paused to request Sara's cloak from Ellison, the butler.

Ellison flushed in excitement as he saw her. "Miss Mathilda! Surely you're not leaving so soon."

Sara gave him an impish smile. "I've had a more intriguing invitation. To another club, as a matter of fact."

"I see," The butler's face drooped with disappointment. "You'll want your cloak, then."

"Yes, please."

As an attendant rushed to fetch the required cloak, Jenner pulled Sara a foot or two away. " 'E called you Mathilda," he said in a strange voice.

"So he did."

"That's who you are? Mathilda? The one they wrote the book about?"

"In a way," Sara said uncomfortably. It was definitely a twisted version of the truth. She couldn't tell him her real name. No one must know that well-behaved, proper Miss Sara Fielding had ever gone to a ball and become intoxicated, and consorted with men of ill-repute. If word somehow ever got back to Perry Kingswood, or his mother . . . She shuddered at the idea.

Seeing the involuntary movement of her shoulders, Jenner received the cloak and draped it about her reverently. Lifting the rippling mass of her hair, he pulled it free of the velvet mantle. "Mathilda," he breathed. "The woman ewery man in England wants."

"That's a great exaggeration, Mr. Jenner . . . er . . . Ivo."

"*Jenner?*" Having overheard the last few words, the butler looked sharply at Sara's masked companion. "Oh, no. Miss Mathilda, don't say you're going off with this debauched, dangerous ruffian—"

"I'm all right," Sara soothed, patting the butler's arm. "And Mr. Jenner is really very sweet."

Ellison began to protest vigorously. "Miss Mathilda, I cannot allow—"

"She's with me," Jenner interrupted, glaring at the butler. "No one can say nofing about it." Masterfully he pulled Sara along with him and ushered her down the front steps toward the line of waiting carriages.

With the assistance of Jenner and a footman dressed in a slightly frayed uniform, Sara climbed into a black and burgundy carriage. Though the interior was clean and presentable, it hardly matched the luxuriously outfitted vehicles she had become accustomed to at Craven's. Sara smiled slightly, reflecting on how spoiled she had become in a matter of days. Fine food, French wine, impeccable service, and all the opulence of Craven's club . . . It certainly was a contrast to Greenwood Corners.

Uneasily she gazed down at her borrowed finery. It had been willful, frivolous, inconsiderate of her to have put Worthy and Lady Raiford to trouble. It wasn't like her. She had changed in the last few days, and not for the better. Craven was right—she should return to the village as soon as possible. Her parents would be ashamed if they knew of her conduct, and Perry . . . Sara bit her lip in dismay. Perry would condemn her for such behavior. He was of the old school, believing that natural feelings and animal urges should be strictly governed, never to take precedence over the intellect.

Wearily Sara leaned her head back against the flat cushions. Mr. Craven must despise her now, she thought. Unwillingly she remembered the searing delight of his hands on her skin, and the hot brand of his mouth. A shiver chased across her shoulders, and her heart gave an extra thump. God forgive her, but she wasn't sorry for any of it. No one would be able to take it away from her, the memory that would remain even when she was safely tucked away in her country village. When she was an old woman, rocking serenely in a corner of the parlor and listening to her granddaughters giggling about their handsome swains, she would smile privately at the thought that she had once been kissed by the most wicked man in London.

Her thoughts were interrupted by a crowd gathering outside the club. Frowning, she looked at the amassing vehicles and the darkly garbed figures encircling the building. "What's happening?" She continued to stare as Jenner's carriage pulled away. "Are those police officers?"

"Could be."

"Then they're going to raid the club? During an assembly ball?"

Jenner's pale blue eyes glittered with enjoyment. "Looks like it."

"You're responsible for this!" she exclaimed.

"Me?" he asked innocently. "I'm just a simple 'azard operator, love." But his satisfied smirk betrayed him.

"Oh, Mr. Jenner, this is too bad of you," she scolded as the carriage rattled along the street. "I fail to see what this will accomplish! Poor Mr. Craven has had enough on his hands tonight—"

"Poor Mr. Crawen?" he echoed indignantly. "Ah . . . women! You've taken 'is side now?"

"I'm taking no one's side," Sara bent a long, disapproving stare on him. "As far as I can see, the two of you are exactly alike."

"A raid!" someone called inside the club as officers swarmed in through the doors. The happy disorder of the ball turned into pandemonium. Guests milled through the rooms in disoriented groups while employees deftly covered up tables, hid cards and dice, and concealed cribbage boards and bowls of counters. Police officers swarmed inside the club with swaggering aggressiveness, pausing to eye the scantily dressed whores. Inconspicuously they helped themselves to samples of the lavish buffet and expensive wines, a rare opportunity for the poorly paid members of the city force.

Sourly Derek watched the proceedings from a corner of the central room. "What a night," he muttered.

Ivo Jenner had timed his prank to perfection, crowning an evening already rife with indignity. The raid was nothing. It was what had gone before that had proved his undoing. Derek hadn't been left high and dry since his early days of chasing after saucy street wenches. He liked it even less now than he had then. His skin prickled as if he'd been ice-burned. Every muscle in his body was tight. Everyone knew it was unhealthy for a man to be kept in such a condition. He counted the ways he'd like to punish Sara Fielding for her antics. Now he was finally rid of her, thank God. No more temptation, no more hazy blue eyes, no more note-taking and questions and "research" that provided an excuse for her to poke her nose into every corner of his unsavory life. Fumbling in his coat pocket, he sought the tiny pair of spectacles. His hand closed around them tightly.

"Mr. Craven." Worthy approached him with great hesitation. The factotum's long forehead was plowed in deep furrows. "Jenner," he said succinctly, gesturing to the police.

Derek fixed a brooding stare on the invading officers. "I pay those bastards enough under the table to keep this from happening."

"It looks as though Jenner pays them more," Worthy said, and became the recipient of a frosty glare. Nervously he cleared his throat. "I've just spoken to Ellison. He's in quite a pucker."

"My butler's never in a pucker."

Worthy craned his neck to stare at his towering employer. "He is tonight."

"We've had plenty of raids before."

"It's not the raid. The reason Ellison is upset is because he just saw a woman he identified as 'Mathilda' leaving the club with Ivo Jenner."

"So Jenner's gone? Good. That'll save me the trouble of pounding the slimy little bastard into the ground."

"Mr. Craven, forgive me, but you're missing the point. He—"

"What point? That he's with some woman named Mathilda? I could find a dozen women for you, all pretending to be frigging Mathilda. It's a *masquerade*, Worthy." He began to walk away, speaking brusquely over his shoulder. "Pardon me, but I have a few police officers to knock heads with—"

"Miss Fielding is Mathilda," the factotum said bluntly.

Derek froze. He shook his head as if to clear his ears. Slowly he turned to face the smaller man. "What did you say?"

"Somehow Miss Fielding evaded me. She must have used the concealed passageway that leads to the card rooms. The 'Mathilda' who just left with Ivo Jenner is described as wearing a blue dress and having long brown hair, not to mention a notable pair of . . . of . . ." Worthy spluttered into silence and made an explicit gesture with his hands.

"Holy hell!" Derek exploded, turning several shades darker. "No, *no*, not with Jenner. I'll kill him if he touches her. I'll kill *her* . . ." Swearing obscenely, he raked both hands through his hair until it was in wild disarray.

"I believe they left in Jenner's carriage," the factotum murmured, falling back a few steps. In all the years of their acquaintance, he had never witnessed such a volcanic display from Craven. "Ellison seems to believe they went to Mr. Jenner's club. Sir . . . perhaps you'd like a drink?"

Derek stormed back and forth in uncoiling fury. "I tells 'er to go back to bloody Greenwood Corners, an' instead she traipses off with Ivo Jenner. She'd be safer walking naked through St. Giles!" He glared at Worthy. "You stay here," he growled. "Pay off the bloody police and get rid of 'em."

"You're going to Jenner's?" the factotum asked. "You can't leave with the officers surrounding the club—"

"I'll get through the police," Derek said coldly. "And when I find Miss Fielding—" He stopped and stared at Worthy, his green eyes gleaming with a vengeful light that caused the factotum to blanch. "You helped her with this, didn't you? She couldn't come to the assembly without you knowing. If anything happens to her . . . I'll fire you and ewery employee in this club. The whole bloody lot of you!"

"But Mr. Craven," Worthy protested, "no one could have known she would behave so recklessly."

"The hell you couldn't," Derek said in a blistering tone. "It was obvious since the day she got here. She's been itching for a chance to land herself in trouble. And you made it bloody easy for her, didn't you?"

"Mr. Craven—"

"Enough," Derek said curtly. "I'm going to find her. And you'd better pray nothing happens to her—or I'll send you to the devil."

During the carriage ride through the city, Sara listened patiently as Jenner boasted about his prize-fighting days, his past victories and defeats, and all his life-threatening injuries. Unlike Derek Craven, Ivo Jenner was a simple man who knew exactly where he belonged. He preferred the world he had come from, with its assortment of coarse people and coarser pleasures. It didn't matter to him if his money was taken from silk purses or greasy pockets. He sneered openly at Derek Craven's pretensions . . . "Talkin with those 'igh-kick words, pretending 'e was born a gentleman. All clean an' dandified . . . Why, 'e walks through 'is fancy club like the sun shines from 'is arse!"

"You're jealous of him," Sara said.

"Jealous?" His face crinkled in distaste. "I'm not jealous ow a man what's got one foot planted in Mayfair an' the other in the East End. Pox take 'im! Bloody fool doesn't know who the 'ell 'e is."

"So you believe he shouldn't mingle with social superiors? I'd call that reverse snobbery, Mr. Jenner."

"Call it what you likes," he said sullenly.

Oh, he was jealous indeed. Now Sara understood the bitter rivalry between the two men. Jenner represented all that Craven had tried to escape from. Every time Craven looked at him, he must see the mocking reflection of his past. And Jenner was clearly annoyed by the way Craven had reinvented himself from a street urchin into a rich and powerful man.

"If you're so indifferent to Mr. Craven and his success, then why—" Sara began, but she fell silent as the carriage stopped abruptly. Her mouth fell open as she heard a cacophony of sound: shouts and screams, breaking glass, even explosions. "What's happening?"

Jenner shoved aside the curtain at his window and stared at the tumult outside the carriage. He made a startling sound, something between a howling laugh and a roar of encouragement. Sara shrank back into the corner of her seat. "It's a mob!" Jenner cried. He opened the door to confer with the pasty-faced driver and footman. " 'Ow many streets does it cover?" he asked. Another snatch of conversation, and then Sara heard him say, "Try a roundabout way, then."

The door closed and the carriage started again, turning sharply. Sara gulped with fear. A few rocks pelted against the side of the vehicle, and she jumped in her seat. The shrieking mob sounded like a demon chorus. "What's going on?"

Jenner continued to gaze out the window, grinning at the carnage that surrounded them. His enjoyment increased with every second that passed. "I likes a good mob, I do. I led one or two in my time. We're in the middle ow it now."

"Why are they rioting?"

Jenner kept his eyes on the window as he replied. "Does the name Red Jack ring a bell?"

Sara nodded. Red Jack was a notorious highwayman who had earned his nickname by murdering at least a dozen people on the busy coach route from London to Marlborough. "I've heard of him. He's being held at Newgate, waiting to be executed."

A bark of laughter escaped him. "Not anymore. Offed 'imself yesterday—cheated the 'angman's noose.

Can't say as I blame these lively bastards for runnin' riot."

"You mean they're angry because he committed suicide? Why should they care, as long as he's dead?"

"Why, 'anging's a good spectacle. Ewen the old women an' the chiwdren come to watch 'em piss an' twist in the wind. Would've been a good show. Now they want a taste ow 'is blood." He shrugged and regarded the rioters sympathetically. "They dug 'im up tonight to pull 'is guts out. I say let 'em 'ave a bit ow fun."

"F-fun to publicly dismember a c-corpse?" Sara gagged at the notion and stared at him in horror. Her disgust was lost on him, however. Jenner cheered lustily for the drunken mob engaged in looting, breaking windows, and setting fires. Several heavy thumps caused the carriage to lurch and rock. The vehicle ground to a halt. As Jenner pushed the curtain aside, Sara saw hands and faces wedged against the window. They pushed and shoved, threatening to turn the carriage over.

"Driver's gone," Jenner said. "I wondered 'ow long 'e'd last."

"Oh, God!" Sara cowered in the corner, staring at him with wide eyes. "They'll tear us to pieces!"

"Don't worry. You're safe with these to look after you." He held up his heavy fists as if they were dangerous weapons.

The ceiling shuddered and sank downward as people piled on top of the carriage. Sara scrambled wildly for a way to protect herself. God knew what she had done with her reticule. She was defenseless without her pistol. The door burst open like a clap of thunder, and Sara screamed at the nightmarish sight of dozens of hands reaching for her.

Enthusiastically Jenner flung himself through the opening, landing on three men at once. His arms swung in a steady rhythm, plowing through the rioters like a scythe through grain. Sara leapt after him. Reaching for the back of Jenner's coat, she clutched handfuls of the thick fabric and followed him with her head lowered. She gritted her teeth as she was jostled and elbowed by the crowd. Miraculously they broke through the free-for-all. Sara gripped her companion's burly arm.

"Mr. Jenner," she begged, "get me away from here."

He laughed down at her, his eyes bright with excitement. "No taste for a little brawl, eh?"

Sara glanced back at the carriage, which was being demolished. "The horses," she said anxiously fearing for the animals' safety. The rioters had unhitched the team from the carriage and were leading them away.

Some of Jenner's amusement faded. "My 'orses! I paid a king's ransom for 'em!" He left her to stride after the thieves. "Stop, you thieving scum, those are mine!"

"Mr. Jenner," she pleaded, but he appeared not to hear.

It seemed she was going to have to fend for herself. Carefully Sara made her way through the street while looters rushed by her with armfuls of stolen goods. A bottle flew past her ear and shattered on the pavement nearby. Sara flinched and drew closer to the shadows. She looked in vain for a night watchman or a stray police officer. Fire cast a ruddy glow over the ramshackle buildings. She didn't know what direction she was

walking in, only hoped the path she was taking
wouldn't lead to a thieves' kitchen. She passed a gin
shop and an evil-smelling ditch. People swarmed from
one street to another, scuffling, quarreling, giving
bloodthirsty cries as they hurled rocks and sticks
through the air. Sara pulled the hood of her cloak over
her face and stumbled around a row of wooden posts
rising from the flagged pavement. All the giddy
warmth of the wine she had drunk was driven away.
She was sober and terrified.

"Damn," she said under her breath with each step
she took. "Damn, damn, damn . . ."

"Egads, what have we here?"

Sara stopped short as she saw a man's broad silhou-
ette before her. He was dressed in a dandy's clothes,
fine and disheveled. Precisely the kind of young buck
who frequented Craven's club and went slumming to
attend blood sports in Covent Garden and visit prostitutes at the Strand. They gambled, drank, and went
"skirt-hunting" to relieve their boredom. Profligates,
libertines, yes . . . but gentlemen by birth. Sara began
to feel relieved, knowing that this man would be
honor-bound to see her to safety.

"Sir—"

He interrupted her with a cry to unseen companions. "*À moi*, my good fellows—come meet the enchanting wench I've discovered!"

Immediately Sara was surrounded by three
chortling young men, all reeking of liquor. Crowding
around her, they gloated over their new acquisition.
Alarmed, Sara spoke to the first one. "Sir, I've lost my
way. Please guide me safely away from this place,
or . . . at least stand aside and allow me to pass."

"My sweet bit o' skirt, I'll lead you 'zactly to the

place you belong," he promised with a lecherous grin, sliding his hands down the front of her body. Sara jumped back with a muffled cry and found herself restrained by the rake's companions. They held her tightly, laughing at her struggles.

"Where shall we take her?" one of them asked.

"To the bridge," came the ready suggestion. "I know just the spot to have her. We'll wait our turns politely—as gennelmen should—an' if she makes a fuss, we'll toss her in the Thames."

The other two burst out laughing.

"Let me go! I'm not a prostitute. I'm not—"

"Yes, you're a good girl," he soothed. "A young, pretty wench who shouldn't mind a bit of folly with a few randy bucks."

"*No*—"

"Don't worry, darling, you'll like us. Splendid fellows, we are. Never given a wench reason to complain before, have we?"

"I should say not!" the second man chimed.

"You'll likely offer to pay *us* after!" the other added and the three rocked with drunken hilarity as they dragged her along with them. Sara screamed and fought with her nails and teeth, lashing out with all her strength. Annoyed by her frantic clawing, one of them cuffed her across the face. "Don't be a little fool. We're not going to kill you—just want a tail-tickle."

Sara had never made sounds in her life as she did now, mad screams that rent the air. She found unexpected strength in her terror, feeling her nails rip across skin, her half-closed fists striking hard against the bonds that held her . . . and yet it wasn't enough. She was half-carried, half-dragged. Her lungs shuddered, drawing in enough air for another ear-splitting

scream. Suddenly she was dropped to the street, landing hard on her buttocks. The scream was knocked out
of her throat. She sat on the ground in stupefied silence.

A slim, dark figure passed before her eyes, moving
with a peculiar catlike grace. Sara heard heavy thuds as
a weighted cudgel swung in vicious arcs. Two of the
men who had assaulted her collapsed, groaning sickly.
The third screamed in outrage and skittered back.
"What are you doing?" he shouted. "What in blazes?
You ignorant *swine* . . . I'll see you hanged for this!"

Sara passed a hand over her eyes and gazed at the
apparition in trembling wonder. At first she had
thought Jenner had come back to rescue her. But it
was Derek Craven's scarred face she saw, harsh as a
primitive war mask, lit by red fire-glow. He stood with
his legs splayed and his chin lowered. One hand was
wrapped around a neddy, the weighted club preferred
by rookery brutes. He didn't spare a glance for Sara,
only stared at the remaining man like a hungry jackal.

He spoke through his teeth. "Take your friends and
leave."

The fallen libertines struggled to their feet, one of
them clasping a hand to his bleeding head, the other
holding his side. The third, divining the accent in
Derek's voice, did not move. "Well-dressed for a cockney, aren't you? So fine feathers are to your taste, eh?
I'll give you money for more. You'll be the Beau
Brummell of the East End. Just let us have the
woman."

"Go."

"I'll even share, if you want a taste of her first—"

"She's mine," Derek growled, and raised the club a
few inches.

By tacit agreement the two injured men lurched away. The third stared at Derek in angry indecision. "Thickheaded knave!" he finally exclaimed. "Have the little bitch all to yourself, then!" After biting his thumb in a contemptuous gesture, he hastened to join his companions as they shuffled down the street.

Sara stood up and staggered toward Craven. He was upon her in three strides, with a swirl of black cloak and a face so harsh that she half-believed he was the devil. Her shoulders were seized in a brutal grip. She was ushered without ceremony to an ebony horse waiting nearby, its sides gleaming with sweat. Silently she endured Craven's rough handling as he more or less threw her into the saddle. He took the reins and swung up behind her in a lithe movement, his left arm clamping hard about her.

The horse sprang into a canter. Dismal shacks, broken storefronts, and swarming streets flew past them. Closing her eyes against the biting rush of air, Sara wondered dully if he was taking her back to the club. Miserably she turned her face into the fine wool fabric of his cloak. Each rising surge of the horse's gait urged her closer against him. She had never been held so tightly, her body caught hard against his, her lungs squeezed until her breath was short. But strangely she found a measure of solace in his painful grip. With the sinewy strength of him braced behind her, nothing and no one would harm her. *She's mine*, he had said . . . and her heart had throbbed in answer . . . recognizing it as truth.

Strange, unknowable man, who had once deliberately driven the woman he loved into someone else's arms. Worthy had told her the story of how Derek had practically thrown Lily into Lord Raiford's bed.

"Mr. Craven feared that he himself was falling in love with her," Worthy had confided, "and so he virtually gave her away to the earl. He did everything possible to encourage their liaison. Mr. Craven doesn't know how to love. He recognizes it only as weakness and folly. That's part of his attraction for women, I believe. They each hope to be the one who will finally capture his heart. But it's not possible. He'll never allow it, no indeed . . ."

Weakness and folly . . . Tonight she had indulged in a hearty share of both. Words of apology and gratitude hovered on her lips, but she was too ashamed to say them. Instead she closed her eyes and clung to him, desperately pretending that time had vanished and they would keep riding forever, off the edge of the earth and into a sea of stars . . .

Her fantasy was short-lived. Soon they reached a small park bordered by quiet streets. The glass globes of suspended oil lamps cast ovals of feeble light across the road. Reining the horse to a halt, Derek dismounted and held up his hands to her. Awkwardly Sara slid down from the saddle, guided by his hands at her waist. He let go of her as soon as her feet touched the ground and walked to the edge of the park.

Sara approached him and stopped a few feet away. Her lips parted and her throat worked, but no sound came out.

Derek swung around, rubbing his jaw as he gazed at her.

She was swamped by a feeling of utter hopelessness as she waited for him to destroy her with a few caustic words. But he continued to watch her silently, his face unreadable. It seemed almost as if he were waiting for some cue from her. The dilemma lasted for several seconds, until Sara solved it by bursting into tears. She jerked her hands up to her face, blotting her streaming eyes. "I'm so sorry," she gasped.

Suddenly he was next to her, touching her shoulders and arms lightly and then jerking his hands back as if burned. "No, don't. Don't. You're all right now." Gingerly he reached out to pat her back. "Don't cry. Everything's fine. Bloody hell. Don't do that."

As she continued to weep, Derek hovered over her in baffled dismay. He excelled at seducing women, charming and deceiving them, breaking down their defenses . . . everything but comforting them. No one had ever required it of him. "There, now," he muttered, as he had heard Lily Raiford say a thousand times to her crying children. "There, now."

Suddenly she was leaning on him, her small head resting at the center of his chest. The long skeins of her hair draped everywhere, entangling him in a fine russet web. Alarmed, he lifted his hands to ease her away. Instead his arms slid around her until she was pressed against him length to length. "Miss Fielding," he said with great effort. "Sara . . ." She nestled deeper against him, muffling her gulping sobs in his shirt-front.

Derek swore and furtively pressed his lips to the top of her head. He concentrated on the chilly night air, but his loins began to throb with an all-too-familiar pain. It was impossible to stay indifferent to the feel of her body molded to his. He was a bloody charlatan . . . no gentleman, no chivalrous comforter of women, only a scoundrel filled with raw desire. He smoothed his hand over her hair and urged her head into his shoulder until she was in danger of being smothered. "It's all right," he said gruffly. "Everything's fine now. Don't cry anymore."

"I sh-should never have gone off with Mr. Jenner, but I was angry with you for . . . for . . ."

"Yes, I know." Derek searched in his coat and found a handkerchief. Clumsily he plastered it against her wet face. "Here. Take this."

She peeled the linen from her cheeks and used it to blow her nose. "Oh, th-thank you."

"Did Jenner hurt you?"

"No, but he *left* me, right in the middle of that m-mess—" Her chin wobbled, heralding fresh tears, and Derek interrupted in alarm.

"Easy. Easy. You're safe now. And I'm going to wring Ivo Jenner's neck—after I wring yours for going with him." His hand slipped under her cloak to her velvet-covered back, kneading the knotted muscles.

Sara gave a last hiccup. She drooped against him, shivering. "You saved me tonight. I'll never be able to thank you enough."

"Don't thank me. We're even now."

"I am grateful," she insisted.

"Don't be. I'm responsible for some of this. I should have known it was you behind the mask." His eyes swept over her luminous, tear-streaked face. "Perhaps I did, somehow."

Sara was very still, soaking in the warmth that mingled beneath their cloaks. The heel of his hand rested on the side of her breast, while his other spread across the small of her back. "Where did the dress come from?" he asked, his breath a puff of white mist in the air.

"Lady Raiford."

"Of course," he said sardonically. "It looks like something she would wear." He glanced into the open neck of the cloak, where the shadow of her cleavage was visible. His thumb moved high on her breast, lingering at the edge where velvet ended and soft skin began. "Except you fill it out differently."

Sara pretended not to notice the gentle fondling, even as her blood quickened and her nipples contracted within the velvet sheath. "Lady Raiford was very kind. You mustn't blame her. Coming to the assembly ball tonight was my idea. It was all my fault, no one else's."

"I suspect Worthy and Lily were damn eager to help you." His knuckles brushed over the top of her breast and around the side, until a tremor of pleasure went through her. He spoke softly against her hair. "Are you cold?"

"No," she whispered. Liquid fire raced through her veins. She felt as if she had drunk some heady concoction a hundred times more potent than wine.

Derek eased her head back and stared into her eyes. "I want you to forget everything that happened tonight."

"Why?"

"Because you're going back to your village tomorrow. You're going to marry your Kingsfield."

"Kings*wood*."

"Wood," he repeated impatiently.

Sara moistened her dry lips. "Will you forget, Mr. Craven?"

"Yes." His gaze flickered to her mouth, and he let go of her.

Momentarily disoriented, Sara swayed and found her balance. She half-expected him to tell her it was time to leave, but he seemed in no particular hurry. Wandering to the wooden fence nearby, he leaned against the highest rail.

"Shouldn't we return to the club?" Sara asked, following him.

"For what? There's not much left of the assembly, after the raid your friend Jenner arranged. No more guests, no gambling . . . and fortunately for you, no more rum punch."

Sara blushed deeply. "That punch was quite intoxicating," she admitted.

He laughed, inspecting her flushed cheeks and her uncertain balance. "You're still flying high as a kite, angel."

Relieved that he was no longer angry with her, Sara folded her arms and glanced at the quiet streets. The wind seemed to carry the faint howl of the distant mob, though that was only a trick of her imagination. She wondered if their gruesome purpose had been accomplished, if they had reveled in pulling apart the highwayman's corpse. The thought made her shudder, and she told Craven what Jenner had said about the mob. He listened without surprise. "How can people behave in such a way?" Sara asked. "How can they watch executions for entertainment? I can't understand it."

"I did, when I was a boy."

Her jaw dropped. "You went to hangings, a-and floggings, and disembowlings, and . . . but you didn't *enjoy* it. You couldn't have."

Derek met her gaze without blinking. "Now I take no pleasure in death. But at the time I had quite a fascination for it."

Troubled by the admission, Sara reminded herself

that as a child he had lived in an underworld of crime and sin, brought up in brothels, flash houses, and the streets of the rookery. But still she found it difficult to accept the image of him cheering as a man strangled at the end of a rope. "What did you think, as you watched them being hanged?" she asked.

"I considered myself lucky. At least I wasn't up there. I was hungry, and didn't own so much as a piss pot . . . but at least there was no rope around my neck."

"And that made you feel better about your situation?"

"I had no 'situation,' Miss Fielding. I fought, cheated, stole for everything: the food I ate, the gin I drank . . . for women, sometimes."

Sara colored slightly. "What about honest labor? You worked sometimes. Worthy told me you did."

"Labor, yes. Honest?" He shook his head and snorted in bitter amusement. "You'd rather not know."

Sara was quiet for a moment. "I would," she said suddenly. "I would like to know."

"More material for your research?"

"No, it's not that at all." Impulsively she touched his arm. "Please. You must believe I would never betray a private confidence."

Derek stared at the place on his sleeve she had touched, even after her hand was withdrawn. He crossed his long legs and kept his eyes on the ground. A heavy swath of black hair spilled over his forehead. "I was a climbing boy until I got too big. Some of the chimneys were only two or three bricks wide. I was small for a boy of six, but one day I couldn't squeeze myself through the flue." A reminiscent smile crossed his face. "You don't know what hell is until you've been stuck in a chimney."

"How did they get you out?" she asked, horrified.

"They lit a bundle of hay underneath me. I tore half my hide off, scrambling up that chimney." He laughed shortly. "After that I worked on the docks, loading crates and boxes. Sometimes I skinned and gutted fish, or shoveled manure and hauled it from stableyards to the wharf. I never knew what a bath was." Sliding a glance at her, he grinned at her expression. "Stank until even the flies wouldn't come near me."

"Oh, my," she said faintly.

"Sometimes I mudlarked—stole cargo from the waterside, sold it under the table to crooked merchants. I wasn't much different from the other lads in the rookery. All of us did what was necessary to survive. But there was one . . . Jem was his name . . . a scrawny boy with a face like a monkey. One day I noticed he was doing better than the rest. He had a thick coat to wear, food to fill his belly with, even a wench on his arm now and again. I went up to him and asked where he was getting his money." His face changed, becoming coarse and hard, all trace of handsomeness wiped away. "Jem told me. On his advice, I decided to try my hand at the resurrection business."

"You . . . joined a church?" Sara asked, bewildered.

Derek gave her a startled look and then began to choke with laughter. When she asked what was the matter, he actually doubled over, gasping for breath. "No, no . . ." After dragging a sleeve over his eyes, he was finally able to control himself. "I was a bone-grubber," he explained.

"I don't understand—"

"A grave-robber. I dug up corpses from cemeteries and sold them to medical students." A peculiar smile crossed his lips. "You're surprised, aren't you? And revolted."

"I . . ." Sara tried to sort through her scattered thoughts. "I can't say I f-find the thought very pleasant."

"No. It was far from a pleasant business. But I'm a very good thief, Miss Fielding. Jem used to say I could steal the twinkle from the devil's eye. I was a good resurrection man—efficient, dependable. I averaged three a night."

"Three what?"

"Bodies. By law, surgeons and medical students can only use the corpses of convicted felons. But there's never enough to go around. So they paid me to go to burial grounds near hospitals and asylums and bring them the newest corpses I could find. The surgeons always called them 'specimens.' "

"How long did this go on?" Sara asked with a horrified shiver.

"Almost two years—until I began to look like the corpses I stole. Pale, scrawny, like walking death. I slept during the day and only went out at night. I never worked when the moon was full. Too much light. There was always a danger of being shot by groundskeepers, who naturally didn't look kindly on the business. When I couldn't go about my work, I would sit in a corner of the local tavern and drink as much as my belly would hold, and try to forget about what I'd been doing. I was a superstitious sort. Having disturbed many an eternal rest, I began to think I was being haunted."

He spoke in a flat voice, as if he were talking about something that had no connection with him. Sara noticed that his color was high. Embarrassment, self-disgust, anger . . . She could only guess at the emotions that stirred within him. Why was he confessing such personal and unspeakable things to her?

"I think I was dead inside," he said. "Or at least only half-human. But the money kept me going back, until I had a nightmare that put a stop to it all. I never set foot near another graveyard after that."

"Tell me," Sara said softly, but he shook his head.

"After my resurrection days I turned to other ways of making a profit—all of them nearly as unsavory. But not quite. Nothing's as bad as what I did. Not even murder."

He was quiet then. The moon was veiled by clouds, the sky painted in muted tones of gray and violet. Once it might have been the kind of night he had gone out to desecrate graveyards. As she stared at the man next to her, his hair gleaming like ebony in the lamp-light, Sara realized that her heart was pounding and her palms were clammy. Cold perspiration trickled down her back and beneath her arms. He was right—she was revolted by the things he had done. And without a doubt there was more he hadn't told her.

She struggled with many feelings at once, trying to understand him, trying most of all not to fear him. How terribly naive she had been. She would never have imagined him capable of such terrible things. The families of his victims, how they must have suffered—and it could just as well have been *her* family, *her* relatives. He was responsible for causing pain to many people. Had someone described such a man to her, she would have said that he was beyond re-demption.

But . . . he wasn't completely bad. He had come after

her tonight, fearing for her safety. He had refused to take advantage of her at the club, when there had been nothing to stop him but the remnants of his own conscience. Just now when she had been crying, he had been kind and gentle. Sara shook her head in consternation, not knowing what to think.

Craven's face was turned away, but challenge was clear in every line of his posture. It seemed as if he were waiting for her to condemn him. Before she was quite aware of what she was doing, she reached out to the black hair that curled slightly on the back of his neck. At the touch of her hand, he seemed to stop breathing. Muscle flexed beneath her fingertips. She sensed the smoldering beneath his stillness, and his battle to keep his emotions closed away.

After a minute he looked up at her with blazing green eyes. "You little fool. I don't want your pity. I'm trying to tell you—"

"It's not pity." Hastily she snatched her hand back.

"I'm trying to tell you that all that stands between me and becoming *that* again is a pile of money."

"You have a mountain of it."

"Not enough," he said heatedly. "Never enough. If you had the sense of a frigging sparrow, you'd understand."

Sara's brows knitted together. She felt the tightness in her chest expand until she burst with an anger that almost equaled his. "I *do* understand! You have the will to survive, Mr. Craven. How could I blame you for that? I don't like the things you've done, but I'm not a hypocrite. If I'd been born in the rookery, I probably would have become a prostitute. I know enough to understand that there were few choices for you in that place. In fact . . . I . . . I *admire* you for lifting yourself out of such depths. Few men would have had the will and the strength to do it."

"Oh?" He smiled darkly. "Earlier today you were asking about my committee of patronesses. I'll tell you. Most of their husbands keep mistresses, leaving them alone in their beds night after night. I used to service those fine ladies for a price. I made a fortune. I was as good a whore as I was a thief."

The blood drained from Sara's cheeks.

Seeing her reaction, he jeered softly. "Still admire me?"

Numbly Sara remembered the conversations she'd had with the prostitutes she'd interviewed for *Mathilda*. They had the same look on their faces as Craven did now . . . bleak, hopeless. "When I needed more money to finance the club," Craven continued, "I blackmailed a few of them. No proper lord would like to find out his wife had taken flash gentry like me into her bed. But the odd thing was, the blackmail did little to dull my charms. The 'friendships' continued until the club was built. We have very civilized understandings, my patronesses and me."

"Lady Raiford—" Sara said hoarsely.

"No, she wasn't one of them. She and I never . . ." He made an impatient gesture and retreated unexpectedly, beginning to pace around her as if a circle of fire separated them. "I didn't want that from her."

"Because you cared about her." When the comment drew no response, Sara pressed further. "And she's one of many people who care about you . . . including Mr. Worthy, Gill, even the house wenches—"

"It comes along with paying their salaries."

Ignoring his sneering sarcasm, she regarded him steadily. "Mr. Craven, why have you told me all of this? You won't accept my sympathy—and I won't give you scorn. What do you want from me?"

Stopping in the middle of another pass, he crossed the invisible barrier between them and seized her. His hands clenched her upper arms painfully. "I want you to leave. You're not safe here. As long as you're in London you're not safe from me." His gaze raked over the rippling mass of her hair, her delicate face, her bewildered eyes. With a sudden groan he pulled her against him, burying his face in her hair. Sara closed her eyes, her mind spinning. His body was solid and powerful, hunching over hers to accommodate their difference in height. She felt him tremble with the force of his need. He spoke just beneath her ear, his voice thick with tormented pleasure. "You have to leave, Sara . . . because I want to hold you like this until your skin melts into mine. I want you in my bed, the smell of you on my sheets, your hair spread across my pillow. I want to take your innocence. God! I want to ruin you for anyone else."

Blindly Sara flattened her hand on his cheek, against the scratch of newly grown beard. "What if I want the same?" she whispered.

"*No,*" he said fiercely, and turned his mouth to the tender skin of her neck. "If you were mine, I would make you into someone you didn't recognize. I would hurt you in ways you'd never dream of. I won't let that happen. But don't ever think I didn't want you." His hands gripped her closer, and they both began to breathe harshly. The hard jut of his arousal burned against her stomach. "That's for you," he muttered. "Only for you." He groped for her wrist and brought her palm to his chest. Even through the thickness of linen, broadcloth, and wool, she could feel the resounding thump of his heart. She squirmed to press harder against him, and he caught his breath. "A man should never come so close to hell as this," he said raggedly. "But even with the devil whispering in my ear to take you, I can't do it."

"Please," she gasped, not knowing if she was asking him to let go or to keep her with him.

The word seemed to drive him to the edge of madness. He fitted his mouth over hers with a tortured groan, his tongue searching in urgent forays. Sara curled her arms around his head, tangling her fingers in his dark locks as if she could hold him to her forever. She could still feel his heartbeat pounding against her flattened breasts. His thigh was a hard intrusion amid her skirts, bearing firmly against an unspeakably intimate place. She didn't know how long he stood there kissing her, his mouth sometimes gentle, sometimes brutal, his hands wandering freely inside her cloak Her legs turned weak, and she knew she couldn't have stood upright without his arms around her.

"Mr. Craven," she moaned when his lips left hers to slide hotly down her throat.

He smoothed her hair back from her face and pressed his forehead to hers until she could feel the stitches of his wound against her skin. "Say my name. Say it just once."

"Derek."

For a moment he was immobile. His breath fanned over her chin. Then he brushed a soft kiss on each of her closed eyes while her lashes trembled against his lips. "I will forget you, Sara Fielding," he said roughly. "No matter what it takes."

* * *

There was one last moment of that night that lingered in Sara's memory. He had taken her to the Goodmans' home, riding with her perched sideways across the saddle. She burrowed her head against his chest, clinging to him tightly. Even in the wintry rawness of the air, his body seemed to blaze with the heat of a coal fire. They stopped on the side of the street, and he disentangled her arms in order to dismount.

A light snow had begun to fall. Tiny flakes swirled downward, making a delicate, audible patter on the street. Craven helped her to the ground. A few snowflakes had fallen on his hair, melting points of lace caught in the dark locks. His scar was more pronounced than usual. She longed to press her lips against the wound, a lasting reminder of the night she had met him. Her throat was unbearably tight. Her eyes stung with unshed tears.

He was so far from the gallant knights in her romantic fantasies . . . He was tarnished, scarred, imperfect. Deliberately he had destroyed any illusions she might have had about him, exposing his mysterious past for the ugly horror that it was. His purpose had been to drive her away. But instead she felt closer to him, as if the truth had bonded them in a new intimacy.

Walking her to the Goodmans' front steps, Craven paused to survey her tangled hair, whisker-burned cheeks, and puffy lips. He smiled slightly. "You look like you've been done over by a squadron of sailors on leave."

Sara looked into his intent green eyes, knowing they would haunt her forever. "I'll never see you again, will I?" she asked dazedly.

There was no need for him to reply. He took her

hand as if it were a priceless object, raising it to his
mouth so lightly that she felt as if her arm were floating. The warmth of his breath penetrated her skin.
She was aware of the movement of his lips as he
pressed soundless words in her palm. He released her,
and the look he gave her seemed to reveal the depths
of his lustful, longing, bitter soul. "Good-bye, Miss
Fielding," he said hoarsely. He turned and strode
away. Sara watched in frozen silence as he hoisted
himself easily into the saddle and rode down the street,
until he had disappeared from sight.

Chapter 7

*T*he day after her return to Greenwood Corners, Sara walked a mile across the frozen cart trails and patches of woodland that separated her family's cottage from the Kingswoods' smaller village manor. Along the way she breathed deeply of the clean country air, crisp with the scents of pine and snow. "Miss Fielding!" She heard a boy's high-pitched voice behind her. "How was London?"

Sara turned to smile at young Billy Evans, the miller's son. "London was very exciting," she replied. "Why aren't you in school at this hour?" She gave him a mock-suspicious glance, for this wouldn't be the first time Billy had been caught playing truant.

"Sent to borrow a book from the rectory," he said cheerfully. "How's your novel, Miss Fielding?"

"Barely begun," Sara admitted. "I think I'll have it finished by summer."

"I'll tell my mother. She loves your books—though she has to hide 'em from Pa."

"Why is that?"

"He doesn't like her to read. Says it might give her the notion to run off like Mathilda did."

They both laughed, and Sara rumpled the boy's red hair. "She would never do that, Billy. Besides, Mathilda ended up nearly jumping off a bridge—see what comes of running away?"

He gave her a sly, bucktoothed grin. "Guess you won't be leaving Mr. Kingswood anymore, then."

Sara leaned close to him. "Do you think he missed me?" she asked in a conspiratorial whisper. To her delight, Billy blushed until his face was bright pink underneath his carrot-colored hair.

"Ask 'im yourself!" he said, and scampered down the road.

"I intend to." Resuming her walk at a leisurely pace, Sara sighed with a mixture of pleasure and sadness. This was where she belonged, in a place where everything was familiar to her. She knew the patterns of every path, meadow, and stream. She was acquainted with everyone in the village, and the histories of the families who lived there. Greenwood Corners was a lovely place. But this homecoming was different from her others. Instead of relief and joy, she felt hollow, as if she had left some vital part of herself behind. Not even her parents and their smiles of loving welcome had been able to take away her unease. She was eager to see Perry this morning, hoping he would provide the comfort she needed.

Her heart picked up a faster beat as she approached the Kingswood home. It was a charming village manor of classical design, with ivy creeping over its scored stucco front. Inside, the rooms were decorated with simple plasterwork and refined shades of ocher, brown, and pea-green. In the warm seasons Perry's mother, Martha, was most often found in the kitchen garden at the back of the manor, tending to her herbs and vegetables. During the winter months she spent her time doing needlework in the parlor, close to the light and warmth offered by the fireplace. And Perry, of course, was in the library, poring over his beloved history and poetry books.

Sara knocked at the door and scraped her feet at the side of the step. After a minute or two Martha Kingswood appeared. She was an attractive woman with blue-gray eyes and hair that had once been blond but had faded to a pale vanilla color. Her welcoming expression melted as she recognized the visitor. "Back from your gallivanting, I see."

Meeting the older woman's sharp eyes, Sara smiled cheerfully. "Not gallivanting. Researching." She couldn't help thinking of the warning her own mother, Katie, had given her a few years ago. *"Be careful of what you tell that woman, Sara. I've known Martha since she was a girl. She'll encourage you to confide in her, and then find a way to use your words against you."*

"But I've never given her a reason to dislike me," Sara had protested.

"You have Perry's affection, dear. That's reason enough."

Since then Sara had come to realize that her mother was right. Widowed a few years after Perry was born, Martha had centered her life around her son. Whenever she was in the same room, she hovered over him with an indiscreet jealousy that made Sara uncomfortable. Perry had resigned himself to his mother's possessiveness, knowing that she disliked anyone who took his attention away from her. But he claimed that after he was married, Martha would soften her tightly controlling grip. *"We'll all be able to come to an under-standing,"* he had told Sara countless times. *"Remember not to take anything she says personally. She would behave like this with any girl I chose to court."*

Martha blocked the doorway with her sticklike fig-ure, as if she wished to prevent Sara from entering. "When did you return?"

"Last evening."

"I suppose you're here to see my son." Martha's tone was smooth, but it carried an edge of hostility that made Sara wince.

"Yes, Mrs. Kingswood."

"Perhaps next time you could arrange your visit so as not to disturb his midmorning studies." Martha's tone implied that it was the height of inconsideration to have called at such an hour. Before Sara could reply, Martha opened the door wider and motioned her into the house.

Hoping Martha was not following her, Sara quick-ened her step through the hallway. It would be nice, she thought wryly, if her reunion with Perry was pri-vate, at least for a minute or two. Thankfully she didn't hear Martha's footsteps behind her. She reached the library, a comfortable room decorated with papered panels of pink, red, and brown birds, and fitted with rows of mahogany bookshelves.

The young man seated at the rosewood desk by one of the windows stood up and smiled at her.

"Perry!" she cried, and ran to him.

Chuckling at her impulsiveness, Perry caught her in his arms. He was slender and of moderate height, with the most elegant hands Sara had ever seen on a man. His every gesture was infused with grace. She had al-ways loved to watch him write, play the piano, or merely turn the pages of a book. Closing her eyes, she inhaled the scent of his cologne and smiled in contentment. "Oh, Perry." The feel of his compact body was familiar and comfortable, making it seem that the past days in London had never happened.

But all at once a memory blazed across her mind . . . Derek Craven's powerful arms crushing her close, his softly growling voice in her ear. *"I want to hold you like this until your skin melts into mine . . . I want you in my bed, the smell of you on my sheets . . ."*

Startled, Sara drew her head back.

"Darling?" Perry murmured. "What is it?"

She blinked hard, while a shiver crossed her shoulders. "Just . . . a chill from outside." Staring at him, she tried to blot out the memory with the sight of Perry's face. "You're so handsome," she said sincerely, and he laughed, pleased.

Everyone acknowledged that Perry was the best-looking man in Greenwood Corners. His hair, a little too long at the moment, was a coppery shade of gold. The rich jewel-blue of his eyes was far more striking than her own. His nose was small and straight, his lips fine, his forehead high and pale, all in the mode of a romantic Byronic hero.

After glancing around to make certain they were unobserved, Perry leaned forward to kiss her. Sara lifted her chin willingly. But suddenly all she could think of was a scarred face close to hers, the gleam of wicked green eyes, a hard mouth that searched and plundered ruthlessly . . . so different from Perry's gentle lips. Closing her eyes tightly, she willed herself to respond.

Finishing the kiss with a slight smacking noise, Perry lifted his head and smiled at her. "Where is your cap?" he asked. "It always looks so pretty with the lace framing your cheeks."

"I decided not to wear it today," Sara frowned as his arms loosened from around her. "No . . . don't let go just yet."

"Mother will interrupt us soon," he warned.

"I know." Sara sighed and stood back from him reluctantly. "It's just that I missed you so."

"As I missed you," Perry replied gallantly, gesturing to the painted beechwood settee. "Let's sit down and talk, darling. I believe Mother means to bring in some tea—I hear her stirring about in the kitchen."

"Couldn't we have some time alone?" she whispered, mindful of Martha's acute hearing. "I have some things to tell you privately."

"We'll have a lifetime of privacy, you and I," Perry promised, his blue eyes twinkling. "Surely an hour here and there spent with my mother isn't too much to endure?"

"I suppose not," she said reluctantly.

"That's my darling girl."

Glowing at his praise, Sara allowed him to take her cloak. She seated herself on the heavily embroidered cushions of the settee. Perry took her hands, stroking his thumbs over her knuckles. "Well," he said fondly, "it appears your visit to London did you no harm." His lips parted in a teasing smile. "Mother has some absurd notions about your research trips. 'How does that girl know all about such indecent things as harlots and thieves?' she asks. I've had a difficult time convincing her that you haven't been roving through back-street gin shops and bordellos! Mother simply doesn't understand what a marvelous imagination you have."

"Thank you," Sara said uncomfortably, fixing her

gaze on the pair of black and gilt sconces on the opposite wall. Although she had never lied to him about her research in the city, she had gently misled him, glossing over most of her dangerous activities and making it all sound rather dry and dull. Perry had always accepted her descriptions without question, but his mother had a suspicious nature.

"After all," Perry continued, "my darling Sara spends most of her time sorting through book collections and touring old buildings. Isn't that so?" He beamed at her, while Sara felt heat creeping up from her neckline.

"Yes, indeed. Er . . . Perry . . . there's something I must tell you. During my stay in London, there was a night or two when I came in very late. Mrs. Goodman threatened to write to my mother and her other friends in Greenwood Corners that I'm a 'reckless hoyden.' "

Perry collapsed with amusement at the notion. "Sara Fielding, a reckless hoyden! Anyone who knows you would laugh at that."

She smiled in relief. "I'm glad you won't pay attention to anything Mrs. Goodman might say."

Perry squeezed her hands. "Perhaps some old biddy might spread gossip about you because you've written some foolish story about Mathilda. But I know you better than anyone, darling. I know the fondest wishes of your heart—and I'm going to make them come true. After that, there'll be no need for you to worry with all your daydreaming and scribbling. You'll have me and a houseful of your own children to occupy your time with. All a woman could want."

Sara looked at him in surprise. "Are you saying you would want me to stop writing?"

"I've brought tea," came Martha's voice from the doorway. She entered the room bearing an engraved silver tray and a tea service that had been in the Kingswood family for three generations.

"Mother," Perry said with a brilliant smile. "How did you know that was exactly what we wanted? Come join us while Sara regales us with an account of her visit to the wicked city."

Prodded by Martha's disapproving gaze, Sara inched away from Perry until they were seated at a more circumspect distance from each other.

Martha placed the tray on the round boulle table in front of them. She settled into a nearby chair. "Why don't you pour, Sara?" Martha invited, in a tone that implied she was bestowing an honor on a favored guest. But somehow Sara had the feeling she was undergoing a test. Carefully she strained the tea into one of the delicate china cups, and added milk and sugar. Her suspicion that she was being tested was confirmed by Martha's sourly pleased expression. "That is not how Perry likes it," Martha said.

Sara turned a questioning gaze to Perry. "You take milk and sugar, don't you?"

He shrugged slightly. "Yes, but—"

"You poured the milk in *last*," Martha interrupted, before Perry could enlighten her. "My son prefers the milk *first* and tea added second. It makes a distinct difference in the flavor."

Thinking that perhaps she was joking, Sara looked back at Perry. He gave her a helpless smile. Sara forced herself to shrug prosaically. "Well," she said with a faint tremor of laughter in her voice, "I shall try to remember that, Mrs. Kingswood. I can't think why it has escaped my notice all these years."

"Perhaps you should try to be more observant of my son's needs." Martha nodded in satisfaction at the lesson she had just delivered. "You might remember that I prefer mine the same way, but without the sugar."

Obediently Sara prepared the beverages the proper way, and settled back with her own cup of tea—no milk, extra sugar. After she took the first sip, she met Martha's inquisitive gaze. The older woman's lips compressed until thin vertical lines were scored all along the edges. "I assume you attended church when you were in London, Sara?"

The temptation to lie was strong. Sara gulped more tea and shook her head apologetically. "There wasn't time."

"There wasn't time," Martha repeated softly. "Hmph. I'm certainly grateful the Lord doesn't give us such excuses when we entreat Him with our prayers. As busy as He is, He always finds the time for us. I should think we would all be willing to do the same for Him."

Sara nodded ruefully, reflecting that Martha Kingswood's record for regular church attendance was unmatched by anyone. Martha always arrived fifteen minutes early and sat in the front row. It was also her habit to leave fifteen minutes after everyone else, for she felt it was her special responsibility to give Reverend Crawford her opinions on how the sermon could have been improved. "Neither Perry nor I has ever missed a Sunday for any reason," Martha was saying. "And neither did Mr. Kingswood when he was alive. 'I had rather be a doorkeeper in the house of my God, than to dwell in the tents of wickedness.' Do you know where that quote comes from, Sara?"

"Job?" Sara guessed.

"Psalms," Martha replied with a frown. "No woman aspiring to be Perry's wife would ever consider missing a service, unless it was for some unavoidable reason."

"Death? Natural disasters?" Sara suggested innocently, feeling Perry's knee shove against hers in warning.

"Precisely so," Martha said.

Sara was silent, all of her exuberance at being with Perry fading. She had come here to be with him, not to receive a lecture from his mother, no matter how well-intentioned. Why was Perry allowing it without a word? He was being complacent while his mother dominated their time together. Ignoring a twinge of resentment, Sara tried to steer the conversation in a new direction. "Tell me what happened in Greenwood Corners while I was away. How is old Mr. Dawson's gout?"

"Much better," Martha replied. "He actually put his shoes on the other day and went for a stroll."

"His niece Rachel became engaged to Johnny Chesterson the day before last," Perry added.

"Oh, that's wonderful," Sara exclaimed. "The Chestersons are lucky to have such a nice girl in their family."

Martha nodded primly. "Rachel is the kind of spiritual, self-effacing girl that Mr. Kingswood always hoped his son would marry. She would never dream of drawing attention to herself . . . as some young women do."

"Are you referring to me?" Sara asked quietly.

"I am making a point about Rachel."

Slowly Sara set her cup and saucer on the table and looked at Perry, who had colored at his mother's rudeness. "It's a wonder you never courted such a paragon," Sara told him, smiling although her chest was tightening with anger.

Martha answered for her son. "Perry was never free to court her or any other girls in the village. Someone else was always taking up his time with her demanding possessiveness."

Sara felt her face turn red. "Was that you or me, I wonder?" Standing abruptly, she snatched up her cloak. "Excuse me. I think it's time I left."

Behind her, Martha gave a sharp exclamation. "What a rude display. I was only making conversation!"

As Perry bent to soothe his mother, Sara strode out of the house. She had never been angry in front of Perry before—she had always tolerated his mother with patience and courtesy. For some reason she had finally reached her limit. Swearing under her breath, she began the walk home. Her spine stiffened as she became aware of Perry hurrying to catch up with her. He had rushed outside without even stopping to put on a coat.

"I can't believe you would storm off in such a manner," Perry exclaimed. "Sara, stop and let me talk to you for a minute!"

She continued without even breaking stride. "I don't feel like talking."

"Don't be angry with Mother."

"I'm not angry with her. I'm angry with you for not defending me!"

"Sara, I can hardly tell her she's not free to express her own opinions in her own house! You're making too much of this."

"She was insufferable!"

Perry gave a harassed sigh and adjusted his pace to

match hers. "Mother was in high dudgeon today," he admitted. "I don't know what put her in such a state."

"I think it's safe to say *I* did. I *always* do, Perry. Haven't you ever realized how much she dislikes me and any other woman that you associate with?"

"What has made you so sensitive?" he asked in astonishment. "It's not like you to take offense easily. I must say it's not an attractive side of you, Sara, not at all!"

Now that she had begun to let the barricades down, she felt an immense relief at being able to speak her mind. "Oh? Well, I don't find it attractive when you let your mother needle me like that. And what's worse, you expect me to swallow it with a smile!"

Perry's face turned sullen. "I don't wish to argue with you, Sara. We never have before."

Her eyes began to sting. "That's because I thought if I was understanding and long-suffering enough, you would finally be moved to propose to me. I've had to wait four years, Perry, hanging all my hopes on your mother's approval. Well, she's never going to give her blessing to a marriage between you and me." Impatiently she brushed away a few angry tears. "You've always asked me to wait, as if we had time in abundance. But time is too precious, Perry. We've wasted *years*, when we could have been with each other. Don't you understand how much even one day of loving each other is worth? Some people are separated by distances they can never cross. All they can do is dream about each other for a lifetime, never having what they want most. How foolish, how *wasteful* to have love within your reach and not take it!" She damped her teeth on her trembling bottom lip to steady herself. "Let me tell you something, Perry Kingswood—it would be unwise of you to assume that I'll be happy to wait forever!"

"What do you mean by that?" he asked, stunned by her tirade.

She stopped and faced him squarely. "If you truly wanted me, you wouldn't be able to stand being apart from me. You wouldn't let anyone come between us. A-and you would have seduced me by now!"

"*Sara*," he exclaimed, staring at her in disbelief. "I've never seen you like this. You're not yourself. What happened to you in London?"

"Nothing. I've just been taking stock of things." Regaining control of herself, she gazed at him with a mixture of resolve and longing. "I've made a decision, Perry."

"Oh, you have," he said, the sulky curve of his lips deepening. "Well, I won't be dictated to, my girl!"

"I hope that's true. I'm afraid you'll let your mother's wishes guide you in this. You know as well as I that she has done her best to stand in our way. I have always tried to avoid making you choose between us, but I can't see any other way to resolve this." Sara took a long breath. "I want to marry you, Perry. I want to take care of you, and be a loving helpmate. But this 'courtship,' or whatever it is that has been going on for the past four years, must end one way or another. If you don't propose to me soon—*very* soon—I will end our relationship for good."

His face turned pallid. They stared at each other in silence, both of them amazed that such forceful words had come from her. Sara read the dawning anger and hurt in his eyes, but she continued to stare at him resolutely.

A breeze cut through Perry's shirt and vest, and he shivered. "I'm cold," he muttered. Without another word, he turned and left her, hurrying back to the manor where his mother waited.

As always Sara felt soothed by the sight of her family's cottage, perched at the top of a gentle hill. There were four rooms in the little house, a privy with a thatched roof in the garden, and a combination stable and cart shed. Her elderly parents had lived there for nearly forty years, after inheriting it from Sara's grandparents. No matter what troubles befell them in the outside world, home meant safety and peace.

As she approached the cottage, Sara saw that the small rectangular windows were glowing with light. The silhouettes of many heads showed plainly. Visitors. Her heart sank. Sometimes her parents' elderly friends would stay for hours, socializing over countless cups of tea. Sara didn't want to face a crowd at the moment, but there was no way to avoid it. Pulling her lips into a halfhearted smile, she opened the front door and walked in. As she had expected, every piece of worn furniture was filled with guests . . . the Hughes, the Brownes, and Archie Burrows, a recent widower.

"Sara, you're back early," her father, Isaac, exclaimed. He was a short man with broad shoulders and a shock of silver-gray hair. His leathery face creased with an infectious smile. He patted the cushioned footstool near his chair. "Have one of the delicious cakes Mrs. Hughes brought."

"No, thank you," Sara said while her mother helped to remove her cloak. "I believe I'll have a rest after my walk."

"Why, look," Mrs. Browne exclaimed. "The poor girl's cheeks are all red from the cold. The wind has a vicious bite today, doesn't it?"

"It certainly does," Sara murmured, declining to explain that it was emotion, rather than cold, that had brought the color to her cheeks.

"How is young Mr. Kingswood?" one of the elderly ladies inquired, and they all watched her with great interest. "As handsome as ever, isn't he?"

"Oh, very." Sara managed to give the group a strained smile before she retreated to the privacy of her room.

Sitting on her narrow bed, she folded her hands in her lap and stared at the picture on the wall, a watercolor landscape that had been painted by one of her friends years ago. The artist was Mary Marcum, a friend exactly her age who had married the local blacksmith and was now the mother of three children. A wave of self-pity came over Sara. She had never felt so much like a spinster. Gritting her teeth with frustration, she wiped her dampening eyes with her sleeve. At that moment her mother entered the room and closed the door.

"What happened?" Katie asked quietly, easing her plump body onto the bed and folding her hands on her lap. Although her skin was lined with age, her brown eyes were youthful and warm. A halo of soft white curls framed her face becomingly.

"What about your guests—" Sara began.

"Oh, they're perfectly happy to listen to your father telling his ancient jokes. We've finally reached the age when they all sound new again."

They chuckled together, and then Sara shook her head miserably. "I think I may have made a mistake," she confessed, and told Katie about the scene with the Kingswoods and the ultimatum she had given Perry afterward.

Katie's forehead was wreathed in concern. She held Sara's hand comfortingly. "I don't believe it was a mistake, Sara. You did what you felt was right. You won't go wrong by listening to your heart."

"Oh, I don't know about that," Sara said ruefully, dragging her sleeve across her wet face. "My heart was telling me some very strange things a few days ago."

Her mother's hand loosened slightly. "About your Mr. Craven."

Sara glanced at her, startled. "How did you know?"

"It was the way you talked about him. There was something in your voice I'd never heard before."

Although Sara had mentioned just a few scant details about the gambling club and the man who owned it, she should have known her mother would sense the things that were left unsaid. She lowered her head. "Mr. Craven is a wicked man, Mama," she whispered. "He's done terrible things in his life."

"But you found something in him to care about, didn't you?"

A few tears splashed into Sara's lap. "If he'd had someone to teach him about right and wrong, someone to love and care for him as a child, he would have grown up to be a fine man. A very fine man." She wondered what Derek Craven might have been like if he'd been born to one of the families in Greenwood Corners. He would have been a handsome little boy with innocent green eyes and a sturdy, well-nourished body, running through the meadows with the other village children. But the image dissolved, and she could only see him as a scrawny climbing boy, choking on soot as he crawled upward through chimney stacks. Sara twisted her fingers together in agitation. "The

club factotum told me that Mr. Craven is a man of ruined potential. He was absolutely right."

Katie watched her closely. "Sara, did this man admit
to having feelings for you?"

"Oh, no," Sara said hastily. "At least . . . not the kind
of feelings you and Papa would approve of."

She flushed, while her mother took unexpected
amusement in the comment. "Of course I approve of
those feelings," Katie said, chuckling. "Within the
bonds of matrimony."

Sara dragged her fingers through her own hair, ruining the smooth coiffure and pulling out the pins that
seemed to jab into her scalp. "There's no point in talking about Mr. Craven," she said dully. "Perry is the
only man I want, and the only one I was likely to get,
and it's possible I've just ruined all chance of marrying
him!"

"No one can know for certain," Katie mused. "But I
think you might have given him the prodding he
needed. Deep in his heart, Perry doesn't want to be
alone with his mother forever. He can never really be
a man until he leaves her and begins to make decisions
for himself—and she's made that well-nigh impossible.
In a way she's created a prison for him. What worries
me, Sara, is that instead of escaping the prison, he may
want you to join him there."

"Oh, no." Sara's chin wobbled. "I couldn't bear a
lifetime of being under Martha Kingswood's thumb!"

"It's something you should think about," Katie said
gently. "Lord bless you both, it may be the only way
you can have Perry." Giving Sara's arm a squeeze, she
smiled warmly. "Dry your face, dear, and come out to
visit with the guests. Mrs. Browne has been asking

about Mathilda again, and I never remember what I'm supposed to tell her."

Sara gave her a dark look and obediently followed her to the front room.

The following day was spent washing clothes and preparing a "pepper pot" for supper. Cutting carrots, turnips, and onions into small pieces for the stew, Sara talked and laughed with her mother. As they worked, they sang a selection of the love ballads with sweetly tragic endings that were so popular in the village. Finally Isaac called to them from the parlor, where he sat on the floor fixing the cracked leg of a chair. "Don't the two of you know any songs in which no one dies or loses his sweetheart? I began the day in a happy mood, and now after these dirges I'm hard-pressed not to be wiping a tear from my eye!"

"Will hymns do?" Sara asked, scraping the vegetables into a pot of boiling water. Later they would add equal parts of mutton and fish, and season the whole with cayenne pepper.

"Aye, something to uplift the soul!"

They launched into a vigorous hymn, pausing to giggle as they heard Isaac's off-kilter baritone join in. "Your father has his share of faults," Katie murmured to Sara in the lull after the hymn was finished. "He gave me a trying time, to be sure, especially in his youth. He had a quick temper back then, and a tendency to brood." A reminiscent smile curved her mouth. "But that dear man has loved me every day of his life. He's been true to me all these forty years. And after all this time, he still makes me laugh. Marry a man like that, Sara . . . and if it pleases God, you'll be as happy as I've been."

* * *

Retiring early for the night, Sara lay very still in her bed and waited for her ice-cold toes to warm. Perry had been in her thoughts all day. Fervently she prayed that she hadn't driven him away for good. She had loved him for so many years. He had always been a part of her life. When he was in one of his boyish moods, teasing her and pressing careless kisses on her lips, she sometimes feared she would expire of happiness. The afternoon picnics with him, long walks through the countryside, snuggling against his shoulder as he read aloud to her . . . the memories had brought her hours of pleasure as she recounted each golden moment. If by some miracle she became his wife, she would be able to wake up every morning and find him next to her, his blond hair softly tumbled, his sleepy blue eyes smiling at her.

Tense with anxious hope, Sara clenched her arms around her pillow. "Perry," she said aloud, her voice muffled. "Perry, I can't lose you. I *can't*."

She fell asleep with Perry's name on her lips. But when she dreamed, it was of Derek Craven, his dark presence filtering through her sleep like a ghost.

She played a game of hide-and-seek with him, running through the empty club, giggling wildly as she sensed him drawing near. He followed her intently, closing in until she knew there was no chance of escape . . . except one. After finding a secret door, she disappeared into a tunnel of darkness, concealing herself. But suddenly she heard the sound of his breathing. He was with her in the shadows. He caught her easily and pinned her against the wall, laughing at her startled gasp. *"You'll never get away from me,"* he whispered, his hands sliding roughly over her body. *"You're mine forever . . . only mine . . ."*

Sara was awakened suddenly by a tapping on her door. Her father's voice was groggy and tempered with annoyance. "Sara? Sara, we have company. Dress yourself, daughter, and come to the front room."

She stirred heavily, wishing only to sink back into the dream. "Yes, Papa," she mumbled, and dragged herself out of the cozy warmth of her bed. She found a heavy robe and tied it over her high-necked night rail. "Papa, who on earth is . . ." Her voice faded as she saw the visitor. Automatically her hand flew to her wild hair, smoothing back the tangled skeins. "Perry!"

Looking haggard and ill-at-ease, Perry stood by the front door, hat in hand. He kept his eyes on Sara as he spoke to her father quietly. "Sir, I know this has the appearance of impropriety, but if I could have a minute alone with your daughter—"

"A minute, no more," Isaac said reluctantly. He gave Sara a meaningful glance just before he left the room. She nodded in answer to the silent warning to keep the interlude short.

Her heartbeat was heavy and fast. Clearing her throat, she wandered to a nearby chair and sat on the edge. "Why are you here at such a late hour, Perry? You know how unseemly it is."

"I've been half-mad for the past two days." His voice was strained. "I didn't sleep at all last night. I thought about everything you said. You hardly seemed like the same person yesterday morning—the way you looked and spoke—you should have told me how you truly felt long ago, Sara. It was a disservice to me every time you covered your thoughts with a smile."

"I suppose it was," she admitted, noticing that his eyes were smudged with the shadows of lost sleep.

"You were right about a few things," Perry said, surprising her by dropping on his knees before her. Carefully he took her hands. "Mother will not approve of our union, not at first. But she'll get used to it after a while. It's possible you and she may even become friends someday." Sara began to reply, but he gestured for her to wait. "You were right about something else, darling. It is wasteful not to take love when it's within my grasp. I do want to be with you." He held her hands tightly, looking into her flushed face. "I love you, Sara. And if you'll have me, I would like for us to be married in the spring."

"Yes, *yes!*" Sara left the chair and flung her arms around his neck, nearly toppling them both over in her excitement.

Laughing and kissing her, Perry tried to hush her exclamations. "Quiet, darling, or we'll wake your parents."

"They probably have their ears pressed to the door," she said, tightening her arms in a stranglehold. "Oh, Perry, you've made me so happy."

"You've made me even happier." They grinned at each other, and Perry stroked the wild tendrils of her hair.

"Come back tomorrow morning and talk to my father," Sara urged. "It's only a formality, but it will please him."

"Yes, and then you'll come with me to break the news to my mother."

"*Ugh,*" Sara couldn't resist saying.

He gave her a reproving glance. "If you approach her in a spirit of love and goodwill, she'll reciprocate in kind."

"All right," Sara said with a grin. "I'm so happy I'd be willing to kiss the devil hims—"

Perry didn't seem to notice the odd catch of her voice. Nor could he know the cause of it.

They talked for another minute or two. After they exchanged a few hasty kisses, Perry left the cottage. Sara's mind buzzed with strange, fearful notions all the while, but she concealed her turmoil until he was gone. Then she let herself think about the flashing memory . . . Derek Craven's snarling grin, his dark head bending over hers. She exhaled unsteadily, feeling as if she were being haunted. It must not happen again. She must drive every thought of Craven out of her mind forever. He had said he would forget her. Bitterly she wondered how he intended to accomplish that, if it would be easy for him . . . if he would turn to another woman.

It was ridiculous, letting herself brood over a man like him. What had gone on between them was finished—and the episode had been so brief, really, it had all been like a dream. Perry was real, and so was her life in Greenwood Corners. She would content herself with family and friends, and embark on a future with a man who loved her.

"I still can't bring myself to believe our young Mr. Kingswood finally came up to scratch." Mrs. Hodges shook her head with a smile, watching as Katie cleaned the grate for her and Sara piled kindling in her kitchen fireplace. Because Mr. and Mrs. Hodges were elderly and Mr. Hodges had bouts of rheumatism, they sometimes required help with their household chores. Dusting her prized kitchen dresser with its display of pewter and china, Mrs. Hodges spoke in jovial tones. "Heaven's sake, I'm surprised his mother allowed it." As she saw Katie and Sara's guarded expressions, her smile faded and her round cheeks sagged with dismay. She had meant to make them laugh. Instead she seemed to have touched on a sore point.

Sara broke the tension with a shrug. "Mrs. Kingswood had no choice in the matter. And she seems to have reconciled herself to the idea. After all, she can hardly fault me for loving Perry."

"That's right," Mrs. Hodges agreed quickly. "It will do both the Kingswoods a world of good for Perry to take a wife of his own. Martha nearly ruined that boy with her spoiling, if you ask me."

Biting off a heartfelt agreement, Sara hung freshly scrubbed pots and kettles on the fireplace bracket. A frill of lace hovered just above her eyebrow, and she pushed it back irritably. At Perry's urging she had gone back to wearing her lace caps, but they no longer seemed to fit the way they once had. She walked over to the stone-paved sink in order to wash her sooty hands and arms, shivering at the icy gush of water from the pump.

"That girl isn't afraid of work," Mrs. Hodges said to Katie. "She's nothing like the rest of these flighty village chits, with nary a thought in their heads but how to dress their hair and make eyes at the men."

"Sara has a pair of able hands and a quick mind," Katie agreed. "She'll be a good wife to Perry. And a blessing to his mother, if Martha will allow it."

Mrs. Hodges watched Sara closely. "Is she still insisting that you and Perry live with her after the marriage?"

Sara's back tensed. She continued to rinse her hands until they were white and numb. "I'm afraid so," she said evenly. "We haven't resolved the issue yet."

"Oh, dear." Mrs. Hodges turned to exchange a few quiet murmurs with Katie.

Paying no attention to their exchange, Sara dried her frozen hands and thought about the past month. Martha Kingswood had received the news of the engagement with remarkable calmness. Sara and Perry had told her together. They had been astonished by her lack of protest. *"If marrying Sara will bring you happiness,"* Martha had said to Perry, holding his face in her narrow hands, *"then I give my blessing to the both of you."* She had bent and pressed a brief kiss on her son's lips, and then straightened to look at Sara with a slitted gaze.

Since then, Martha had interfered with and criticized every decision they made. Perry seemed oblivious of his mother's badgering, but it never failed to send Sara's mood plummeting. She was afraid that her marriage would be an endless battleground. The last week, especially, had been a trying one. Martha was preoccupied with the idea that Perry was abandoning her. She had declared her intention of living with her son and his wife after the wedding.

"It's hardly an unorthodox idea," Perry had told Sara. "Many couples reside with their parents—and grandparents, too. I don't see that there's any need for us to live in seclusion."

Sara had been aghast. "Perry, you're not saying you *want* to share a home with her, are you?"

A frown crept across his boyishly handsome face. "What if your mother were all alone and she asked us to live with her?"

"It's not the same. Mine isn't demanding and impossible to please!"

Perry looked hurt and sullen. He was not used to arguments from her. "I'll thank you not to use such words about Mother, and to remember that she brought me up and took care of me with no help from anyone."

"I know that," Sara said ruefully, trying to think of a solution. "Perry, you have some money of your own, don't you? Some savings put away?"

He bristled at the question, for it wasn't a woman's place to ask questions about money. "That not your concern."

Excited about her idea, Sara ignored his offended masculine pride. "Well, I have a little nest egg. And I'll make enough from the sale of my next book to buy a cottage of our own. I'll work my fingers to the bone if necessary, so that we can hire someone to keep your mother company and look after her."

"No," he said instantly. "A housemaid would not care for her the way her own family would."

A vision of herself waiting hand and foot on Martha Kingswood, and giving up her writing forever, caused Sara to flush angrily. "Perry, you know how miserable I would be if she lived with us. She'll complain about everything I do, how I cook, how I keep the house, how I teach my children. You're asking too much of me. Please, we must find some other way—"

"You are going to marry me for better or worse," he said sharply. "I thought you understood what that meant."

"I didn't realize it was going to be better for you and worse for me!"

"If the worst thing that could ever happen to you is living with my mother—and I rather doubt that—you should love me enough to accept it."

They had parted company without making up, each of them refusing to listen to the other's side. "You're changing," Perry had complained. "Day by day you're becoming a different person. Why can't you be the sweet, happy girl I fell in love with?"

Sara hadn't been able to answer. She knew better than he what the problem was. He wanted a wife who would never question his decisions. He wanted her to make difficult sacrifices in order to make his life pleasant. And she had been willing to do that for years, for the sake of love and companionship. But now . . . sometimes . . . love didn't seem worth the price he demanded from her.

He's right, I have changed, she thought unhappily. The fault was with her, not him. Not long ago she had been the kind of woman who would have been able to make Perry happy. *We should have married years ago*, she thought. *Why didn't I stay in the village and earn money some other way than writing? Why did I have to go to London?*

During the evenings when she sat at her desk and labored over her novel, she sometimes found herself gripping the pen handle so tightly that her fingers ached with the strain. She would look down to find splotches of ink across the paper. It was difficult to summon Derek Craven's face clearly now, but there were reminders of him everywhere. The timbre of someone's voice, or the greenish color of someone's eyes, sometimes gave her a jolt of recognition that reached to her very foundations. Whenever she was with Perry, she struggled to keep from comparing the two men, for it would be unfair to both of them. Besides, Perry wanted her as his wife, while Derek Craven had made it clear that he had no desire to be a candidate for her affections. "*I will forget you*," he had assured her. She was certain that he had wiped his memory clean of her, and oh, how the thought stung . . . for she longed to do the same.

Pushing all negative thoughts aside, she tried to envision the home she would share with Perry. They would spend quiet evenings before the fire, and on Sundays they would attend church with friends and family. During the week Sara would linger over the produce at the marketplace, exchanging light gossip with friends, sharing small jokes about married life. It would be pleasant. Overall, Perry had the makings of a good husband. There was affection between them, and the comfort of common interests and shared beliefs. They might even have the kind of marriage her parents had.

The thought should have brought her comfort. But inexplicably, Sara could find little joy in the prospect of what awaited her.

The Christmas season passed in the same warm spirit it always did in Greenwood Corners. Sara enjoyed the caroling, the gathering of old friends, the exchanging of gifts, and all the rituals she remembered from childhood. She was busy with wreath-making, holiday baking, and the task of helping to sew costumes for the children's pageant. There wasn't much time to see Perry, but during the few hours they did spend with each other, they made a concerted effort to avoid arguing. On Christmas Eve, she gave Perry a box of six fine handkerchiefs she had embroidered with his initials, and he gave her a delicate gilt brooch engraved with the pattern of tiny birds. Sitting together before the fire, they linked hands and talked about fondly remembered moments of their pasts. No mention was made of Martha, or of Sara's writing. In fact, neither of them dared to speak of the future at all, as if it were some dangerous and forbidden topic. Only later did

Sara allow herself to think that it was very odd for a betrothed couple, this inability to talk about their plans for the life that awaited them.

On a bright day in January when the air was dry and the ground hard-frozen, Katie and Isaac took the horse and cart to purchase supplies at the village market. Afterward they would pay a visit to Reverend Crawford and engage in a sociable chat. Remaining at home to do chores, Sara stood at the lead-lined kitchen sink and cleaned a large pewter pot. Energetically she scrubbed with a muslin bag filled with powdered whiting, until the dull pewter surface took on a new brightness. She paused in the middle of the task as she heard someone knocking at the front door.

Wiping her hands on the large cloth knotted around her waist, Sara went to greet the caller. Her eyes widened as she opened the door and saw the woman standing there. "Tabitha!" she exclaimed. A driver and one of the unmarked carriages used by Craven's employees waited at the side of the road. Sara's heart twisted painfully in her chest at the reminders of the gambling club.

It was difficult to recognize the house wench, who was now dressed like a simple country maid. Gone were the gaudy spangled skirts and low-cut bodice she had always worn at Craven's. Instead she was clad in a demure lavender gown not unlike those that Sara owned. The usual wanton disorder of her hair was tamed into a neat coif and topped off with a modest bonnet. The faint resemblance between them was more marked than usual, except that Tabitha's face was still etched with the coarseness that betrayed her profession. Her mouth curled in an engaging grin, but there was a hesitancy in her posture, as if she feared

Sara would turn her away. "Miss Fielding, I came to say 'ello. I'm on the way to stay with my family a week or so. They lives in 'Ampshire, y'see."

Sara gathered her scattered wits. "Tabitha, what a pleasant surprise it is to see you! Please come inside. I'll make some tea. Perhaps the driver would like to sit in the kitchen—"

"No time for all that," Tabitha said, at once gratified and embarrassed by Sara's welcoming manner. "I'll be gone in a blink ow an eye—just stopped to 'ave a bit ow a chat. Won't stay but a minute."

Sara urged her inside the warm house and closed the door against a gust of wind. "Is everything all right at the club?"

"Oh, aye."

"How is Mr. Worthy?"

" 'E's fine."

"And Gill?"

"Fine, as allus."

The urge to ask about Derek Craven was overwhelming. Somehow Sara held the words back. She motioned for Tabitha to join her on the settee in the front room and watched her without blinking, wondering why the house wench had taken it upon herself to visit.

Tabitha took exaggerated pains to arrange her skirts and sit like a lady. She grinned at Sara as she smoothed the material of her gown. "My ma thinks I'm a maid for a grand lord in London, carrying coal an' water, polishing silwer an' such. It wouldn't do for 'er to know I works on my back at Crawen's."

Sara nodded gravely. "I understand."

"Mr. Crawen would cull me good if 'e knowed I'd come 'ere today."

"I won't tell a soul," Sara promised, while her heart climbed up into her throat. She stared at Tabitha, who shrugged and glanced around the cottage as if she were waiting patiently for something. The house wench wanted her to ask about Craven, Sara realized. Agitatedly she tangled her hands in her makeshift apron. "Tabitha . . . tell me how he is."

The house wench needed no further prompting. "Mr. Crawen's short in temper these days. Doesn't eat or sleep, acts like 'e's got a bee up 'is arse. Yesterday 'e went to the kitchen an' told Monsieur Labarge 'is soup tasted like bilgewater. Why, it took Gill an' Worthy both to keep Labarge from gutting 'im with a big knife!"

"I-is that why you've come here, to tell me that? I'm very sorry to hear it, but . . ." Sara paused awkwardly and lowered her head. "His mood has nothing to do with me."

"It 'as *everything* to do with you, miss—an' no one knows it better than me."

Sara's fists knotted tighter in her apron. "What do you mean?"

Tabitha leaned forward, speaking in a theatrical whisper. "Mr. Crawen came to my bed two—no, three—nights ago. You know 'e newer does that. Not with the 'ouse wenches."

Suddenly it was impossible to breathe. Sara remembered having felt like this long ago, when her horse Eppie had shied at some movement in the grass and thrown her to the ground. Sara had fallen flat on her stomach and had wheezed and gasped sickly for air. Oh, God, how could it matter this much to her that he had taken his pleasure within this woman's body, held her and kissed her—

" 'Is eyes were so strange," Tabitha continued, "like 'e was looking through the gates of 'ell. 'I 'as a special request, 'e says, 'an' if you tells anyone about it, I'll 'ave you skinned an' gogged.' So I says awright, an' then—"

"No." Sara felt as if she would shatter to pieces if she heard one more word. "Don't tell me. I—I don't want to hear—"

"It was about *you*, miss."

"Me?" Sara asked faintly.

" 'E came to my bed. 'E told me not to say anyfing, no matter what 'e did. No matter what 'e said. Then Mr. Crawen turned the lamp down an' took me against 'im . . ." Tabitha averted her gaze as she continued. Sara was frozen in place. " 'Let me hold you, Sara,' 'e says, 'I need you, Sara' . . . all night long it was, 'im pretending I was you. It's because we look alike, you an' me. That's why 'e did it." She shrugged with a touch of embarrassment. " 'E was gentle an' sweet about it, too. In the morning 'e left wivout a word, but there was still that terrible look in 'is eyes—"

"Stop," Sara said sharply, her face ashen. "You shouldn't have come here. You had no right to tell me."

Instead of being offended by Sara's outburst, Tabitha looked sympathetic. "I says to myself . . . it wouldn't 'urt no one if I told Miss Fielding. You 'as the right to know. Mr. Crawen loves you, miss, like 'e's newer loved no one in 'is blessed life. 'E thinks you're too good for 'im—'e thinks you're as fine as an angel. An' you are, God's truf." Tabitha stared at her earnestly. "Miss Sara, if you only knew . . . 'e's not as bad as they say."

"I know that," Sara choked. "But there are things

you don't understand. I'm betrothed to another man, and even if I weren't . . ." She stopped abruptly. There was no need to explain her feelings, or speculate on Derek Craven's, in front of this woman. It was useless, not to mention painful.

"Then you won't go to 'im?"

The girl's bewilderment caused Sara to smile in spite of her misery. Like the other house wenches, Tabitha felt inordinately proud and not a little possessive of Derek Craven, almost as if he were a favorite uncle or a kindly benefactor. If he wanted something, if something would please him, there was no question that he should have it.

Woodenly Sara stood up and made her way to the door. "I know you came here with good intentions, Tabitha, but you must leave now. I . . . I'm sorry." Those were the only coherent words she could form. Oh, God, she was sorry for things she couldn't name or even admit to herself. She was consumed by loneliness, burning with it. She ached with grief for what she would never have.

"I'm sorry too," Tabitha murmured, her face reddening guiltily. "I won't bother you again, miss. I swear it on my own life." She left quickly, forbearing to say another word.

Chapter 8

Stumbling to the fireplace, Sara sat down on the hard floor and buried her face against her knees. Wildly she tried to convince herself that she would be a fool to give away what happiness she might be able to find with Perry. She tried to imagine going to Derek Craven and telling him . . . telling him what? A bubble of senseless laughter escaped her. "I want to see you one more time," she whispered. She wanted to be near him again, if only for a few minutes. And he felt the same way, or he wouldn't have made love to another woman and pretended it was she.

"I will forget you, Sara Fielding. No matter what it takes . . ."

What good would it do even if she were able to steal a few precious moments with him? He would not want to see her. What could she say to him, when she couldn't explain her feelings even to herself?

Resting her head on her forearm, she groaned in frustration. She was treading on the edge of disaster.

She must forget her dangerous infatuation with Derek
Craven and turn to the man she had loved ever since
she was a girl. Suddenly it seemed as if Perry
Kingswood had the power to save her from herself.
She struggled to her feet. Quickly she banked the fire,
snatched up her cloak and mittens, and bolted out the
front door. She hurried to the Kingswood manor as
fast as her feet would take her. During the long walk,
the cold air drove deep into her lungs and seemed to
freeze her bones. Her chest ached from a knot of pain
that had settled in the center. *"Perry, make it all go
away,"* she wanted to beg. *"Make me feel safe and loved.
Tell me we were meant to be together."*

She didn't care if he thought she had taken leave of
her senses. All she needed was for him to put his arms
around her and reassure her that he loved her. And he
would, she thought, drawing strength from the image
of him holding her. He would be calm and gentle, and
soothe her fears.

Her breath caught in excitement as she came upon
the Kingswoods' home, and she saw Perry leading a
horse from the paddock to the stable in back. "Perry!"
she cried, but the wind was blowing, making it impossible for him to hear. Eagerly she hurried around the
house to the stable. The sturdy structure was warm
and sheltered from the wind, filled with the familiar
smells of hay and horses.

Perry, who was clad in a heavy wool coat and a knitted hat, was busy leading the horse into a hay-lined
stall. Aware of her approach, he turned to face her. His
color was high from exercise, and his eyes were like
sapphires. "Sara? Why are you in such a state? Is
something wrong?"

"I had to see you this very minute." She launched

herself forward and clung to him, dropping her head into the curve of his neck. "Perry, I've been so unhappy, wondering how to get rid of this distance between us! I'm sorry if I've been demanding or unreasonable. I want everything to be right between us. Tell me you love me. Tell me . . ."

"What's brought this on?" he asked in astonishment, his arms closing around her.

"Nothing. Nothing in particular . . . I just . . ." Floundering in her excitement, she fell silent and held on to him more tightly.

After a minute of wordless surprise, Perry eased her away and spoke in a softly chiding tone. "You never used to carry on so, darling. Running about the countryside with your hair flying and your eyes wild . . . there's no need for it. Of course I love you. Have I given you reason to doubt that? I'll be glad when you stop writing. It makes you emotional, and that wouldn't do for our children, or me, for that matter—"

He stopped with a muffled sound as Sara took his face in her mittened hands and pressed her mouth to his. She felt his body tense. There was a tentative response, the slightest movement of his lips . . . but then he pulled back and looked down at her in shocked dismay. "What has happened to you?" he asked sternly. "Why are you behaving this way?"

"I want to belong to you," Sara said, her face flushed. "Is it so wrong of me, when we'll be married in just a few months?"

"Yes, it *is* wrong, and you know it." His cheeks turned as red as hers. "Decent, God-fearing people should have the moral strength to control their animal urges—"

"That sounds like something your mother would

say, not you." Sara pressed against him ardently. "I
need you," she whispered, brushing swift, dancing
kisses over his cheek and jaw. The blood raced in her
veins. "I need you to love me, Perry . . . here . . . now."
Urgently she pulled him toward a stack of neatly
folded blankets and a few blocks of hay. Perry took a
few uncertain steps forward. "Make me yours," Sara
murmured, and lifted her mouth, parting her lips
enough to let her tongue drift over the surface of his.

Abruptly Perry sucked in his breath and pushed her
away. "*No!*" He stared at her with a mixture of accusa-
tion and desire. "I don't want this! And I certainly
don't want to kiss you as if you were some French
whore!"

Sara fell back a step and felt her face stiffen. It was
as if she were standing outside herself, watching the
scene from a distance.

"What is it you're after?" he asked heatedly. "Proof
that I love you?"

"Yes," she stammered. "I . . . I suppose I am."

The admission earned no sympathy or understanding. Instead, it seemed to outrage him further. "Such
boldness! When I think of the modest, innocent girl
you once were . . . By God, you're acting more like
your blasted Mathilda than yourself! I'm beginning to
suspect you succumbed to the advances of some knave
in London. What else would explain your behavior?"

Once she might have begged his forgiveness. But
now his accusations sparked her own emotions into a
white-hot explosion. "Perhaps it's just that after four
years I'm tired of loving you chastely! And if you're
wondering about my virginity, I still have it—much
good it does me!"

"You seem to be far more knowledgeable now than before you left."

"Maybe I am," she said recklessly. "Does it bother you to think that other men might want me? That I may have been kissed by someone other than you?"

"Yes, it bothers me!" Perry was so enraged that his handsome face was mottled purple and white. "It bothers me enough that I've reconsidered my proposal to you." He enunciated each word like the snap of a leather strap. Flecks of spittle fell to his chin. "I loved you the way you once were, Sara. But I don't want you as you are now. If you want to be the next Mrs. Kingswood, you'll have to find some way to change yourself back into the girl I fell in love with."

"I can't." Sara began to storm from the stable, throwing words over her shoulder. "So you may as well tell your mother that the engagement is broken! She'll be delighted, I'm certain."

"She'll feel only sorrow and pity for you."

Sara stopped abruptly and looked back at him. "Is that what you really think?" She shook her head disbelievingly. "I wonder why you thought you needed a wife at all, Perry. Why marry when you've got *her* to take care of you? If you decide to court other girls in the village, you'll soon discover how few of them are willing to abide your mother's high-handed ways. In fact, I can't think of a single one who would agree to take on the pair of you!"

As she ran out of the stable, Sara thought she heard him call her name, but her pace didn't slow. She was grateful for the flood of righteous indignation that sustained her. Making her way back home, she replayed the scene several times in her head, feeling alternately furious and ill. When she reached the cottage, she slammed the front door as hard as she could. "It's over," she told herself repeatedly, sinking down into a chair and shaking her head in disbelief. "It's over, it's over."

She wasn't aware of exactly how much time passed before her parents returned home. "How was Reverend Crawford?" she asked dully.

"Splendid," Katie replied. "Still has his chest complaint, though. His cough is no better than last week. I fear we're due for another half-heard sermon on Sunday."

Sara smiled wanly, remembering how hoarse the reverend's voice had been the previous Sunday. It had been impossible for most of the congregation to hear, especially the elderly parishoners. She began to rise from the chair, but Isaac dropped a letter into her lap. It was addressed to her. "This was delivered to the village yesterday," he said. "Fine paper, a scarlet wax seal . . . it must be from a very important person."

Slowly Sara turned the letter over in her hand, regarding the delicate handwriting and the elaborate crest stamped on the back. Conscious of her parents' interested gazes, she broke the seal and unfolded the smoothly textured parchment. Silently she read the first few lines.

My Dear Miss Fielding,

Since the delightful occasion when we met, I have remembered you often, and I must confess, with a great deal of curiosity. I would dearly love to hear your account of the assembly, and perhaps take some time to further our acquaintance during an upcoming weekend . . .

Sara read further and then looked up at her parents' quizzical faces. "It's from the countess of Raiford," she said in astonished wonder. "I had the opportunity to meet her while I was in London."

"What does the letter say?" Katie asked.

Sara looked back down at the letter. "She . . . she has invited me to stay at Raiford Park for a weekend in Hertfordshire. There will be a ball, grand dinners, fireworks . . . more than two hundred guests . . . She writes that they have need of someone 'bright and fresh' like me to liven the conversation . . ." Sara gave an incredulous laugh. "She can't really mean to invite someone like me to a gathering of the *haut ton*."

Reaching down for the letter, Katie held it at arm's length and squinted at it in an effort to read. "How extraordinary."

"I couldn't possibly accept," Sara said. "I don't have the right kind of clothes, or a private carriage, and I wouldn't know a soul—"

"And Perry would hardly approve," her father pointed out.

Only half-hearing the comment, Sara shook her head in confusion. "Why would she desire my presence at an event of this sort?" Sara caught her breath as a terrible thought occurred to her. Perhaps Lily thought that inviting a country bumpkin would serve as entertainment for her sophisticated guests. They would find no end of amusement in baiting a shy, plainly dressed novelist in their midst. The drumming of her pulse seemed to fill her ears. But as she recalled Lily's sparkling smile, she was ashamed of her own suspicions. She would regard Lily's invitation as the kind-hearted gesture that it was.

"Imagine the gentry who'll attend," Katie said, examining the letter. "I must show this to the Hodges—they'll scarcely believe their ears when I tell them my daughter has befriended a countess!"

"No difference between a countess and a milkmaid in God's eyes," Isaac pointed out, bending to stir up the coals in the grate.

"Lady Raiford is a unique woman," Sara mused. "She is lively, kind, and very generous."

"A woman of her means can afford to be generous," her father remarked, his eyes twinkling.

"I imagine there will be a colorful assortment of people at her home," Sara continued. "Perhaps even . . ." She bit her lip and tried to quiet the sudden chaos of her thoughts. It was possible Derek Craven would be there. He was a close friend of the Raifords. All the more reason not to go, she told herself . . . but her heart whispered a different message.

Hours later, when her parents were toasting their feet before the fire and reading passages from the Bible, Sara sat with a lapdesk and a leaf of her best letter paper. Carefully she clipped a pen into a tiny pot of ink and began to write. Her hand shook a little, but somehow she was able to keep the words even and neatly formed.

My Dear Lady Raiford,

It is with pleasure that I accept your gracious invitation to the forthcoming weekend at Raiford Park . . .

The astringent smell of gin permeated the air of the apartments above the gambling club. Despite the maids' best efforts to keep the place as immaculate as always, they could do little to repair the destruction

Derek had wrought over the past weeks. The thick velvet drapes and elaborate carpets were ruined by liquor stains and cigar burns. A table encrusted with semi-precious stones had been marked by boot heels resting casually on its fragile surface. Litter and discarded clothing were strewn across the floor. The windows were covered to keep out any light.

Cautiously Worthy ventured deeper into the apartment, having the vague sensation of intruding into the cave of an ill-tempered beast. He found Derek sprawled on his stomach across an unmade bed. Long legs and bare feet dangled well over the edge of the mattress. There was an empty gin bottle on the floor, drained over several hours of steady drinking.

Derek's back tensed beneath the thick ocher silk of his robe as he became aware of the visitor. "You took your bloody time," he sneered without looking up. "Bring it here."

"Bring what, sir?"

The rumpled black head lifted. Derek fastened a bleary glare on the factotum. His mouth was bracketed with deep lines. The pallid color of his skin made the scar on his face more noticeable than usual. "Don't play games with me. You know I sent for another bottle."

"Sir, won't you have a tray from the kitchen instead? You haven't eaten anything since yesterday morning . . . and you despise gin."

"It's mother's milk to me. Get me what I asked for, or you'll find your interfering arse on the streets."

Having been threatened with dismissal nearly every day for the past month, Worthy dared to ignore the remark. "Mr. Craven, I've never known you to behave this way. You haven't been yourself since—"

"Since when?" Derek prompted, suddenly looking like a panther tensed to strike. The effect was spoiled by an inebriated burp, and he lowered his head to the wrinkled counterpane once more.

"It's clear to everyone that something is wrong," Worthy persisted. "My regard for you prompts me to speak frankly, even if it means losing my position at Craven's."

Derek's voice was muffled in the covers. "I'm not listening."

"You are a better man than you know, sir. I will never forget that you saved my life. Oh, I know you forbade me ever to mention it, but it is true, nonetheless. I was a stranger to you, and yet you took it upon yourself to spare me from the hangman's noose."

Years ago Worthy had been the under-butler of an aristocratic household in London. He had been in love with one of the parlormaids, who had stolen a pearl and ruby necklace from the mistress of the house. Rather than allow his love to be arrested and hanged for the theft, Worthy had claimed responsibility. He had been held at Newgate for execution. Hearing the story of Worthy's plight through one of the servants at the club, Derek had approached a local magistrate as well as a prison official, using equal parts of bribery and coercion to free the under-butler. It was said in London that Craven could talk the hind leg off a horse. Only he could have plucked a hapless convict right from the bowels of Newgate.

The first time Worthy had ever seen Derek Craven was at the door of his prison cell, wearing an expression of sardonic amusement. "So you're the fool what's going to 'ang for some light-fingered bitch?"

"Y-yes, sir," Worthy stuttered, watching as Derek handed a wad of money to the prison guard.

"More loyalty than wits," Derek had observed with a grin. "Just as I 'oped. Well, little gallows-bird, I could use you as a factotum for my club. Unless you'd rather let the 'angman string you up tomorrow?"

Worthy had done everything short of kissing his feet in gratitude, and had served him faithfully ever since. Now, as he saw the state to which his strong-willed, prosperous employer had fallen, he was at a loss to know how to help him. "Mr. Craven," he said tentatively, "I understand why you're doing this to yourself." A spasm of pain crossed his face. "I was in love once."

"I remember. Your noble affair with the light-handed parlormaid."

Worthy ignored the gibe and continued in a quiet, earnest tone. "For ten years not a day has gone by that I haven't thought of her. I can still see her face before me, as clear and bright as nothing else in my memory."

"Bloody fool."

"Yes, sir. There is no logic to it. No one can explain why one woman can tear a man's very heart from his chest, and never let go. For you that woman is Miss Fielding, isn't it?"

"Get out," Derek said harshly, his fingers digging into the mass of crumpled bedclothes.

"Sir, even if you have lost her, you must conduct your life in a manner that will honor your feelings for her. It would sadden her to see you like this."

"*Out!*"

"Very well, sir."

"And send up another bottle of gin."

Murmuring his acquiescence, the factotum left the room.

Perhaps later Derek would notice that the gin was never delivered, but for now he fell into a drunken oblivion. Senseless dreams floated through his head while he twitched and muttered incoherently.

In the middle of the seething shadows, he became aware of a woman's body pressed against his. Small hands slipped inside his robe and eased the fabric apart. His body stiffened in arousal. Hungrily he pressed himself against her, seeking the exquisite friction of her palms clasped around him. Gathering her close, he cupped the silken weight of her breasts in his hands.

Burning with the need to thrust inside her, he rolled on top of her and pushed her knees wide to position her for his entry. He dragged his mouth over her throat and breathed hotly against the moist trail he had left behind. Moaning passionately, she arched against him and wrapped her arms around his shoulders. "Sara," he groaned against her ear as he began to push inside her. "Oh, Sara—"

All at once knifelike talons raked over his back, digging vengefully deep. Derek gasped in painful surprise. Rearing back to escape the stinging scratches, he caught the woman's slim wrists and pinned them on either side of her head. Lady Ashby lay beneath him, glaring up at him. Her fingers were curled into claws, the tips wet with his blood. "You rutting bastard," she spat. "Don't *ever* call me by another woman's name!"

Derek heard a dull roar that he didn't recognize as his own. His hands fastened around her neck. A thick red haze surrounded him. His fingers dug into her throat, choking off the pathways of blood and air until her face turned purple. She stared at him with a twisted grimace of triumph, as if she welcomed his murderous grip on her throat. Just as her eyes began to roll back in her head, he released her with a feral snarl and leapt off the bed.

Joyce curled in a heap amid the tangled covers. The room was filled with the sound of her violent choking.

Clenching a shaking hand around the tasseled bellpull, Derek rang for Worthy. Dazedly he walked to the window and gathered the open robe around himself. He rubbed his unshaven jaw, the bristles as rough as wire. "Mad as a weaver," he muttered. It wasn't clear if he was referring to Joyce or himself.

She finally regained enough breath to speak. "What st-stopped you from killing me?"

He didn't look at her. "I won't hang for your murder."

"I'd like to die," she wheezed sickly, "and take you with me."

The scene disgusted Derek, nauseated him. It was an echo of his past, a reminder that the years of depravity would always haunt him, making any sort of normal life impossible. The sour taste of defeat filled his mouth.

Worthy appeared, wearing an expression of blank surprise as he saw the naked blond woman on Derek's bed and her discarded gown on the floor.

"It's Lady Ashby," Derek said curtly, walking to the door. Blood from the nail marks on his back soaked through his robe. "Find out how she got in here. Get rid of whoever's responsible for letting her inside." His narrowed eyes swerved from the woman on the bed to the factotum. "If she ever sets foot in Craven's again,

I'll kill her—right after I clean and bone you like a mackerel."

Joyce raised herself on her hands and knees like a golden cat. Strands of her hair fell over her face, and she watched Derek intently through the gleaming wisps. "I love you," she mewled.

Something about her tone sent a chill down Derek's spine . . . some insistent, wild note that warned she would never admit defeat. "Go to hell," he said as he left the room.

The hired carriage traveled along the mile-long drive that led from the fifteenth-century gatehouse, through a lush, landscaped park. Eventually the vehicle reached the splendid Raiford mansion. Sara's knees turned weak as she stared through a corner of the carriage window. "Oh, my," she breathed. A nerveless shiver went from her head to her toes. She most definitely did not belong here.

The glistening white mansion was fronted with ten towering columns and twenty pairs of Palladian windows, and ornamental carved stone balustrades that ran the entire width of the building. A regal procession of chimney stacks and towering domed projections on the roof gave the mansion the appearance of reaching for the sky. Before Sara had the presence of mind to direct the driver to return to Greenwood Corners, the carriage stopped. Two gigantic footmen with carefully blank expressions helped her alight from the vehicle. Sara was ushered to the row of circular steps leading to the front portico. A tall, gray-bearded butler appeared at the door, accompanied by the groom of the chambers.

The butler had a stern face that might have been

carved from granite. She smiled at him and began to fumble in her reticule for the letter from Lily. "Sir, I have an invitation from Lady Raiford—"

He seemed to recognize her, perhaps from Lily's description. "Of course, Miss Fielding." He glanced over her plain gray gown and traveling bonnet, and the brightly embroidered shawl that one of the village women had loaned to her. Some of his haughtiness seemed to melt away. "We are honored by your presence."

Before she could thank him for the sentiment, she was interrupted by Lily Raiford's exuberant voice. "You're here at last! Burton, we must go to special lengths to make Miss Fielding feel at home." Dressed in a lemon-colored gown made of cashmere, with sleeves of a silk so thin it was referred to by dressmakers as *peau de papillon*, or "butterfly skin," Lily was breathtakingly beautiful.

"Oh, please don't go to any trouble—" Sara protested, but the words were lost in the flood of Lily's busy chatter.

"You haven't arrived a moment too soon, my dear." Lily kissed her on both cheeks in the continental fashion. "Everyone is lounging inside making cynical observations and thinking themselves quite witty. You'll be a breath of fresh air. Burton, see that Miss Fielding's bags are brought to her room while I take her around."

"I should put myself to rights," Sara said, knowing her clothes were travel-rumpled and her hair disheveled, but Lily was already dragging her into the entrance hall. Burton gave Sara a surreptitious wink and turned to welcome another arriving carriage.

"We're all quite informal today," Lily said. "New guests will appear every hour. There are no activities planned until the dance tonight. Entertain yourself in any manner you choose. The horses and carriages, the books in the library, the music room, and anything else you fancy are all at your disposal. Ring for whatever you want."

"Thank you." Sara gazed in admiration at the domed white marble entrance hall. A grand staircase with the most elaborate gilded balustrade she had ever seen split into two majestic curving arches that led to the mansion's upper floors.

Lily whisked her through the great hall, a cavernous room with a barrel-vaulted ceiling, ornate plaster-work, and the solemn atmosphere of a cathedral. "The men will go on a shooting excursion in the morning and play billiards in the afternoon. The women sip tea, gossip, and nap. We all gather to play charades and cards every evening. It's positively stultifying. You'll be bored to tears, I assure you."

"No, not at all." Sara strove to match Lily's brisk pace as they progressed through a long gallery in the back of the mansion, lined with mirrors and paintings on one side and French doors on the other. Through the glass-paned doors she could see the borders of a large formal garden.

As Lily led Sara past rooms designed for small gatherings, groups of men and women glanced at them curiously. The music room was filled with a duster of giggling, chattering girls. Lily waved to them cheerfully without breaking pace. "Some of the county families will be presenting their daughters at the ball for their first Season," she told Sara. "It will be less of a trial for them here than in some stuffy London drawing room. I'll show you the ballroom presently, but first . . ."

They paused at the doorway of the billiards room, an exclusively masculine alcove adorned with burgundy damask, leather, and dark wood panelling. Gentlemen of assorted ages lounged around the carved mahogany billiards table. Smoke from their cigars circled the shaded lamps overhead.

"Gentlemen," Lily informed the room at large, "I came to tell you I must abandon the game to show my new guest 'round the house. Lansdale, perhaps you would take my place at the table?"

"He will, but not half so attractively," someone remarked. There were assorted chuckles around the room.

Lansdale, a middle-aged man of unusually short stature but possessing a handsome aquiline face, regarded Sara with bold interest. "Perhaps, Lady Raiford, you would keep to the billiards game and allow *me* to show your guest around."

Sara blushed at the suggestion, while several of the men laughed.

Rolling her eyes, Lily addressed a remark to Sara. "Watch out for that one, my lamb. In fact, don't trust a single one of these men. I know them all, and I can vouch for the fact that underneath those attractive exteriors is a pack of wolves."

Sara could see how Lily's remark pleased the men, who clearly liked to think of themselves as predators, paunches and receding hairlines notwithstanding. "At least allow us a brief introduction," Lansdale suggested, coming forward. "Your Miss Fielding is quite the loveliest creature I've seen all day." Taking Sara's hand, he bowed and imprinted a deferential kiss on the back.

Lily obliged readily. "My lords Lansdale, Over-

stone, Aveland, Stokehurst, Bolton, and Ancaster, I
should like to present Miss Sara Fielding—a talented
author and a charming new acquaintance of mine."

Sara mustered a shy smile and a curtsey as they
bowed to her individually. She remembered having secretly observed some of them at the gambling club.
And if she wasn't mistaken, she had met the duke of
Ancaster during her masquerade as Mathilda. In spite
of his noble heritage and dignified bearing, he had behaved quite badly at the assembly, fawning drunkenly
over her and then chasing after one of the house
wenches. Her lips twitched at the corners, but her
amusement was wiped away by Lily's next casual
words. "Oh, and that surly-looking one pouring a
brandy is my beloved husband, Lord Raiford. Next to
him is Mr. Craven, who as you can see has a fondness
for lurking in dark corners."

Sara barely noticed Lily's large blond spouse. Her
round blue eyes flew to the lean, sinister form that de-
tached from the shadows. He bowed as the others had,
the movement impeccably graceful for such a large
man. There was no sign of recognition on his face.

The air of toughness and vital masculinity was the
same as she remembered. His skin looked as swarthy
as a pirate's against the snowy linen of his cravat. The
scar on his face had faded, so that his intense green
eyes dominated every other feature. Closed in a small
room with these gently-born men, he seemed like a
panther keeping company with house cats. Sara
couldn't have said a word to save her life. Her mouth
felt as if it were filled with dust.

The other occupants of the room couldn't help but
notice the sudden electric silence. A few glances were
exchanged, and brows were raised an expressive

quarter-inch or so. Sara's raw nerves jangled in warning as Lord Raiford approached her. Slowly she raised her eyes to stare at Lily's imposing husband, whose broad shoulders blocked them from the gentlemen's view.

Lord Raiford's hawklike features were softened by a pair of warm gray eyes and a crop of golden hair the color of ripe wheat. He smiled and took her hand, pressing it between his huge palms in an unexpected breech of formality. "We're fortunate to have our home graced by your gentle presence, Miss Fielding." He slanted an ironic glance at Lily. "I suspect my wife hasn't yet allowed you a few minutes to restore yourself after your journey."

"I was just showing Sara to her room," Lily protested, lowering her voice as the men returned to their game. "But I had to stop here first. I couldn't abandon the lot of you without a word, could I?"

Letting go of Sara, Alex gathered his petite wife close and ducked her underneath the chin. "I know exactly what you're up to," he warned softly, in a tone the others couldn't hear. "My beautiful, meddlesome little bully—for once couldn't you allow others to manage their own affairs?"

Lily grinned at him cheekily. "Not when I can manage them so much better."

Alex traced his thumb lightly over Lily's jaw. "An opinion Craven doesn't share, my sweet."

Lily leaned closer to him and replied in a barely audible murmur. Sara averted her gaze as the two drew aside and engaged in a whispered exchange. She didn't want to eavesdrop on a private conversation. Nevertheless, she caught a few revealing snatches as they talked at the same time.

"—Derek doesn't know what's good for him," Lily was saying.

"—concern should be what's good for Miss Fielding—"

"But you don't understand how—"

"—understand all too well," Alex finished, and they stared into each other's eyes challengingly.

Sara felt her color rising. There was a palpable attraction between the two that made her feel like an intruder on an intimate scene.

It was clear that Lord Raiford would have liked to say more to Lily, but he let go of her reluctantly and gave her an admonishing glance. *"Behave yourself"* was the silent but unmistakable message. Lily made a face and looked around him to wave at Lansdale and Aveland. "Enjoy the game, gentlemen," she called. They responded with agreeable murmurs. Derek Craven was silent, coldly ignoring the womens' departure.

Dejectedly Sara followed Lily through the carpeted hallway. Craven's icy manner had been a rude surprise. She scolded herself silently for thinking that he might actually be glad to see her. Instead it seemed likely that he would ignore her for the entire weekend.

They approached a row of guest suites in the west wing, each with its own dressing and sitting room. Sara's room was decorated in pastel shades of lavender and yellow. The elaborate garden below was visible from a pair of windows hung with divided curtains. Wandering to the tent bed with fluted columns, Sara touched a fold of the bedhangings. They were embroidered to match the delicate floral pattern of the wallpaper.

Lily opened an armoire to reveal Sara's clothes. In a

remarkably short time, the housemaids had unpacked her meager belongings with faultless efficiency. "I hope this room pleases you," she said, frowning slightly as she saw Sara's expression. "If you'd prefer another—"

"It's lovely," Sara assured her, and made a wry face. "It's just that . . . perhaps I should leave. I don't wish to cause trouble. Mr. Craven is annoyed by my presence here. And he is angry with you for inviting me. The way he looked at you . . ."

"He'd like to strangle me," Lily admitted cheerfully. "Slowly. But the way he looked at *you* . . . Good God, it was priceless!" She gave a peal of laughter. "How does it feel to have the most unattainable man in England at your feet?"

Sara's eyes widened. "Oh, he's not—"

"At your feet," Lily repeated. "Believe me, Derek has had this coming for years! When I think of all the times he's infuriated me by acting superior and cold-hearted, so utterly in control of himself and everything around him . . ." She shook her head, chuckling. "Don't misunderstand me. I adore the big, hardheaded cockney. But it will be the best thing in the world for him if he's taken down a peg."

"If anyone's going to be taken down a peg, it's *I*," Sara said under her breath. Lily didn't appear to have heard.

After Lily left to attend to her guests, Sara rang for a maid to help with her toilette. A French maid a few years older than herself appeared. The woman was blond and small, with round pink cheeks and a droll smile. "*Je m'appelle Françoise,*" the maid informed her, setting a pair of curling tongs near the coals beyond the fireplace grate. Busily Françoise bustled about the room, selecting a fresh gown from the armoire and holding it up for Sara's approval.

"Yes, that one will be fine," Sara said, removing her jacket and bonnet and unbuttoning the front of her wrinkled traveling gown. She sat at the small satinwood dressing table and pulled the pins from her disheveled hair.

The russet and golden-brown locks fell down her back. There was a pleased exclamation behind her. *"Comme vos cheveux sont beaux, mademoiselle!"* Reverently Françoise brushed out the heavy length of hair until it was a smooth, shining curtain.

"Do you speak any English, Françoise?" Sara asked the maid doubtfully. Françoise met her eyes in the mirror and shook her head with a smile. "I wish you did. Frenchwomen are supposed to know all about matters of the heart. I need some advice."

Hearing the disconsolate note in her voice, Françoise said something that sounded sympathetic and encouraging.

"I shouldn't have come here," Sara continued. "By leaving Perry I've thrown away what I thought I always wanted. I hardly recognize myself, Françoise! The feelings I have for another man are so compelling . . . I'm afraid that I might take whatever I can have of him, no matter how fleeting the moment is. If I heard some other woman confessing to such thoughts, I would condemn her as a fool and worse. I've always considered myself a sensible person, guided more by reason than by passion. I can't explain what's come over me. All I know is that from the moment I met him—" She broke off, unable to finish the sentence. Sighing, she rubbed her aching forehead. "I don't think time will help. It hasn't so far."

There was a long silence as the maid brushed her hair in soothing strokes. Françoise wore a thoughtful expression, as if she were contemplating the situation. It didn't matter that they spoke different languages— any woman who had ever suffered heartbreak could recognize it easily. Finally the maid paused in her brushing and gestured toward Sara's heart. *"Faire ce que le coeur vous dit, mademoiselle."*

"Follow my heart?" Sara asked in bewilderment. "Is that what you're saying?"

"Oui, mademoiselle." Placidly the girl reached for a narrow blue silk ribbon and began to weave it through the loose locks of hair.

"That could be very dangerous," Sara whispered.

Several minutes later Sara finished buttoning the high collar of her gray gown and checked her appearance in the mirror. She was pleased by the results of the maid's efforts. Her hair had been neatly confined on top of her head in a heavy plait, while a few wisps at her temples had been curled into ringlets. Thanking Françoise, Sara left the room and wandered toward the grand staircase. Nervously she considered joining one of the ladies' gatherings downstairs for some tea and conversation. She hoped the women would be friendly, or at least tolerant of her presence.

Pausing in the hallway to stare at a marble sculpture poised in a semi-circular niche, Sara tried to bolster her courage. She was in awe of the guests downstairs, and half-afraid of them. Lily had said the gathering included ambassadors, politicians, artists, and even a visiting colonial governor and his family. Sara was well-aware that she had nothing in common with them. No doubt they would consider her gauche and unsophisticated. Perhaps this was how Derek Craven felt, hobnobbing with aristocrats who were disdainfully aware of his origins. Poor Mr. Craven, she thought sympathetically. Suddenly she was aware of an icy tingling on her neck, and every hair on her body stood erect. She turned around slowly.

Derek was standing behind her, looking far from deserving of anyone's sympathy. He stared at her like a jaded sultan surveying his latest female acquisition. His dark handsomeness was matched only by his extraordinary self-possession. "Where is your fiancé?" he asked in a distinctly unfriendly tone.

Sara was unnerved by his threatening stillness. "I don't have a . . . That is, h-he . . . We're not going to marry."

"He didn't propose?"

"No . . . well, yes, but . . ." Sara stepped back instinctively. Derek moved to close the distance between them. As they talked, she continued to edge away, and he followed like a stalking cat. "Mr. Kingswood proposed a few nights after my return," Sara said breathlessly. "I accepted. I was very happy at first . . . well, not precisely *happy*, but—"

"What happened?"

"There were problems. He said I had changed. I suppose he was right, although—"

"He broke the engagement?"

"I . . . I think a case could be made that we broke it together . . ." As he advanced on her, she found herself backing into a nearby room, almost stumbling over a delicate gilded chair. "Mr. Craven, I wish you would stop prowling after me this way!"

His hard stare was relentless. "You knew I would be here this weekend."

"I didn't!"

"You planned this with Lily."

"I most certainly did *not*—" She broke off with a startled squeak as he reached her and clamped his hands on her shoulders.

"I can't decide whose neck to wring first—yours or hers."

"You're offended that I'm here," Sara said in a small voice.

"I'd rather stand in a bucket of coals than spend one night under the same roof with you!"

"You dislike me that much?"

Derek's lungs began to work hard as he stared into her small, lovely face. The violent joy of being near her caused his blood to sizzle. His fingers flexed repeatedly into the softness of her shoulders, as if relishing the texture of her flesh. "No, I don't dislike you," he said, nearly inaudible.

"Mr. Craven, you're hurting me."

His grip didn't loosen. "That night after the assembly . . . you didn't understand a bloody thing I told you, did you?"

"I understood."

"And still you came here."

Sara stood her ground, although it took all her strength not to wilt beneath his scorching glare. "I had every right to accept Lady Raiford's invitation," she said stubbornly. "A-and I won't leave, no matter what you say to me!"

"Then I will."

"All right!" To her amazement, an urge to taunt him overcame her, and she added, "If you have so little control over yourself that you find it necessary to run away from me."

His face was wiped clean of all expression, but she

could sense the fury that blazed within him. "They say God protects fools and children—for your sake I hope it's true."

"Mr. Craven, I thought you and I could at least manage to be civil to each other for one weekend—"

"Why the hell would you think that?"

"Because we managed it quite well before the assembly, and . . ." Sara sputtered into silence as she realized how tightly he was holding her. The tips of her breasts grazed his chest. Her skirts flowed gently around his legs.

"I can't manage it now." He gripped her inflexibly, until she felt the hot, leaping pressure of his arousal against her stomach. His eyes blazed like emeralds in his austere face. "I can protect you against everything except myself."

She knew that his grasp was deliberately painful. But instead of resisting, she relaxed against his hard body. More than anything she wanted to twine herself around him and crush her mouth against the place where the white linen of his cravat met smooth brown skin. Her hands crept up his broad shoulders, and she stared at him wordlessly.

Derek feared he was a hairsbreadth away from attacking her. "Why didn't you marry him?" he asked hoarsely.

"I don't love him."

He shook his head in baffled anger, and opened his mouth to deliver a scathing reply. Apparently thinking better of it, he closed his mouth abruptly, only to open it again. Were the moment not so tense, Sara would have laughed. Instead she stared up at him helplessly. "How could I have gone through with it when I don't love him?"

"You little fool. Isn't it enough that you'd be safe with him?"

"No. I want more than that. Or nothing at all."

His dark head bent lower over hers. One of his hands released her shoulder, and his fingertips grazed the delicate curls at her temple. He was tight-lipped, as if enduring an exquisitely painful torture. Sara made an inarticulate sound as she felt his knuckles brush the highest edge of her cheek. The brightness of his gaze was like harsh sunlight. She felt as if she were drowning in the depths of burning green. His large hand cradled her cheek and jaw, his thumb testing the downy surface. "I'd forgotten how soft your skin was," he murmured.

She stood there trembling against him, beyond all sense of pride and propriety. Impulsive words hovered on her lips. Suddenly she was distracted by the feel of a strange object underneath her palm, pressed flat against his chest. There was a hard lump in the inside pocket of his coat. She frowned curiously. Before Derek realized what she was doing, she reached inside the garment to investigate.

"No," he said swiftly, his large hand gripping her wrist to stop her.

But it was too late; her fingers had already encountered the object and identified it. With a disbelieving look on her face, Sara pulled out the tiny pair of spectacles she thought she had lost at the club. "Why?" she whispered, amazed that he was carrying them in his breast pocket.

He met her gaze defiantly, his jaw set. A small muscle twitched in his cheek.

Then she understood. "Are you having problems with your sight, Mr. Craven?" she asked softly. "Or is it your heart?"

Just then they both heard the sound of distant voices down the hall. "Someone's coming," he muttered, and released her.

. "Wait—"

He was gone in an instant, as if the hounds of hell were nipping at his heels. Still clutching the spectacles, Sara bit her lip. In her wild mixture of emotions—relief that he still wanted her, fear that he would leave—nothing was as strong as the desire to comfort him. She wished she had the power to reassure him that his love wouldn't hurt her . . . that she would never ask for more than he could give.

Harrassed by a flood of minor difficulties, Lily searched for her husband and found him alone in the hunting room. He was seated at a desk with an empty cigar box in his hand. Alex smiled at the sight of her, but his expression changed to a questioning frown. "What is it, sweetheart?"

Lily talked even more quickly than usual, a sure sign of her frustration. "To begin with, Mrs. Bartlett is demanding that she have her room changed, claiming the view doesn't suit her, when it's perfectly obvious that what she *really* wants is to be located next to Lord Overstone, with whom she's carrying on a flaming affair—"

"So let her have the room."

"It's already occupied by Stokehurst!"

Alex considered the dilemma with apparent seriousness. "I don't think Stokehurst would like to find Overstone in his bed," he mused, and snickered at the image of the two lecherous old rakes sneaking through the mansion at night to find the delectable Mrs. Bartlett.

"Oh, go on and laugh, but I have even worse problems to tell you about. The cook's been taken ill. Nothing serious, thank God, but she's gone to bed and the rest of the kitchen staff is trying to organize themselves, and I can't guarantee that supper will be edible tonight."

Alex made a dismissive gesture, as if that were the least of their worries. He held up the empty box. "My stock of cigars is out. Did you remember to order more?"

"I forgot," she admitted with a rueful sigh.

"Hell." He frowned. "What are the men and I supposed to smoke while we're having our after-dinner port?"

"You wouldn't like my suggestion," Lily replied pertly. "Oh, the children have lost the puppy again—its somewhere in the house, Nicole says."

In spite of his annoyance over the cigars, Alex laughed. "If that blasted animal ruins any more family heirlooms—"

"It was only one chair," Lily protested.

They were interrupted by Derek Craven's explosive entrance. The edge of the door careened into the wall as he came into the room and fixed Lily with a violent glare. "I'm going to stuff you down the nearest well."

Driven by a strong instinct for self-preservation, Lily skittered hastily to Alex and settled herself on his lap. "I can invite whomever I want to my weekend parties," she defended herself, watching Derek from within the protective circle of her husband's arms.

Derek's eyes blazed green fire. "I told you never to interfere in my life the way you do others—"

"Easy, Craven," Alex said calmly, squeezing Lily tightly to keep her silent. "I agree that Lily occasionally goes a step too far with her meddling. But it's always with the best of intentions . . . and in this case I don't see why the presence of one small, shy woman should affect you so greatly." He arched a tawny brow in the mocking tradition of his aristocratic ancestors. "With all your experience, surely you don't perceive Miss Fielding as a threat?"

Both the Raifords were amazed to see a dark flush cover Derek's face. "You have no idea in hell about the trouble she can cause."

That remark earned a skeptical look from Alex. "She won't cause any trouble this weekend," he replied evenly. "We're all here to socialize, enjoy the scenery, and take the fresh air."

Glaring at them both, Derek hesitated as if yearning to say something else. Instead he left with a muffled curse, raking his hands through his hair.

There was silence as the Raifords looked at each other. Alex let out a long breath of amazement. "Christ. I've never seen him behave this way."

"*Now* do you believe what I've been telling you?" Lily demanded in satisfaction. "He adores her. He's gone mad over her."

Alex didn't argue, only shrugged. "He'll deny it to his last breath."

Lily snuggled against him. "Thank you for defending me. I actually thought he might try to box my ears!"

Alex grinned and fondled her slim body. "You know I'll never let anyone raise a hand to you. I reserve that privilege for myself."

"I'd like to see you try," she warned, and smiled as he kissed the soft, perfumed space behind her earlobe.

"Lily," he murmured, "for my sake as well as yours, leave the two of them alone. They'll resolve the matter on their own—without any help from you."

"Is that a request or a command?"

"Don't test me, my sweet." Although his tone was gentle, there was no mistaking the note of warning in it.

Knowing better than to cross her husband when he was in this mood, Lily toyed flirtatiously with the crisp points of his shirt collar. "I've always suspected I would have been better off married to a milksop," she grumbled.

Alex laughed. "I'm exactly the husband you deserve."

"I'm afraid you're right," she replied, and kissed him lovingly.

Suddenly he interrupted the kiss and drew his head back. "Lily . . . have you mentioned to Derek yet that the Ashbys are attending?"

She grimaced and shook her head. "I couldn't summon the nerve to tell him. He'll never believe that I agreed to invite them with the greatest reluctance."

"My father and Lord Ashby were close friends. And Lord Ashby has been a powerful ally of mine in Parliament. I couldn't offend the old man by withholding an invitation—even if his wife is a poisonous bitch."

"Why don't *you* explain it to Derek? Good God, with him and Joyce under the same roof, I'm expecting bloodshed at any moment!"

For the better part of the afternoon Sara was cloistered with a group of young matrons whose eager gossip reminded her of the quote, "Love and scandal are the best sweeteners of tea." Quickly she discovered that her fears of being snubbed were groundless. The women were pleasant and friendly, and far more outspoken than Sara's village friends. Among them were Mrs. Adele Bartlett, a wealthy widow with an opulent figure and brilliant red hair, and Lady Mountbain, a mellow-voiced brunette with an earthy sense of humor. Two lively young women were seated next to Lily Raiford; Lady Elizabeth Burghley and Lady Stamford, Lily's own sister. The group talked with shocking frankness about their husbands and lovers, exchanging *bon mots* and giggling quietly. It was not lost on Sara that the conversations of these aristocratic ladies bore a strong resemblance to those of the house wenches at Craven's.

Although Lily seemed to enjoy the gathering, her gaze often strayed to the window. Sara guessed that she would have preferred walking outside or riding, rather than being confined indoors. Noticing Lily's lack of participation in the discussion, one of the women addressed her nonchalantly. "Lily, darling, why don't you tell us about *your* husband? After all these years of domesticity, how often does Lord Raiford demand his conjugal rights?"

Lily surprised them all by blushing. "Often enough," she said with a private smile, refusing to say any more. They teased and laughed, and regarded her with envy, for Lily wore the look of a happily married woman—a rarity among the *ton*.

Lady Mountbain curled in a corner of a cushioned settee. Her wide, scarlet-hued mouth stretched into a speculative smile. "Enough talk about husbands," she declared in her silky-rough voice. "I much prefer the subject of *un*married men—their activities are so much more interesting. Derek Craven, for example. There is something positively *animal* about him. Whenever he's near, I can't take my eyes from the man. Perhaps it's that black hair . . . or the scar . . ."

"Yes, the scar," Adele Bartlett added dreamily. "It makes him look even more of a brute."

"Wickedly unprincipled," someone else added in a tone of relish.

Adele nodded emphatically. "I'm so pleased you invited him to the weekend, Lily. It's so exciting, having a dangerous man nearby. It makes one feel anything could happen."

"Nonsense," Lily said in reply to the comments. "Derek is no more dangerous than . . . than that cat near the hearth!"

A few gazes settled doubtfully on the sleeping animal, a fat and lazy tom who had far more interest in chasing after supper than after other felines. Reading their disbelief, Lily changed the subject adroitly. "No more talk about men—they're bothersome creatures, and that is that. We have more important things to discuss!"

"Such as?" Adele was clearly wondering what could be more important than men.

"Did I happen to mention that we have an author in our midst?" Lily asked brightly. "You must talk to Sara—you loved the novel *Mathilda*, didn't you?"

In order to keep from drawing attention to herself, Sara had taken an inconspicuous place in a chair near the corner. Suddenly she found herself the focus of every pair of eyes. A flood of excited questions erupted all at once.

"You wrote *Mathilda?*"

"My dear, you must tell us all about her! How did you meet?"

"How is she these days?"

Sara smiled and made a valiant attempt to reply, but she soon found that it didn't matter what she said, for they all answered their own questions and went right on talking. Ruefully Sara glanced at Lily, who grinned and shrugged helplessly to show that the group was incorrigible.

Two hours before the appointed suppertime, the women began to disperse in order to change their gowns and ready themselves for a long evening. As she gazed around the room, Sara became aware of a new arrival, a blond woman to whom she hadn't yet been introduced. Although the others gave the newcomer lackluster greetings, no one seemed inclined to claim her as a friend. Sara turned in her chair to glance at her.

The woman was slender and very striking. Her face was sharply sculpted, the nose aristocratically thin with a delicate point. Changeable eyes that held tones of blue, gray, and green were set deep below her plucked brows. A wealth of rich golden hair was cut with a fringe across her forehead and drawn on top of her head in a profusion of careless curls. Were there any warmth in her expression, she would have been stunningly beautiful. But the woman's eyes were strangely flat and hard, like chips of stone. Her unswerving stare made Sara uneasy.

"And who are you?" she asked in a silky voice.

"Miss Sara Fielding, ma'am."

"Sara," the woman repeated, looking at her speculatively. "Sara."

Uncomfortably Sara set her cup of tea down and

began to brush invisible crumbs from her skirts. Noticing the others leaving the room, she wondered how she could follow suit without seeming rude.

"Where are you from?" the woman continued softly.

"Greenwood Corners, ma'am. It's a small village not far from here."

"But how sweet you are. Greenwood Corners. Of course. With a complexion as pure as a milkmaid's, you would have to be from the country. And that delightful air of innocence . . . You make me feel quite protective. You're not married, I see. Tell me, Sara, has any man yet claimed your affections?"

Sara kept silent, not knowing what to make of the woman's interest.

"Oh, you'll capture a score of hearts," Lady Ashby said. "Even the most hardened ones. No one could resist a pretty innocent like you. I believe you could make an old man believe he's young again. Why, you could probably make a scoundrel renounce the devil—"

"Joyce," came Lily's calm voice. They both glanced at Lily, who wore an unusual look of hauteur. Sara stood up from the chair, silently grateful for the rescue. "I'm certain my friend appreciates all these flattering observations," Lily continued coolly, "but she's rather shy. I wouldn't like you to make any of my guests uncomfortable."

"What an accomplished hostess you've become, Lily," Joyce purred, staring at Lily with active dislike. "One would never suspect you've led such a colorful life. You hide it so well. But you can't conceal the fruits of your past entirely, can you?"

"What do you mean by that?" Lily asked, her eyes narrowed.

"I mean that your adorable daughter Nicole is a constant reminder of your liaison with Derek Craven." Joyce turned to Sara and added smoothly, "Why, you look surprised, darling. I thought everyone knew that Nicole is Derek Craven's bastard child."

Chapter 9

Sara sensed Lily's inner struggle to keep her temper in check. For a moment it seemed she would lose the battle. Sara touched her arm in a silent gesture of support, while Lady Ashby noted the gesture with a mocking gaze. Mastering herself, Lily compressed her lips until they were white. She glanced at Sara. "Shall we go upstairs?" she asked in a voice that shook slightly.

Hastily Sara nodded, and they left Lady Ashby, who wore a calculating smile.

They reached the second landing of the grand staircase before Lily was able to speak. "Nicole is a bastard child, but Derek isn't the father."

Sara made a small, consoling sound in her throat. "Lily, there's no need to tell me—"

"I-I made a mistake, several years ago, before I was married. Alex couldn't love my daughter any more if she were his own. I don't care what anyone may say about me, but Nicole is a precious, innocent child. I can't bear to think of her being punished for my sins. Thank God there are few people who would dare to cast stones. Lady Mountbain has so many children by different fathers that her brood is called the Mountbain Miscellany. And Lady Ashby has enough ex-lovers to form a complete regiment. Damn that woman! I hadn't intended to tell you, but Joyce is the one who arranged to have Derek attacked in the rookery."

Sara caught her breath in a mixture of surprise and anger, not only at Joyce but at Derek. How *could* he have carried on an affair with a woman like that? Well, he and Lady Ashby were two of a kind! This is what it would be like, her mind slyly whispered . . . always being confronted with evidence of his sins . . . always having to make excuses for him. Not for the first time Sara wondered what she was doing here. Unhappily she considered telling Lily that she wanted to leave Raiford Park.

". . . stay away from Lady Ashby," Lily was saying. "If she suspects that Derek has feelings for you, she'll make things very unpleasant." Mumbling something under her breath, Lily stomped up the stairs at an aggressive pace that Sara labored to follow. "Come with me—I want to show you something."

They went to the third floor, approaching a set of bright, thickly carpeted rooms that Lily explained were the schoolroom, the nursery, and the bedchambers for the nurse and the two nursery maids. The sound of childish babble and laughter drifted from the nursery. Standing in the doorway, Sara saw two beautiful black-haired children, a girl of eight or nine, and a boy who appeared to be about three. They were sitting on the carpet, surrounded by towers of blocks, games, and books.

"These are my two darlings," Lily said proudly.

At the sound of her voice, both of them looked up and rushed forward eagerly. "Mama!"

Lily embraced her children and turned them to face Sara. "Nicole, Jamie, this is Miss Fielding. She's a very nice friend who writes stories."

Nicole curtseyed neatly and regarded her with interest. "I like to read stories."

"Me too!" Jamie chimed in, hovering behind his sister's skirts.

"Jamie can't read yet," Nicole said with dignity.

"Yes, I can!" Jamie said, his temper sparking. "I'll show you!"

"Children," Lily interceded, forestalling her son's efforts to fetch a book, "it's a grand day outside. Come have a romp in the snow with me."

The nurse wore a disapproving frown. "M'lady, they'll catch their deaths of cold."

"Oh, I won't keep them out long," Lily said cheerfully.

"You won't have time to ready yourself for the ball—"

"It never takes me long to change." Lily grinned at her children. "And besides, playing outside is *much* more fun than going to a boring old ball."

Sniffing haughtily, the nurse went to fetch her charges' coats.

"May I take one of my dolls, Mama?" Nicole asked.

"Certainly, darling."

Sara had to smile at Nicole's quaint charm as the girl opened a painted toy cupboard and rummaged through a row of dolls. The child was an excessively ladylike little creature. Lily leaned toward Sara confidentially. "I encourage her to be as wild as she pleases, but she'll have none of it. A little angel, she is. Completely unlike me." She laughed quietly. "Wait until you have children, Sara—they'll probably be perfect hellions!"

"I can't imagine it," Sara said, trying to picture herself as a mother. A wistful smile crossed her lips. "I don't know if I will. Some women aren't meant to have children."

"*You're* meant to," Lily replied firmly.

"How do you know?"

"With your patience and kindness, and all the love you have to give . . . Why, you'll be the best mother in the world!"

Sara laughed wryly. "Well, now that's been established, all I need is someone to father them."

"The ball tonight will be swarming with eligible bachelors. For supper I've seated you between two of the most promising ones. Have you brought the blue gown? Good. I expect you'll have your pick of any man you desire."

"I haven't come for husband-hunting—" Sara began anxiously.

"Well, that doesn't mean you'll ignore any good prospects that come your way, does it?"

"I suppose not," Sara murmured, deciding not to leave the weekend party. Now that she was here, she supposed there wasn't much harm in staying.

Clad in their splendid evening finery, the guests assembled in the drawing room and began the long and complicated procession into the dining hall, an opulent room with a fifty-foot ceiling. With the couples arranged by order of rank, importance, and age, the ladies lightly held the gentlemen's right arms and promenaded to the two long tables, each of which would accommodate one hundred guests. The tables were laden with innumerable crystal goblets, silver, and fine patterned porcelain.

Seated between two charming young men, Sara found herself enjoying the dinner greatly. The conversation was fascinating, for the table included poets quoting from their latest works and ambassadors telling amusing stories of life abroad. Every few minutes glasses were raised in a round of toasts, praising the host and hostess, the quality of the food, the health of the king, and every other notion that struck the guests as meritable. White-gloved servants moved quietly among the diners, bringing dishes of seasoned patties, tiny soufflés, and crystal plates of bonbons to sample between courses. After the great silver tureens of turtle soup and the plates of salmon were removed, large platters of roast, poultry, and game were brought out. The meal was concluded with iced champagne, pastries, and a luscious selection of fruits.

The cloths were removed from the tables, and the gentlemen leaned back in their chairs to enjoy Lord Raiford's excellent stock of hock, sherry, and port, and to puff on cigars as they talked of masculine interests such as politics. Meanwhile the ladies retired to separate rooms for more tea and gossip. They would all rejoin in the ballroom an hour or two later, when dinner had settled.

Seated to Alex's left, Derek nursed a glass of port and listened to the conversation with deceptive laziness. It was not his wont to take an active part in after-dinner arguments, no matter how good-natured they were. Certainly none of the men made the mistake of engaging him in a debate. He was far from a great or-

ator, for he disliked making speeches of any length.
But he had a way of cutting to the heart of a matter
with a few well-chosen words. "And besides," one of
the men murmured to his neighbor, "I would never be
fool enough to debate with a man who knows how
much I'm worth."

"How does he know that?"

"He knows how much *everyone* is worth, down to
the last farthing!"

As the gentlemen drank deeper into their cups, the
conversation turned to a bill that had recently been
dismissed in Parliament. It would have abolished the
practice of using climbing boys to clean chimneys. But
Lord Lauderson, a fat, long-winded earl who had a
habit of turning almost everything into an occasion for
jokes and amusement, had made a humorous speech in
the House of Lords that had killed the bill. A few of his
witticisms were recounted at the table, and many of
the men were laughing in appreciation. Proud of his
own cleverness, Lauderson beamed until his face
turned as pink as a cherub's. "I say, I was in good form
that day," he said with a chuckle. "Glad to entertain,
my good fellows . . . always glad of it."

Slowly Derek set down his glass in order to keep it
from splintering in his hand. He had supported the bill
with as much money and behind-the-scenes manipula-
tion as possible. With all that and Raiford's support,
the bill had been guaranteed to pass—until Lauderson's facetious speech. All at once Lauderson's boast-
ing was too much to take.

"I hear you were quite amusing, my lord," Derek
said. His tone was soft, undercutting many of the boisterous jests that were being tossed back and forth.
"But I doubt a group of climbing boys would have

been as appreciative of your wit as Parliament was." The table quieted immediately. Many gazes turned to his impassive face. Derek Craven always gave the appearance of never caring about anything . . . but it seemed that this issue was of more than passing importance to him. More than a few guests recalled the rumors that Craven himself had been a climbing boy. Their smiles faded noticeably.

"It's clear that your sympathy rests with the boys," Lauderson commented. "I pity the poor little wretches m'self, but it's a necessary evil."

"The work they do could easily be taken care of with long-handled brushes," Derek said evenly.

"But not as efficiently as the small boys do it. And if the chimneys aren't properly cleaned, our valuable homes could catch on fire—would you have us put our own lives and property at risk for the sake of a few cockney brats?"

Derek stared at the gleaming mahogany surface of the table. "With that one entertaining speech, my lord, you sentenced thousands of innocent boys to death for years to come. To something worse than death."

"They are sons of day laborers, Mr. Craven, not sons of the gentry. They will never amount to anything. Why not put them to good use?"

"Craven," Alex Raiford muttered, fearing that an ugly scene was about to take place.

But Derek lifted his eyes and regarded Lauderson in a cool, almost pleasant manner. "You almost tempt me to give you back a pig of your own sow, my lord."

"What does that mean?" Lauderson asked, chuckling at the crude cockney expression.

"It means the next time you defeat a bill I'm partic-

ular to, using one of your frivolous high-kick speeches,
I'll stuff your gullet full of soot and mortar and shove
your fat arse up a chimney. And if you get stuck there,
I'll light straw beneath you, or jab pins into your feet
to get you going. And if you complain of burns from a
hot flue, or of suffocation, I'll flay your hide with a
leather strap. *That's* what a climbing boy goes through
every day of his miserable existence, my lord. That's
what the bill would have prevented." Giving him a
chilling glance, Derek stood up and left the dining hall
with a measured tread.

Lauderson had turned scarlet during the contemptuous speech. "What gave Craven the idea that his
opinion is worth a farthing?" His voice echoed in the
deadly quiet of the room. "A man of no blood, no ed-
ucation, and certainly no refinement. He may be the
wealthiest bastard in England, but that gives him no
right to speak to *me* in that insolent manner." He
glanced at Alex in rising indignation. "An apology is
due me, sir! Since you're responsible for inviting the
man, I'll accept yours in lieu of his."

The assemblage froze. Not even a creak of a chair
disrupted the silence. Alex's face was like carved marble as he returned Lauderson's stare. "Excuse me, gentlemen," he finally said. "The air in here has suddenly
turned foul." He left the table with an expression of
distaste, while Lauderson's eyes bulged.

Alex couldn't find Derek until the ball had begun. He
walked into the ballroom, pausing to observe the orchestra nearly concealed behind huge banks of roses. A
row of French crystal chandeliers, each weighing a
thousand pounds, shed sparkling light over the gleaming floor and the huge columns of *fleur de peche* mar-

ble. Lily presided over the ball with her usual warmth and grace, effortlessly making everyone feel welcome.

Catching sight of Derek taking a drink from the tray of a passing servant, Alex went to join him. "Craven, about that scene in the dining hall—"

"I hate the upper class," Derek muttered, and took a large gulp of wine.

"You know we're not all like Lauderson."

"You're right. Some are worse."

Following Derek's gaze, Alex saw Lauderson's bulky form join a group of peers who were all engaged in toadying up to Lord Ashby. A haughty, irascible gentleman of the old school, Lord Ashby was usually making some speech or another. He believed that every word he uttered was like a pearl dropping from his lips. Because of his rank and wealth, the obsequious fools around him would never have dared to contradict that opinion. "Has Lady Ashby approached you yet?" Alex asked.

Derek shook his head. "She won't."

"How can you be certain?"

"Because I almost strangled her the last time I saw her."

Alex looked startled, and then smiled grimly. "I wouldn't have blamed you if you had."

Derek continued to stare at Lord Ashby. "Joyce was fifteen when she married that old bastard. Look at him, surrounded by those highborn lickspittles. I can see why Joyce turned out the way she did. Married to him, a girl in her teens would turn into either a trembling rabbit or a monster."

"You sound as if you have some sympathy for her."

"No. But I understand her. Life makes people what they are." A scowl settled between Derek's dark brows.

He gestured to a corner of the room. "If any one of those fine barons or viscounts had been born in the rookery, they wouldn't have turned out any better than I did. Noble blood counts for nothing."

Following Derek's gaze, Alex saw a growing coterie of men around Sara Fielding. Her small but lushly curved body was clad in a blue velvet gown a few shades darker than her eyes. Her hair was pulled into a mass of chestnut curls. She was uncommonly pretty tonight, exuding a shy charm that any man would find irresistible. Alex looked back at Derek's expressionless face. "If that's true," he asked slowly, "then why let one of *them* have Miss Fielding?"

Derek ignored the question, but Alex persisted. "Would any of them treat her more kindly than you? Take better care of her? Would one of those young fops value her as you would?"

The green eyes glinted coldly. "You of all people know what I am."

"I know what you *were*," Alex replied. "Even five years ago, I would have agreed that you didn't deserve someone like her. But you've changed, Craven. You've changed enough. And if she finds something in you that's worthy of her affection . . . for God's sake, don't argue with a gift that fate has handed you."

"Oh, very simple," Derek jeered. "It doesn't matter that I was born a bastard. She deserves nothing better than a man with a false name, fine clothes, and a sham accent. It's not important that I have no family and no religion. I don't believe in sacred causes, or honor, or unselfish motives. I can't be innocent enough for her. I never was. But why should that matter to her?" His lips pulled into a sneer. "A match between us wouldn't be a gift of fate, Raiford. It would be a bloody joke."

Alex dropped the argument immediately. "Apparently you know best. Pardon, but I have to go search for my wife, who's probably fending off her own set of admirers. Unlike you, I have a jealous streak as wide as the Thames."

"More like the Atlantic," Derek muttered, watching his friend wander off.

He turned his attention back to Sara and the bucks who hovered around her. "Jealous streak" couldn't begin to describe how he felt. He despised the men who sought her favor. He wanted to snarl and gnash his teeth at them, and take her far away from their roving hands and leering gazes. But what could he do with her? The idea of making her his paramour was an unthinkable as marrying her. Either way, he would ruin her. The only choice was to stay away, but that seemed as simple a solution as stopping himself from breathing. The physical attraction was powerful, but more irresistible than that was the alarming feeling he had when he was near her . . . a feeling that came perilously close to happiness. No man on earth was less entitled to that than he was.

He was nowhere in sight, but Sara had the feeling that Craven was watching her. Earlier he had been mingling and exchanging pleasantries with guests. It hadn't been lost on Sara that women were sending him all manner of signals; flirtatious glances, playful taps on his shoulder with their fans, and in one case the bold, deliberate brush of a thinly covered breast against his arm. Women were fascinated by his mix-

ture of earthiness and elegance. It was as if there was a
dark, smoldering fire buried beneath a layer of ice, and
each woman hoped to be the one to break through his
reserve.

"Miss Fielding," Viscount Tavisham interrupted her
thoughts. He stood an inch too close and stared at her
with soulful brown eyes. "Perhaps you would honor
me with another waltz?"

Sara smiled at him blankly while she thought of a
suitable reply. She had danced with Tavisham twice already; a third time was out of the question. It would be
noticed by the guests, and it would lead to improper
speculation. Not that she didn't like the impulsive
young rake, but she didn't wish to encourage his attentions. "I'm afraid the dancing has made me rather
fatigued," she said with an apologetic smile. Actually,
it was true. Several waltzes and vigorous quadrilles had
made the soles of her feet sore.

"Then we will find a quiet place to sit and talk." He
offered his arm in a courtly gesture. Clearly there was
no way to avoid him. Sighing inwardly, Sara accompanied him to the long gallery with its multitude of
French doors, and sat on a polished wooden bench
with an ornately carved back. "Would you like some
punch?" Tavisham offered, and she nodded. "Don't go
anywhere," he admonished. "Don't even bat an eye.
I'll return momentarily. And if any man approaches
you, tell him you're spoken for."

Giving him a mock salute, Sara pretended to freeze
in place, and he grinned at her before leaving. Couples promenaded back and forth along the gallery,
admiring the view of the terrace and the fountain in
the snow-covered garden outside. Toying with the
sparkling beadwork on her gown, Sara thought of the

last evening she had worn it. A soft smile curved her lips.

He had been carrying her spectacles right next to his heart. A man wouldn't do something like that unless . . .

The thought filled her with nervous energy. She stood up, ignoring the protesting twinge of her feet. The garden was visible through the frosted windows, the hedges delicately coated with ice, the shadows cold and quiet. Pale blue moonlight gleamed over the frozen fountain and the bordered walkways. After the crowded, music-filled ballroom, the quiet garden was an inviting sanctuary. Obeying a sudden impulse, Sara slipped to the French doors and turned one of the gilded knobs. She shivered as a winter breeze caressed her bare shoulders, and closed the door behind her.

The garden was like a snow palace. Carefully she made her way along a graveled path, filling her lungs with refreshing air. Lost in her thoughts, she wandered until she heard a sound behind her. It might have been the rustle of another breeze . . . or her name, whispered in a low voice. Sara turned around, the ice-dusted hem of her skirt whirling and settling at her feet. He *had* been watching her, she thought, and a winsome smile broke over her face as she looked at the man standing a few yards away.

"Somehow I thought you might follow me," she said breathlessly. "At least, I hoped you would."

The stern cast of Derek's face concealed a torrent of repressed emotion. How could she smile at him like that? He was shaking with cold and heat and need. God, he couldn't bear the way she looked at him, as if she could see down to the darkest recesses

of his soul. She began to approach him. Without
meaning to he reached her in three strides and
snatched her in his arms. Her joyous laugh tickled his
ear as he lifted her off her feet. Urgently his mouth
roved across her face with rough kisses that stung her
cheek, her chin, her forehead. She caught his lean jaw
in her hands to hold him still. The moonlight was
captured in her glistening eyes as she stared up at him.
"I want to be with you," she whispered. "No matter
what happens."

No one in his life had ever said such a thing to him.
Derek tried to think above the pounding of his heart,
but she brought her soft mouth to his, and all reason
was lost. Hungrily he bent over her, trying not to hurt
her with the force of his kisses, trembling with an
emotion as ferocious as it was tender.

Lily's teeth chattered from the cold as she crept
stealthily through the garden and positioned herself
behind a frozen tree. Catching sight of Derek and Sara
in the distance, locked in a passionate embrace, Lily
broke into a wide grin. She had to restrain herself
from doing a little victory dance. Rubbing her hands
together to warm them, she considered a variety of
matchmaking strategies.

"Lily."

The quiet whisper gave her a start, just before her
husband's arms closed around her. "Why the hell are
you out here?" Alex murmured, pulling her back
against his tall body.

"You've been following me!" Lily exclaimed indignantly, keeping her voice low.

"Yes—and you've been following Derek and Miss
Fielding."

"I had to, darling," she explained innocently. "I've been helping them."

"Oh," he said sardonically. "At first it appeared as if you were spying on them." Ignoring her protests, Alex began to drag his wife away from the scene. "I think you've 'helped' enough, my sweet."

"Spoilsport," Lily accused, pulling against his firm grip. "I just want to watch a moment longer—"

"Now. Leave the poor devil alone."

Determined to have her way, Lily braced her feet against the stone border of a pathway. "Not yet . . . Alex . . . *oof!*" With one easy tug, he had jerked her off balance, causing her to fall against him.

"Watch your step," he advised mildly, as if the stumble had been her fault.

Her dark eyes met his twinkling gray ones. "You heavy-handed, overbearing *tyrant*," she accused, and began to giggle as she pounded his chest.

Grinning, Alex subdued her struggles and kissed her amorously. He stopped only when she was out of breath. "At the moment Derek doesn't need your help." His hands wandered boldly over her tulle and satin ball gown. "But I have a problem that needs immediate attention."

"Oh? What problem is that?"

His lips wandered to her neck. "I'll have to show you in private."

"*Now?*" she asked, scandalized. "Really, Alex, you can't mean—"

"Now," he assured her, and capturing her hand in his, began to walk her back to the mansion.

Lily's fingers laced with his, while her heart beat in anticipation. In spite of his obstinate, overbearing nature, she thought him the most wonderful husband in the world, and was about to tell him so, when suddenly they nearly bumped into the solitary woman who crossed the path before them.

Lady Ashby whipped around and eyed them both like a baleful cat. From the seething anger on her face, Lily guessed that she had also followed Derek, and had seen him kissing Sara Fielding. "Lady Ashby," Lily said sweetly. "Rather a cool night for a stroll, isn't it?"

"It's a relief from all the mismatched clutter inside," Joyce replied.

Lily, whose taste in decorating was universally praised as being the epitome of elegance, took offense at hearing her home described as a "mismatched clutter." "Now see here—" she began, and winced as Alex's grip became painful.

"Sheathe your claws, ladies." Alex pinned Joyce with an autocratic stare. "My wife and I would be delighted to accompany you back to the ball, Lady Ashby."

"I don't wish—" Joyce objected, but was presented with Alex's rock-solid arm.

"I insist," he said, ignoring his wife's glare. It was clear that given the choice, the two women would much rather sneak back to the garden and spy on the embracing couple. In that moment Alex almost pitied Derek Craven, who was apparently neck-deep in trouble. On the other hand, Craven had brought it all on himself. Alex smothered a wry laugh as he was reminded of a quote he had once read . . . "These impossible women! How they do get around us!"

Too absorbed in each other to notice anything around them, Derek and Sara wound together, exchanging kisses of greedy violence, until the heat of desire was stoked to a sweltering blaze. Derek's feet spread to contain her body more closely within his embrace. His lips forged a path down her exposed throat. "Oh . . ." The catch of sound came from her throat as she felt the hot swipe of his tongue on her skin. Derek bent his knees and pulled her high against him, and breathed deeply in the perfumed vale where her breasts were pushed together.

Suddenly he lifted his head and buried his lips in the mass of her curls. "No," he said, his voice muffled. His large body was still except for the rhythmic force of his breathing. Somehow it seemed as if he were waiting for her to convince him of something he wanted very badly to believe.

Honesty was too much a part of Sara's nature for her to keep her feelings hidden. Although it might result in disaster, she had no choice but to lay her heart before him. "I need you," she said, combing her fingers through his black hair.

"You don't even know me."

She turned her face and pressed her lips to the thin, healed-over scar, lingering in the space between his thick brows. "I know that you care for me."

Derek did not pull away from her tender ministrations, but his tone was savage. "Not enough, or I wouldn't be here with you. I wish to hell I had the decency to leave you alone."

"I've been alone for far too long," she said passionately. "There's no one for me; not Perry, not any of the men in the village, or anyone inside that ballroom. No one but you."

"If you'd seen anything of the world, you'd know there's a hell of a lot more to choose from than Perry Kingswood and me. Thousands of ordinary, honorable men who would fall to their knees in gratitude for a woman like you."

"I don't want anyone honorable. I want you."

She felt him smile unwillingly against her ear. "Sweet angel," he whispered. "You can do far better than me."

"I don't agree." Ignoring his attempt to ease her away, she snuggled under his chin.

Reluctantly Derek folded her against his warm body. "You're getting cold. I'll take you inside."

"I'm not cold." Sara had no intention of going anywhere. She had dreamed of this moment for too many nights.

Derek glanced over her head at the light coming from the ballroom. "You should be in there dancing with Harry Marshall . . . or Lord Banks."

She frowned at the mention of the two callow youths. "Is that what you think I deserve? You would pair me with some shallow, conceited dandy and claim that I've made a splendid match? Well, I'm beginning to think it's a convenient excuse, this notion of yours that I'm too good for you! Perhaps the truth is that I'm lacking something. You must think I wouldn't satisfy your needs, or—"

"No," Derek said swiftly.

"I suppose you would rather be consorting with all those married women who keep whispering in your ear and making eyes at you, and touching you with their fans—"

"Sara—"

"Writers are very observant, perceptive people, and I can tell exactly which women you've consorted with, just by watching— "

Derek smothered her tirade with his mouth. When

she was quiet, he lifted his head. "None of them mattered to me," he said roughly. "There were no promises, no obligations on either side. I felt nothing for them." He looked away from her and swore, aware of the futility of trying to explain it to her. But she had to understand, so that she would have no illusions about him. He forced himself to go on. "Some of them claimed to love me. As soon as they said it, I left without looking back."

"Why?"

"There's no place in my life for that. I don't want it. I have no use for it."

Sara stared at his averted face. In spite of his unemotional tone, she sensed the tumult inside him. He was lying to himself. He needed to be loved more than any person she had ever met. "Then what *do* you want?" she asked softly.

He shook his head without answering. But Sara knew. He wanted to be safe. If he were rich and powerful enough, he would never be hurt, lonely, or abandoned. He would never have to trust anyone. She continued to stroke his hair, playing lightly with the thick raven locks. "Take a chance on me," she urged. "Do you really have so much to lose?"

He gave a harsh laugh and loosened his arms to release her. "More than you know."

Clinging to him desperately, Sara kept her mouth at his ear. "Listen to me." All she could do was play her last card. Her voice trembled with emotion. "You can't change the truth. You can act as though you're deaf and blind, you can walk away from me forever, but the truth will still be there, and you can't make it go away. I love you." She felt an involuntary tremor run through him. "I love you," she repeated. "Don't lie to either of us by pretending you're leaving for my good. All you'll do is deny us both a chance at happiness. I'll long for you every day and night, but at least *my* conscience will be clear. I haven't held anything back from you, out of fear or pride or stubbornness." She felt the incredible tautness of his muscles, as if he were carved from marble. "For once have the strength *not* to walk away," she whispered. "Stay with me. Let me love you, Derek."

He stood there frozen in defeat, with all the warmth and promise of her in his arms . . . and he couldn't allow himself to take what she offered. He'd never felt so worthless, so much a fraud. Perhaps for a day, a week, he could be what she wanted. But no longer than that. He had sold his honor, his conscience, his body, anything he could use to escape the lot he'd been given in life. And now, with all his great fortune, he couldn't buy back what he'd sacrificed. Were he capable of tears, he would have shed them. Instead he felt numbing coldness spread through his body, filling up the region where his heart should have been.

It wasn't difficult to walk away from her. It was appallingly easy.

Sara made an inarticulate sound as he extricated himself from her embrace. He left her as he had left the others, without looking back.

Somehow Sara made her way to the ballroom, too dazed to think about what would happen next. Derek was not there. The elegant clamor of the ball made it easy for her to maintain an appearance. She danced several times with different partners, pasting a shallow smile on her face. She made conversation in a light voice that sounded odd to her own ears. Evidently her pain wasn't visible, for no one appeared to notice that something was wrong.

But then Lady Raiford appeared. The expression on Lily's face changed from a smile to an uncertain frown as she approached. "Sara?" she asked quietly. "What happened?"

Sara was quiet, while panic assailed her. Any hint of sympathy would push her over the edge. She would have to leave the ball immediately, or she would burst into tears. "Oh, I've had a lovely time," she said rapidly. "I just have a touch of the headache. It's rather late— I'm not used to such hours. Perhaps I should retire."

Lily made a motion to touch her, then withdrew her hand. The velvety eyes filled with sympathy. "Would you like to talk?"

Sara shook her head. "Thank you, but I'm very tired."

While the two women conversed, Lady Ashby watched them from across the room. She had secluded herself in a corner with Lord Granville, one of many admirers who had unsuccessfully sought her favors for years. The hope of gaining access to her bed kept him coming back time after time, but she had always disdained him. In spite of his reputed virility and his fleshy handsomeness, he'd never had anything she wanted. Until now.

She smiled into his narrow blue eyes. "Granville, do you see that woman standing next to Lily Raiford?"

Indifferently Granville glanced away from her, his gaze alighting on the pair. "Ah, the delightful Miss Fielding," he commented. "Yes, indeed." Contemplating Sara's bountiful charms, he moistened his lips with a thick tongue. "A pretty little bonbon." He looked back at Joyce, savoring her golden beauty, displayed in a diaphanous lavender gown. "However, I prefer a woman of worldliness and experience—who could satisfy a man of my varied tastes."

"Indeed." Joyce's lovely face took on a hard cast. "We've known each other a long time, haven't we, Granville? Perhaps it's time we made our friendship more intimate."

A flush of sexual greed worked up from his throat. "Perhaps it is," he breathed, stepping closer to her.

Delicately she propped her fan against his chest, keeping him at bay. "But first I would ask a favor of you."

"A favor," he repeated warily.

"You'll find it quite pleasant, I assure you." Joyce's lips curved in a malicious smile. "When that 'pretty little bonbon' as you call her, retires for the evening, I want you to go up to her room and . . ." Standing on her toes, Joyce whispered her plan to him, while his flush grew deeper. "Consider her a morsel to whet your appetite," Joyce finished, "before you enjoy the main course later tonight. First Miss Fielding . . . then me."

Granville shook his head with momentary dismay. "But there's a rumor," he protested. "They say that Derek Craven is enamored of her."

"She won't tell him. She won't tell anyone. She'll be too ashamed."

Contemplating the proposition, Granville finally nodded with a chortle of lecherous delight. "All right. As long as you tell me why you want this favor. Has it something to do with your former liaison with Craven?"

Joyce's chin dipped in a small nod. "I'm going to ruin everything he values," she murmured. "If he is attracted by innocence, I'll see that it's debauched. If any woman is fool enough to care for him, I'll ruin her. I won't let him have *anything* . . . unless he crawls on his knees to beg me for it."

Granville stared at her in fascination. "What an extraordinary creature you are. A tigress. You swear by all that's sacred to you that you'll yield yourself to me tonight?"

"I hold nothing sacred," Joyce smiled thinly. "But I'll yield to you tonight, Granville . . . after you've finished with Miss Fielding."

Gently repelling Lily's attempts to talk to her, Sara bade her good night and slipped from the ballroom. She went upstairs alone. The music and laughter from the ballroom faded with each step, until she reached the silence of her room. Declining to ring for a chambermaid, Sara managed to struggle from her gown unaided. She left the rich heap of beaded velvet on the floor, along with her white lawn underclothes. It seemed too much of an effort to pick the garments up. After donning her nightgown, she sat down on the edge of the bed and allowed herself to think for the first time since Derek had left her alone in the garden.

"He was never mine to lose," she said aloud. She wondered if there was anything she could have done differently, any more she could have said. No . . . she didn't have reason for regret. It had not been wrong to love him, nor had it been wrong to tell him so. A sophisticated woman might have played her hand more cleverly, but Sara knew little about games. It was best to be open and giving . . . and if her love wasn't returned, at least she couldn't be faulted for cowardice.

Kneeling by the bed, she folded her hands and

closed her eyes tightly. "Dear Lord," she said in a
strangled whisper. "I can bear it for a while . . . but
please don't let it hurt forever." She was motionless for
a long time, while her mind swam with painful
thoughts. In the welter of her emotions, there was a
trace of pity for Derek Craven. For an instant tonight,
quick as a lightning flash, he had been tempted to take
the risk of loving someone. Somehow she doubted
that he would ever come that close again.

And me? she wondered wearily, extinguishing the
lamp and crawling into bed. *I'll just muddle through all
of this, and carry on. And someday, with the grace of
God . . . I might be strong enough to love someone else.*

For a while Derek lingered in the billiards room with a
glass of brandy, only half-listening to the languid conversations of the men who had retreated there for a
gentlemanly smoke. The cloying atmosphere made
him feel like a caged tiger. He left silently, taking the
brandy with him. As he wandered around the first floor
of the mansion, Derek saw a flash of white on the grand
staircase. Welcoming any distraction over the prospect
of returning to the ballroom, he went to investigate.
Halfway up the stairs he saw Nicole in her white ruffled nightgown, her long hair a mass of tangles. She
huddled by the banister in an effort to conceal herself.
Upon seeing him, she held a finger to her lips in a gesture to keep quiet. Casually Derek made his way up the
stairs and sat next to her. He rested his arms on his bent
knees. "What are you doing out of bed at this hour?"

"I'm sneaking downstairs to look at all the pretty
gowns," Nicole informed him in a whisper. "Don't tell
Mama."

"I won't, as long as you go back upstairs to your room."

"After I see what the ball looks like."

He shook his head firmly. "Little girls shouldn't roam through the house in their nightgowns."

"Why?" Nicole looked down at herself, tucking her bare feet beneath the hem of the garment "It covers everything. See?"

"It isn't proper." Derek resisted the urge to smile grimly as he heard himself delivering a statement on propriety.

"Mama doesn't have to be proper."

"Neither will you, when you're older."

"But Uncle Derek . . ." Nicole pleaded, and then sighed heavily as she saw his brows lower threateningly. "All right, I'll go back upstairs. But someday I'm going to have a ball gown of silver and gold . . . and I'll stay up and dance all night!"

Derek looked down at her small face. Nicole's features were slightly more exotic than her mother's. With her lustrous black eyes and striking dark brows, she had the promise of stunning beauty. "That day isn't long coming," he said. "Someday you'll have every man in London begging to marry you."

"Oh, I don't want to marry anybody," she said earnestly. "All I want is my own stable full of horses."

Derek smiled slightly. "I'm going to remind you of that when you're eighteen."

"Maybe I'll marry *you*," she said with a childish giggle.

"That's very kind of you, sweet." He rumpled her hair. "But you'll want to marry someone your own age, not some old cheeser."

A new voice interrupted from the foot of the stairs.

"He's right," Lady Ashby said silkily. "I was forced to marry an old man—and look what became of me."

Nicole's smile vanished. With a child's natural perceptiveness, she sensed the corruption beneath Joyce's beautiful exterior. Warily she inched closer to Derek as Joyce ascended the steps in fluid, graceful movements. Pausing before them, Joyce regarded the little girl with distaste. "Run along, child. I want to talk with Mr. Craven alone."

Hesitantly Nicole glanced at Derek. He leaned over and whispered to her. "Back to bed, miss."

As soon as the child was gone, all warmth faded from Derek's face. Raising his brandy glass, he downed the last of the warm amber liquid. He remained sitting, affecting no pretense of courtesy.

"Why the somber face?" Joyce purred. "Thinking about your tender scene in the garden with Sara Fielding?" She smiled as his gaze shot to hers. "Yes, darling, I'm fully aware of your preoccupation with that modest country violet—and so is everyone else. It's provided a fair amount of amusement for all of us. Derek Craven falling for a timid little nobody. You should have told me you liked your women to play innocent—I could have obliged you." Sinuously she draped herself against the balustrade and smiled at him.

Derek watched her, tempted either to shove her down the stairs or to tell her to go to hell . . . but something stopped him. He didn't like the smug look on her face. Something was very wrong. Patiently he waited while she continued her speech. His hard green eyes didn't move from hers.

"How does it feel to make love to a woman like that, darling? She can't be very satisfying to a man of your robust appetite. I can't imagine she would know the first thing about pleasing you." Joyce sighed thoughtfully. "Men are such fools. I daresay you fancy yourself in love with her. Need I remind you that you're not capable of love? You're nothing but a great, lusty animal . . . and I wouldn't have you any other way." She pursed her red lips provocatively. "Leave the sentiments and the romantic foolishness to other men. What you have is much better than a heart . . . a nice, big cock. That's all you've got to offer your country bumpkin. She probably doesn't know enough to appreciate it . . . although now . . . at least she'll have a basis for comparison." She waited with a feline smile for her last words to register.

Comparison? Slowly Derek stood up, staring at her intently. A jolt of anxiety caused his heart to pump unpleasantly hard. His voice was scratchy. "What have you done, Joyce?"

"I've done her a favor, actually. I've enlisted someone to help her learn more about men. As we speak, she's in her room 'taking a flier' as you cockneys put it, with our virile Lord Granville. Not so innocent anymore."

The brandy snifter dropped from Derek's hand and rolled, unbroken, down the thickly carpeted stairs. "Jesus," he whispered, turning to lunge up the steps. He took them three at a time, while Joyce called after him.

"Don't bother to charge to her rescue, my poor gallant. It's too late." She began to laugh wildly. "By now the deed is already done."

.

At first Sara's dazed mind could only recognize it as a nightmare. It couldn't be real. She had been awakened by a huge hand clapped over her mouth. The bloated, ruddy face of a stranger was barely visible in the darkness. The weight of his body dropped over her as he joined her on the bed. She went rigid with terror and tried to scream, but all sound was smothered by his pawlike hand. His heavy bulk crushed her down, flattening her breasts painfully and forcing the air from her lungs.

"Quiet, quiet," he grunted, eagerly raking up her gown. "Lovely creature. I watched you tonight . . . those magnificent breasts swelling out of your gown. Don't struggle. I'm the best cocksman in London. Relax, you'll enjoy it. You'll see."

Frantically she tried to bite and claw him, but nothing could stop his heavy thighs pushing between hers. The pungent sweat-and-perfume odor of his skin filled her nostrils, while groping hands searched over her half-clad body. Choking on her own smothered cries, Sara felt herself sinking in a dark, airless void.

Suddenly the punishing hand left her mouth, and the massive weight was lifted from her. She was finally able to scream with bloodcurdling force. Scrambling off the bed, she ran without direction until she found herself cowering in a corner. There was a terrifying snarling noise in the room, as if a wild beast had been let loose. Blinking rapidly, she tried to understand what was happening. Her hand flew to her mouth, holding in another scream.

Two men rolled over and over across the floor, crashing into the washstand. The porcelain pitcher and basin fell and shattered. Growling murderously, Derek drove his fists into Granville's face. With a howl of pain, Granville managed to throw him off. Derek rolled easily and came to his feet.

Granville struggled up and stared at him in horror. "Good God, man, let's discuss this like civilized beings!"

Derek's teeth gleamed in the dim room, his lips twisting in a demonic sneer. "After I take your head off and pull your guts out through your neck."

Granville whimpered in fear as Derek came after him again, slamming him to the floor. Brutal fists descended on him relentlessly, until Granville got in a blow of his own and gained another second's respite. He raised a hand to his own face, discovering it was streaming with blood. "My nose is broken!" he cried in panic, crawling backward to the door as Derek stalked him mercilessly.

To Granville's relief, a house steward appeared, staring into the room with alarm and bewilderment. "Please," Granville sobbed, clutching at the servant's ankle, "keep him away from me! He's trying to kill me—"

"You won't be that lucky," Derek interrupted, snatching up a shard of broken pottery and advancing on him.

Bravely the house steward placed himself between Derek and his intended victim. "Mr. Craven," the servant quavered, staring at the enraged giant before him, "you must wait until—"

"Get out of my way."

Conscious of the blubbering aristocrat seeking his protection, the servant didn't move. "No, sir," he said unsteadily.

More servants and several guests began to appear, all crowding to see what the commotion was about. Derek pinned Granville with a bloodthirsty stare. "The next time I see you—and the coldhearted bitch who sent you—I'll kill you both. Tell her that."

Granville shrank back in fear. "There are witnesses who will testify as to your threats—"

Derek slammed the door, closeting himself alone in the room with Sara. He dropped the piece of broken pottery and turned to her, swiping his heavy black hair out of his eyes. She clutched the thin gown around herself as if it would protect her. Her face was blank, as if she didn't recognize him. When he saw that her entire body was trembling, he went to her and scooped her up in his arms.

Silently he carried her to the bed and sat down with her in his lap. She was still against his broad chest, her arms gripped around his neck, her head wedged against his shoulder. They both breathed in hard spurts, one from fear, one from rage. As his anger diminished, Derek became aware of the multitude of voices gathering outside the door. No one dared come in. God only knew what they thought was going on in there. It would be better if he relinquished Sara to someone else's care.

He didn't realize she was crying until her wet cheek brushed his neck. No sobs, just quiet tears that slipped down her face and broke his heart. Slowly he unclenched his hands and caressed her loose hair and her back. "Did he hurt you?" he finally brought himself to ask.

She knew what he meant. "No," she said in a watery voice. "You arrived in time. How did you know? How—"

"Later." At the moment he couldn't bring himself to explain that she had been assaulted because of him.

Sara relaxed against him with a ragged sigh, her tears drying. It was impossible to believe that the same man who had attacked Lord Granville so brutally could hold her with such tenderness. She had never felt so safe, cradled against his broad chest, feeling his breath filter through her hair. One of his hands was splayed over her side, his thumb resting against the curve of her breast. It was wrong for him to hold her so intimately, for her to allow it, but she couldn't bring herself to deny him. His head moved, and his mouth brushed hers in a gentle kiss. Closing her eyes, Sara felt his lips touch her delicate eyelids, her wet lashes.

A decisive rap on the door heralded Lady Raiford's entrance. She slipped inside and turned to admonish the cluster of people around the portal. "Go on, all of you," she said pertly. "Everything's all right now. I wish everyone would go downstairs and try to refrain from gossiping about things that are not their concern." Firmly she closed the door and stared at the pair on the bed. "Damnation," she muttered, coming over to light the bedside lamp.

Aware of the scandalous appearance of the situation, Sara tried to crawl from Derek's lap. He deposited her beneath the covers, tucked her in carefully, and sat on the bed beside her.

Lily's gaze moved from Sara's distraught face to Derek's impassive one. "That filthy goat Granville," she muttered. "I've always known he was a lecherous bastard, but that he would dare attack a guest under *my* roof . . . Well, Alex is booting him off the estate right now, and after I'm through, Granville won't be received by anyone in the *ton*. Here, I thought this might help." She handed a glass of whiskey to Derek. "Between the two of you, I can't decide who needs it more."

He gave it to Sara, who sniffed cautiously and shook her head.

"No—"

"Drink some for me," he insisted gently.

She tried a small swallow and coughed as it burned her throat. "*Ugh.*" She made a face at the vile taste. Gingerly she took another sip, and then another.

Derek pushed the whiskey back as she tried to give it to him. "Keep sipping."

Lily pulled a chair to the bed and sat down. Removing the jeweled bandeau from her forehead, she rubbed her temples distractedly. Catching Sara's worried glance, she produced a wry smile. "Well, now you've had your first scandal. Don't worry, Derek and I are old hands at this sort of thing. We'll take care of everything."

Sara nodded uncertainly, lifting the glass to her lips. The more she drank, the easier it was to swallow, until she felt unsteady and very warm, as if heat were radiating from her bones. At first she thought she would never sleep again, but soon the frenzied thoughts in her mind were replaced by exhaustion. Derek and Lily began to talk idly, making noncommittal remarks about the ball, the guests, even the weather.

Derek softened his voice as he watched the whiskey taking effect. Gradually Sara's eyes closed, and she gave a small yawn. Her breathing became even and deep. She looked like a child nestled beneath the covers, her hair rippling over the pillow, her long lashes fanning her cheeks. Assured that she was asleep, Derek stroked the palm of her hand with his fingertip, marveling at the softness of her skin.

Lily watched him with a trace of amazement. "You do love her. Until this moment I never really thought it could happen to you."

He was silent, unable to admit the truth.

Lily spoke again. "She's in serious trouble, Derek."

"No, I got here in time. He didn't hurt her."

Although Lily's voice was low, it didn't alter her intensity. "*Think*, Derek. It doesn't matter if Granville actually raped her or not. No one will have her now. No one will believe she hasn't been ruined. The rumors will follow her back to the village. People will gossip and torment her for the rest of her life. Mothers will keep their children away from her 'corrupting influence'—she'll be a pariah. You have no idea how backward these people are. I grew up in the country, I know what it's like. If some man does condescend to marry her, he'll consider her secondhand goods. She'll have to be grateful the rest of her life, and endure whatever kind of treatment he decides to mete out. God, if only I hadn't invited her here!"

"If only," he agreed coldly.

"Well, how was I to know Granville would take it in his head to do something like this?"

Derek swallowed hard, dropping his accusing stare. He looked at the slumbering innocent beside him, and fingered a silken lock of hair. "Tell me what's to be done now."

"To make Sara respectable again?" Lily shrugged helplessly. "We find someone for her to marry. The sooner the better." She gave him a sarcastic glance. "Any candidates in mind?"

Sara awakened early, staring blankly at the unfamiliar ceiling. It took several minutes for her to recall where she was. Rubbing her eyes, she groaned miserably. Her temples throbbed with a sharp ache. She felt more than a little queasy. Carefully she crept out of bed and fumbled for her gray gown. When she was fully

dressed, her hair tied back at the nape of her neck, she
rang for a maid. Françoise appeared, wearing an expression so sympathetic that it was clear she knew
about the previous evening.

Pale and controlled, Sara smiled at her briefly.
"Françoise, I need your help to pack my belongings."
She gestured to her clothes. "I'm going home as soon
as possible."

The maid began to chatter, gesturing to the door
and mentioning Lady Raiford's name.

"The countess wishes me to see her?" Sara asked,
puzzled.

Françoise made a careful effort to speak in English.
"If you please, mademoiselle . . ."

"Certainly," Sara said, although she had no desire to
talk with Lily or anyone else this morning. She would
rather slink away and try to forget that she had ever
come to Raiford Park.

The house was quiet as Sara followed Françoise to
the east wing, where the Raifords' private suites were
located. At nine o'clock, it was too early for most of
the guests to have risen. Only the servants were up and
about, dusting, emptying slops, carrying armloads of
kindling, cleaning grates, and lighting fires.

Françoise led her to a small sitting room decorated
in shades of white and powder-blue, filled with elegant
furniture of Sheraton design. Giving her an encouraging smile, the maid left. Sara entered the empty room
and wandered to the half-moon table against the wall.
The table bore a display of carved jade, ivory, and lapis
animals. Picking up a tiny jade elephant, Sara examined it carefully. She started as she heard Derek
Craven's voice behind her.

"How are you this morning?"

Setting down the carved piece, Sara turned slowly. "I-I was expecting Lily."

Derek looked as if he hadn't slept at all. Sara doubted he had even changed his clothes, which were rumpled and wrinkled. His black hair was completely disheveled, as if he had raked his hands through it a hundred times during the night. "As matters stand, Lily can't do much to help you. But I can."

Sara was perplexed. "I don't need anyone's help. I'm leaving this morning, and . . . What's that in your hand?" She stared at the piece of paper he held, covered with his heavy black scrawl.

"A list." Suddenly businesslike, Derek walked toward her and pushed the display of carved figures aside. He flattened the paper on the table, motioning for her to look at it. "These are the twenty most eligible bachelors in England, listed in order of preference. If none of them are to your liking, we'll expand the list, although these are the most appropriate in age and character—"

"What?" Sara stared at him incredulously. "You're trying to marry me off now?" A sputter of dazed laughter escaped her. "Why on earth would any of these men offer for me?"

"Pick a name. I'll get him for you."

"How?"

"There's not a man in England who doesn't owe me one favor or another."

"Mr. Craven, there's no need for this . . . this *absurdity*—"

"You don't have a choice," he said brusquely.

"Yes, I do! I can choose not to marry anyone, and return to Greenwood Corners where I belong." Sara backed away as he tried to give her the list. "I won't look at any names. I don't know any of those men. I don't want to marry some stranger just for the sake of propriety. My reputation doesn't mean that much to me . . . or to anyone else, really."

"News of this will reach the village. You know the things they'll say about you."

"I don't care what they say. I'll know the truth, and that will sustain me."

"Even when your precious Kingswood looks down his nose at you for being a ruined woman?"

That caused Sara to flinch, the image of Perry and his mother treating her with contemptuous pity under the guise of Christian virtue . . . but she nodded resolutely. "I'll bear any burden the Lord sees fit to give me. I'm stronger than you think, Mr. Craven."

"You don't have to be strong. Take someone's name. Let him be your shield. Any one of the men on this list has the means to support you and your parents in luxury."

"I don't care about luxury. I can still afford my principles. I won't be bartered off to some unwilling suitor merely to save my name."

"No one can afford principles all the time."

She became even calmer in the face of his growing impatience. "I can. And I could never marry someone I didn't love."

Derek ground his teeth together. "Everyone else does!"

"I'm not like everyone else."

Biting back an unflattering reply, Derek struggled for self-control. "Would you at least look at this?" he asked through his teeth.

She went to him and glanced at the neatly written list, discovering that Lord Tavisham's name was at the top. " 'Viscount' is spelled with an 's,' " she murmured.

An impatient scowl crossed his face. "What do you think of him? You danced together last night."

"I rather liked him, but . . . are you certain *he's* the most eligible bachelor in England? I find that hard to believe."

"Tavisham's young, titled, intelligent, kind-hearted—and he has a yearly income that makes even my fingers itch. He's the best catch I've ever seen." Derek pasted a fake, unnatural smile on his face. "I think he likes books too. I heard him talking about Shakespeare once. You'd like to marry someone who reads, wouldn't you? And he's handsome. Tall . . . blue eyes . . . no pockmarks . . ."

"His hair is thin."

Derek looked offended, his coaxing panther-grin disappearing. "He has a high forehead. It's a sign of nobility."

"If you're so enthralled with him, *you* marry him." Sara walked away to the window, turning her back to him.

Abandoning all attempts at diplomacy, Derek followed her with the paper clutched in his hand. "Pick one or I'll cram this down your throat!"

She was unfazed by his fury. "Mr. Craven," she said with great care, "you're very kind to take such an interest in my welfare. But it's better that I remain a spinster. I will never find a husband who wouldn't resent my writing. No matter how well-intentioned he was in the beginning, he would be frustrated by my habit of abandoning my wifely duties in order to work on my novels—"

"He'll learn to live with it."

"What if he doesn't? What if he forbids me to write ever again? Unfortunately, Mr. Craven, a wife is at the mercy of her husband's whims in such matters. How can you suggest I should entrust my life and my happiness to a stranger who may not treat me with respect?"

"He'll treat you like a queen," Derek said grimly. "Or he'll answer to me."

Sara gave him a chiding glance. "I'm not so naive as that, Mr. Craven. You would be powerless to do anything for me, once I belonged to another man."

Derek felt his color rising. "Anything's better than letting you go back to that stinking hole of a village to live alone and be scorned by everyone."

"How do you plan to stop me?" she asked gently.

"I'll . . ." Derek halted, his mouth open. Physical harm, blackmail, and financial ruin, his stock-in-trade threats, weren't options in this case. She had no gambling debts, no scandalous past, nothing he could use against her. And she wasn't susceptible to bribery in any form. Restlessly he considered possibilities. "I'll close down your publisher," he finally said.

She infuriated him by smiling. "I don't write for the sake of being published, Mr. Craven. I write because I love the act of putting words on paper. If I can't earn money by selling novels, I'll do odd jobs in the village, and merely write for my own pleasure." Faced with his glowering silence, Sara felt her temporary amusement fade away. She looked into his bright green eyes, understanding the reason for his discomfort. He was determined to find another man to take care of her, but that didn't stop him from wanting her for himself. "I appreciate your concern, but there's no reason for you to worry. You mustn't feel responsible for me. None of this was your fault."

Derek turned pale, as if she'd slapped him instead of

thanking him. A mist of sweat appeared on his forehead. "Last night *was* my fault," he said hoarsely. "I once had an affair with Lady Ashby. Granville attacked you because she asked him to, out of a desire to spite me."

Sara's face turned blank. It took a good half-minute for her to form a reply. "I see," she murmured. "Well . . . that confirms everything I've heard about Lady Ashby. And although you should have had more sense than to conduct an affair with a woman like that, the blame belongs with her—*not* you." She shrugged and smiled faintly. "Besides, you stopped Lord Granville in time. I'll always be grateful for that."

Derek hated her for being so sweetly forgiving. He closed his eyes and rubbed his forehead. "Damn you, what do you want from me?"

"I told you last night."

The mist on his forehead turned to fine droplets, while Derek's pulse drove hard and fast. He'd thought nothing would ever bring him to this. What if he did manage to walk away once more? It seemed he would just come back again.

Sara's gaze was riveted on him, while she waited for what seemed to be endless minutes. She was afraid to speak, her entire body tense with anticipation. All at once he crossed the distance between them and took her in his arms, holding her against his pounding heart. His voice was low and steady as he spoke just above her ear. "Marry me, Sara."

"Are you sure?" she whispered. "You won't take it back?"

It was strange, but with the words said, he felt powerfully relieved, as if some eternally divergent part of himself had just settled into place. "You said you wanted this," he muttered, "even knowing the worst about me. Let it be on your head, then."

Sara nuzzled into the warm side of his neck. "Yes, Mr. Craven," she whispered. "I'll marry you."

Chapter 10

*U*pon being informed of the engagement, Lily was overjoyed and brimming with a multitude of plans. "You must allow Alex and me to give you a wedding, Sara. Something small and elegant in the chapel at Raiford Park, or at our home in London—"

"Thank you," Sara said hesitantly, "but I think we might be married in the village." She looked at Derek questioningly for his reaction to the idea.

His expression was unfathomable, but he answered readily. "Whatever you want." Now that the leap had been taken, he didn't care about the particulars: where, how, or even when. All that mattered was that she was his now . . . and he would pay any price to keep her.

Lily continued excitedly, "We'll give a reception for you, then. I have many wonderful friends to introduce you to, respectable and otherwise. In the meanwhile we'll send you home in one of our carriages, Sara, and Derek can stay here to talk to Lord Raiford—"

"I'm afraid not," Derek interrupted. "Sara and I are both leaving within the hour. In my carriage."

"Together?" Lily looked startled, and then shook her head. "You can't. Don't you realize what people would say when they discovered that both of you were gone?"

"Nothing they haven't said already." He slid a proprietary arm around Sara's shoulders.

Lily drew her slight frame up as tall as possible, adopting the brisk tone of a chaperone defending her charge. "Where are you planning to go?"

Derek smiled slowly. "None of your damn business, gypsy." Ignoring Lily's sputtering protests, he stared down at his fiancée and raised his brows mockingly.

As she met his glinting green eyes, Sara realized he intended to take her to London and keep her with him for the night. Her nerves jangled with alarm. "I'm not certain it's advisable—" she began diplomatically, but he cut her off.

"Go pack your things."

Oh, the arrogance. But it was part of why she loved him, his single-minded determination to get what he wanted. Only blind, bullying stubbornness had enabled him to climb from the gutter. Now that the prospect of marrying her was within his reach, he planned to ensure it by well and truly compromising her. After tonight there would be no turning back. Sara stared at the broad expanse of his chest, conscious of the weight of his arm across her shoulders, the gentle stroke of his thumb and forefinger against her neck. Well . . . reprehensible as it was, she wanted the same thing.

"Derek," Lily said in a steely voice, "I won't allow you to force this poor child into something she's not prepared for—"

"She's not a child." His fingers tightened on the back of Sara's neck. "Tell her what you want, Sara."

Helplessly Sara raised her head and looked at Lily, her face turning a deep shade of crimson. "I . . . I'm leaving with Mr. Craven." She didn't have to look at Derek to know that he was smiling in satisfaction.

Lily sighed shortly. "This entire situation is indecent!"

"A lecture from Lawless Lily on indecent behavior," Derek mocked, leaning over to kiss his long-standing friend on the forehead. "Save it for another time, gypsy. I want to leave before everyone wakes up."

During the carriage ride to London, Derek prompted Sara to tell him about her engagement to Perry. She hedged uncomfortably, not wanting to speak ill of her former fiancé behind his back. "That's all in the past now. I would rather not talk about Perry."

"I want to know how it ended between you. For all I know I'm caught in the middle of a lovers' spat—and you'll go running back to him when the smoke clears."

"But you can't really think that!"

"Can't I?" His voice was dangerously quiet.

Sara frowned at him, although she was inwardly amused. The big, potently masculine creature sitting opposite her was simmering with jealousy, clearly longing to do battle with his unseen rival. "There isn't much to tell," she said evenly. "The trouble began right after Perry proposed. Although we were happy at first, it didn't take long before we discovered that we didn't suit. Perry said I wasn't the same woman he'd known all his life. He said I had changed—and he was right. We'd never argued before, but suddenly it seemed we couldn't agree on anything. I made him very unhappy, I'm afraid."

"So you gave him plenty of lip," Derek commented, looking pleased. His good humor restored, he reached over to pat her familiarly on the thigh. "That's fine. I like my women saucy."

"Well, Perry doesn't." She pushed away his exploring hand. "He wants a woman who will allow him to dictate to her. He wanted me to stop writing, and fill the house with children, and spend the rest of my life waiting on him—and his mother—hand and foot."

"Clodhoppers," Derek said without rancor, exhibiting the typical cockney disdain for simple country folk. He pulled her onto his lap, ignoring her attempts to wriggle free. "Did you tell him about me?"

"Mr. Craven," she exclaimed, protesting the clasp of his hands on her hips.

He locked his arms around her. Their faces were very close, their noses almost touching. "Did you?"

"No, of course not. I tried not to think about you at all." Sara's eyes half-closed as she stared at the tanned hollow at the base of his throat. Disliking the civilized confinement of a cravat, he had removed the starched cloth and unfastened the top button of his white shirt. "I did dream about you," she confessed.

Derek smoothed his hand over her chestnut hair and brought her head closer to his. "What was I doing in your dreams?" he asked against her lips.

"Chasing me," she admitted in a mortified whisper.

A delicious grin curved his mouth. "Did I catch you?"

Before she could reply his lips were on hers. His mouth twisted gently, his tongue hunting for an intimate taste of her. Closing her eyes, Sara made no protest as he took her wrists in his hands and twined her arms around his neck. He stretched one of his legs out to rest his foot on the seat. Caught in the lee of his powerful thighs, she had no choice but to let her body rest on the hard length of his. Leisurely he fondled and kissed her, wringing succulent delight from every nerve. As he began to slide his hand into her bodice, the thick wool fabric of her gown resisted his efforts. Foiled in his attempt to reach her breasts, he pushed a lock of her hair aside and dragged his mouth over her throat. She stiffened, unable to hold back a whimper of pleasure. The carriage swayed and jolted suddenly, forcing their bodies closer with the impact.

Derek felt himself approaching a flashpoint beyond which there was no return. With a tortured groan he pried Sara's voluptuous body away from his and held her away, while he struggled to emerge from a scarlet fog of desire. "Angel," he said hoarsely, nudging her toward the opposite seat. "You . . . you'd better go over there."

Bemused, Sara nearly toppled to the floor from his gentle push. "But why?"

Derek lowered his head and tunneled his fingers into his black hair. He started as he felt her hand brush the nape of his neck. "Don't touch me," he said, more roughly than he intended. Raising his head, he stared into Sara's perplexed face with a crooked smile. "Sorry," he muttered. "But if you don't move away, sweet, you're going to be lifting your heels for me right here."

They entered Craven's discreetly through the side door, being zealously guarded by Gill. "Mr. Craven," he said respectfully, and glanced away from the female guest with a show of tact. But the gray cloak she wore was vaguely familiar. Suddenly recognizing the visitor,

Gill exclaimed with pleasure, "Miss Fielding! I thought we would never see you here again! Back for more research, eh?"

Sara flushed and smiled, not knowing how to reply. "Hello, Gill."

"Shall I tell Worthy that you're here? He'll certainly want to know—"

Derek interrupted in a biting voice. "I'll ring for my bloody factotum if I want to see him. Right now I don't want to be disturbed." If the employees were alerted to her presence, they would all come swarming around her in a matter of minutes. He wasn't in the mood for impromptu celebrations over Sara Fielding's return. He had brought her here for privacy.

"Oh. Yes, Mr. Craven." Gill's eyes widened as understanding dawned. Prudently he buttoned his lips and resumed his station at the door.

Derek brought Sara to the apartments above the club, his hand resting on the small of her back as they ascended the stairs. She paused as soon as they entered the cluster of private rooms, and inspected the surroundings curiously. "It looks different," she commented. Far more tasteful, actually. The rich plum draperies had been changed to a cool, powdery shade of blue. The gold-embossed leather on the walls had been replaced with a coat of gleaming ivory paint. Instead of the intricate Oriental rug on the floor, there was an elegant carpet of English floral design.

"I changed some things after you left," Derek said dryly, thinking of all the ruined furniture and textiles that had been replaced. He had wanted her so desperately that he'd been able to ease the ache only by drinking endless bottles of gin and destroying everything in sight. Now she was there. She claimed to love him. All at once the situation seemed so fantastic that he feared he was having an alcohol dream, and he would wake in a dull stupor to discover that she wasn't there.

Sara wandered from room to room, noting all the changes, and he followed her slowly. As they reached the bedroom, Derek was disconcerted by the heavy silence between them. He was accustomed to provocative banter, seductive smiles, experienced partners. None of the women he had known was hampered by inhibition or modesty. But Sara was quiet, her movements wooden as she went to a vase of cut flowers poised on a bronze side table. Suddenly Derek felt an unfamiliar pang of remorse. The impulse to bring her here had been selfish. He should have let her go back to her family. Like the rutting scoundrel he was, he hadn't given her any choice—

"Is it always this awkward?" Sara asked. Her voice was hushed.

Derek turned to look at her, his gaze falling to the white rose in her hands. She had taken it from the arrangement of hothouse flowers. Nervously her fingers ruffled the fragile petals.

Self-consciously Sara sniffed the pale blossom and began to insert it back into the huge vase. "It's nice to have roses in January," she murmured. "Nothing in the world has such a lovely scent."

She was so innocently beautiful, with the disordered waves of her hair falling around her face. His muscles tightened in response. He would like to have her painted this way, standing by the table with her head turned toward him, the white flower caught in her fingers. "Bring it here," he said.

She obeyed, coming to him and handing him the

rose. He closed his fingers around the plump head of the flower and pulled gently, freeing the petals from their tenuous moorings. Tossing aside the desecrated stem, he opened his hand over the bed. The petals scattered in a fragrant shower. Sara drew in a quick breath, staring at him as if mesmerized.

Derek reached for her, taking her face in his large hands. His rose-scented palm was hot against her cheek as his lips found hers. He tasted her lightly, toying, until she opened to allow the sleek plunge of his tongue. His cradling hands left her face and swept down her back and sides, savoring the shape of her body encased within the heavy gown. Sara leaned against him, lifting her arms around his shoulders. There was a tug at the ribbon that confined her hair, and a rippling curtain of russet locks fell down her back. With a growl of enjoyment Derek sank his fingers into her hair, stroking, twining, bringing handfuls to his face.

A fluttering pulse beat in Sara's throat as Derek reached to unfasten her wool gown. She was unmoving beneath his expert hands, even when the dress dropped to the floor to reveal her crumpled linen undergarments and neatly mended cotton stockings. Slowly Derek sank to his knees before her, pulling her body against his face and breathing through her shift. Sara twitched as if she had been scalded, her small hands coming to rest on his shoulders.

Reaching beneath the hem of the shift, Derek found the waist of her drawers and eased them down to her ankles, followed by her stockings. His hands traveled over her bare legs, his fingers dipping in the hollows behind her knees, venturing up her thighs to her buttocks. She fidgeted in unease but allowed the caress . . .

until she felt his mouth encroaching high inside her leg, his tongue crossing her skin in a burning sweep. Jerking from him with an incoherent stammer, she backed away until she felt the edge of the bed against her hips. She stared at him in round-eyed surprise.

For a moment Derek knew a dismay equal to hers. He had frightened her. Holy hell, he thought . . . and wondered for the first time in his life how to make love like a gentleman. He strove for a measure of restraint, while Sara gave him an apologetic glance. Surreptitiously she pulled long sheaves of hair in front of her, concealing her meagerly clad body. Half-suspecting she might bolt, Derek began to unbutton his shirt.

Sara propped herself against the massive bed, grateful for its support. A whirlwind of panic swept through her as Derek stripped off his white shirt. She switched her gaze to the floor, but not before she had seen how large and formidable his body was, his torso heavily muscled, his chest covered with thick black hair. Silvery scars marked his skin, legacies of his life in the rookery. He was a man of vast experience. All that was new and frightening to her was commonplace to him. He had known countless women who were as familiar with this act as he was. How could he help but be disappointed by her? "You've done this many times before, haven't you?" she murmured, squeezing her eyes shut.

She heard his trousers drop to the floor. "Never with someone I . . ." He paused and cleared his throat. "Never with someone like you." His bare feet padded across the floor toward her.

Sara flinched as his hands slid around her waist, pulling her to his naked body. The heat of his skin sank through the insubstantial layer of her shift. He was aroused, throbbing hard and forcefully erect against her. "Open your eyes," he said. "There's nothing to be afraid of."

She forced herself to comply, staring straight ahead into his chest. Her heart thumped so violently that it seemed to batter against her ribs.

As if he could read her mind, Derek lowered his mouth to her hair and held her tightly. "Sara . . . I'm going to take care of you. I'll never hurt you, or force you to do something you don't want." He took a long breath and forced himself to add reluctantly, "If you want this to stop, then tell me. I probably won't be kind. But I'll wait."

She would never know how much the words cost him. It went against his nature to deny himself what he wanted so badly. He had been deprived of too much when he was young—it had made him selfish to the core. But her needs had become too important to him, her affection too precious to risk.

Sara looked up at him, reading the truth in his face. Gradually her body relaxed against his. "You must tell me how to please you," she said softly. "I-I don't know anything . . . and you know too much."

His black lashes lowered over a flick of green fire. A wry smile pulled at the corners of his mouth. "We'll find some middle ground," he promised, and kissed her.

Willingly Sara dropped her arms as he pushed the shift down her hips to the floor. He lifted her naked body onto the bed, and the scent of roses drifted over them. A fierce blush covered her from head to toe, and she moved to gather the covers around herself. Derek spread her beneath him with a muffled laugh, his hands traveling over her shrinking body. "Don't be shy with me." He kissed the translucent skin of her shoulders and the downy slope of her breast, relishing her lush softness. Raising his head, he stared into her eyes. "Sara, you have to believe . . . I've never wanted anyone like this." He paused, aware of the sublime banality of the words. Yet he was driven to continue like an impassioned idiot, trying to make her understand. "You're the only one who ever . . . Oh, bloody hell."

As he struggled with the words, her small hand came up to his face, sliding tenderly over his jaw. She knew what he was trying to tell her. "You don't have to say it," she whispered. "It's all right."

Derek turned his lips against her palm, and she closed her fingers afterward, as if to hold the kiss for safekeeping. "Everything I have is yours," he said raspily. "Everything."

"I only want you." She curved her arms around his neck and drew him down to her.

His gentleness was astonishing. She had expected the same violent passion of their other encounters . . . but tonight he was no pirate to ravage and plunder. Instead he claimed her with sneak-thievery, exploring her with a stealthy patience that set her nerves on fire. He stole away her modesty, her restraint, her every thought, leaving nothing but a smoldering blaze of sensation.

His hand lightly gripped the round weight of her breast, lifting it as he covered the peak with his mouth. Slowly his tongue traced over the awakening bud, causing the tender flesh to contract. He turned to her other breast, sucking and nibbling until Sara writhed against his mouth. Scooping up a fragrant handful of petals, Derek sprinkled them over her body, gently playful as he nudged them across her skin. Sara arched up to him, abandoning herself to his tender passion. A few delicate petal shards caught in the springy crop of curls between her thighs. He reached down to the soft thatch, but Sara stiffened in surprise and tried to push his hand away.

"No," she protested as he used his leg to pry hers apart.

Derek held her down easily and smiled against her throat. "Why not?" He closed his teeth on the small lobe of her ear. Tracing the fragile rim with the tip of his tongue, licking hotly inside the shell-like curve, he spoke to her in the softest of whispers. "Every part of you belongs to me . . . inside and out. You're mine everywhere. Even here." Cupping his hand between her legs, he toyed with her until he felt a sheen of moisture against his palm. Her weak protests faded into silence as he parted the soft curls and searched her with extreme care. He found her sleek and swollen, sensitive to the touch of his fingers. Pressing, stimulating, he carefully worked his fingers into the slickness, until she gasped and pressed the crescents of her nails into his shoulders.

Derek shuddered with desire, raising himself over her, possessing her mouth with a wet, carnal kiss. Sara responded with her own feminine demand, running her hands over the muscled plane of his back, seeking to pull him more heavily on top of her. Unable to wait any longer, Derek urged her knees wide and positioned himself against her. Carefully he pushed himself inside, easing beyond the virginal resistance. Sara cried out as she was sundered, invaded, in a deep thrust.

Derek held her hips steady as he drove even further, immersing himself in her warmth. His senses hovered on the verge of rapture, and he fought to contain himself as she twisted beneath him in discomfort. "I'm sorry," Derek whispered, closing his eyes. "I'm sorry . . . Oh, God, don't move." Sara subsided against him, her breath falling on his shoulder in delicate puffs.

Gradually he mastered himself and pressed his lips to her drawn forehead. "Is it better this way?" he murmured, shifting his weight.

Sara quivered, feeling the altered pressure inside her. "I-I don't know."

He pushed again, a long, gentle slide. "Or this . . . ?" he asked, his voice hoarse.

She couldn't answer, her lips parting in suspended silence as he began an easy rhythm. Each surge brought a flick of pain, but a deep instinct clamored for her to arch upward, her inner muscles grasping to hold him inside. His black head dropped to her breasts, his mouth pulling at her nipples with gently flirting suction. Lost in a tide of building sensation, Sara felt more slickness emerge between them, until the back-and-forth motion became a smooth, frictionless glide. "Please . . . you must stop," she gasped, while her muscles squeezed around him. "I can't bear any more."

The emerald eyes glittered with triumph. "Yes, you can." He plunged deeper into her struggling body, his thrusts relentlessly regular. With a gasping whimper, she went still beneath him while a great wave of pleasure rolled through her, unmatched by anything she'd ever felt before. He wrapped his arms around her, impelling himself more strongly, prolonging the exquisite spasms. When she was finally satiated, he took his own fulfillment, his body shaking with violent release.

They remained locked together for a long time, relaxing amid the rumpled sheets. Derek reclined on his side and kept her against him, his lips drifting over her forehead and the silken edge of her hairline. Sara smiled in drowsy wonder, breathing in the perfume of the crushed petals and the scent of his skin.

"Was it what you expected?" He traced a gentle pattern on her hips.

She blushed and pressed her face against his chest. "No. It was much better."

"For me too. It was different from—" Derek stopped himself, hesitant to speak of his past experiences.

"From all your other women," she finished for him dryly. "Tell me *how* it was different."

Derek shook his head. "You're the one with the fancy words. I can't explain it."

"Try," she insisted, tugging threateningly at his wiry chest curls. "In your own words."

He covered her plucking fingers with his own, pressing her hand flat. "It was just *better*, all the way through. Especially this part." He cuddled her closer. "I've never felt so peaceful afterward."

"And happy?" she asked hopefully.

"I don't know how 'happy' feels." He sought her mouth for a brief, hard kiss, and his voice turned to rough velvet. "But I know I want to stay inside you forever."

As evening approached, Sara closed herself in the seclusion of the tiled and furnished bathing room. She was nonplussed at the arrival of a housemaid who insisted on making the preparations for the bath: warming towels, drawing and testing the water, setting out a tray of soaps and perfume. Although Sara had heard it was common for aristocratic ladies to require help with their baths, she felt it was unnecessary in her case.

"Thank you, that will be enough," she said with a disconcerted smile as she stepped into the warm water. But the maid waited while she bathed, and held up a heated towel when she emerged. Another towel was employed to pat her back and arms dry. It seemed terribly decadent, allowing someone to do what she was perfectly able to do for herself, but there seemed to be no choice. Sara sniffed curiously at the proffered flacons of perfume, detecting rose, jasmine, hyacinth, and violet, but she declined to use any of them. The maid helped her into a large robe of heavy textured silk. Murmuring thanks for the assistance, Sara was finally able to dismiss the maid. She rolled up the long sleeves of the robe and wandered back to Derek's bedroom, the hem of the garment dragging on the floor behind her.

Clad in a similar robe, Derek was standing in front of the fireplace. He poked at a blazing log with a fire iron. As he glanced at her with a half-smile, the golden-red light played over his black hair and swarthy face. "How do you feel?"

"A little hungry," she replied, and then added self-consciously, "*very* hungry."

Derek approached her, taking her shoulders in his large hands. Smiling, he brushed a kiss on the tip of her nose. "I can do something about that." He turned her to face a table laden with trays and silver-domed platters. "Monsieur Labarge outdid himself for your sake."

"How wonderful, but . . ." Color climbed high in her cheeks. "I suppose everyone must know what we're doing."

"Everyone," he agreed. "I think you'll have to marry me, Miss Fielding."

"To save your reputation?"

Derek grinned, bending to kiss the flash of pale throat revealed by the robe. "Someone has to make a respectable man of me." He led her to the table and seated her. "We'll have to serve ourselves. I dismissed the stewards."

"Oh, good," Sara said in relief. Draping an embroidered napkin on her lap, she reached for a platter of tiny molded pates and puddings. "I think it would be tiresome, having servants hover around all the time."

Derek ladled out a broth flavored with vegetables, wine, and truffles. "You'll get used to it."

"What if I don't?"

"Then we'll let some of them go."

Sara frowned, knowing how difficult it was to find employment in London. Many of the prostitutes she had talked to had once been maids dismissed by aristocratic employers. Cast out in the streets, they had no choice but to sell themselves. "I couldn't dismiss anyone just because I'm not accustomed to being waited on," she protested.

Derek was amused by her dilemma. "Then it seems we'll have to keep the servants." He gave her an encouraging smile, handing her a glass of wine. "You'll have more time for your writing this way."

"That's true," she said, brightening at the thought.

They consumed the supper at a leisurely pace, while the level of wine in the bottle dipped lower and the fire on the grate burned to hot red coals. Sara had never eaten such a delicious meal in her life: succulent lobster and quail meat baked in pastry, and chicken breasts rolled in crumbly batter, fried in butter, and covered with a rich Madeira sauce. Derek kept urging her to try different morsels: a bite of potato soufflé dabbed with soured cream, a spoonful of liqueur-flavored jelly that dissolved on her tongue, a taste of salmon smothered in herbs. Finally replete, Sara collapsed in her chair and watched him as he left to stoke the fire. "Do you eat like this all the time?" she asked contentedly, dabbing her spoon in a delicate almond-flavored custard. "I don't understand why you're not fat. You should have a belly the size of the king's."

Derek laughed and returned to the table, pulling Sara into his lap as he sat down. "Thank God I don't . . . or I wouldn't be able to hold you like this."

She curled against his hard chest and sipped from the wineglass he held to her lips. "How did you acquire such a talented chef?"

"I'd heard of Labarge's reputation, and I wanted the best for my club. So I went to France to hire him."

"Was it difficult to convince him to leave with you?"

Derek smiled reminiscently. "Almost impossible. The Labarges had worked for the family of a French count for generations. Labarge didn't want to break tradition, not when his father and grandfather had been employed by the same family. But everyone has a price. I finally offered to pay him two thousand pounds a year. I also agreed to hire most of his kitchen staff."

"Two thousand?" she repeated in amazement. "I've never heard of a chef being paid so much."

"Don't you think he's worth it?"

"Well, I enjoy his dishes very much," Sara said earnestly. "But I'm from the country. I wouldn't know good French food from bad."

Derek laughed at her artlessness. "What do people eat in the country?"

"Root vegetables, stews, mutton . . . I make a very good pepper pot."

Slowly he stroked the rumbled cascade of her hair. "You'll have to make it for me someday."

"I don't think Monsieur Labarge would allow it. He's very possessive of his kitchen."

Derek continued to play with her hair. "We'll go to a cottage I have in Shropshire." A smile crossed his face. "You'll put on an apron and cook for me. I've never had a woman do that before."

"That would be nice," she said dreamily, lowering her head to his shoulder. But the mention of the cottage had awakened her interest. After a moment she looked up at him with a question in her eyes.

"What is it?" he asked.

She seemed to choose her words carefully. "Mr. Worthy once told me that you own a great deal of property. And everyone says you've made a fortune from the club. I've heard people claim that you're one of the wealthiest men in England. I've just been wondering . . ." She hesitated, recalling Perry's admonition that it wasn't a woman's place to ask about finances. "Oh, never mind."

"What is it you want to know? How much I own?" Derek read the answer in her abashed expression, and he smiled wryly. "There isn't a simple answer to that. As well as my personal holdings, there are estates, mansions, and tracts of land deeded to Craven's in payment of gambling debts. Also a yacht, jewelry, artwork . . . even some Thoroughbreds. Those things aren't strictly mine, since they belong to the club . . ."

"But the club belongs to you," she finished.

"Exactly."

Sara couldn't resist probing further. "What do you count among your personal holdings?"

Derek had the grace to look slightly embarrassed. "Four estates . . . a terrace in London . . . a chateau in the Loire Valley—"

"A chateau? I thought you didn't like France!"

"It came with excellent vineyards," he said defensively, and resumed his list. "A castle at Bath—"

"A castle?" she repeated in bemusement.

He made a gesture as if it were nothing. "It's in ruins. But there are wooded hills with deer, and streams full of fish—"

"I'm sure it's very picturesque," Sara said in a strangled voice. "You needn't go on."

His eyes narrowed on her. "Why do you look like that?"

Sara nearly choked on a mixture of laughter and dismay. "I've just begun to realize how wealthy you are. It's rather frightening."

"You'll get used to it."

She shook her head. "I don't think so."

There was a teasing lightness to his tone, but his eyes glinted oddly as he replied. "You've been compromised, sweet. It's too late to change your mind."

Sara shook her head and stood up from his lap. "I can live with being compromised. Where are my clothes?" She was only jesting, not reading the sudden tension in his face.

"You said you would stay with me no matter what."

"At the time," she said, wandering to the fireplace, "I didn't know that a chateau and a castle would be part of the arrangement." She shook her head in bemusement. "It's almost too much to take in. I think I'd better go back to Greenwood Corners." She didn't know that he had followed her until he spun her to face him. His hand grasped her upper arms with bruising force. Sara was alarmed as she looked up at his harsh face.

"What?" she gasped. "What in the world—"

"I won't let you leave me." His voice was even, but his large body was rigid, his hands hurtful.

She blinked in astonishment. "I don't want to leave you. You must know that I was teasing you!" As his eyes bored into hers, she realized that she had discovered a vulnerable spot, like a thin patch on the surface of a frozen river. In a few careless words she had broken through to the dark depths he concealed so well. He was deadly quiet, still staring at her, while she tried to soothe him. "I won't make a joke of it again. I was just surprised. You . . . you mustn't hold my arms so tightly."

His fingers loosened, and he began to breathe again, in rough surges. All the comfortable ease of the evening was gone. Abruptly they had become strangers. "Nothing would make me leave you," Sara murmured. "You don't trust me yet, do you?"

"I've known too many deceitful women." Derek was bitterly surprised by his own actions. He'd just demonstrated beyond a doubt why they didn't belong together. Trust was only one of many things he couldn't give her.

"All I ask is that you try." Sara leaned toward him, against the slight pressure he exerted to hold her back. She pressed her ear to his wildly beating heart. Faith, constancy, trust . . . He'd known little of such things. He would need time to learn them. "You're far too worldly," she whispered. "You don't want to believe in anything you can't see or touch. It's not your fault. I know why you've had to be that way. But you must try to have faith in me."

"I don't know if I can change."

"You've already changed." She smiled as she thought of the way he'd been when they first met.

Derek was silent for a long moment. "You're right," he said with a touch of surprise.

She kissed his silk-covered chest and sighed. "Perhaps it's odd, but I'm not afraid of being poor. It's what I've always been used to. I am a little afraid of being rich, though. I can't imagine myself living in a mansion."

He wrapped his arms around her. "I used to walk through the rookery, and instead of seeing thieves' kitchens and beggars, I would imagine gold palaces and servants. Rooms full of candles, tables piled with food."

"And you made it all come true."

"I had some luck."

"It wasn't luck." She held him more tightly. "It was you. You're a remarkable man."

He touched her as if he couldn't stop himself. "I want you," he muttered, although the fact was becoming obvious, with her body flattened against his. His palms skimmed the deep curves of her hips, waist, breasts. Roughly he tugged at the silk robe until it parted in the front. Firelight danced over her exposed skin, gilding the porcelain whiteness.

Sara made a hesitant move toward the bed, but he pulled her back to stand before him. He removed her robe, dropping it to the floor. His long fingers wrapped around her breasts, thumbs passing over her nipples in light circles. There was a new, wicked certainty in his touch, for he had already learned what aroused her. Pushing her down to the floor, he nudged her back into the silken pool of their robes. Sara stretched out at his bidding, and he lowered himself over her, blocking the fire glow from the grate. She shivered at the erotic slide of his tongue as he licked the shadowed undercurve of her breast. His mouth wandered over her in open, wet kisses that sent ripples of sensation across her skin. In some places she felt his teeth close on her, eliciting a twitch of startled reaction.

Derek made a prison of his own body, his muscled legs tangling with hers, his weight caging her against the carpeted floor. She couldn't hold back a quiet moan as he pressed himself intimately against her, stiffness and burning silken skin . . . he made a tantalizing motion, a rhythm that promised relief from the sweet torment. Sara lifted herself to him, eager for his possession. But he held back, his green eyes blazing with deviltry.

"Please," she whispered.

He moved downward to kiss her navel, his tongue intruding in the tiny hollow. A few delicate swirls, and he blew softly against the damp circle. He fitted his hands around the deep curve of her waist, then shaped the roundness of her hips in his palms, kneading gently. The feathery brush of curls against his chin was a powerful enticement. He worked his mouth down in the inviting triangle, ignoring her sudden jolt of unwillingness. Hungrily he breathed in the scent of her, his nerves stimulated by the earthy sweetness.

Spurred into action, Sara struggled frantically to escape him. He wrapped his arms up around her thighs, mastering her, and his head dipped low into the space he had made for himself. He swept through the lush curls with short, wheedling touches of his tongue. Sara groaned a denial as he reached deeper into the soft cleft, searching for the intoxicating taste of her body. His fingers wove gently through the patch of curls, separating them. He found the delicate center of sensation and stroked with his tongue, teasing, insinuating deep in the softness. Steeped in pleasure and shame, Sara lay motionless.

The taste of her was maddeningly erotic. He covered the enticing female flesh with his mouth and tugged firmly. At the same time he slid his fingers inside the moist passage, stroking in counterpoint to the steady rhythm of his mouth. Sara cried out suddenly, pulled into a whirling upheaval, her senses overflowing.

As the last tremor subsided, Derek levered his body over hers and pushed himself inside her, gripping her hips in his large hands. He gave a pleasured groan and began to thrust in a sustained motion. Their bodies converged until there was no space left between them. Feeling the shudder of his climax resounding deep against her womb, Sara enfolded him in her arms. She rubbed her face against his gleaming black hair. "I do love you," she whispered in his ear. "And I'll never leave you."

They passed through the center of Greenwood Corners at midmorning. Sara kept away from the windows, knowing the gossip it would cause for her to be seen in the magnificent private carriage. Strolling merchants and village women carrying large baskets on their arms stopped to watch the vehicle's progress. Shopkeepers came outside to remark on the lacquered carriage, the pair of outriders, and the liveried footman in attendance. Such an equipage had rarely, if ever, been seen in Greenwood Corners. A few people followed the vehicle far enough to determine its direction and ran back to report that it was traveling toward the Fieldings' cottage.

When they reached her parents' home, Derek helped Sara from the private carriage. He spoke briefly with the footman before walking Sara along the path that led to the cottage door.

"I wish the night wasn't over," she said, holding his arm tightly.

"There'll be other nights for us."

"Not for a while."

That earned her a piercing glance. "You'll arrange the wedding as soon as possible. Accept Lily's offer of help if necessary."

"Yes, sir." Sara smiled at his commanding tone. "It almost sounds as if you're anxious to marry me."

"It won't be a moment too soon," he muttered.

Sara was glad of his sudden fretfulness, knowing it meant that he was reluctant to be parted from her. She was half-afraid that she had dreamed the last two days. "If you don't come back for me, I'll find you in London," she threatened. "Or I'll send Papa—and he'll bring you here at the end of his old musket."

Derek grimaced. "I'm not certain any man in his right mind would choose me for his daughter."

"Oh, Papa's a wise, dear man. You'll adore each other. Just make certain to speak loudly so he can hear you." They stopped at the door, and Sara turned the handle to open it. "Mama?" she called.

Katie appeared in the doorway with a delighted exclamation, and made a move to embrace her daughter. "Sara, how was the ball? You must tell me everyth—" She stopped at once as she saw the man beside Sara, his dark, broad-shouldered form filling the doorway.

"Mama, this is Mr. Craven," Sara said softly.

Taken aback, Katie stared at the two of them with round eyes. "Isaac," she called, her voice higher-pitched than usual. "Sara's brought someone home with her. A man."

"Has she? Well, let me have a look at him."

Abruptly Derek found himself confronted by two small gray-haired people. Scrutinizing him closely, they welcomed him into the tidy, worn little cottage. There were sprays of dried flowers and herbs, painted pottery, and piles of books everywhere. He had to duck his head to avoid a low overhead beam as he crossed the threshold. As Sara introduced him to her father, they shook hands cordially. The old man's face was engraved with lines of good humor and character, his blue eyes lit with a friendly twinkle.

"Papa," Sara chattered, "you'll remember I mentioned Mr. Craven before. We met during my research in London. He owns a social club." She proceeded to bustle her mother toward the kitchen. "Mama, let's make some tea while the men become acquainted."

They went into the kitchen and closed the door. Dazed, Katie fumbled for the jar of tea while Sara began to pump water energetically at the sink. "You've taken my breath away," Katie remarked, hunting for a spoon.

"Mr. Craven was at Raiford Park this weekend," Sara said, her face mantled with the high color of excitement. "It's a complicated story, but the long and the short of it is . . . I love him, and he proposed to me, and I said yes!"

Katie's mouth dropped. She sat in a chair, fanning her hands over the center of her chest as if to calm her heart "Your Mr. Craven proposed," she repeated numbly.

"He's the most wonderful man in the world. You and Papa are going to love him as much as I do."

"Sara . . . isn't this terribly sudden? Think of all the years you've known Perry—"

"Mr. Craven makes me a thousand times happier than Perry ever could. Don't look worried, Mama. Haven't you always known me to be sensible?" She smiled confidently. "I've made the right choice. You'll see." As Katie began to ask something else, Sara motioned for her to be quiet, while portions of the men's conversation filtered from the other room. Carefully Sara pressed her ear to the door.

". . . you're a little too late in asking, Mr. Craven. Sara already has a fiancé. Young Kingswood."

Sara couldn't stop herself from interrupting. She opened the door enough to stick her head through the space. "He's not my fiancé anymore, Papa. Perry and I became unengaged before I left this weekend."

Isaac looked perplexed. "You did? Why?"

"I'll explain later." She gave Derek an encouraging look and retreated behind the door.

Katie watched her daughter with wry amusement. "There's no need to pop back and forth like a turtle in its shell. I have a feeling your Mr. Craven is quite capable of talking to Papa without any help from you."

Sara rested her ear against the panels again. "Shhh."

". . . I can't say I approve of my daughter marrying a gambler," came Isaac's voice.

"I don't gamble, sir. I own a club where others gamble."

"Splitting hairs, my boy. I don't approve of the whole business. On the other hand . . . I don't approve of men drinking too much, and I suppose I don't hold it against our local tavern owner. Tell me more about this social club. You have fancy women working there, do you? Has Sara met any of these poor fallen creatures?"

"I can't keep her away from them," Derek said dryly.

"My Sara has a kind heart. Drawn to unfortunates. The city is a dangerous place for a girl like her."

Sara opened the door again. "I've never come to any harm there, Papa!"

Derek spoke before Isaac could reply. "Is there any bread to go with the tea, Sara?"

"Yes," she answered, slightly perplexed. "Would you like some toast?"

"Lots of it. Very thin slices." Derek held up his thumb and forefinger to demonstrate.

She frowned at him, realizing he intended to keep her too busy to interrupt again. "Very well," she said grudgingly, and went back into the kitchen.

Isaac regarded the man sitting across from him in a new way, a smile creasing his leathery face. "You're patient with her," he said approvingly. "I'm glad of that. She was always a wilful child. She has her own ideas about things." Derek was tempted to make a sardonic remark, but he kept silent and watched the old man sitting there in his comfortable chair, gnarled hands resting on the knitted blanket over his knees. A fond look came over Isaac's face, and he continued as if to himself, "She was a miracle for Katie and me, born to us long after the time for childbearing had passed. We thank God every day for giving her to us. I could never entrust her to someone who might cause her harm. Young Kingswood is a self-indulgent man . . . but at least he's a gentle sort." The blue eyes met Derek's in a direct, guileless stare. "Mr. Craven, I've brought up my daughter to think for herself. If I were twenty years younger, I wouldn't have allowed her such freedom. But her mother and I are elderly, and as nature takes its course, there will come a time when we won't be here to protect her. I thought it was best to teach Sara to trust her own judgment. If Sara wants to marry you, she will, whether I approve or not."

Derek met his eyes without blinking. "Your approval may not be necessary, sir, but I still would like to have it."

A faint smile came to Isaac's face. "All I want is your assurance that you'll treat my daughter with kindness."

Derek had never talked to another man so earnestly; no maneuvering or shrewdness, nothing but humble honesty. "I want to be more than kind to Sara. I want to keep her safe, and happy, and provide whatever will please her. I don't pretend to deserve her. I'm not educated or wellborn, and even the devil wouldn't have my reputation. My one saving grace is that I'm not a fool. I would never interfere with her writing, or any of the projects she chooses for herself. I would never try to separate Sara from her family. I respect her too much for that. I don't want to change her."

Isaac seemed to find the words reassuring, but there was lingering doubt in his expression. "I believe you are sincere. But marriage, a wife, children . . . That's a load of responsibility you've never had before."

"I wouldn't be here if I weren't prepared for it."

Their conversation was interrupted by an enthusiastic knocking on the front door of the cottage. Isaac's gray brows quirked in curiosity as he rose to answer.

Derek stood up also, and watched intently as a slender young man with pale, longish hair entered the room. His fair forehead was puckered with worried impatience. "I heard that a fine carriage had passed through town," he said rather breathlessly. "Was it Sara? If she's returned, I would like to talk to her immediately."

Hearing the arrival of another visitor, Sara emerged

from the kitchen, followed by her mother. She stopped short in amazement. "Perry," she said weakly.

Somehow Sara had never thought that the two men would have occasion to be in the same room together. The silence was ponderous. She sought the right words to break it, while one part of her mind marveled at the striking differences between the two men.

Perry's handsomeness was fit for poetry. He was as pale and golden as a fairy-tale prince. A crest of pink color extended from his cheekbones across the bridge of his refined nose. His eyes gleamed bright and blue. Derek, by contrast, looked dark and surly, exhibiting all the charm of a sullen cat. He didn't return Sara's glance, all his attention focused on the newcomer.

Mustering her nerve, Sara stepped forward. "Perry . . . I would like to introduce you to Mr. Craven, a . . . a visitor from London."

Perry glanced at the swarthy stranger, and then back at Sara. "Why is he here?" he asked with a petulant frown.

"He and I . . . Well, we . . ." She cleared her throat and said baldly, "He's my fiancé."

"What nonsense," Perry said curtly. "*I'm* your fiancé. You left the village before we could resolve our differences."

"We did resolve them," Sara said, inching closer to Derek. "And I realized that I'm much better suited to Mr. Craven."

"Is this by chance *Derek* Craven?" Perry demanded in outrage. "Why, he's a complete blackguard! Everyone in decent society knows it. I can scarcely believe your father would let him in the house!"

Sara bristled defensively. "I'm beginning to wish he hadn't let *you* in!"

"If this is the company you've been keeping, no wonder you changed so greatly," Perry sneered. "It certainly explains your attempts to satisfy your insatiable lust with me. I've wracked my brains all weekend trying to make excuses for your wanton advances—"

Derek started for Perry with a snarl. "You pompous little runt—"

Yelping with fright, Perry charged outside, his legs a blur as he hurried back to the safety of his home and his mother.

Swiftly discarding the idea of pursuit, Derek turned to Sara. "What did he mean, 'insatiable lust'?"

She hastened to explain. "Well, 'insatiable' means unable to satisfy—"

"I know that," he said in a biting tone. "Why did he say it about you?"

Sara rolled her eyes and shrugged. "It was nothing. I merely tried to kiss him once the way you kissed me, and he . . ." Her voice faded as she realized that her parents were watching the pair of them in dumbfounded silence.

Isaac was the first to speak, a smile twitching the corners of his mouth. "I've seen and heard enough, Mr. Craven. If you and my daughter are already talking about 'insatiable lust,' I think I'd better give you my approval . . . and hope for a quick wedding."

They were married in the village church, the ceremony small and simple. Sara's only concession to Lily's grandiose plans was to allow the church to be filled with fresh flowers and greenery. Surrounded by family and friends, she exchanged vows with a man far different than the one she had always expected to marry.

With Perry, the future had been predictable. Now the coming weeks, months, and years loomed before her in a tangle of possibilities. She sensed the bewilderment of her friends, who had never dreamed that she would spurn Perry Kingswood in favor of a man she barely knew.

But Sara saw Derek for exactly what he was, no more and no less, and she was aware that he might never change. It was enough that he loved her. In spite of his faults, he would take care of her and defend her to the last breath of life. Separately they had different strengths. Together they were complete.

Chapter 11

*L*ate at night it gave Sara a cozy feeling to rest against Derek's hard chest and listen to the sounds of the club below them. If she was very still, she could barely make out the clink of dishes, the drone of patrons and employees, the faint rattle of cribbage counters in bowls, even the sultry murmurs of house wenches as they welcomed guests into their rooms. The club was like a living creature, a splendid monster with a ceaseless pulse of activity. "I like being up here," she murmured. "Quiet and hidden away, while everyone is busy downstairs."

"Enjoy it while you can," Derek advised.

Sara lifted her head in surprise. "What? Why do you say that?"

"I promised your father we wouldn't live at the club."

"But I like living here. Why would my father object?"

Derek smiled sardonically. "He has some strange

notion about not wanting you to stay under the same roof with whores and gamblers."

She propped herself up on her elbows, while a small pucker of worry insinuated itself between her brows. "But how will we manage? You've always lived at the club in order to keep a close eye on everything." Her voice lowered in suspicion. "Are you planning to install me in one of your mansions and forget about me?"

Derek laughed and flipped her to her back, his broad shoulders looming over her. "Much good you'll be to me that way," he said dryly. "I married you to keep you in arm's reach." He drew his hand down her body in a leisurely caress. "Closer if possible."

Sara pushed at his chest in a show of pretended annoyance. "Why do you always try to make love to me when I want to talk about something?"

Derek eased her legs apart. "You always try to talk while I'm making love to you," he countered, kissing her throat.

Sara wriggled out from beneath him and crawled to the opposite side of the bed. "I want this settled," she insisted, pulling the sheet around herself protectively. "I don't want you to move away from the club on my account."

"It's not just for you. I might like to try living in a place where I'm not surrounded by wenches, drunken swells, and thieves all the time. Maybe I'd like to sleep at night without keeping one ear out for a police raid."

"What about your business?"

"I'll still have my thumb on it. Worthy will watch over the place when I'm not here." He began to tug the sheet away from her. "Give me this."

"Where are you planning for us to live?" Sara asked warily.

Derek gave a casual shrug. "I thought we'd start by touring the places we already own. If none of them please you, we'll buy something. Or we'll have it built." In a sudden move he snagged her ankle in his hand and began to pull her toward him. "Come here . . . You have wifely duties to attend to."

She grabbed the edge of the mattress to stop the inexorable slide. "I'm not finished talking!"

"I am. Let go of that." He yanked gently at her leg.

Sara rolled to her stomach, gasping with laughter as she felt him crawl over her. His considerable weight lowered enough to keep her pinned flat. The startling male length of him, roughness, heat, and sinew, pressed from her shoulders to her feet. She giggled suddenly. "You can't do anything this way," she gloated. "And I'm *not* going to turn over."

Derek smiled at her innocence. Pushing her long hair aside, he kissed the downy nape of her neck. "I don't want you to turn over," he whispered. He hoisted himself up enough to settle his hands on her shoulders, manipulating the soft muscles. His touch was deft and easy.

Sara sighed in pleasure. "That's nice. Oh . . . don't stop that."

The soothing pressure traveled over her back, his thumbs finding vulnerable points on either side. She turned her head to the side, breathing deeply. He crouched over her again, his strong hands resting on the swell of her hips, his mouth at her ear. The tip of his tongue edged the fine curve and then ventured inside to flick in a shallow, delicate thrust. For a second all sound was blocked. Sara quivered at the peculiar sensation. After his tongue withdrew from her moist ear, the heat of his breath and the low timbre of his voice seemed more acute than before. "Do you like that?" he whispered.

"I-I don't know."

He laughed quietly and did it again. Sara would have turned over for him then, her body filled with restless impulses. But he kept her face down and forced his hand gently beneath her hips. She gasped as he found the damp triangle between her thighs, his fingers searching expertly. When she tried to twist around, he sank his teeth into the back of her neck, holding her still. "Stay there. I like this view of you."

"Don't," she murmured, thinking he was teasing her.

His voice was vibrant with lust. "Round, sweet, firm . . . You have the prettiest backside I've ever seen."

Her protesting laugh ended in a groan as he goaded her with his hips, pushing her down against his hand. She reached forward and curled her fingers around the mattress, digging deeply. The provocative devil on top of her kept whispering, praising her with earthy accolades, nudging her in a slow rhythm. Caught between his body and his tormenting hand, she felt the tension build inside until a frustrated whimper broke from her throat. Instead of turning her to face him, he straddled her from behind. She floundered in a moment of confusion as she felt his thighs brace against hers. "This way," he said quickly, pulling her hips high. "Let me . . . my sweet Sara . . . I won't hurt you."

He pushed inside her, a heavy, exciting surge. Shocked and aroused, she curved her spine to make it easier for him. He rode her gently, the muscled force of him surrounding her while his hands coasted over her breasts and smooth belly. Sara dropped her head,

smothering her cries against the mattress. A few
strokes more, and she climaxed in shivering ripples
that emptied her of all strength. His hands tightened
powerfully on her hips as he followed her into the
depths of thoughtless rapture.

It wasn't long before their marriage had taken on a
wilful character of its own. Having never experienced
family life, Derek didn't know how to behave like a
husband, at least not the ordinary kind. He seemed
like a half-tamed creature to Sara, unaware of regular
hours for eating or sleeping. The only structure in
their life was what she imposed. Sara tried to make the
changes gradual, unwilling to require too much of him
at once.

One night after waiting up for him past two o'clock,
she dressed in a simple gown and ventured out of their
private apartments, wondering what kept him downstairs. The club was infused with particular excitement,
the drone of voices punctuated with exclamations and
encouragements. Standing inconspicuousy at the edge
of the doorway, she watched the tightly knit crowd
around the hazard table. All of them concentrated on
the roll of ivory dice as if life or death depended on it.
Derek's slim, dark form was visible in their midst. He
was laughing quietly at some quip that had been made
to ease the tension.

"Mrs. Craven." Sara heard Worthy's voice beside
her, and she turned with a smile. She had come to rely
on the factotum almost as much as Derek. Worthy had
been more overtly pleased about their marriage than
anyone else, reassuring her in his quiet way that she
had made the right decision. They had talked for a few
minutes at the reception the Raifords had given after

the wedding. Together they had watched Derek's attempts to wheedle her elderly mother into a dance. "I've never seen him care about anyone the way he does you," Worthy had told Sara. "After you left, it was like watching a man crumble inside. The only reason he went to the weekend at Raiford Park was because he was too pickled to protest when Gill and I loaded him into the carriage."

"Oh, dear." Sara had smiled in sympathetic amusement. "He was drinking quite a bit?"

"Blue ruin," Worthy had confirmed. "But ever since he returned, knowing you were going to be his wife . . . well, he's been a different man. You bring out the best in him. He is determined to be a good husband to you—and he never fails, once he decides to accomplish something."

Just then Derek had managed to coax Katie into a sedate waltz, the pair of them circling the corner of the ballroom with great dignity. "You don't have to convince me of that," Sara had remarked, her eyes gleaming with laughter.

Since the wedding Worthy had done all that was possible to make her comfortable at the club and afford her time and privacy with Derek. The servants were irreproachable in their goodwill and efficiency. Whatever she needed was provided almost before she could ask for it. When she was in the vicinity of the club patrons, Worthy or Gill hovered protectively nearby, ensuring that she was safe from any improper advances.

As another roll of the dice caused the group at the hazard table to murmur excitedly, Sara leaned closer to the factotum. "What's happening?" she asked.

"Lord Alvanley is at the hazard table, playing very

deep. He tends to spend large amounts and run up heavy losses. Naturally he is a great favorite of Mr. Craven's."

"Naturally," Sara repeated wryly. No wonder Derek was following the game closely. Derek's presence tended to encourage spending at the tables, almost as if the players wished to impress him by throwing around their wealth.

"Is there something you require, Mrs. Craven?" Worthy asked.

She shrugged slightly, watching Derek. "I was just wondering . . . do you think it will be very long before the game is over?"

Worthy followed her gaze. "I'll go and ask him. Wait right here, Mrs. Craven."

"Perhaps you shouldn't bother him . . ." Sara began, but he was already gone.

While the factotum made his way to the hazard table, some of the house wenches approached her, led by Tabitha. Although Sara and Tabitha had tacitly agreed never to mention their meeting in Greenwood Corners, the girl seemed to feel partially responsible for Sara's good fortune. She had thanked Sara for not "turning her nose up" at all the house wenches after becoming Derek's wife. "Ye're a fine, gracious lady," she had told Sara, "just like I said you was."

This evening the three house wenches came up to Sara, all of them dressed in brightly spangled finery. Sara greeted them pleasantly.

" 'Tis a slow night," Tabitha commented, sticking a hip out and resting her hand on it as she eyed the assortment of soldiers, aristocrats, and diplomats. "Always is when the play's deep. But after, they rush for the nearest wench, an' sometimes pay double for a flier."

"You'd better take care to 'ide yourself when the game's done," Violet advised Sara sagely. "Mr. Craven would blow up good, were another man to try an' riddle you."

"I'm just waiting for Mr. Worthy to return—" Sara began, but Tabitha interrupted with a gusty laugh.

"I've a notion to bull-bait yer 'usband, Mrs. Crawen, an' show 'im why a man should keep close to 'is wife's bed at night."

Sara shook her head in confusion. "I don't know what you mean, Tabitha. But I won't participate in any attempts to trick Mr. Craven, especially not in front of his friends . . . no . . . *really* . . ."

Laughing merrily, bent on mischief, the house wenches dragged her with them to the hazard table. They took care to keep her concealed in their midst. "Mr. Crawen," Tabitha said casually, "we brung a new girl for ye to try out. She's been waiting to give ye a little knock."

Eyebrows were raised and a few glances exchanged across the table, for the prostitutes usually knew better than to intrude on a game.

Derek gave Tabitha a quizzical frown. "Tell her I don't tumble the house wenches." He turned away dismissively.

Tabitha persisted with glee. "But she's a nice, fresh one. Why don't you take a look?" Giggling, the wenches brought Sara forth. She was flushing and protesting, trying to remove the spangled tuft of plumes they had tucked behind her ear.

Derek laughed suddenly, his expression lightening. He pulled Sara into the crook of his arm. "This one I'll take," he murmured, bending to kiss her temple.

Pausing in the middle of the game, Lord Alvanley

inquired as to the identity of the newcomer. When informed that she was Craven's new bride, Alvanley temporarily deserted his position at the hazard table. The crowd of men watched in amusement as he approached Sara. "My sincerest compliments, Mrs. Craven." Alvanley bowed over her hand and addressed Derek languidly. "You don't have the intelligence I suspected, Craven, if you choose to leave such a pretty creature waiting upstairs in favor of our boorish company."

Derek grinned and bowed in acknowledgment. "At Your Lordship's advice, I'll oblige my wife and retire for the evening." He eased Sara through the crowd and walked away with her.

A rumble of masculine laughter and off-color comments accompanied their exit. "There's a mannerly fellow!" . . . "Oblige her once for me, Craven!"

Red as a beet, Sara apologized as they entered the hall. "I'm so sorry! I didn't intend to take you away. Worthy said the game was important . . . Please, you must go back and attend it."

A smile played on Derek's lips. "It's too late. If you take it upon yourself to fetch me from a high-stakes game, you'll have to face the consequences." Pulling her to the side of the stairs that led to their apartments, Derek bent and covered her mouth with a lusty kiss. "Poor little wife," he murmured, cupping his hands over her bottom and urging her hard against his body. "I haven't done well by you, if you've been left so unsatisfied you had to come looking for me." He nibbled at the tender spot just beneath her ear. "I'll just have to work harder to keep up with your appetite."

"Derek," she protested, her hands working aimlessly over his shoulders as he kissed her again. Her heart began to race, and she couldn't suppress a little moan of pleasure. "I-I was just concerned that you wouldn't have enough sleep for the night."

He strung a necklace of kisses around her throat. "You were right about that. I won't. And neither will you."

"I'll never take you away from a game again," she said, feeling the need to apologize. "I didn't mean to disrupt your evening—"

"I'm glad you did," Derek murmured. He grinned as he stared into her soft blue eyes. "Any time you want me, Mrs. Craven . . . I'm at your service." Sliding his arm around her hips, he nudged her up the stairs.

At first it was a shock for Sara to live so intimately with a man. She had been brought up with modesty and discretion in matters of personal habits, whereas Derek had no inhibitions at all. Although Sara admired the lithe power of Derek's body as he walked across the room naked, she knew she would never be able to expose herself so nonchalantly. He was a physical man, easily aroused and adventurous. One night he could be protective and sweetly tender, taking hours to explore her body with gentle caresses, holding her afterward as if she were a treasured child. The next he would be lusty and insolent, introducing her to sensual arts she had never imagined possible. His range of moods was infinite. She was never precisely certain what to expect from him. His humor could be ribald or exquisitely subtle. He could be quietly understanding or mocking. She had never known anyone so self-controlled, but at odd moments she had a sense of the deep-felt emotions locked inside him. And when she found her new life overwhelming, his arms were the safest haven she had ever known.

They had long conversations in bed at night, talking until they could barely keep their eyes open. Their opinions were sometimes drastically opposed, but Derek claimed to enjoy looking at the world through her eyes, even as he teased her for being an idealist. Perhaps she had affected him more than he knew, for his bitterness seemed to be eroding slowly. At times Sara noticed a trace of boyishness about him, a wont to tease and engage her in bits of nonsense, a new free and easy laugh.

"Mr. Crawen looks 'specially fine these days," Tabitha and the other house wenches had remarked, and Sara knew that it was true. The vital, charismatic quality that had always made Derek attractive seemed to have doubled. Women stared at him covetously wherever they went, causing Sara twinges of jealousy. She took reassurance in his devotion to her. Females might flutter and simper when he was near, but he treated them all with polite indifference. Sara alone was entrusted with his secrets, his affection, his needs, and no other woman had ever come close to holding such a position in his life.

They had a well-deserved reputation for reclusiveness, though it wasn't intentional. In the first whirlwind month of marriage, there simply wasn't time to attend many social events. Sara was busy every waking moment. She set aside a few hours of solitude in the mornings for her writing, and spent the rest of each day making nerve-wracking decisions about the house they were to live in. They had agreed on a place Derek already owned, a handsome town mansion of three stories, surrounded by high-walled gardens. It was a house designed for entertaining. The floor plan centered around a spacious colonnaded hall, which opened into a huge drawing room and dining room. The house was serene and airy, filled with delicate white plasterwork of garlands and ribbons, the walls painted icy shades of green, mauve, and blue.

Derek had dropped the entire project of decorating it into her lap, claiming cheerfully that he had no taste. The truth of that was indisputable. His idea of elegance was to load as much gilt and carving as possible on every spare inch of space. But Sara feared that her own taste might be no better. She enlisted the advice of Lily Raiford and a small number of young society matrons with whom she was becoming friends. Cautiously she chose furniture of simple design, upholstered with pale, richly emboidered brocades. Bed hangings and window draperies were made of light-colored damask and chintz. Sara had ordered splendid framed pier glasses for several rooms, and at Lily's suggestion, small writing tables to hold books, prints, and newspapers for guests to glance at. Her own writing desk was made of glowing rosewood, fitted with rows of compartments and drawers.

Occasionally her labors were interrupted by an evening out with Derek. They attended a play, a musical evening hosted by the Raifords, and a reception for a visiting foreign royal. Suffering under intense scrutiny at these social functions, Sara became aware of the need for suitable clothes. She was reluctant to go to the dressmaker, knowing how expensive it would be. After years of counting pennies, the act of spending large amounts of money made her feel slightly queasy. Buying furnishings for the house was necessary. Buying purely for herself was much more difficult to justify. To her surprise, Derek insisted on accompanying her to Madam Lafleur's shop.

Monique welcomed them extravagantly, her dark eyes smiling in her round face. "*Voici*, the most talked-about couple in London," she proclaimed, meeting them personally at the front of the shop instead of sending her assistants. "How well you look, the both of you! Everyone wonders why you have gone into hiding, but I tell my clients *bien sûr*, of course they will keep to themselves at first! That is the privilege of the newly-married, *n'est-ce pas?*" She regarded Derek speculatively. "You have accompanied your wife here, Monsieur Craven. How generous it is of you to take such an interest!"

Derek gave her a charming smile. "I'm here because my wife has a little problem she won't admit to you."

"*Oh?*" Monique's gaze instantly dropped to Sara's stomach.

Derek grinned and winced as Sara dug her elbow into his side. Leaning toward the dressmaker, he said in a confidential tone, "The problem is she's afraid to spend my money."

"I see." There was a flash of disappointment in Monique's eyes. Clearly she had hoped for a juicy bit of gossip she could spread around London. Her good humor was restored as Derek continued.

"I don't intend for my wife to waste the afternoon trying to talk you into making gowns with less costly fabric and no trimmings. I want her to have the best, and look as elegant—more elegant than any woman in England. Price is no object."

The last four words sent the dressmaker's pulse soaring. "Oh, monsieur . . ." Monique nearly kissed him in her excitement. "She is such a *lovely* woman, your wife."

"Lovely," Derek agreed, his warm gaze falling on Sara. Idly he picked up a stray tendril that had fallen to her shoulder, and curled it around his finger. "There's only one requirement I have. Show enough of her, but not too much. I want certain parts kept for my private admiration."

"I understand," Monique said with an emphatic nod. "Men are tempted by a beautiful bosom, they lose their heads, *et alors* . . ." She shrugged prosaically.

"Exactly."

Monique touched his arm inquisitively. "How many gowns do you have in mind, monsieur?"

Sara was annoyed that the two were conducting the transaction as if she weren't there at all. "Four day gowns," she interrupted, "and two for evening. Six in all. And perhaps a cambric nightgown—"

"Twenty-five," Derek told the dressmaker. "Don't forget gloves, slippers, unmentionables, and everything she'll need to go with the order." Gently he covered Sara's mouth with his hand as she sputtered in protest. His sly green eyes met the dressmaker's over her head, and he winked as he added, "Nightgowns aren't necessary."

Monique chuckled and glanced at Sara's reddening face. "I think perhaps, madam, your husband is part French!"

After interminable weeks of consultations and fittings, Sara found herself in possession of an array of gowns more beautiful than she had ever imagined. They were made of vibrantly hued silks, velvets, and brocades, with small belted waists and flowing skirts worn over crisp petticoats. The deep scoops of necklines were finished with lavish lace borders. Underneath she wore thin, almost transparent drawers that reached only to the knees, and chemises so sheer they could be pulled through her wedding ring. From the milliner she had bought several provocative hats with tiny eye-length veils, bonnets lined with silk, and a turban to which Derek took a violent dislike.

"It covers all of your hair," he complained, lounging on the bed and watching as she tried it on. "And it looks lumpy."

Sara stood before the looking glass as she stuffed coils of unruly locks beneath the headdress. "The problem is that I have too much hair. The milliner said if I cut a fringe across my forehead and took several inches off the bottom, the turban would fit better."

He shook his head decisively. "You're not going to cut any of it."

Sara sighed in frustration as a chestnut curl sprang from beneath the turban and fell over her shoulder. "All my new hats would sit more becomingly if my hair were short. Madam Lafleur said that I have just the right bone structure to wear it in a smart crop."

Derek actually paled. "If you cut all your hair off, *I'll* take a crop to you." Leaping off the bed, he snatched the offending turban from her head before she had time to move.

"Now look what you've done," she exclaimed while her hair tumbled around her. "And I almost had it finished. Give me the turban." Derek shook his head and backed away, clutching the small bundle. Sara made her voice very patient. "The turban, if you please."

"Promise me you won't cut your hair."

Sara couldn't believe he was being so ridiculous. "If I did, it would grow back." She advanced on him and made a quick grab. His arm shot up in the air, holding the turban well out of her reach.

"Promise," he insisted.

"If you knew the price that had been paid for that turban, you wouldn't treat it so cavalierly!"

"I'll pay it a hundred times over, for your promise."

An incredulous smile flitted across her lips. "Why?" she asked, combing a hand through the wild ripples of her hair. "Does my appearance mean so much to you?"

"It's not that. It's . . ." Derek dropped the turban to the floor and circled her slowly. "I like to watch you braid it . . . and the way you let a few curls fall on your neck after you've pinned it up . . . and when you brush it out at night I know I'm the only man who sees it loose and long over your back. It's a part of you that only I can have." He grinned and added, "Among other things."

Sara watched him for a moment, touched by his admission. Although he couldn't admit out loud that he loved her, he said it in more subtle ways . . . his gentleness, his constant praise of her, his generosity. "What other things?" she murmured, backing up against the bed and draping herself over it.

Needing no further invitation, Derek crawled up beside her. He unbuttoned her bodice as he answered. "Your skin . . . especially here. Pure and white as a moonbeam." His fingertips moved tenderly over the firm slopes of her breasts. "And these . . . beautiful . . . I want to cover them with diamonds and kisses . . ."

"Kisses are sufficient," she said hastily.

Derek raked up her skirts. Her hips lifted willingly as he pulled her drawers down. Softly his hand found her. "And this part of you . . . mine alone." His thick lashes lowered, and his breath touched her throat in unsteady surges. He reached for the fastening of his trousers. "Sometimes," he whispered, "I'm so deep inside you I can feel your womb . . . and I'm still not close enough. I want to share every breath . . . every beat of your heart."

Sara quivered as she felt him move against her suddenly, entering her in a thrust that stretched her exquisitely tight. Derek cradled her head in both his hands, his mouth hot on her neck. "Sometimes," he murmured, "I want to punish you a little."

"Why?" She groaned at his purposeful stokes, her head falling back on the pillow. His hands pressed down on her shoulders, holding her steady as he pushed into her center.

"For making me want you until I ache with it. For the way I wake at night just to watch you sleeping." His face was intense and passionate above her, his green eyes harsh in their brightness. "I want you more each time I'm with you. It's a fever that never leaves me. I can't be alone without wondering where you are, when I can have you again . . ." His lips possessed hers in a kiss that was both savage and tender, and she opened to him eagerly.

He had never been so demanding, his body hard and heavy as it met hers in solid blows. She rocked upward to receive him, straining to match his rapid pace, breathing in sobs of frantic need. Her blood pumped furiously, and the sensations sharpened as she sought release. Compulsively she answered his rhythm over and over, until her muscles ached and trembled. He reached down to grip her bottom tightly, pulling her against him, forcing himself even deeper inside her. Their skin was slick with the mingled sweat of their efforts. The friction between them was a slippery, powerful motion that teased their senses to an excruciating pitch. All at once violent spasms of pleasure tore through Sara, and she screamed against his shoulder. The inward ripples of her response wrapped around him tightly, and Derek let his passion burst forth in a glorious rush. In the aftermath he held her tightly, his hands smoothing over her back in repeated strokes. Words dammed up in his chest while he battled silently to drag them out. Sara seemed to understand, for she laid her head against his chest and sighed. "It's all right," she whispered. "Just keep holding me."

"I've never seen you look so fine," Katie exclaimed as Sara entered the cottage. She helped Sara off with her high-necked pelisse and reached out to finger one of the long banded sleeves of the new gown. "What beautiful fabric. It shimmers like a pearl!"

Smiling, Sara turned in a circle and swished the skirts of the corded silk gown. "Do you like it? I'll have one just like it made for you."

Katie regarded the geranium-colored silk doubtfully. "It might be a touch too elegant for Greenwood Corners."

"No, it will be perfect for church on Sunday." Sara grinned mischievously. "You can sit a row or two ahead of Mrs. Kingswood in all your finery, and she'll whisper to everyone that you've gone to blue blazes just like your daughter!"

Katie ruffled her white hair in distraction. "If a new gown doesn't convince everyone I've gone to blue blazes, the new house will for certain!"

Sara smiled at that, recalling the entire afternoon of persuasion it had taken for Derek to convince them to accept his gift of a new house. He had finally won through a mixture of charm and sheer stubbornness. "It's your choice," he had told Isaac and Katie pleasantly. "Either you'll have it here or in London." The next afternoon they had found themselves conferring with Graham Gronow, Derek's preferred architect. Gronow had designed a lovely, classical Georgian house of comfortable size for them. Under construction on a choice plot of land close to the center of the village, the house was a subject of conversation for everyone in Greenwood Corners. Wryly Katie had told Sara that she thought Derek had deliberately made certain the house would be larger than the Kingswoods' manor. Sara hadn't argued, knowing full well that he wasn't above such behavior.

"Derek plans to hire a cookmaid and gardener for you," Sara said, following her mother into the kitchen. "I told him you might want to choose someone familiar from the village. If not, we'll send someone from London."

"Heavens above," Katie exclaimed. "Tell your Mr. Craven we don't need hired help."

"But you do," Sara argued. "What about the days when Papa's joints are too stiff for him to work outside? And now that I won't be able to do my share of the household tasks, you'll need someone to help, and perhaps bring you a cup of tea in the afternoon. Wouldn't you like that?"

"Sara, the whole village is already expecting us to put on airs. Mrs. Hodges says her head spins every time she thinks about us living in a new house. Forty years we've been here, and never thought to leave."

Sara smiled. "Everyone knows it's not in you or Papa to put on airs. And Mrs. Hodges will become accustomed to the idea of you living in another home, just as the rest of Greenwood Corners will. This cottage is too small and old, and when it rains there are more leaks in the roof than I can count. And you may as well brace yourself for another surprise, because I told Derek yesterday that I would like for you to visit us in London. He's going to furnish you with a carriage, horses, and a driver, so you'll be able to travel whenever you want."

"Oh, my." Katie sagged against the kitchen table. "Imagine poor Eppie stabled next to an elegant pair of chestnuts!"

"It'll do her good to associate with higher-ups."

They both laughed, and then Katie's face changed. Her voice was suddenly filled with motherly concern. "How is it for you, Sara? I can't help but worry at times, thinking of you living with him in . . . that place."

" 'That place' is a gambling club," Sara said dryly. "And I'm perfectly comfortable there. But to ease your worry, the mansion will be finished soon, and I'll be living in a proper home."

They began to prepare a tea tray as they talked, the familiar ritual making the conversation easier. "What about Mr. Craven?" Katie asked. "What kind of husband is he?"

A comical expression came over Sara's face. "A *peculiar* one is the best way to put it." Carefully she measured spoonfuls of tea leaves into a chipped yellow pot. "Derek is a very complicated man. He's not afraid of anything . . . except his own feelings. He isn't able to admit that he loves me, but at times I see it on his face, and it's as if the words are trying to burst from him."

Katie wore a perturbed look. "Is there any likeness

between the two of you, Sara? Anything at all you have in common?"

"Yes, but it's difficult to explain." Sara smiled thoughtfully. "We're eccentric in our own ways, but somehow we fit together. I'm certain that an ordinary marriage wouldn't have done for either of us. We're often in each other's company, but we have our separate interests. I have my books and my writing, and Derek busies himself with the club and all his intrigues—"

"Intrigues?"

"Oh, it's a constant amazement, the assortment of people who visit him at all hours. One moment I'll see him conferring with urchins and ruffians right off the street, and the next he's talking to the ambassador of France!"

Katie shook her head in wonder. "I'm beginning to understand what you meant by 'complicated.'"

Sara hesitated and then set down the spoon and the jar of tea. "I'm going to tell you something, Mama, but it mustn't go past these walls, or Derek will have my head. The other day I happened to find receipts and records of charity donations in a drawer of his desk. I couldn't believe my eyes when I saw the figures written out. He has given *immense* sums of money to schools, orphanages, and hospitals, and that doesn't include what he spends on his political causes!"

"Did you ask him about it?"

"Of course! I asked him why he would give all of it in secret, and deliberately let everyone think that he never cares about any cause but his own. It's as if he wants people to have a bad impression of him. If they only knew how much good he's done . . ."

Katie leaned forward in fascination. "What did he say?"

"He laughed and said that if people were told he had made a charitable contribution, no matter how great or small, they would claim he was trying to polish his own reputation. And there was a time, he said, when he gave money to orphans for just that reason—to make certain others thought well of him. He said he's done more bootlicking in his life than any man should have to, and that now he can afford to do what he wants without giving a damn . . . er . . . without giving a thought to what others say. He said that he's entitled to his privacy, and that as his wife I'm obliged not to tell anyone." She raised her brows significantly. "Now what do you think of that?"

Katie was frowning. "He sounds quite odd, if you ask me."

Sara felt a carefree laugh bubbling up from inside her. "From what I can tell, the *ton* considers Derek and me to be an odd pair."

"So do the villagers," Katie said bluntly, and Sara laughed again.

Without a doubt the *ton* would have disdained the Cravens had they sought to court its favor. Between them they didn't have a thimbleful of blue blood. No families of distinction, no histories of any merit . . . nothing but a vulgarly large fortune built on the habits of wealthy men who liked to gamble. However, the Cravens cared so little for the *ton*'s approval that it had reluctantly been given to them by default. And as Derek remarked crudely but accurately, money was a good grease for social acceptance.

But while the *ton* accorded them grudging admission into their elevated circles, the public gave the Cravens outright adoration. It astonished everyone, including the celebrated couple themselves. "The day has finally come when pigs fly," the *Times* acerbically noted, "and a cockney and a country maid have become the center of all fashionable observation in London."

Derek was at first puzzled and then wryly resigned to the small uproar they created whenever they appeared in public. "Next month they'll take an interest in someone else," he assured Sara. "We're a temporary curiosity."

What he didn't expect was the fascination of the populace for a pair of commoners who lived like royalty. They were labeled "refreshing" by one source, "upstarts" by another. A caricature by George Cruikshank depicted them as flash gentry trying to ape the rarefied manners of the elite. The Cravens were a window through which ordinary people could view the lives of the upper crust and imagine themselves in such a position.

The interest was stirred even more when it became known that Sara was the reclusive author of *Mathilda*. There was speculation in coffeehouses and pubs across the city about whether Mrs. Craven was Mathilda in disguise. Sara heard the name being called out from a crowd observing the arrival of theatergoers as they attended a production at Drury Lane. "Look 'ere, Mathilda!" a man called out as she emerged from the carriage. "Show us yer face!" As Sara glanced toward him in bewilderment, a cheer scattered across the gathering. "Mathilda! Ye're a lovely sight, dearie!"

" 'Show us your face,' " Derek muttered beneath his breath as he escorted Sara up the front steps. "Soon you'll be declared public property."

Sara began to laugh. "I think they just want to believe there is a Mathilda somewhere."

Before going to their box seats, they drifted apart to exchange social pleasantries with the multitude of acquaintances who swarmed around them. Husbands who were assured that Derek was no longer crawling into their wives' beds had begun to treat him with cautious pleasantness. People Sara barely knew or had never met took special care to fawn over her. Her hands were repeatedly decorated with kisses from dandies and smooth-voiced foreigners, while she was overwhelmed with praises for her hair, her gown, her charm. For the most part they were respectful . . . except for one insolent knave whose voice was all too familiar.

"Damn my sparklers if it ain't Mathilda!"

Sara turned warily to confront Ivo Jenner's cheeky grin. "Mr. Jenner," she said, acknowledging him with a polite nod.

His sly gaze roved over her. "Fancy little warming pan, you are. Crawen's a lucky bastard to 'ave you in his bed ewery night. 'E doesn't deserve such a fine splice as you."

"Mr. Craven is an exemplary husband," she murmured, trying to edge away from him.

"Fine-feathered gentleman, your 'usband," Jenner scoffed. "Tell 'im 'e's nofing but an apple-polishing cockney bastard—"

"If you don't leave right now," Sara interrupted, "you'll have a chance to tell him yourself."

Jenner followed her gaze, his insolent smile broadening as he saw Derek shouldering his way toward them. By the time he reached them, Jenner had melted into the crowd.

Derek seized Sara's arm. "What did he say to you?"

She blinked in wary surprise at his rough tone. "Nothing of any import."

"Tell me."

"It was *nothing*," she said, wincing in pain. She twisted her arm free. "Derek . . . please, don't make a scene."

He seemed not to hear her. His gaze was riveted on Jenner's retreating figure. "I'll teach that weedy bastard to lay a blasted finger on what's mine," he growled.

Sara's lips tightened in annoyance. He was behaving like a mongrel fighting over a bone. She knew why Jenner always angered him so easily—Jenner's swaggering cockiness reminded Derek of his own past. "I'm not your property," she said.

Although Sara's voice was as gentle as always, there was a cool note in it that raised Derek's hackles. He looked at her sharply. She had never spoken to him that way before. He didn't like it. "The hell you're not," he said gruffly, daring her to argue.

She kept her gaze averted from his. "I would like to go to our seats now."

For the rest of the evening Derek was infuriated by the reserve in her manner. She virtually ignored him, all her attention focused on the play. It was clear he had displeased her. Sara's withdrawn manner was worse punishment than any argument could have been. He steeled himself to be just as cool to her. If she was expecting to wring an apology from him, she could wait until the devil went blind. She was *his*—he had a perfect right to defend her against the advances of scum like Ivo Jenner!

After they returned home and retired for the evening, they kept to their own sides of the bed. It was the first night of their marriage that they didn't make love. Derek was miserably conscious of her soft body so close by, his own acute desire for her, and, even worse, his need for her affection. In the morning he was vastly relieved when Sara awoke in her usual good humor, the previous night apparently forgotten.

Derek lounged in the bathing tub while she perched on a nearby chair and read the daily paper to him. The *Times* carried detailed descriptions of Sara's ivory gown and the five-carat blue diamond on her finger, the Cravens' reported opinions of the play, and speculation on whether Derek was truly a "reformed rake." "There's not a word of truth in any of it," Derek said. "Except the part where they said you were resplendent."

"Thank you, kind sir." Sara set down the paper and reached over to toy with one of the large soapy feet propped on the porcelain rim of the tub. She wriggled his big toe playfully. "What about the part that says you're reformed?"

"I'm not. I still do everything I used to do . . . except now only with you."

"And quite impressively," she replied, her tone demure.

He liked that, she could see. His green eyes gleamed, and he drew his foot down into the bath. "The water's still hot," he said, making inviting swirls with his hands.

Sara smiled and shook her head. "No."

He slid lower into the water, watching her steadily. "I need help with my bath. There's a spot I can't reach."

"Where?"

"Come in here and I'll show you."

Unable to resist his roguish appeal, Sara relented. Standing up from the chair, she dropped her robe and night rail to the wet tiles and blushed under his inter-

ested gaze. Carefully she stepped into the tub. Derek
reached up to help her and lowered her gently into the
warm water. She shivered at the feel of him beneath
her, slippery and strong, his muscled arms and legs
wrapping around her. His black hair gleamed like the
pelt of a wet seal.

"Where is the soap?" she asked, brushing a clot of
foam away from his jaw.

"I dropped it," he said regretfully, and drew her
hand down into the cloudy water. "You'll have to find
it."

She giggled and splashed him. Puddles of water col-
lected on the floor of the bathing room as they played.
Linking her dripping arms around his neck, she
pressed a wet kiss to his lips. "I'm afraid I can't find the
soap," she whispered, her body drifting buoyantly
against his.

"Keep looking," he encouraged throatily, and
sought her mouth for another kiss.

In his private moments Derek acknowledged to himself that all Lily had ever claimed about marriage was
true. The sheer convenience of it was stunning. His
wife was always close at hand, her small presence grac-
ing his home, her hand on his arm when they appeared
in public, the lingering scent of her perfume haunting
him sweetly when they were apart. He knew it would
be impossible ever to tire of her, for she was as vital to
him as the very air he breathed. And yet he felt himself to be an imposter with every husbandly kiss he
placed on her forehead. It was as if he had been given
a handsome suit of clothes that didn't quite fit. He
found himself studying Sara intently, waiting for the
clues that he had made mistakes. He wasn't fool

enough to think he was behaving the way most husbands did—whatever that was. But she gave him precious little guidance, and he was left to walk blindly along a steep and unfamiliar path.

Frequently Derek felt a deep sense of unease, as if some invisible, monumental debt were being accumulated in his name. There was also the occasional bite of resentment when he realized she had become the source of all pleasure to him, all comfort and peace. She was the first human being he had ever needed. He had lost his freedom in a way he had never imagined possible, bound more securely by her love than by a mile's length of iron chains.

Missing Derek's presence in bed, Sara crept downstairs in the early hours of the morning and found him alone in the central gaming room. It was eerily quiet and cavernous without the usual crowd of patrons and employees. Derek was at Worthy's corner desk with several decks of cards aligned carefully across the polished surface. Sensing her presence, he glanced over his shoulder with a noncommittal grunt.

"What are you doing?" Sara asked with a yawn, curling into a nearby chair.

"Worthy suspects one of my dealers is cheating. I wanted to look at the cards he was using tonight, just to be certain." Derek's mouth twisted with displeasure as he indicated one of the shallow stacks. "That's a marked deck if I've ever seen one."

Sara was perplexed. She had seen all the elaborate rituals at the tables, the ceremonious openings of fresh boxes of cards. "How could any of the dealers mark the cards? There's no time or opportunity . . . is there?"

Derek picked up a new deck, shuffling so expertly that the cards were nothing but a blur. He dealt a hand to her, facedown. "Tell me which is the queen."

Sara squinted at the backs of the cards. "I can't. They're all the same."

"No, they're not. I just marked the queen." Derek picked up the card and showed her the tiny, nearly indistinguishable notch he had made with his thumbnail on the edge of the card. "There are other ways of marking. I could use ink on the tip of my finger to leave smudges. I could bend them just a little. Or keep a bit of glass-work up my sleeve."

"A mirror?" she asked.

He nodded, continuing to toy with the cards. "If a deck has been professionally marked, you can tell by riffling the deck and watching the backs. Any line work or blockouts will jump out." The cards seemed to come to life in his hands as he shuffled once more. "Here's how to stack the deck . . . but the motion has to be smooth. It takes practice in front of a mirror." The cards were a flowing stream in his hands. He held them tenderly, his long fingers manipulating and flexing until the deck formed a bridge, a waterfall, a snapping fan.

Sara watched in awe. As agile as the dealers in the club were, she had never seen any of them handle cards with such ease. That, coupled with his extraordinary mind for numbers, would make him an invincible opponent. "Why don't you ever play?" she asked. "I've never seen you in a casual game with Lord Raiford or your other friends. Is it because you know you would always win?"

Derek shrugged. "That's one reason," he said without conceit. "The other is that I don't enjoy it."

"You don't?"

"I never did."

"But how can you be so good at something and not enjoy it?"

"Now there's a question," he said, and laughed softly, setting aside the cards. Leading her to the hazard table, he took her by the hips and lifted her up. She sat on the edge of the table, her knees pushed apart as he stood between them. Derek leaned forward, his mouth a warm, gentle brand. "It's not like your writing, sweet. When you sit at your desk, you put your heart and your mind into your work, and it gives you satisfaction. But cards are just patterns. Once you learn the patterns, it's automatic. You can't enjoy something if it doesn't demand a little of your heart."

Sara caressed his black hair. "Do I have a little of your heart?" A moment after she asked, she regretted the question. She had promised herself not to push him, not to demand things he wasn't ready for.

Derek's eyes were shadowed green as he stared at her without blinking. He leaned forward, and his lips sought hers, kindling a warmth inside her that rapidly leapt to bright flame. Sara shivered as she felt him raise her skirts to her waist. He wedged himself tighter between her spread knees. They kissed ardently, groping underneath confining clothes, clumsily plucking at buttons in impetuous haste.

Sara gasped as she felt his hot, intimate flesh rising against her body. "Not here . . . Someone will see . . ."

"They're all gone." Gently he bit into her neck.

"But we can't . . ."

"Now," he insisted, pulling her head against his shoulder as he took her there on the hazard table, making her shudder in helpless pleasure.

*   *   *

Sara was alone in the private apartments over the club, viewing herself in the long mirror of the bedroom. She was dressed to attend the birthday dinner of Lord Raiford's seventeen-year-old brother Henry. On private occasions such as this the Raifords surrounded themselves with warm, enjoyable company. Sara knew the evening would be filled with wit and laughter. Derek had gone with Alex to help deliver Henry's present, a shining Thoroughbred horse, to Swans' Court before the boy arrived home from Eton.

Sara smoothed the skirt of her green velvet gown. Low-cut and severe in its simplicity, the gown was adorned only by a row of six golden clasps that held the split front of the skirt together. She was wearing a necklace Derek had given her to mark their first month of marriage, a gorgeous creation of diamonds and tumbled emeralds that lay in intricate strands over her chest. Admiring the sparkling necklace in the mirror, Sara smiled and turned to view it from another angle.

Suddenly her heart stopped.

The reflection showed there was someone behind her.

Whirling around, Sara stared with wide eyes at the golden-haired woman who held a pistol pointed directly at her.

Chapter 12

*L*ady Ashby's face was taut, her eyes brilliant with madness and hatred.

Sara was the first to speak, hearing her own calm voice with a sense of amazement. "You must have come through the hidden passages."

"I knew about them long before you ever met him," Joyce sneered, her gaze darting to the huge gilded bed. "I was with him in that bed too many times to count. We were magnificent together. We invented things that had never been done before. Don't move." Her grip on the gun was steady.

Sara took a quick, shallow breath. "What do you want?"

"I want to have a look at the woman he's taken as his wife." Joyce smiled contemptuously. "Covered in velvet and jewels . . . as if that might fool others into thinking you're a lady of consequence."

"A lady such as yourself?"

Joyce ignored the jab, staring mesmerized at the

necklace that glittered against Sara's pale skin. "Those emeralds are the exact color of his eyes. No one else has eyes like that." She glared at Sara in crackling fury. "I said don't move!"

Sara froze, having begun to inch toward the long tasseled rope that would ring the servants' bell.

"You must be pleased with yourself," Joyce said, "admiring yourself in your fine gown, with his ring on your finger. You think you have what I covet most. You think he belongs to you. But your marriage means nothing. He belongs to *me*. I put my mark on him."

"He doesn't want you," Sara whispered, her eyes locked on Joyce's vindictive face.

"You country simpleton! Do you actually think you've had any more of him than a hundred women could claim? I know him every bit as well as you do. I know the pattern of hair on his chest, the smell of his skin. I've felt his scars beneath my hands, and the muscles moving on his back. I know what it is to have him inside me . . . the way he moves . . . slow and deep . . . just before he finds his release." Joyce's eyes half-closed. "A gifted lover, your bastard husband. No other man on earth understands a woman's body as he does. A big, sensual beast, with no conscience and no scruples. He is my perfect counterpart—and he knows it."

Swiftly Sara darted to the bellpull and gave it a frantic jerk, expecting to hear the explosion of the pistol. But Joyce didn't fire. Trembling and white, Sara faced her. "The servants will be up here right away. I suggest that you leave, Lady Ashby."

Joyce regarded her with contempt. "What a ridiculous creature you are." Deliberately she reached over and knocked the lit oil lamp from the dresser.

Sara gave a cry of horror as the globe broke and the puddle of oil ignited. Immediately the pool of fire spread outward, flames licking hungrily at the carpet, woodwork, and draperies. "Oh, God!"

Joyce's face was painted gold and red by the rearing, malevolent light. "You can die by smoke and fire," she said in a guttural voice, "or a bullet. Or . . . you can choose to do exactly as I tell you."

Derek and Alex were several streets from St. James when they realized something was terribly wrong. Bells were tolling. Carriages, horses and pedestrians clogged the area. The sky was filled with a dull red glow that came from a blaze somewhere on the horizon. "Fire," Alex said tersely, staring out the window of the carriage.

"Where?" A cold feeling settled over Derek, collecting in the pit of his stomach. The carriage progressed with excruciating slowness while the outriders did their best to forge a way through the crowded streets. His sixth sense, always accurate, warned of disaster. "It's the club," he heard himself say.

"I can't say for certain." Alex's voice was calm, betraying none of the anxiety he was feeling. But one of his hands was gripped around the curtain at the window, exerting so much tension that the stitches in the fabric began to pop.

With a muffled curse Derek opened the door of the carriage and leapt out. The vehicle moved so slowly that it was faster to walk. He shouldered his way through the mob that was gathering to watch the fire. "Craven!" He heard Alex behind him, following at a distance. He didn't pause. The insistent tolling of the bells filled his ears, reverberating in thunderous crashes. It couldn't be his club. Not after he'd spent years of his life working, stealing, suffering for it. He'd built it with his own sweat and blood, with pieces of his soul. God, to watch it all disappear into smoke and ashes . . .

Derek turned the corner and made an incoherent sound. The gambling palace was roaring. The growl of fire was everywhere; the sky, the air, even the ground seemed to tremble. Derek staggered to the scene and watched as his dreams burned in an unholy blaze. He was mute, breathing and swallowing, trying to understand what was happening. Gradually he became aware of familiar faces in the awestruck crowd. Monsieur Labarge sat on the side of the pavement, numbly holding a copper pot he must have carried from the kitchen, too panicked to set it down. Gill was standing with the house wenches, some of them angry, some crying.

Worthy was nearby, the flames reflected in his spectacles. Sweat trickled down his cheeks. He turned and saw Derek. His face twitched convulsively. He tottered forward, his voice unrecognizable as he spoke. "Mr. Craven . . . it spread too quickly. There was nothing they could do. It's all gone."

"How did it start?" Derek asked hoarsely.

Worthy removed his spectacles and mopped his face with a handkerchief. He took a long time to answer, having to choke the words forth. "It began on the top floor. The private apartments."

Derek stared at him blankly.

Two police officers rushed by them, a snatch of hasty conversation floating in the air behind them.

". . . knock down the next building. . . make a fire gap . . ."

"Sara," Derek heard himself say.

Worthy bent his head and shivered.

Derek drew close to Worthy, gripping the factotum's shirtfront. "Where is she? Where is my wife?"

"I've questioned the employees," Worthy answered, gasping as if it were painful to talk "Several of them . . . confirmed she was in the club."

"Where is she now?"

"Sir . . ." Worthy shook his head and began to make an odd gulping sound.

Derek let go of him and reeled back a few steps, staring at him dazedly. "I have to find her."

"It happened too quickly," Worthy said, trying to control his tears. "She was in the apartments when it started. She couldn't have gotten out."

There was jangling confusion in his head. Disoriented, Derek swerved in a half-circle. He felt very strange, all his skin prickling. "No, I . . . *No.* She's somewhere . . . I have to find her."

"Mr. Craven?" Worthy followed him as he made his way into the street. "You mustn't go in there. Mr. Craven, wait!" He took hold of Derek's arm.

Derek shook him off impatiently, his purposeful strides gaining momentum.

In a sudden panic, the factotum flung himself at Derek, using his slight weight and wiry strength to hold him back. "Help me stop him!" Worthy screamed. "He'll run straight into the middle of it!"

Derek growled and shoved him away, but other hands descended on him, shoving him down to the ground. He cursed and tried to rise again, only to find himself surrounded by a crowd of men intent on restraining him. Enraged, he began to fight like a rabid animal, roaring and struggling to break free. Distantly he heard Alex Raiford's voice. "Derek . . . for God's sake, man . . ."

"Sara! Sara—"

Someone clubbed him, a violent blow to his skull. Derek arched against the pain with an animal whimper. "My . . . wife," he gasped, his brain on fire, his thoughts collapsing like a house of cards. He gave a quiet groan and plummeted into blackness.

Lady Ashby had taken Sara to the underground wine cellar at gunpoint. They left the club through one of the hidden doorways. It had been designed to allow patrons an easy escape route to avoid the embarrassment of being caught in the club during a police raid. As she emerged from the cellar to the fresh outside air, Sara was surprised to see a hired carriage waiting for them. "Get in," Joyce muttered, jabbing her in the back with the muzzle of the pistol. "And don't try to appeal to the driver. He's being paid well to keep his mouth shut and do as I bid him."

Once inside, they sat on opposite seats. Joyce kept the pistol pointed at Sara, relishing the power of life and death over her prisoner. The carriage began to move.

Sara clasped her trembling hands in her lap. "Where are we going?"

"To an Ashby holding in the country. An old medieval house." Now that her plan was progressing exactly as she'd intended, Joyce was casual, even conversational. "Most of it has crumbled over the centuries, except for the central core and the tower. No one ever goes there."

"How far is it?"

"We'll travel a good hour and a half. Perhaps two."

She smiled mockingly. "Would you like to know why I'm taking you there? I'm not going to tell you. I'm saving it as a surprise."

Sara wondered if the fire had spread throughout the club, or if by some miracle the employees had been able to contain it. Soon Derek would return from his errand with Alex. She felt ill at the thought of what he might face. He would discover that she was missing . . . He might be injured in the attempt to find her. Suddenly she was terrified for his sake, wondering if he would be in danger, if he would think she was dead . . . Agitatedly she touched the heavy necklace at her throat, worrying the smooth emeralds between her fingers.

"Give that to me," Joyce said sharply, watching her.

"The necklace?"

"Yes, take it off." Joyce watched as Sara unhooked the glittering treasure from her neck. "A peasant woman with a necklace fit for a queen," she sneered. "You don't have the grace or bearing to wear it properly. Give it to me." Her eager fingers wrapped around the necklace, and she snatched it away. Setting it on the seat beside her, she toyed lovingly with the web of emeralds and diamonds. "He gave me presents . . . a bracelet, a necklace, jeweled combs for my hair . . . but nothing as fine as this." She smiled at Sara tauntingly. "The day he gave me the combs, he said that he'd imagined making love to me wearing jewels in my golden hair and nothing else. He much prefers blond hair to dark, did you know that?"

Sara kept her face blank, refusing to let the other woman see that her remark stung. Joyce began another sneering litany of insults and boasted about Derek's sexual prowess until anger and jealousy roiled unpleasantly in Sara's stomach.

* * *

A woman's voice touched Derek gently, luring him from the welter of darkness. Something was wrong . . . Some strange coldness was all around him, inside him, a sinister shadow that had soaked through every inch of his body. He stirred groggily, wanting comfort. "Sara . . ."

"I'm here, darling." It was Lily's voice, sounding thick and odd.

Derek shook himself awake and groaned at the throbbing pain in his head. "Jesus." He blinked and sat up clumsily, squinting at his surroundings. He was in the Raifords' carriage, pulled to a halt in front of Swans' Court. Alex was next to him, resting a steadying hand on his shoulder. Derek's chest hurt. He felt as if he'd been beaten. "What happened?" he mumbled, rubbing his eyes.

Lily stood at the door of the carriage, her tear-streaked face illuminated by the side lamps. Her eyes were swollen. "Come into the house with us, Derek. Careful—let Alex help you."

Derek obeyed without thinking, discovering as he stumbled out of the carriage that he wasn't steady on his feet. Standing next to the vehicle, he braced a hand against the smooth lacquered side and tried to clear his head. Alex and Lily were on either side of him. Both of them looked at him strangely. He began to remember . . . the fire, the club . . . Sara.

"Where is she?" he asked. He was infuriated by the glance they gave each other. "Damn the both of you, answer me!"

Alex's gray eyes were compassionate. He replied in a quiet voice, "She's nowhere to be found, Derek. She was caught in the fire. She couldn't have survived."

Derek made a rough sound, backing away from them. The nightmare was upon him again. He began to tremble.

"Derek," Lily said softly, her eyes glistening, "you're not alone. We'll help each other through this. Come inside. Come, we'll get a drink."

He stared at her without expression.

"Derek—" she coaxed, but suddenly he had vanished, moving swiftly into the night until it swallowed him whole.

Startled, Lily called out after him, and then turned to Alex. "You must follow him," she said urgently. "Alex, bring him back!"

He slid his arms around her. "And then what? Short of knocking him unconscious, I can't make him stay." Lifting her chin, he stared into her eyes. "He'll come back," he reassured her gently. "He has nowhere else to go."

Exhausted by her own frantic thoughts, Sara was wearily surprised when the pace of the carriage eased and then stopped. It had seemed as if the wheels would never cease turning, taking her farther away from London with every torturous minute that passed. Midway through the journey Joyce had lapsed into silence, fumbling awkwardly to clasp the emerald necklace around her throat while retaining possession of the gun.

Sara had contemplated her quietly, pondering the woman's obsession with Derek. Joyce Ashby was insane, or at the very least mentally unbalanced. She seemed like a cruel, selfish child in an adult body. She valued no life but her own, and felt no sense of remorse for her actions. In her mind there would be no consequences for anything she did.

Why had Joyce been allowed to go about unhindered and cause such harm? Surely Lord Ashby must be aware of his wife's actions. Sara wondered what kind of man he was, and why he hadn't taken Joyce in hand long before now.

The driver opened the door of the carriage and looked inside. The strange young-old look about him defied any accurate guess of his age. He had a thin, whiskery rat face. His colorless eyes shifted nervously from the pistol to Joyce's face. "M'lady?" he questioned.

"We're getting out," Joyce said. "Stay here until I return."

"Aye, m'lady."

Sara spoke swiftly, staring hard at the driver. "You can't allow this. Don't be a fool. The law will hold you responsible for what happens to me here—and if not, then my husband will!"

The man flinched and ducked away, ignoring her.

"Get out," Joyce sneered, gesturing with the pistol.

Sara climbed to the ground, her legs cramped from the long ride. She shot a glance at the driver, who had gone to the front of the carriage with the horses. Since he apparently had no conscience to appeal to, she tried threats. "My husband is Derek Craven, and when he finds out about this, he won't rest until he's made you pay—"

"He won't do anything to help you," Joyce said, prodding Sara with the pistol. "Start walking."

The path was illuminated by the carriage lantern Joyce carried. They approached the medieval structure, little more than a mutilated shell of stonework. The windows and doors had crumbled, giving the fortified house the appearance of a jaw with gaps of missing teeth. Slowly Sara entered the central hall. Mice and vermin scuttled in all directions, alerted to the presence of intruders.

Annoyed by Sara's hesitant pace, Joyce brandished the gun and pushed her toward the broken stone steps that led up to the tower. "Up there," she said brusquely.

Slowly Sara mounted the first step. Her mouth was dry with fear. She broke out into a heavy sweat, liquid fear seeping from her pores. "Why?"

"There's a room at the top with a bar across the door. I'm going to keep you there. You'll be my own private pet. From time to time I'll come and visit you, and tell you all about your husband. We'll find out how long he grieves for you, and how long it takes before he comes back to my bed." Joyce paused and added smugly, "Perhaps I'll even show you ways to pleasure me, and you'll show me exactly what your husband finds so compelling about you."

"You're disgusting," Sara said in outrage.

"You might say that now, but after a few days you'll do whatever I want in return for food and water."

Sara's nerves twitched rebelliously, demanding action. She would rather die at this moment than be at the mercy of a madwoman for some indefinite length of time. She had to do something now, before they reached the tower room. After another few steps she pretended to stumble on the landing. Swiftly she turned and grabbed for Joyce's arm.

Joyce reacted with a hiss of rage, fighting to keep hold of the pistol. She dropped the carriage lantern and tried to claw Sara's face. Feeling the bite of long nails on her neck, Sara screamed and tried to twist the gun away. They grappled desperately and rolled down the steps together. The painful impact of the stone stairs on her head and back dazed Sara, but she didn't let go of Joyce's arm, even as she felt it come down between their writhing bodies.

All at once her ears rang with an explosion.

Sara's first thought was that she had been shot. She had felt a hard, bruising blow against her breast that she gradually identified as the backward kick of the pistol. Slowly she stirred and sat up, holding a hand to the throbbing side of her head.

Joyce lay a foot or two away, moaning. A patch of crimson blood welled over her shoulder. "Help me," she wheezed.

"Help you?" Sara repeated, staggering to her feet. Somehow she managed to collect her wits. The discarded carriage lantern was still intact, the tiny flame sputtering as the lamp rolled lazily across a step. After picking up the lamp, she went to Joyce, who was clutching her injured shoulder. *I should leave you here*, she thought. She was unaware she had said the words aloud until Joyce replied.

"You can't let me die!"

"You're not going to die." Disgusted, terrified, Sara removed her own petticoat, wadded it up, and pressed it firmly against the wound to staunch the blood. Joyce screamed like an enraged cat, her eyes slitted and demonic. Sara's ears rang from the piercing cry.

"Be quiet, you bitch!" Sara snapped. "Not another sound!" Suddenly her entire body was filled with furious energy. She felt strong enough to push down a stone wall with her bare hands. She went to the crumbling entrance of the castle and saw that the hack driver was still waiting, craning his neck curiously. "You!" she shouted. "Come here right away, or you won't get a bloody shilling of what she promised!" She turned back to Joyce, her blue eyes blazing. "And you . . . give me back my necklace."

As Alex had predicted, Derek returned to Swans' Court, disheveled and dirty, smelling of charred wood. His face was tearless and cold, scraped from his earlier scuffles. Lily had been waiting up for him, drinking countless cups of tea. Henry, her brother-in-law, had gone out to roam with his friends in London, seeking trouble as high-spirited young men were wont to do. Alex stayed home, pacing edgily from room to room.

As the butler admitted Derek into the house, Lily rushed to the entrance hall and took his arm. She questioned him anxiously as she led him into the parlor. "Derek, where have you been? Are you all right? Would you like something to eat? A drink?"

"Brandy," Derek said curtly, sitting down on the parlor sofa.

Lily sent maidservants scurrying for hot water, towels, and brandy. All of it arrived in short order. Derek was strangely passive as Lilly dabbed at the dirty scrapes with a moistened towel. He cupped the brandy snifter in his hands without bothering to taste it. "Drink some of that," Lily said in the firm, motherly voice that the children never dared to disobey. Derek took a swallow and set the snifter down, not looking at her as she hovered about him. "Are you tired?" she asked. "Would you like to lay your head down?"

Derek rubbed the lower half of his jaw, his green eyes flat and blank. He appeared not to have heard her.

Carefully Lily smoothed a lock of his hair. "I'll be close by. Tell me if there's anything you want." She went to Alex, who had been watching from the doorway. Their eyes met. "I hope he'll be all right," she whispered. "I've never seen him like this. He lost everything . . . the club . . . and Sara . . ."

Reading the worry in her gaze, Alex pulled her close and rocked her gently. In the years since their marriage they had shared a life of companionship, passion, and incomparable joy. Times like this served as a brutal reminder that they should never take their happiness for granted. He held his wife protectively. "He'll survive," he answered her. "Just as he's survived everything else in his life. But he'll never be the same."

Lily shifted in his arms to glance miserably at Derek's motionless form.

Someone used the brass knocker at the front door. The sharp sound echoed in the entrance hall. Alex and Lily looked at each other in silent question, then watched as the butler went to answer. They heard a thick cockney voice arguing with Burton's well-modulated tones. "If Crawen's 'ere, I bloody well 'as to see 'im!"

The man's voice wasn't familiar to Alex, but Lily recognized it immediately. "Ivo Jenner!" she exclaimed. "Why the hell would he come here? Unless . . ." Her dark eyes widened. "Alex, he's the one who started the kitchen fire at Craven's last year. It was just a prank . . . but perhaps he pulled another prank tonight that got out of hand! Do you think—" She stopped as she felt a sudden breeze rush by her, caused by Derek's form as he shot past them to the entrance hall, lithe as a striking panther.

Alex followed him in a flash, but not before Derek had fastened his hands around Jenner's throat, knocking him to the marble floor. Swearing obscenely, Jenner used his heavy pugilist's fists to batter Derek's sides. It took the combined strength of Alex, the butler, and Lily to pry Derek away. The entrance hall was filled with their combined bellowing. Only Derek was quiet, busily engaged in murder.

"Stop it!" Lily was screeching.

Alex had one powerful arm locked around Derek's neck. "Damn you, Craven—"

"I didn't do it!" Jenner protested loudly "That's why I came 'ere, so as to tell you I didn't do it!"

Gagging from the hard pressure on his throat, Derek was finally forced to subside. "I'll kill you," he gasped, staring at Jenner with bloodlust.

"You 'ammer'eaded madman!" Jenner exclaimed, standing up and shaking himself off. He yanked the hem of his coat back into place.

"Don't you dare call Derek names!" Lily said hotly. "And don't insult me by protesting your innocence under my own roof, when we all know there's reason to believe you're responsible for the fire!"

"*I didn't do it,*" Jenner said vehemently.

"You were behind the kitchen fire at Craven's last year!" Lily accused.

"Aye, I admit to that, but I 'ad nofing to do with this. I came 'ere to do Crawen a frigging *favor*, damn 'is eyes!"

"What favor?" Derek asked in a low, ugly voice. Alex had to tighten his restraining hold once more.

Composing himself, Jenner smoothed his red hair and cleared his throat "My affidavit man came to me tonight at my club, and 'e 'appened to be walking by Crawen's just as the blaze started, an' saw two women leaving the place. Looked odd, 'e said, since it wasn't 'ouse wenches, but ladies dressed in fine gowns. One was blond, the other dark with green jewels all around 'er neck. They took a public coach away from the club . . . an' it was then the place started to burn like the bowels of 'ell." Jenner shrugged and added a touch sheepishly, "I thought . . . maybe the dark one was Mrs. Crawen."

"And maybe I'll find a giant beanstalk in my garden tomorrow morning," Lily said sarcastically. "You're a *fiend*, Jenner, for coming here and tormenting Derek with this tale!"

"It's the truf," Jenner said indignantly. "Dammit, I want you to find 'er! It's all ower London—my own blasted club—that I'm the man what set the fire that killed bloody Mathilda! Bad for my reputation, an' my business, and besides . . . I've a liking for the little wench." He gave Derek a disdainful look. "Deserves better than this black'earted bastard, she does."

"You've said your piece," Alex murmured. "Now leave. I'm getting tired of holding him back." He didn't let go of Derek until Jenner was safely gone, the front door closed behind him. Derek shook him off and retreated several steps, giving him a baleful glare.

Lily released an explosive sigh. "That blustering idiot Jenner! I discount every word he said as nonsense."

Derek had turned his attention to the closed door. His large, rawboned body was very still. The Raifords waited for him to voice his thoughts. His voice was strained and barely audible. "Sara has a green necklace. She was going to wear it tonight."

Alex watched Derek alertly. "Craven . . . would Sara have had any reason to leave the club tonight?"

"With a blond woman?" Lily asked skeptically. "I don't think any of Sara's friends are blond except my sister Penelope, and she certainly wouldn't have—" She broke off at Derek's quiet exclamation. "Derek, what is it?"

"Joyce," he muttered. "It could have been Joyce."

"Lady Ashby?" Lily bit her lip and asked gently, "Derek, are you certain you're not trying to convince yourself of something you want desperately to believe?"

Derek was silent, concentrating on his own thoughts.

Alex frowned as he turned the possibilities over in his mind. "Perhaps we should pay a visit to Ashby House," he conceded. "At this point it wouldn't do any harm. But Craven, don't rest your hopes on discovering anyth—" He turned with surprise to find Derek already striding out the door. Raising his tawny brows, he looked at Lily.

"I'll stay here," she muttered, pushing him after Derek. "Go and keep him safe."

After Sara and the driver helped Joyce into the coach, they began the long journey back to London. Joyce curled in a miserable huddle, groaning and cursing whenever the wheels of the vehicle jostled over a deep rut. Her endless complaining was finally too much for Sara to take. "Oh, good Lord, that's enough," she exclaimed impatiently.

"I'm going to die," Joyce moaned.

"Unfortunately that's not the case. The bullet passed cleanly through your shoulder, the bleeding's stopped, and whatever discomfort you feel isn't nearly enough to make up for all you've done," Sara continued with growing exasperation. "The first time I met Derek was on the night you had his face slashed, and ever since then you've harassed and tormented us both. You brought this on yourself!"

"You're enjoying my suffering," Joyce whined.

"Somehow I can't dredge up much sympathy for a

woman who's just tried to kill me! And when I think of the cruel, callous way you destroyed Derek's club . . ."

"He'll always hate me for that," Joyce whispered in satisfaction. "I'll always have that part of him, at least."

"No," Sara said firmly. "I'm going to fill his life with such happiness that he'll have no room to hate anyone. He won't spare you a thought. You'll be nothing to him."

"You're wrong," Joyce hissed.

They fell into a seething silence that lasted the rest of the journey. Eventually the carriage stopped in front of Ashby House, a magnificent stucco-fronted mansion frescoed in a rich shade of umber. Sara bid the driver to assist her in bringing Joyce into the building. They had to ascend a short flight of steps. Mewling in discomfort, Joyce leaned heavily against Sara, digging her nails punishingly into her shoulder and arm. Grimly Sara resisted the urge to throw her down the stairs. As they reached the front door, an astonished butler admitted them. Sara spoke to the butler tersely. "Pay the driver whatever he was promised, and show us to Lord Ashby. Quickly."

Bewildered, the butler stared at Lady Ashby's blood-stained gown. "Go on," Sara encouraged, and he complied with her orders. After he was paid, the driver scurried back to his coach and left with all due haste.

"What are you going to tell Lord Ashby?" Joyce murmured.

Sara regarded her with cool blue eyes. "The truth, my lady."

Joyce gave a faint cackle, looking like a wild golden witch. "He won't punish me. He lets me do whatever I want."

"Not this time. I'm going to make certain you answer for what you've done tonight."

"Try it," Joyce invited, cackling again.

The butler led them to a nearby sitting room, magnificently fitted in red and black. Since Sara no longer offered her support, Joyce clung to the butler's arm, becoming pale and dizzy as they reached their destination. "Send for a physician," Joyce commanded thinly, holding her shoulder as she eased into a chair. "I require immediate attention."

The butler left, and the heavy rumble of a voice came from the corner of the room. "I've been waiting for you, Lady Ashby. It appears you've been about some mischief tonight."

Joyce glanced at her husband and didn't reply. Cautiously Sara approached Lord Ashby. He was seated in a chair near the fireplace, his knees spread comfortably. A stocky, thick-throated old man with flapping jowls and moist, bulging eyes, he looked like a imperious frog. She felt like an unlucky fly trespassing in his territory. In spite of his fine clothes and his aristocratic heritage, he possessed a grubby, all-engulfing quality that unnerved Sara.

"Explain this," he said, staring at Sara. His broad hand gestured impatiently.

Sara met his eyes and made her tone as crisp as possible. "I wouldn't exactly describe Lady Ashby's actions as 'mischief,' my lord. Tonight your wife set fire to my husband's club, threatened my life, abducted me, and tried to lock me away in your deserted castle to keep me as her own private pet! I'm inclined to have her charged with attempted murder."

Joyce interrupted eagerly. "She's lying, my lord! This . . . this *peasant* creature attacked me without provocation—"

"Quiet!" Ashby thundered. His reptilian gaze returned to Sara. "You don't intend to go to the authorities, Mrs. Craven, or you wouldn't have brought Lady Ashby to me. You and I would rather not expose the distasteful details of this situation in the courts. Your husband, after all, is as much a culprit as my wife."

"I don't agree—"

"Oh? Then what are you doing now, if not trying to protect him from the consequences of his past mistakes? Although you would like to argue the point, Mrs. Craven, you are well aware that your husband should never have taken Lady Ashby to his bed, out of respect for me if for no other reason. Although . . . I will concede that Lady Ashby must have been a potent temptation."

Sara glanced at the feral, bloodstained woman with disdain. "Whatever his taste was in the past, my husband has no interest in anyone but me now."

A slight smile came to Lord Ashby's face. His pendulous jowls twitched. "I do not doubt that in the slightest, Mrs. Craven. And I will consider myself indebted to you—*solely* you, not your husband—if you will allow me to handle my wife in the way I see fit."

The two women spoke at the same time.

"My lord?" Joyce asked sharply.

"What will you do with her?" Sara said.

"I will keep her at a remote location in Scotland," Lord Ashby answered Sara, "away from all society. Clearly she presents a danger to all those she associates with. I would isolate her in relative comfort rather than confine her to an lunatic hospital, where she might be subjected to cruel treatment and also prove an embarrassment to the family."

"*Nooo!*" Joyce erupted in an inhuman howl. "I won't be sent away! I won't be caged like an animal!"

Sara kept her attention on Lord Ashby. "I only wonder why you haven't done it before, my lord."

"My wife has always been a source of amusement for me, Mrs. Craven. Until now she has never caused real harm to anyone."

"My husband's face—" Sara began hotly, thinking of the slashing.

"A punishment he deserved," Lord Ashby declared. "In the past Craven cuckolded many powerful men. He's fortunate that none of them ever decided to make a gelding of him."

He had a point, much as she disliked to admit it. "Your 'source of amusement' nearly cost me my life," Sara said under her breath.

Ashby frowned impatiently. "Mrs. Craven, I see no reason to go over the same ground yet again. I give you my word of honor that the problem will be addressed in the way I have described. Lady Ashby will never set foot in England again. That should be enough to satisfy you."

"Yes, my lord. Of course I trust your word." Sara lowered her gaze deferentially. "If you'll excuse me, I must find my husband now."

"Craven was here with Lord Raiford," Lord Ashby informed her.

Sara was disconcerted by the news. "Here? But how—"

"They suspect that Joyce might have had something to do with your disappearance. I told them I had no knowledge of her whereabouts. They left not ten minutes before your arrival."

"Where did they go?"

"I did not ask. It was of no consequence to me."

Sara was relieved that Derek hadn't been injured.

But he must be distraught, even frantic, not knowing what had happened to her. She bit her lip in consternation. "Well, at least they know there's a chance I'm all right."

"They don't have much hope," Ashby said dryly. "I must say, your husband seemed quite indifferent to the entire situation."

Sara's heart thumped anxiously. She knew it wasn't indifference at all, but a surfeit of emotions Derek couldn't handle. He was keeping it all inside, denying his grief and fear to everyone, even himself. She had to find him. Perhaps the best place to begin her search was the club. With dawn arriving soon, surely the men would want to survey the damaged building by the light of day and comb through the ruins. "My lord," she said urgently, "I would ask that one of your carriages convey me to St. James Street."

Ashby nodded. "With all expediency."

Sara left the room, while Joyce screamed madly after her, "I won't be locked away forever . . . I'll come back! *You'll never be safe!*"

Sara's breath was knocked from her at the first sight of the club. Or rather, the place where the club had been. Thieves and beggars were poking through the rubble in search of fire-damaged goods. Slowly Sara descended from the Ashby carriage. She stood at the side of the street, staring. "Dear God," she whispered, her eyes stinging with tears.

All Derek's dreams, the monument to his ambition . . . razed to the ground. Nothing remained but the marble columns and staircases, sticking up like the exposed skeleton of a once-proud beast. Pieces of the stone facade were scattered on the ground like giant scales. The extent of the destruction was difficult to comprehend. For years the club had been the center of Derek's life. She couldn't imagine how he must be reacting to the loss.

The lavender light of daybreak fell gently over the scene. Sara made her way to the charred ruins at a snail's pace, her thoughts disconnected. Her manuscript had burned, she realized sadly. It had almost been finished. The art collection was gone too. Was Worthy all right? Had anyone perished in the fire? There were hot embers on the ground, and small patches of flame. Tufts of smoke rose from blackened timbers that had fallen at odd angles. What had once been the huge chandelier in the domed hall was a mass of melted crystal lumps.

Reaching what had once been the grand central staircase, now exposed to the open sky, Sara stopped and dragged her sleeve over her face. She gave an aching sigh. "Oh, Derek," she murmured. "What am I going to say to you?"

A breeze rustled past her, stirring ashes around her skirts, making her cough.

Suddenly an odd feeling came over her, a slight shock as if she'd been touched by invisible hands. She rubbed her arms and turned around, somehow knowing Derek would be there.

And he was. He stared at her from a face that was stark-white, paler than the scorched marble columns rising from the ground. His lips formed her name, but he didn't make a sound. The breeze swept over them both, clearing away the wisps of smoke from the ground. Sara was startled by his gauntness, the torment that pulled at his features until he looked like a stranger. His eyes were searing, as if he were flooded with uncontainable rage . . . but suddenly the depths of green overflowed, and she realized with astonishment that it was not rage . . . It was soul-deep terror. He didn't move, or even blink, afraid she would disappear.

"Derek?" she said uncertainly.

His throat worked violently. "Don't leave me," he whispered.

Sara went to him, picking up her skirts, stumbling in her haste. "I'm all right. Oh, please don't look like that!" Reaching him, she threw her arms around him and held on with all her strength. "Everything's all right."

A fierce tremor went through him. Suddenly he clutched her in an embrace that hurt, until her ribs ached from the pressure. His hands slid over her body in a frantic search, while his breath shuddered in her ear. "You said you'd never leave me." He held her as if he feared she would be ripped away from him.

"I'm here now," she soothed. "I'm right here."

"Oh, God . . . Sara . . . I couldn't find you . . ."

She brushed her palms over his cold, wet cheeks. He was off-balance, his considerable weight swaying against her. "Have you been drinking?" she murmured, pulling back to look at him. He shook his head, staring at her if she were a ghost. She wondered how to take away the shattered look in his eyes. "Let's find a place to sit down." As she stepped away toward the marble stairs, his arms tightened. "Derek," she urged. He went with her like a sleepwalker. They settled on a step and he hunched over her tightly, his arms fast around her.

"I love you," he told her, wiping impatiently at the tears that kept trickling down his face. "I couldn't say it before. I couldn't—" He clenched his trembling jaw, trying to control the hot flow of tears. It only made them worse. Giving up, he buried his face in her hair. "Bloody hell," he muttered.

Sara had never seen him so undone, had never imagined it possible. Stroking his dark head, she whispered meaningless words, trying to give him comfort.

"I love you," he repeated hoarsely, burrowing against her. "I would have given my life to have one more day with you, and tell you that."

Watching the reunion from across the street, Alex sighed with tremendous relief. "Thank God," he muttered, and went to his carriage. He couldn't wait to tell Lily the good news. In fact, he might decide never to let Lily out of his sight again. He rubbed his tired eyes and spoke to the coachman. "Well, Craven's got his second chance. As for me . . . I'm going home to my wife now. Step lively about it."

"It's like that, is it, m'lord?" the coachman asked cheekily, and Alex gave him a wry grin.

"Let's go."

Murmuring quietly, Sara kissed her husband's rumpled hair and his neck. He held her for a long time while the shaking in his limbs gradually subsided.

"Is Worthy all right?" Sara asked. "Was anyone hurt?"

"They're all fine."

"Derek, we'll build another club. We'll do it all again, I promise—"

"No." He said it with such vehemence that she was quiet for a few minutes, continuing to stroke his hair. He lifted his head and looked at her with bloodshot eyes. "It'll never be what it was. I'd rather remember the place as it was than build an imitation. I . . . I want something different now."

"What is that?" she asked, her brow wreathed in tender concern.

"I don't know yet." Derek gave a short laugh and hauled her close again. "Don't ask a man questions . . . when he's had the scare of his life." Uncaring of anyone who might see them, he cupped his hands around her head and kissed her. Her mouth was bruised from his desperate, punishing ardor. Sara winced and murmured softly, trying to gentle him. She wasn't aware of the exact moment when he returned to himself, but suddenly his skin was warm and his mouth was once again familiar as it moved tenderly over hers.

After a while Derek ended the kiss and laid his cheek against hers, breathing deeply. His fingers traced the moist curve of her face, the fragile juncture between ear and jaw. "When they said you were dead . . ." He paused while a tremor took hold of him and forced himself to go on. "I thought I was being punished for my past. I knew I wasn't meant to have you, but I couldn't stop myself. In my whole life you were what I wanted most. All along I've been afraid you'd be taken from me."

Sara didn't move or make a sound, but she was amazed. For him to admit he'd been afraid . . . She would have thought no power on earth or beyond could have elicited such a confession.

"And because of that I tried to protect myself," he continued raspily. "I didn't want to give you the one last part of myself that I couldn't take back. And then you were gone . . . and I realized it was already yours. It had been since the very beginning. Except that I hadn't told you. It drove me mad, the thought that you would never know."

"But I'm not gone. I'm here, and we still have a life together."

He kissed her cheek, his stubble scratching her tender skin. "I still couldn't bear to lose you." Suddenly there was a smile in his voice. "But I won't let the thought of it keep me from loving you with everything I have . . . heart, and body . . . and whatever else I can find to throw into the offer."

Sara laughed. "Do you actually think you could get rid of me? I'm afraid I'm a permanent part of your life, Mr. Craven . . . no matter how many ex-mistresses you send after me."

He didn't share her amusement. "Tell me what happened."

She gave him her account of all that had transpired, while Derek grew increasingly tense. His face turned ruddy with anger, and his hands tightened into punishing fists. When she finished the description of her visit with Lord Ashby, Derek dumped her from his lap and stood up with a savage curse.

"What are you doing?" Sara asked, disgruntled, as she picked herself up off the ground.

"I'm going to strangle that gotch-gutted bastard and his bitch of a wife—"

"No, you're not," Sara interrupted stubbornly. "Lord Ashby gave his word that he would lock his wife away where she could do no harm to anyone. Let it be, Derek. You can't go storming off in a temper and create more scandal-fodder just to satisfy your sense of vengeance, and besides . . ." She paused, seeing that her words were having little effect. With feminine shrewdness, she realized there was only one way to dissuade him. "Besides," she continued in a softer tone, "I've endured all I can for one day. I need a few hours of peace. I need to rest." It was the truth, actually. Her bones ached from weariness. "Couldn't you forget the Ashbys for now and take me home?"

Disarmed, his anger overrun by concern, Derek put his arms around her. "Home," he repeated, knowing she meant the mansion they hadn't yet spent a night in. "But it isn't finished yet."

Sara leaned against him, nuzzling against his chest. "I'm certain we can find a bed somewhere. If not, I'll be glad to sleep on the floor."

Derek relented and held her tightly. "All right," he murmured against her hair. "We'll go home. We'll find someplace to sleep."

"And you'll stay next to me?"

"Always," he whispered, kissing her again.

Epilogue

The insistent cry of a hungry baby rang through the mansion, while the nursery maid held the child and tried to soothe her wailing. Aware of the rising clamor, Derek bounded up several flights of stairs to the nursery. The nursery maid started at his sudden appearance, perhaps fearing he would blame her for the baby's fretfulness. His dark face was unreadable. "It's all right," he assured her, reaching for his daughter.

Cautiously the servant retreated to the side of the room, busying herself with a small pile of unfolded baby clothes. "Lydia is hungry, sir. Mrs. Craven must be late from her lecture."

Derek cuddled his daughter against his shoulder and spoke in a mixture of baby words and cockney, a language only she seemed to understand. Gradually the infant quieted, attentive to her father's low voice. A tiny, dimpled hand reached up to Derek's jaw, exploring the scratchy surface. He kissed the miniature fingers and smiled into Lydia's solemn eyes. "What a noisy little girl you are," he murmured.

The nursery maid watched him with awe and curiosity. It was unheard of for a father of means to set foot in the nursery, much less to occupy himself with crying children. "She doesn't do that for anyone else," she remarked. "You do have a way with her, Mr. Craven."

Suddenly Sara's laughing voice came from the door. "He has a way with *all* women." She entered the room and raised her face for Derek's kiss before taking Lydia from him. Dismissing the nursery maid, she settled into a comfortable chair and unbuttoned the bodice of her gown. Her long hair partially shielded the baby at her breast. Derek lounged nearby, watching them closely.

Motherhood had brought a new radiance to Sara's features, while her achievements in her work had given her maturity and confidence. In the past year she had finished another novel, *The Scoundrel*, which was promised to attain the success of *Mathilda*. The story, about an ambitious young man who wished to prosper through honest means but was forced by a callous society to resort to crime, had struck a nerve in the public sensibility. Frequently Sara was invited to speak at salon meetings concerning political reform and social issues. She felt that she wasn't learned or charismatic enough to lecture to such groups of intellectuals, but they virtually insisted on her presence at their gatherings.

"How was your speech?" Derek asked, drawing a gentle finger over the dark fuzz on his daughter's head.

"I just made a few commonsense remarks. I said that instead of hoping the poor will merely 'accept their station' in life, we should give them a chance to make something of themselves . . . or they'll turn to dishonest means, and we'll have more crime."

"Did they agree?"

Sara smiled and shrugged. "They think I'm a radical."

Derek laughed. "Politics," he said, in a tone that conveyed whimsy and scorn at once. His gaze swept over the sight of the nursing baby and lingered on the exposed curve of Sara's breast.

"What of the hospital?" Sara asked. "Has the construction finally begun?"

He tried to look matter-of-fact, but she could see that he was pleased. "The ground's been broken."

Sara's face lit with a smile of delight.

In the last few months the remains of the club had been cleared. Derek had made no decision on what to do with the property. There was, of course, a demand for him to rebuild Craven's, for the place was mourned by such influential figures as the duke of Wellington, Lord Alvanley, and even the king. But Derek resisted the public urgings to reestablish the gambling club and devoted himself to other projects. He was building a large, modern hospital to the north of the city, enlisting voluntary contributions and matching each donation with his own money. He was also developing a plot of land in the West End into a row of elegantly furnished town houses, to be leased to foreign travelers, unmarried men, and families who moved to London for the Season.

Sara had teased him lovingly as they looked over the architect's drawings for the hospital building, a plain but handsome quadrangle. For years Derek had been known as the greatest scoundrel in England, and now he was universally praised for his "reformation." "You're becoming known as a public benefactor," she told him in satisfaction, "whether you like it or not."

"I don't like it," he replied darkly. "I'm only doing this because I'd be bored otherwise."

Sara had laughed and kissed him, knowing he would forever deny having any altruistic feelings.

When Lydia was finished at Sara's breast, the nursery maid returned to take her. Sara used a soft cloth to blot her front. She fastened her dress and blushed slightly at Derek's close regard. His green eyes met hers. "She's lovely," he said. "She looks more like you every day."

Of all the surprises about Derek—and it seemed there was an endless supply—the greatest was his absorption with his daughter. Sara had expected that he would be a kind but uninvolved father. He had never known the relationship between parent and child before. She had thought he might preserve a careful distance between himself and the baby. Instead he loved his daughter with open adoration. Often he would tuck her in the crook of his arm and parade her before guests as if a baby were a lovely miracle none of them had ever seen before. He thought her prodigiously clever for holding his finger, for kicking her legs, for making adorable sounds, for doing all the things that babies usually did . . . except that in his opinion his daughter did them far better.

"Have several more children," Lily had advised Sara dryly, "so that his attention will be divided among them. Otherwise he'll ruin this one."

Sara didn't completely understand the reason for his behavior until a recent afternoon, when she had stood with him over the cradle to watch their sleeping daughter. Derek had taken Sara's hand in his and brought it to his lips. "You're my heart," he had murmured. "You've given me more happiness than I have a right to. But she . . ." He glanced down at Lydia wonderingly. "She's my own flesh and blood."

Moved by the words, Sara had realized how alone he had always been: no parents, sisters, or brothers, no blood ties of any kind. Her fingers tightened, and she nestled against him. "Now you have a family," she had said softly.

Bringing her mind back to the present, Sara answered Derek's earlier comment. "Lydia has black hair, green eyes, and your mouth and chin, and you say she looks like *me?*"

"She has your nose," Derek pointed out. "And your temperament."

Sara laughed, standing up and folding a light blanket into a neat square. "I suppose it's my temperament when she wakes the household in the middle of the night with her screaming?"

Derek advanced on her unexpectedly and cornered her against the wall. "Well, now," he murmured, "in the past you've been known to raise the roof a time or two, haven't you?"

Their gazes locked in an electric moment. Thoroughly disconcerted, Sara blushed deeply. She didn't dare look at the nursery maid in case she had heard. Giving Derek a reproving frown, she ducked beneath his arm and fled, hurrying to the safety of her bedroom. He followed close behind her.

They hadn't made love since well before the baby's birth, and to Derek's credit, he had been patient. Extraordinarily so, considering his strong physical appetites. Although the doctor had indicated that she was fully healed from the birth and ready to resume marital relations, Sara had managed to put Derek off with gentle refusals. Lately, however, she had been the recipient of intense glances that warned she wouldn't be sleeping alone much longer. She paused at the doorway of her bedroom.

"Derek," she said with a pleading smile, "perhaps later—"

"When?"

"I'm not certain," she countered, beginning to close the door against him.

Stubbornly Derek shouldered his way past her and shut the door. He began to reach for her, then hesitated as he saw her stiffen. His face went taut. "What is it?" he asked. "A physical problem? Is it something I've done, or—"

"No," she said swiftly. "None of those things."

"Then what?"

Fiercely Sara concentrated on the fabric of her sleeve. She could find no way to explain her reluctance to him. She had gone through so many changes . . . She was a mother now . . . She wasn't certain that making love with him would be the same at all, and she didn't want to find out. She was afraid of disappointing him, and herself, and it was easier to keep putting off the event than to face it. She shrugged lamely. "I'm afraid it won't be the same as before."   •

Derek was very quiet, absorbing the statement. His hand settled on the back of her neck in a gesture that Sara thought was meant to be consoling. Instead he gripped her nape and pulled her against him, his mouth coming down firmly on hers. She wriggled in surprise as he forced her hand down between his thighs. He was as hard as iron, throbbing at her touch.

"There." He pressed her hand tighter. "Do you feel that? You're my wife, and it's been months, and I'm aching for you. I don't care if it's not the same as before. If you don't come to bed with me now, I'm going to burst."

And that, apparently, was all he intended to say on the matter. He ignored her soft protest and undressed them both. Gathering her small body against his, he groaned in love and pleasure and impatience. "Sara, I've missed you . . . holding you like this . . ." Reverently his hands traced over her, sensitive to the new roundness of her breasts, the fuller curve of her hips.

Hesitant at first, Sara lay still beneath him, her hands resting on his flexing back. He kissed her with gentle greed, savoring her mouth with long, deep forays of his tongue. She stirred in awakening desire, clasping him closer. To her sudden mortification, a few milky droplets seeped from her breasts. Pulling away with an apologetic gasp, she tried to turn from him. Derek pushed her shoulders down and bent over her breasts. His breath flowed in deep gusts as he stared at her. The moist nipples were a darker pink than before, surrounded by a delicate tracing of veins. The lustily maternal sight sent a wave of aching excitement through him. He touched the tip of her breast with his tongue, teasing and circling, then fastening his lips over the tautness. Gently he pulled with his mouth.

"Oh, you mustn't," Sara gasped as she felt a tingling ache in her breast. "It's not decent . . ."

"I never said I was decent."

She gave a breathless moan, caught beneath him as he drew a surge of milk from her body. A demanding pulse began low inside her. He stayed at her breast, his hand cupping underneath the plump roundness, and then he moved to the other. Finally she tangled her fingers in his dark hair and pulled him up, her mouth seeking his. They tangled together, rolling once, twice, across the bed, hands searching with increasing urgency, legs wrapping and twining around each other.

At last, when he slid deep inside her, they both gasped and went still, trying to preserve the moment of oneness. Sara drew her palms slowly from his shoulders down to the tops of his thighs, relishing the powerful length of his body. Derek shivered in bliss and moved against her. She arched languidly, and they began a slow rhythm, drifting in a current of warmth.

"You were right," Derek whispered, shaping his hands over her body, imprinting sweet, hot kisses against her skin. "It's not the same as before . . . It's even better. God, if only . . . I could make it last forever." He thrust more strongly, unable to restrain his movements. Sara clenched her hands and pressed her fists against his back, her body tightening exquisitely. He stared into her eyes, gritting his teeth in the effort to contain his pleasure. She wrapped her legs around his hips and urged him to thrust even harder. Afraid of hurting her, he tried to hold back, but she drove him with her own demanding passion, until he let the tumultuous storm overtake him. His smothered cry followed hers, and together they flowed into the swirling tide of fulfillment, bound together by flesh and spirit, in perfect accord.

Afterward they lay together dreamily, letting hours drift by and pretending time had stopped. Sara draped herself over his chest, tracing his features with her fingertip. A thought occurred to her, and she lifted her head to stare at him expectantly.

Derek returned her gaze, idly stroking her hair and back. "What is it, angel?"

"You told me once you didn't know how 'happy' feels."

"I remember."

"And now?"

Derek regarded her for a long moment, then pulled her flat against him, locking her in his arms. "It's this," he said, his voice slightly hoarse. "Right here and now."

And she rested against his heart, content.